BORDERS

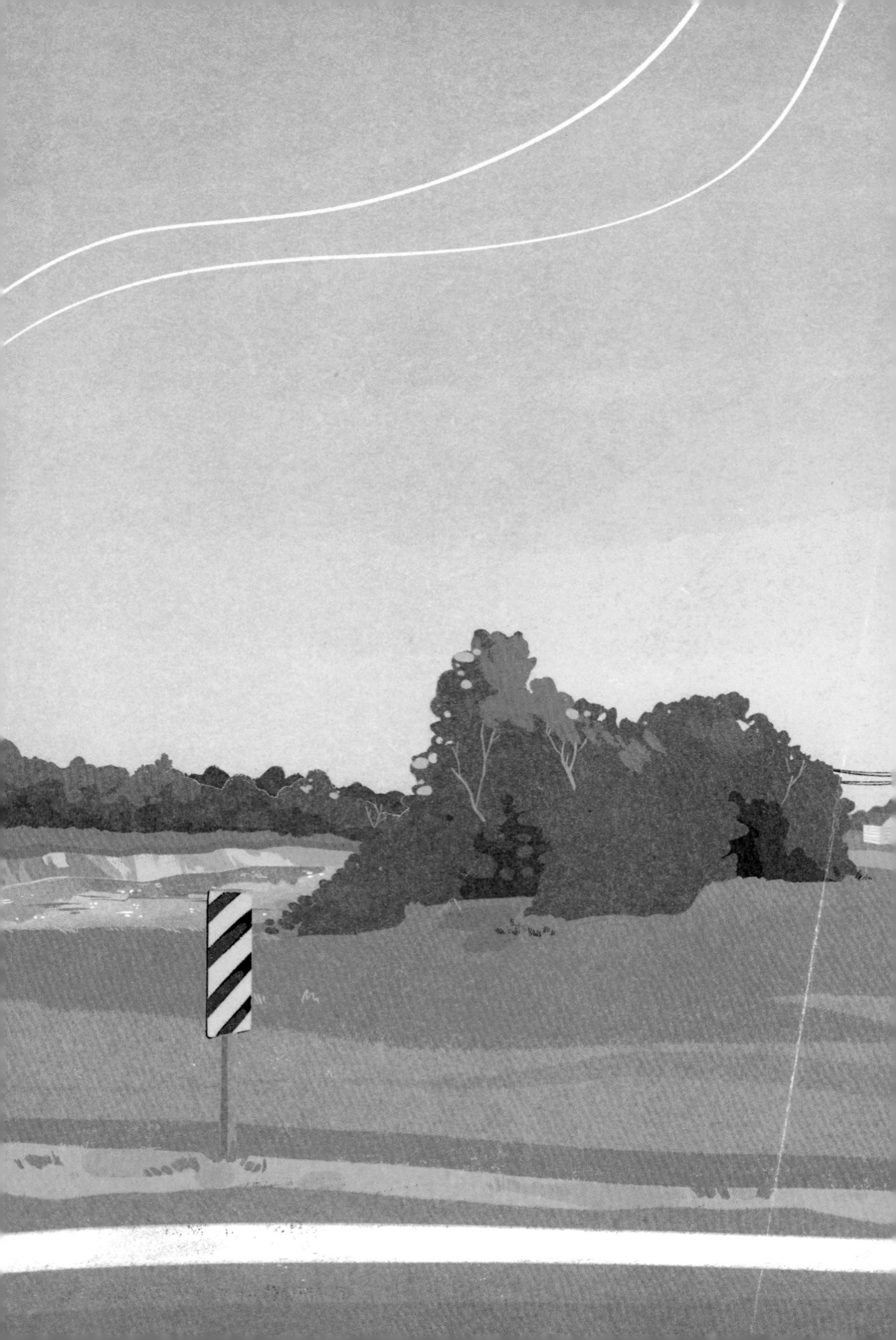

BORDERS

WITHDRAWN

STORY BY
THOMAS KING

ILLUSTRATIONS BY
NATASHA DONOVAN

LITTLE, BROWN AND COMPANY
NEW YORK   BOSTON

30999 9728

C

Text copyright © 1993, 2021 by Dead Dog Café Productions Inc.
Illustrations copyright © 2021 by Natasha Donovan

The text of *Borders* was previously published, in slightly different form, as the short story "Borders" in Thomas King's *One Good Story, That One*, originally published in 1993 by HarperCollins Publishers Ltd.

Cover illustration copyright © 2021 by Natasha Donovan. Cover design by Jenny Kimura.

Little, Brown and Company
Hachette Book Group
1290 Avenue of the Americas, New York, NY 10104
Visit us at LBYR.com

Simultaneously published in 2021 by HarperCollins Publishers Ltd.
First U.S. Edition: September 2021

Little, Brown and Company is a division of Hachette Book Group, Inc.
The Little, Brown name and logo are trademarks of Hachette Book Group, Inc.
The publisher is not responsible for websites (or their content) that are not owned by the publisher.

Library of Congress Cataloging-in-Publication Data
Names: King, Thomas, 1943- author. | Donovan, Natasha, illustrator.
Title: Borders / story by Thomas King; illustrations by Natasha Donovan.
Description: First US Edition. | New York: Little, Brown and Company, 2021. | Summary: A boy and his mother refuse to identify themselves as American or Canadian at the border and become caught in the limbo between nations when they claim their citizenship as Blackfoot.
Identifiers: LCCN 2021019891 | ISBN 9780316593069 (hardcover) | ISBN 9780316593038 (ebook)
Subjects: LCSH: Graphic novels. | CYAC: Graphic novels. | Citizenship—Fiction. | Identity—Fiction.
Classification: LCC PZ7.7.K587 Bo 2021 | DDC 741.5/973—dc23
LC record available at https://lccn.loc.gov/2021019891

ISBNs: 978-0-316-59306-9 (hardcover), 978-0-316-59303-8 (ebook),
978-0-316-29882-7 (ebook), 978-0-316-29892-6 (ebook)

PRINTED IN CANADA

TC

10 9 8 7 6 5 4 3 2 1

For the Blackfoot, who understand that the border
is the figment of someone else's imagination.
—T. K.

For Mona, Marie, and Ann: three generations
of mothers who have provided me with strength
for every journey with love and admiration.
—N. D.

BORDERS

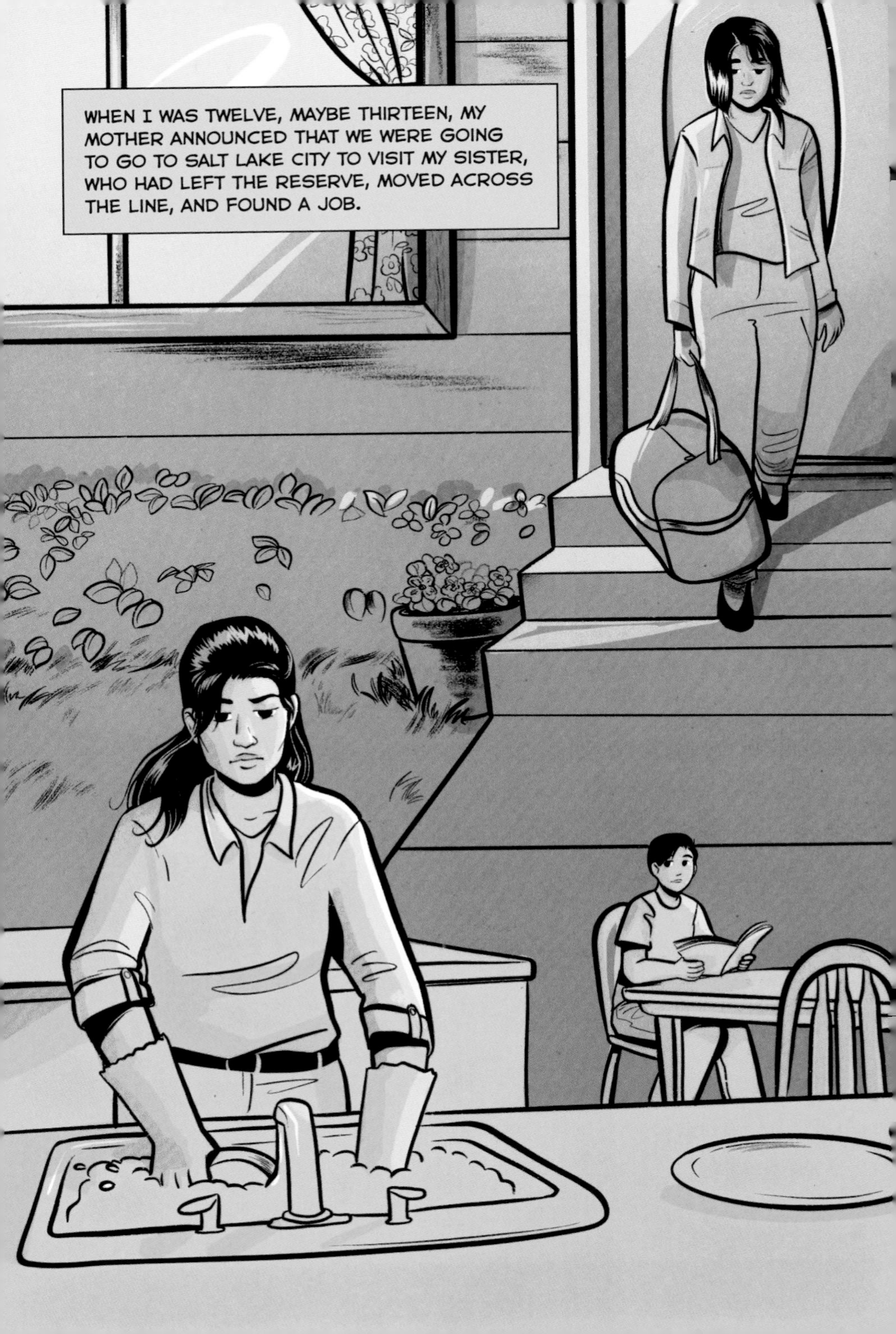
WHEN I WAS TWELVE, MAYBE THIRTEEN, MY MOTHER ANNOUNCED THAT WE WERE GOING TO GO TO SALT LAKE CITY TO VISIT MY SISTER, WHO HAD LEFT THE RESERVE, MOVED ACROSS THE LINE, AND FOUND A JOB.

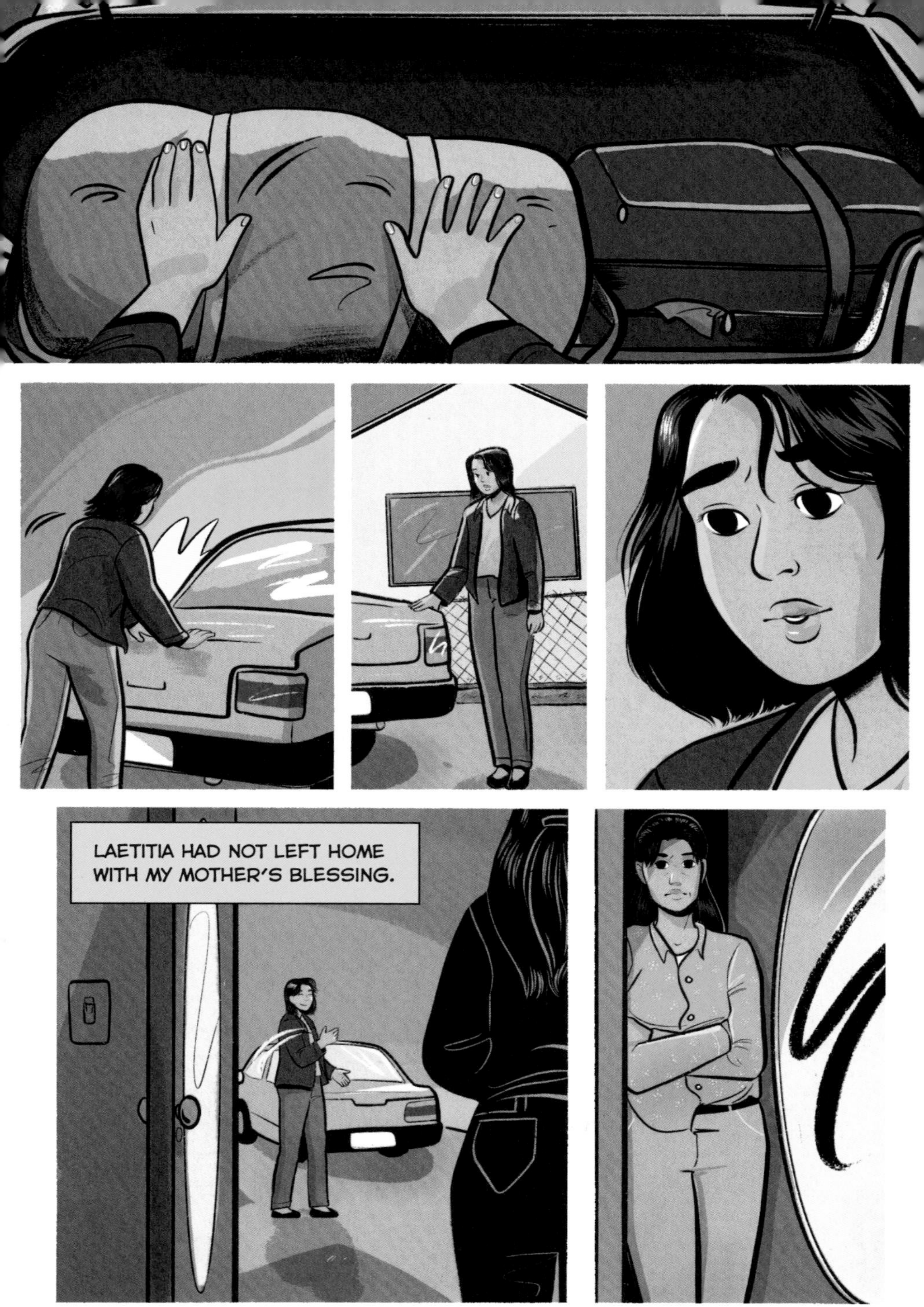
LAETITIA HAD NOT LEFT HOME WITH MY MOTHER'S BLESSING.

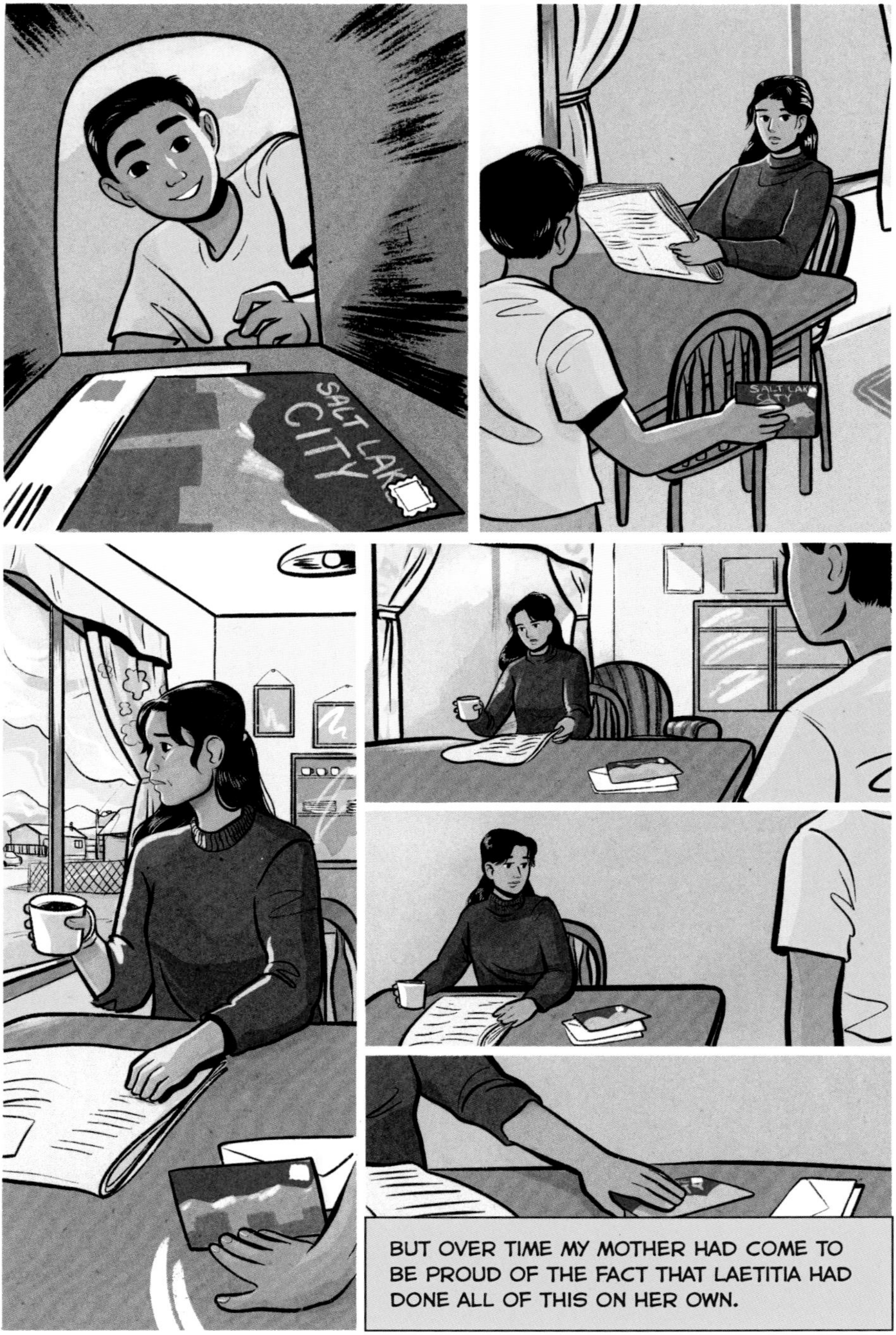
SALT LAK
CITY
SALT LAK
CITY
BUT OVER TIME MY MOTHER HAD COME TO BE PROUD OF THE FACT THAT LAETITIA HAD DONE ALL OF THIS ON HER OWN.

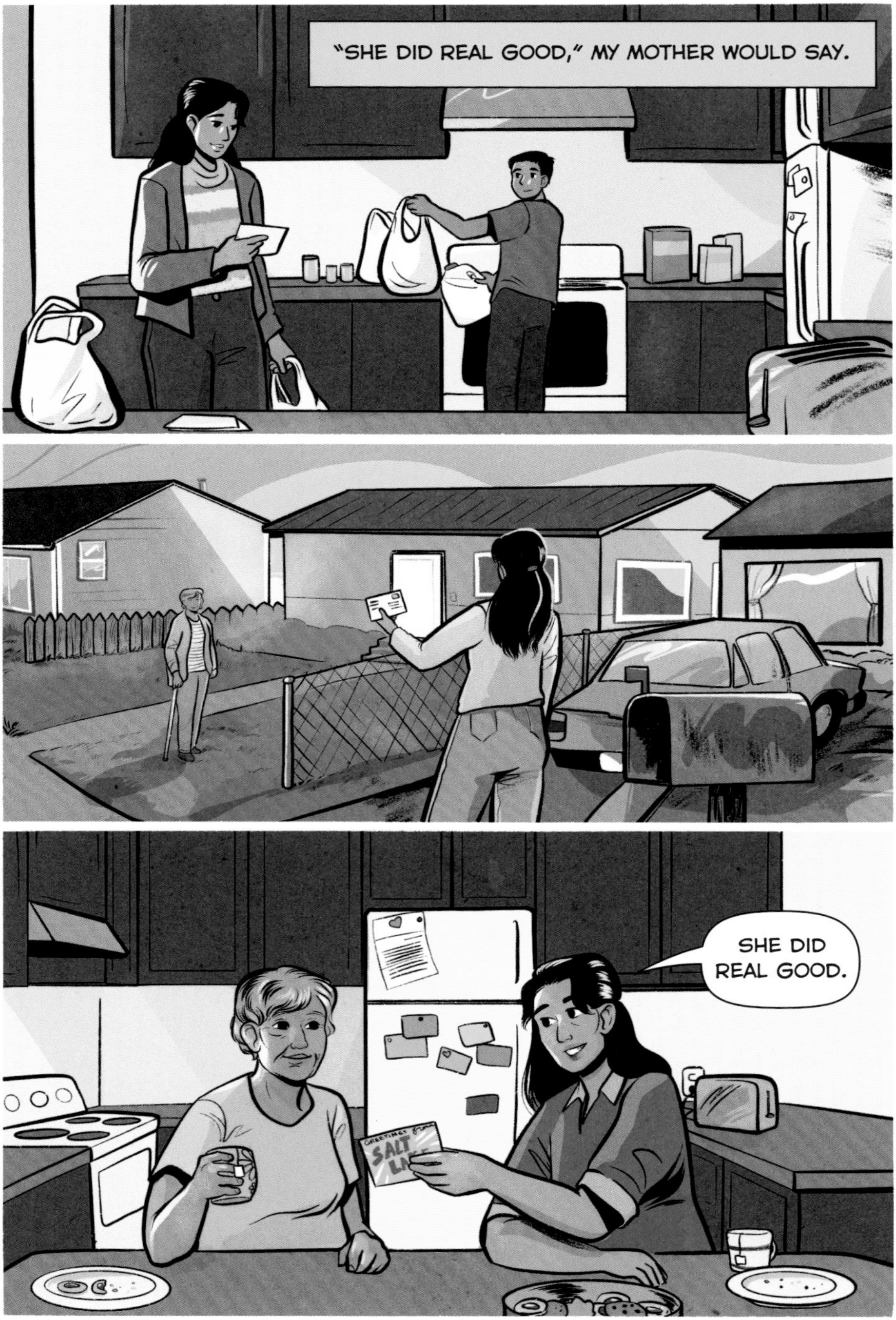
"SHE DID REAL GOOD," MY MOTHER WOULD SAY.
SHE DID REAL GOOD.

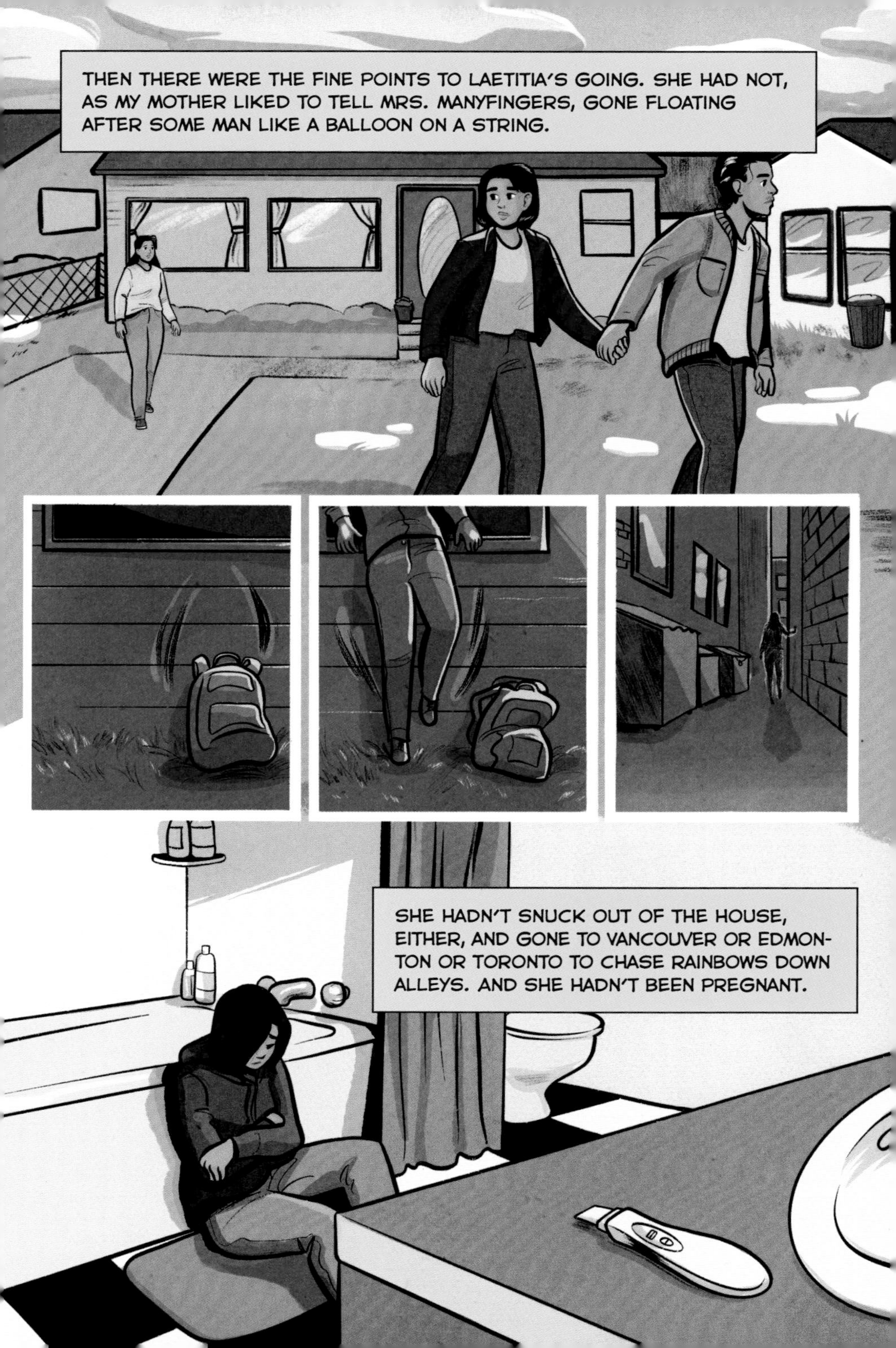
THEN THERE WERE THE FINE POINTS TO LAETITIA'S GOING. SHE HAD NOT, AS MY MOTHER LIKED TO TELL MRS. MANYFINGERS, GONE FLOATING AFTER SOME MAN LIKE A BALLOON ON A STRING.
SHE HADN'T SNUCK OUT OF THE HOUSE, EITHER, AND GONE TO VANCOUVER OR EDMONTON OR TORONTO TO CHASE RAINBOWS DOWN ALLEYS. AND SHE HADN'T BEEN PREGNANT.

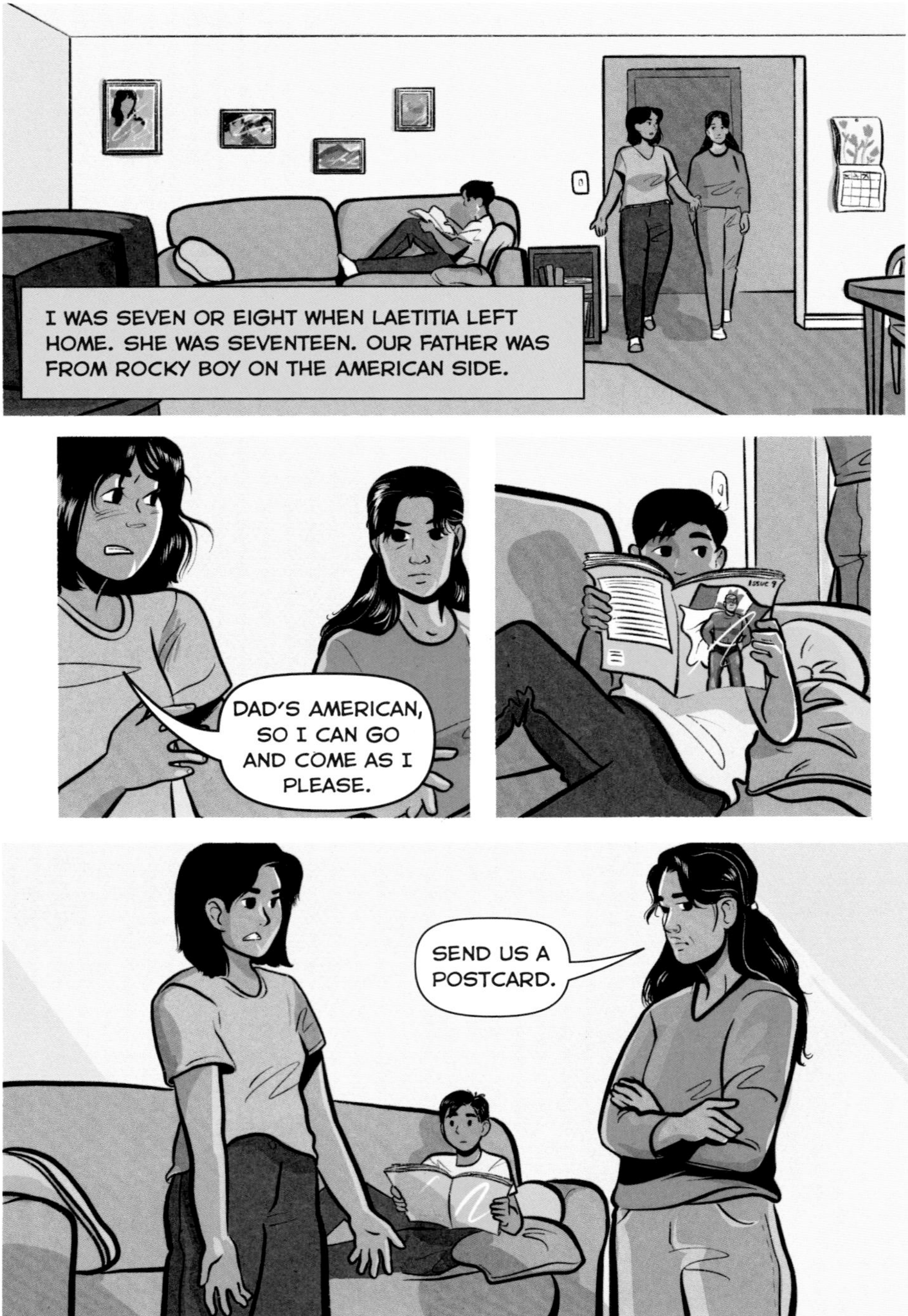
I WAS SEVEN OR EIGHT WHEN LAETITIA LEFT HOME. SHE WAS SEVENTEEN. OUR FATHER WAS FROM ROCKY BOY ON THE AMERICAN SIDE.
DAD'S AMERICAN, SO I CAN GO AND COME AS I PLEASE.
SEND US A POSTCARD.

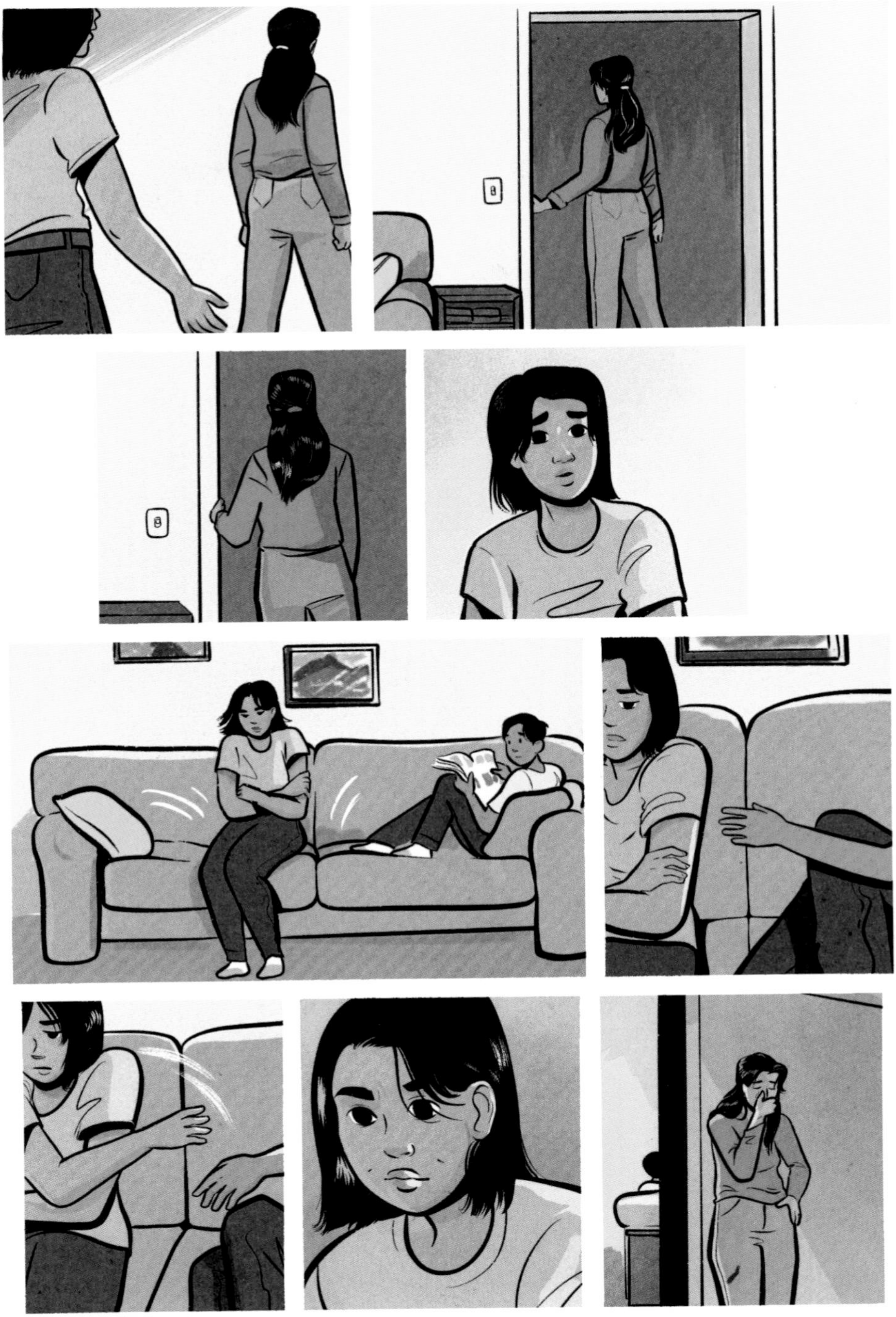

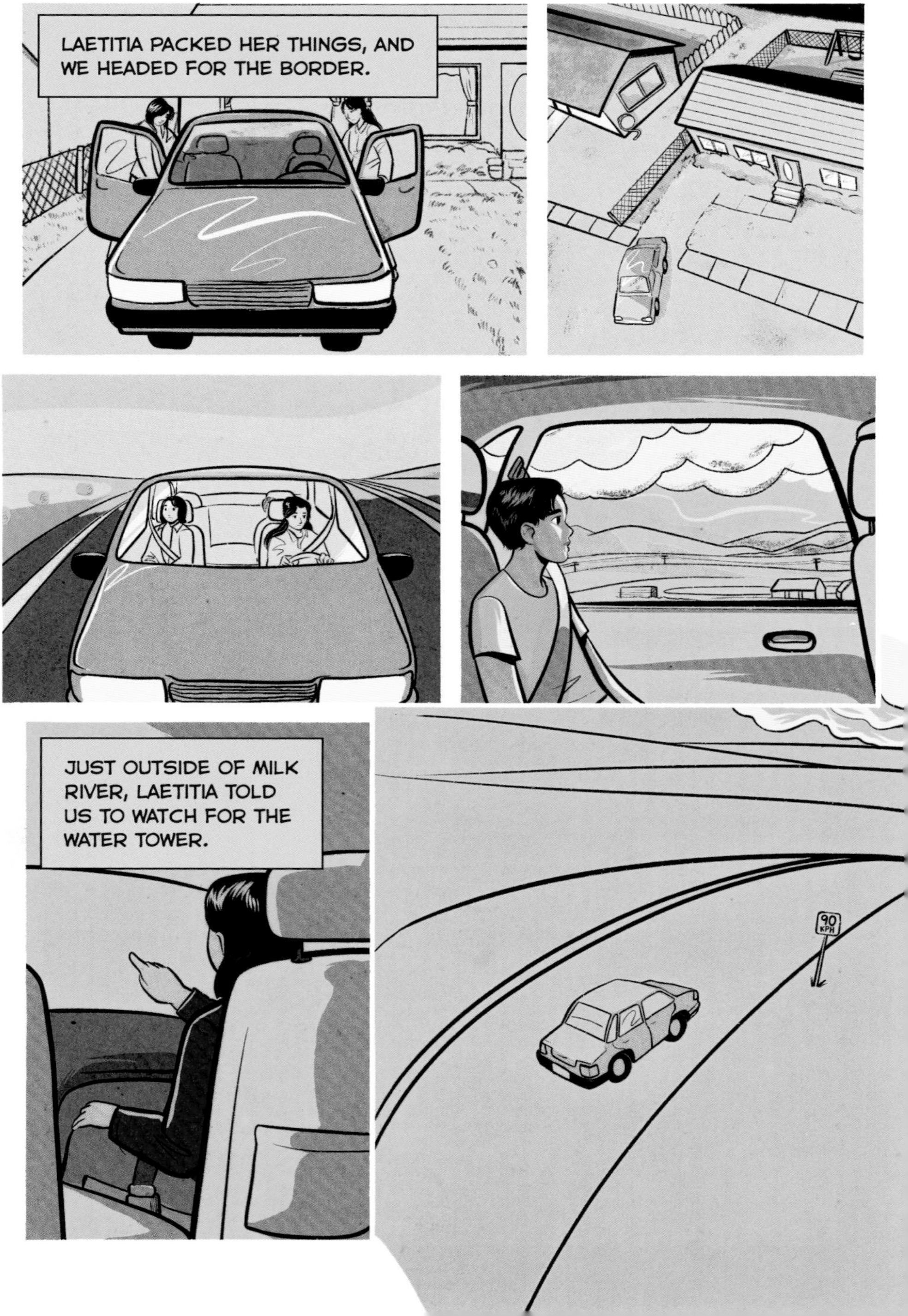
LAETITIA PACKED HER THINGS, AND WE HEADED FOR THE BORDER.
JUST OUTSIDE OF MILK RIVER, LAETITIA TOLD US TO WATCH FOR THE WATER TOWER.
90 KPH

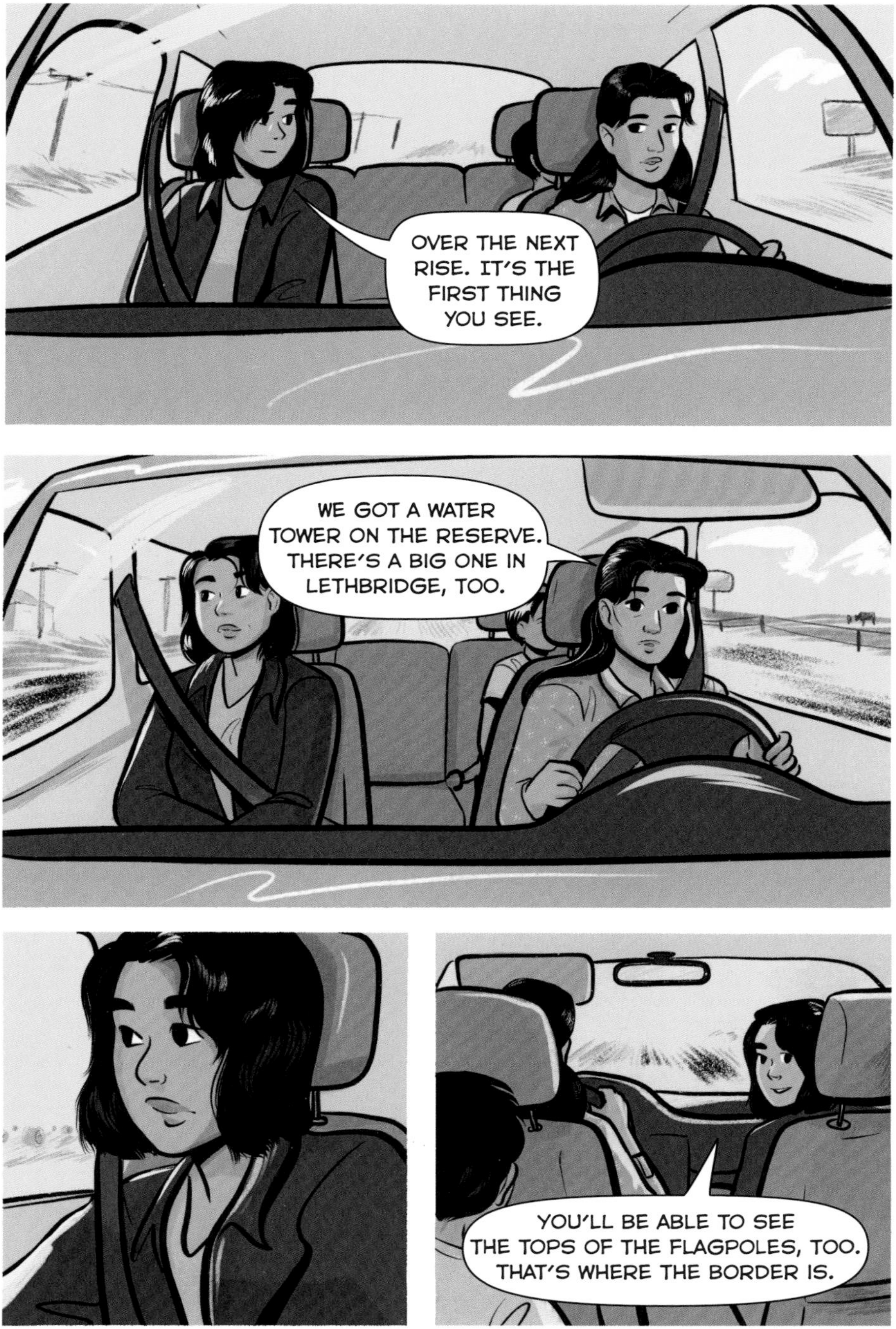
OVER THE NEXT RISE. IT'S THE FIRST THING YOU SEE.
WE GOT A WATER TOWER ON THE RESERVE. THERE'S A BIG ONE IN LETHBRIDGE, TOO.
YOU'LL BE ABLE TO SEE THE TOPS OF THE FLAGPOLES, TOO. THAT'S WHERE THE BORDER IS.

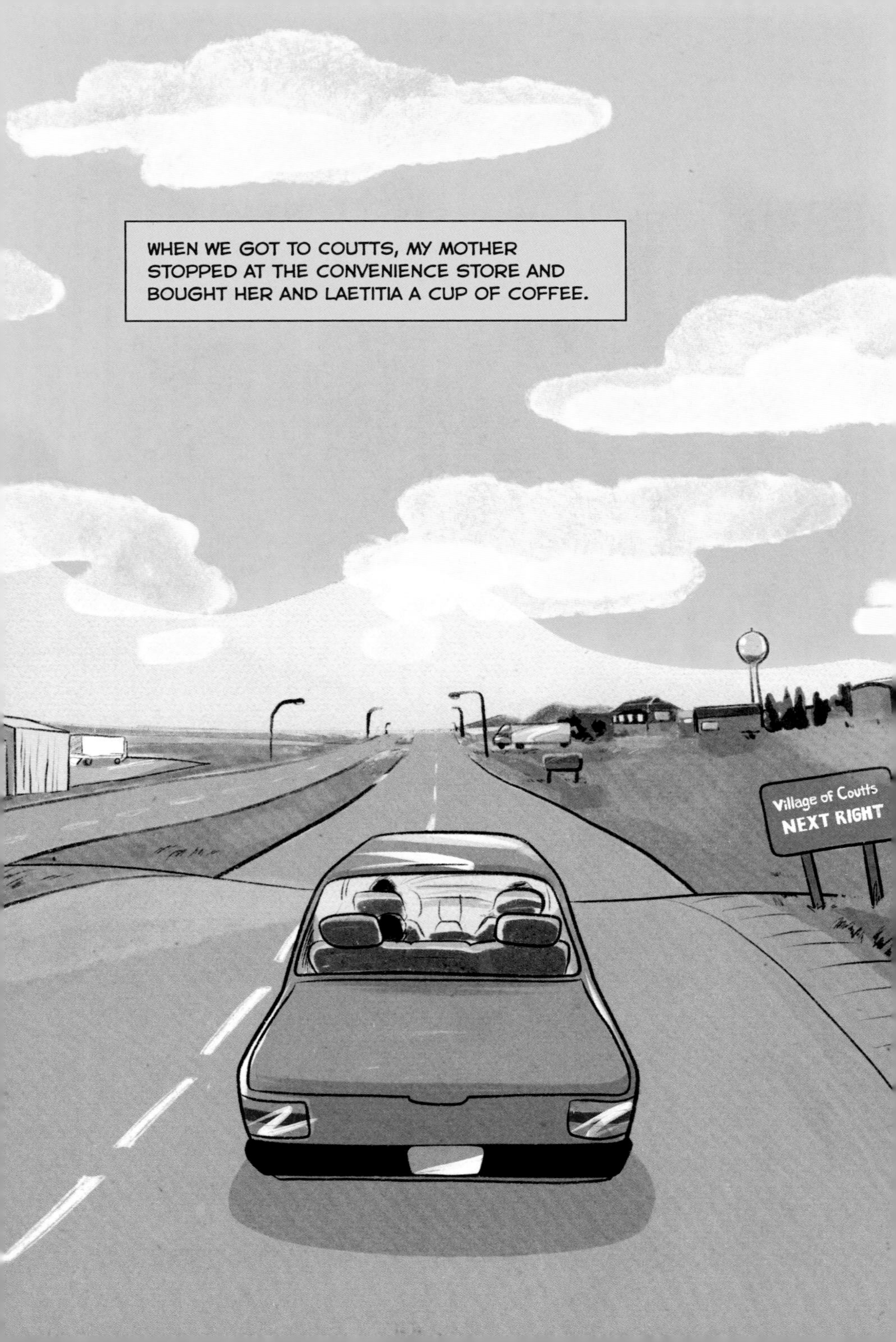
WHEN WE GOT TO COUTTS, MY MOTHER STOPPED AT THE CONVENIENCE STORE AND BOUGHT HER AND LAETITIA A CUP OF COFFEE.
Village of Coutts
NEXT RIGHT

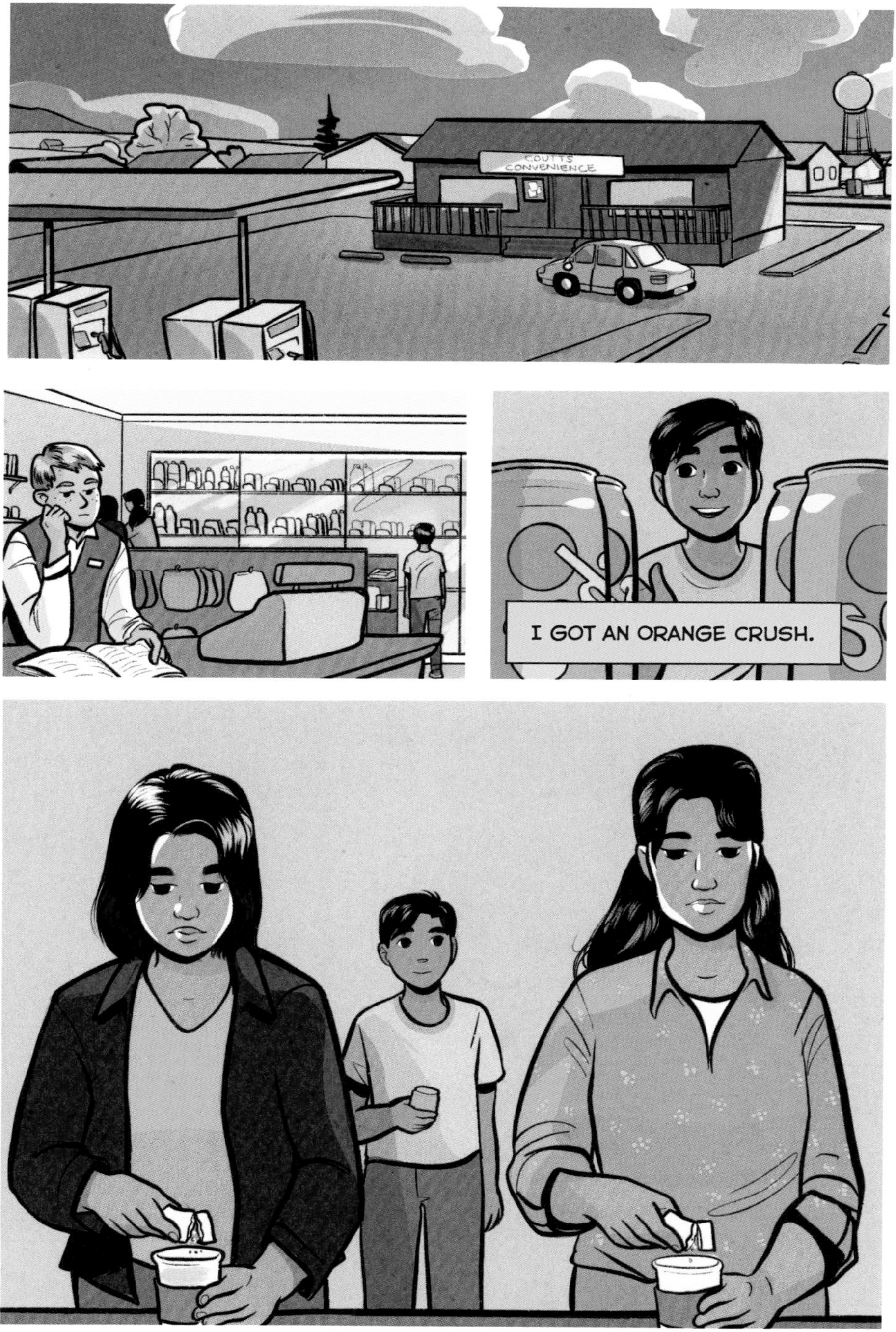
COUTTS
CONVENIENCE
I GOT AN ORANGE CRUSH.

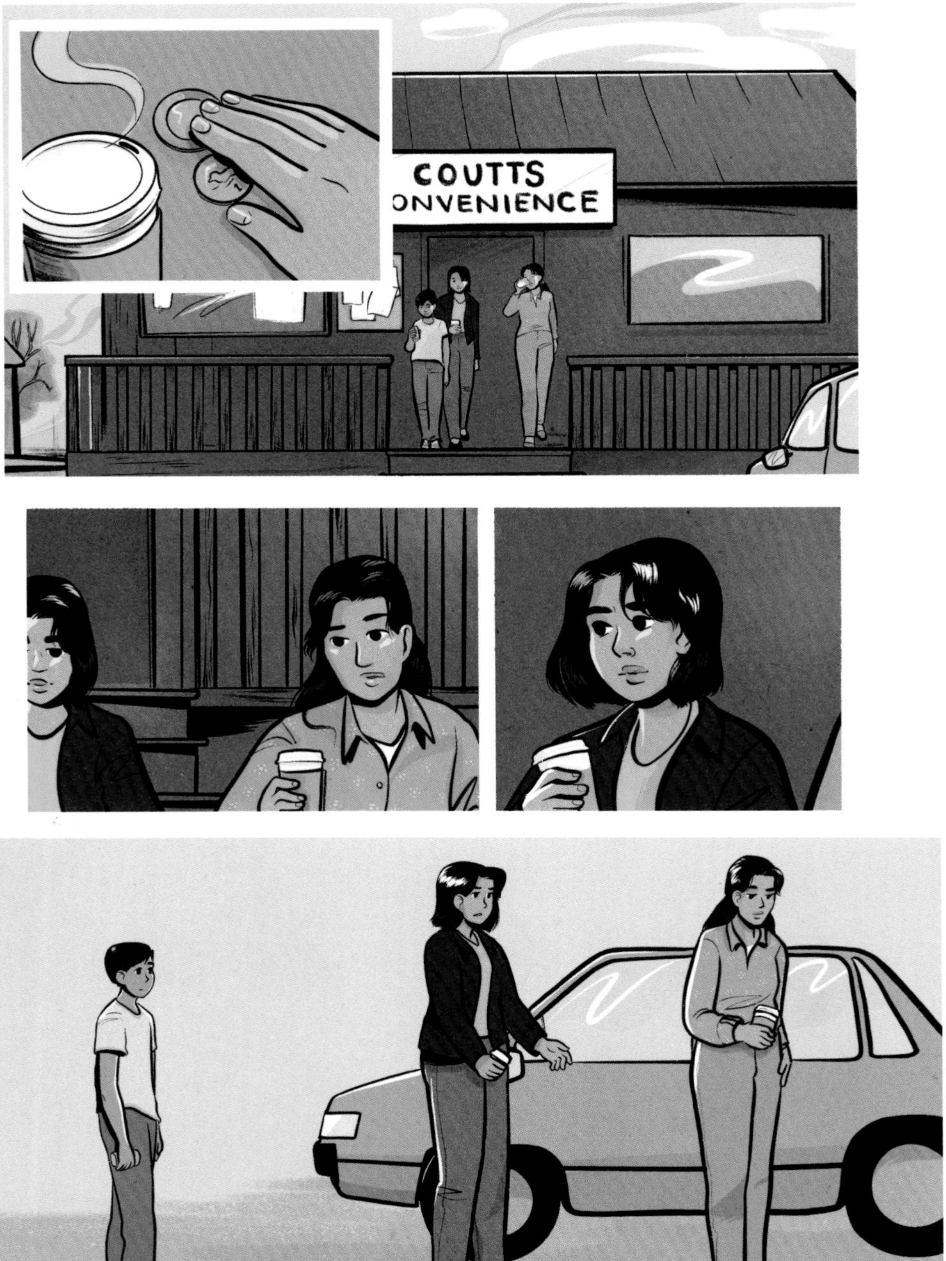
COUTTS
ONVENIENCE

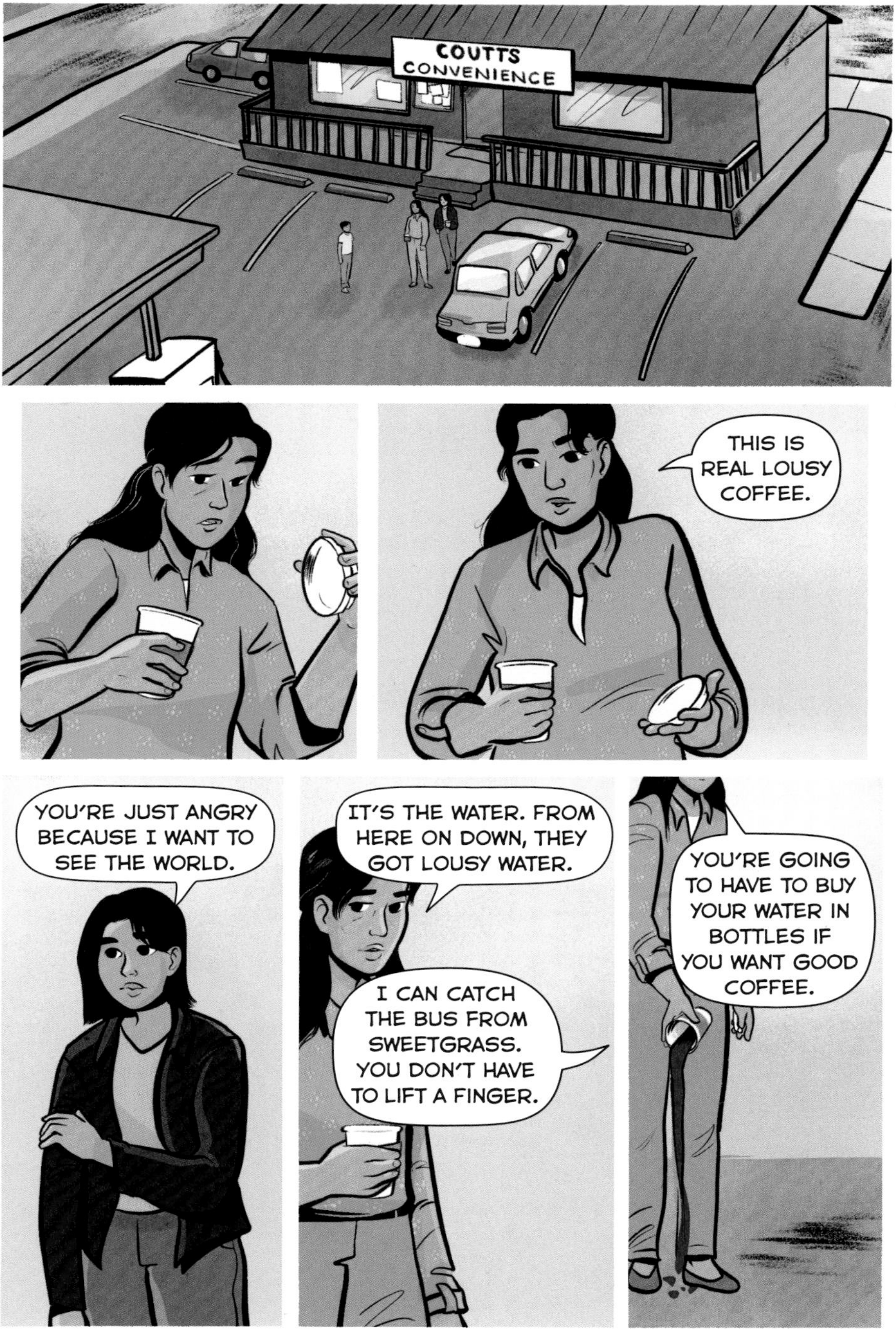
COUTTS
CONVENIENCE
THIS IS REAL LOUSY COFFEE.
YOU'RE JUST ANGRY BECAUSE I WANT TO SEE THE WORLD.
IT'S THE WATER. FROM HERE ON DOWN, THEY GOT LOUSY WATER.
I CAN CATCH THE BUS FROM SWEETGRASS. YOU DON'T HAVE TO LIFT A FINGER.
YOU'RE GOING TO HAVE TO BUY YOUR WATER IN BOTTLES IF YOU WANT GOOD COFFEE.

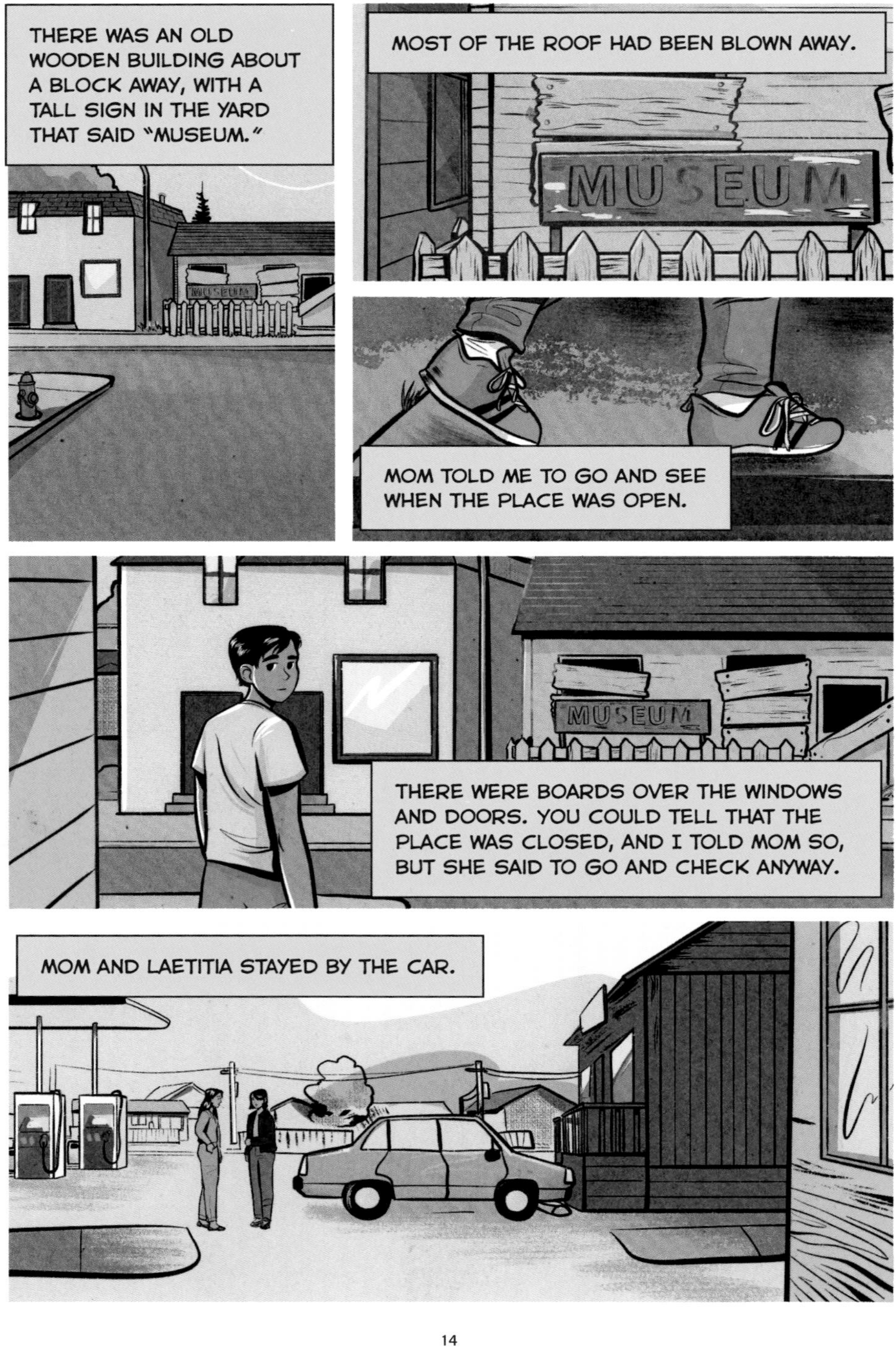
THERE WAS AN OLD WOODEN BUILDING ABOUT A BLOCK AWAY, WITH A TALL SIGN IN THE YARD THAT SAID "MUSEUM."
MOST OF THE ROOF HAD BEEN BLOWN AWAY.
MUSEUM
MOM TOLD ME TO GO AND SEE WHEN THE PLACE WAS OPEN.
MUSEUM
THERE WERE BOARDS OVER THE WINDOWS AND DOORS. YOU COULD TELL THAT THE PLACE WAS CLOSED, AND I TOLD MOM SO, BUT SHE SAID TO GO AND CHECK ANYWAY.
MOM AND LAETITIA STAYED BY THE CAR.

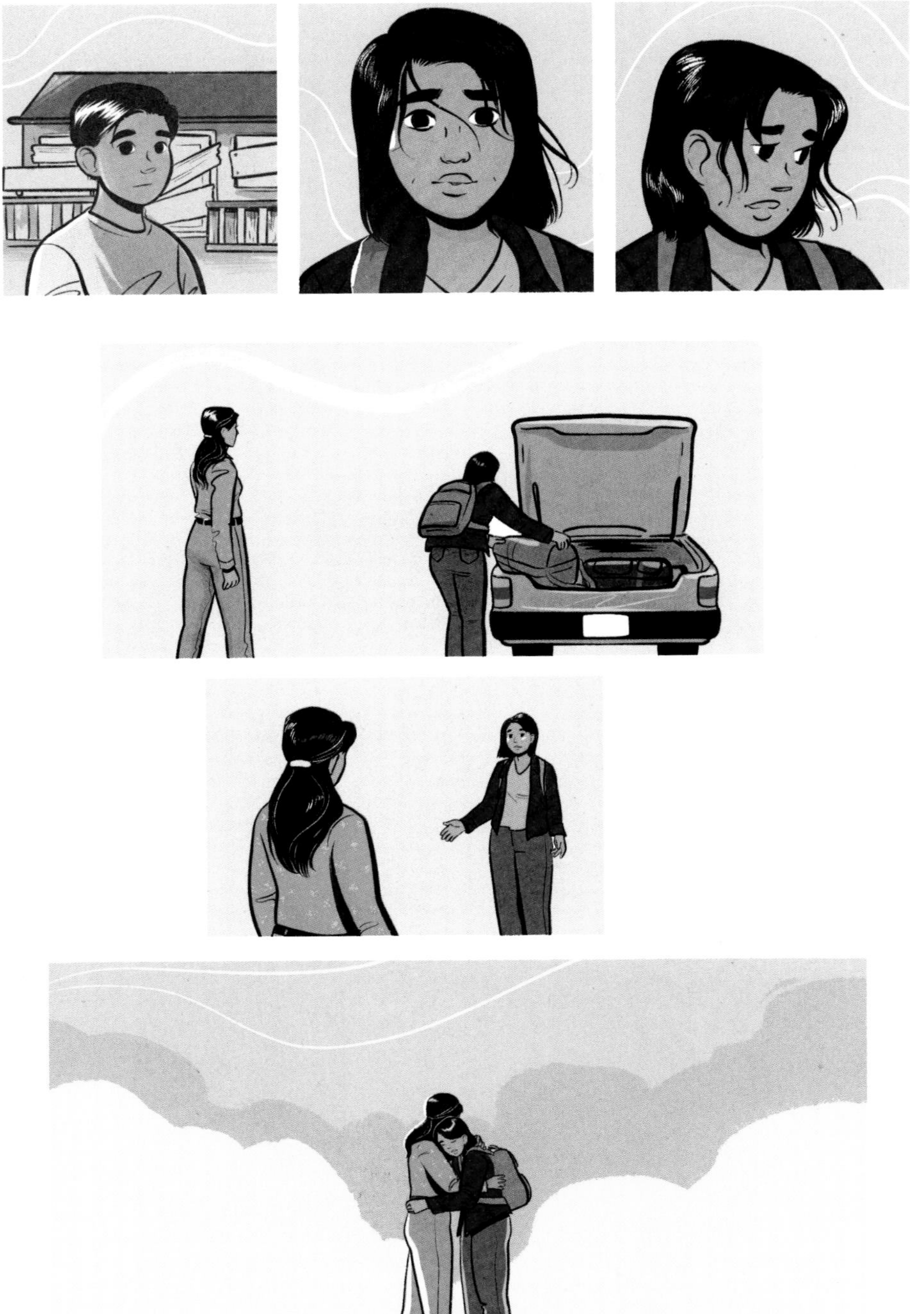

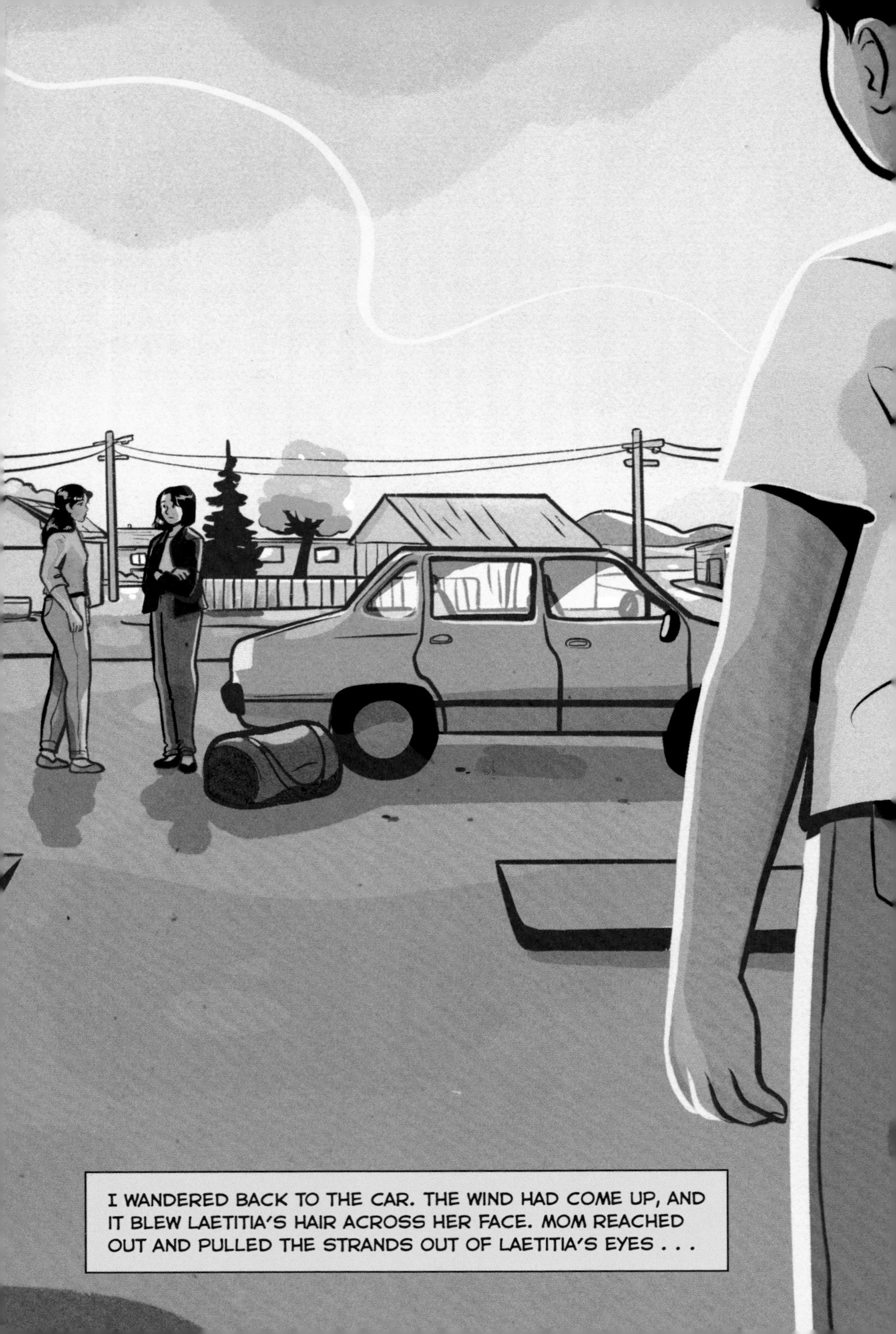
I WANDERED BACK TO THE CAR. THE WIND HAD COME UP, AND IT BLEW LAETITIA'S HAIR ACROSS HER FACE. MOM REACHED OUT AND PULLED THE STRANDS OUT OF LAETITIA'S EYES . . .

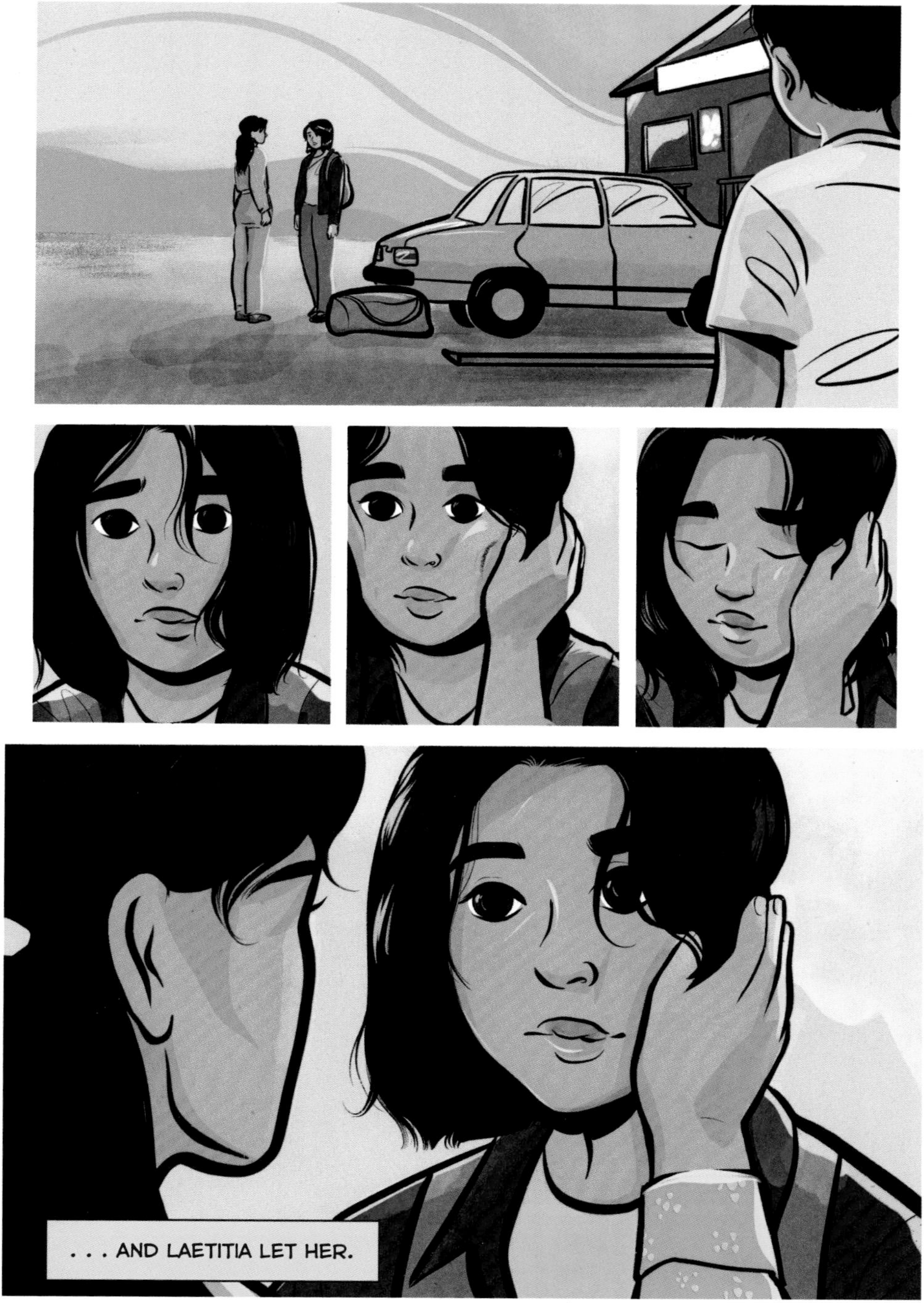
. . . AND LAETITIA LET HER.

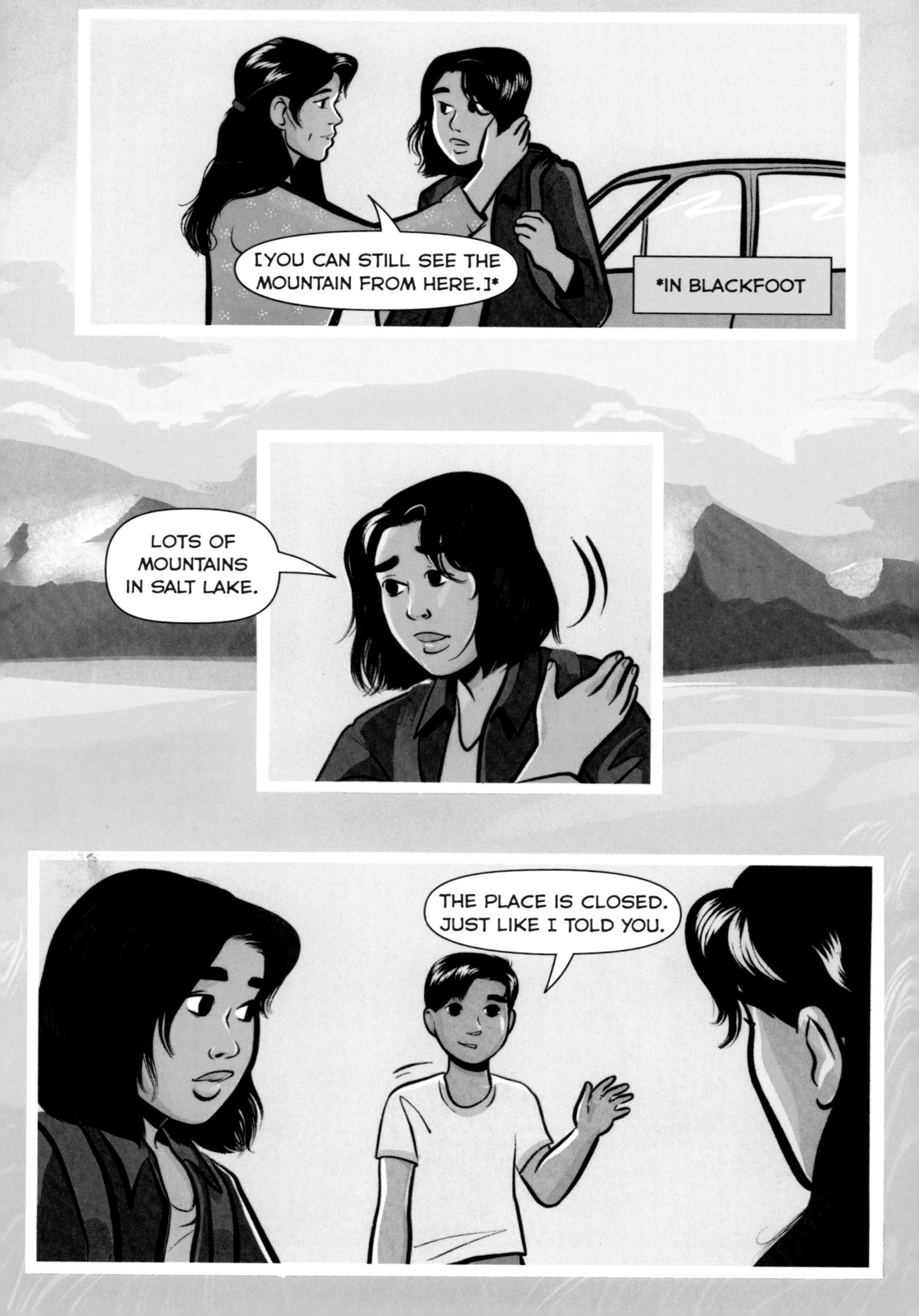
[YOU CAN STILL SEE THE MOUNTAIN FROM HERE.]*
*IN BLACKFOOT
LOTS OF MOUNTAINS IN SALT LAKE.
THE PLACE IS CLOSED. JUST LIKE I TOLD YOU.

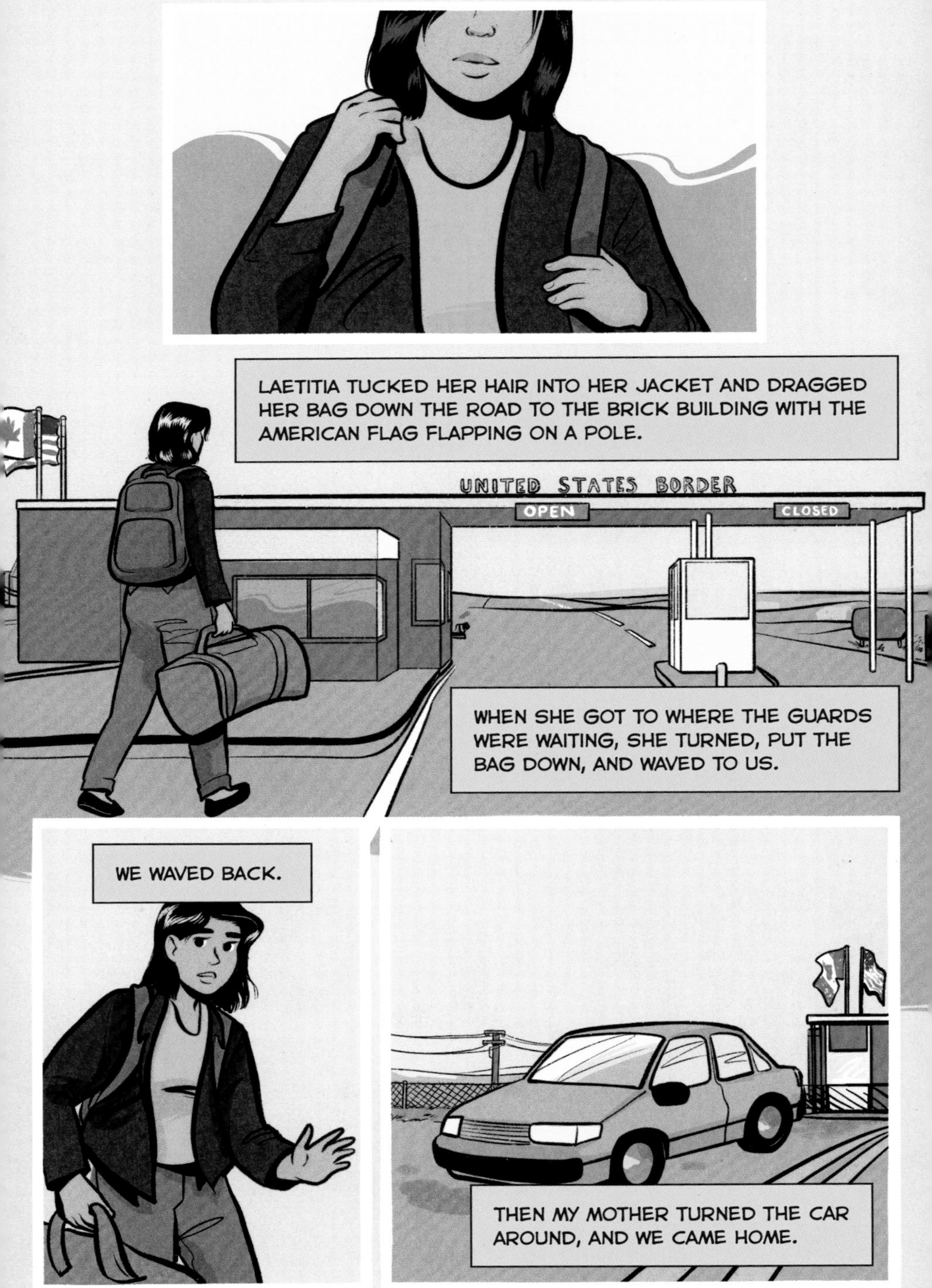
LAETITIA TUCKED HER HAIR INTO HER JACKET AND DRAGGED HER BAG DOWN THE ROAD TO THE BRICK BUILDING WITH THE AMERICAN FLAG FLAPPING ON A POLE.
UNITED STATES BORDER
OPEN
CLOSED
WHEN SHE GOT TO WHERE THE GUARDS WERE WAITING, SHE TURNED, PUT THE BAG DOWN, AND WAVED TO US.
WE WAVED BACK.
THEN MY MOTHER TURNED THE CAR AROUND, AND WE CAME HOME.

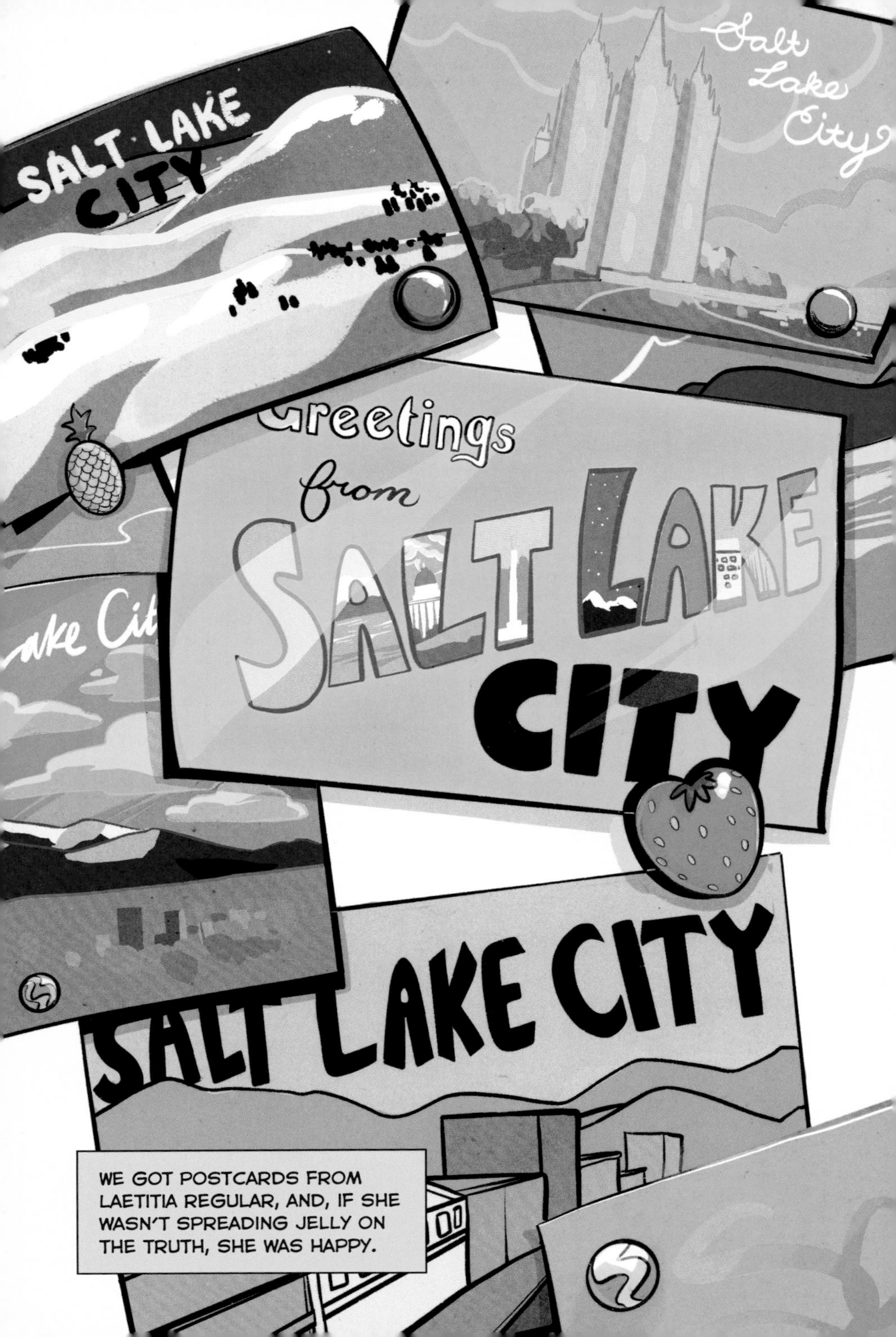
SALT LAKE CITY
Salt Lake City
Greetings from SALT LAKE CITY
SALT LAKE CITY
WE GOT POSTCARDS FROM LAETITIA REGULAR, AND, IF SHE WASN'T SPREADING JELLY ON THE TRUTH, SHE WAS HAPPY.

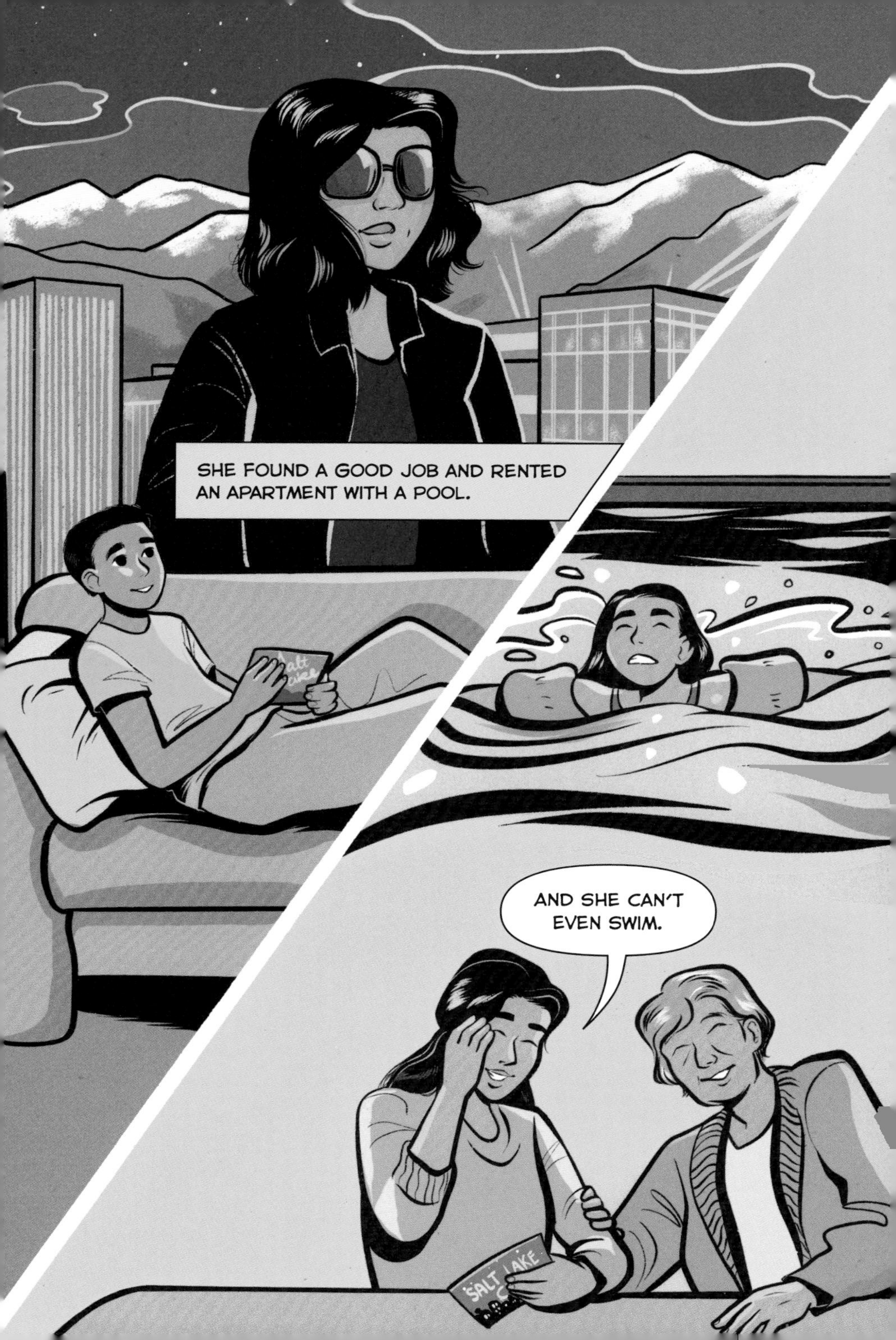
SHE FOUND A GOOD JOB AND RENTED AN APARTMENT WITH A POOL.
AND SHE CAN'T EVEN SWIM.

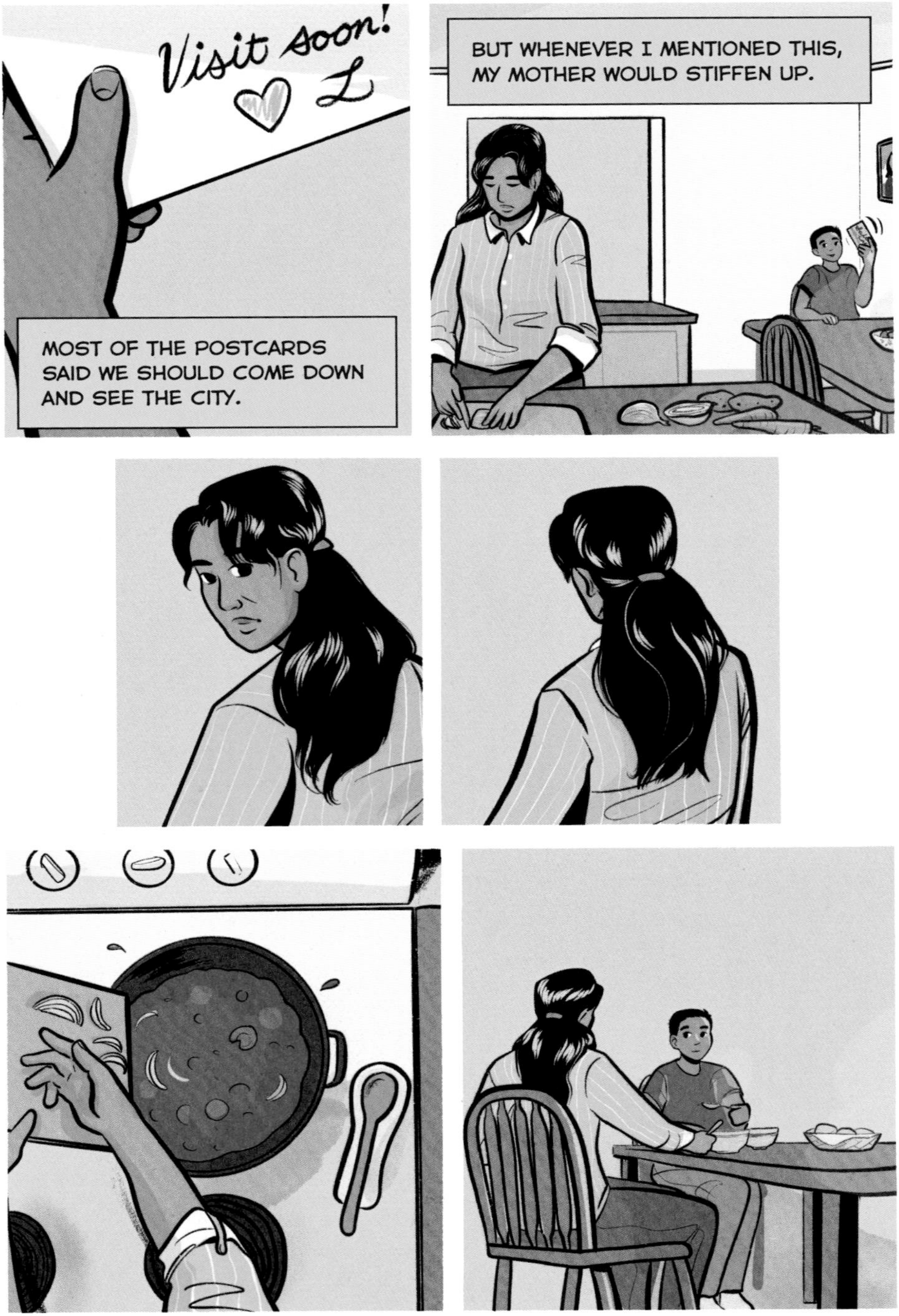
Visit soon!
L
MOST OF THE POSTCARDS SAID WE SHOULD COME DOWN AND SEE THE CITY.
BUT WHENEVER I MENTIONED THIS, MY MOTHER WOULD STIFFEN UP.

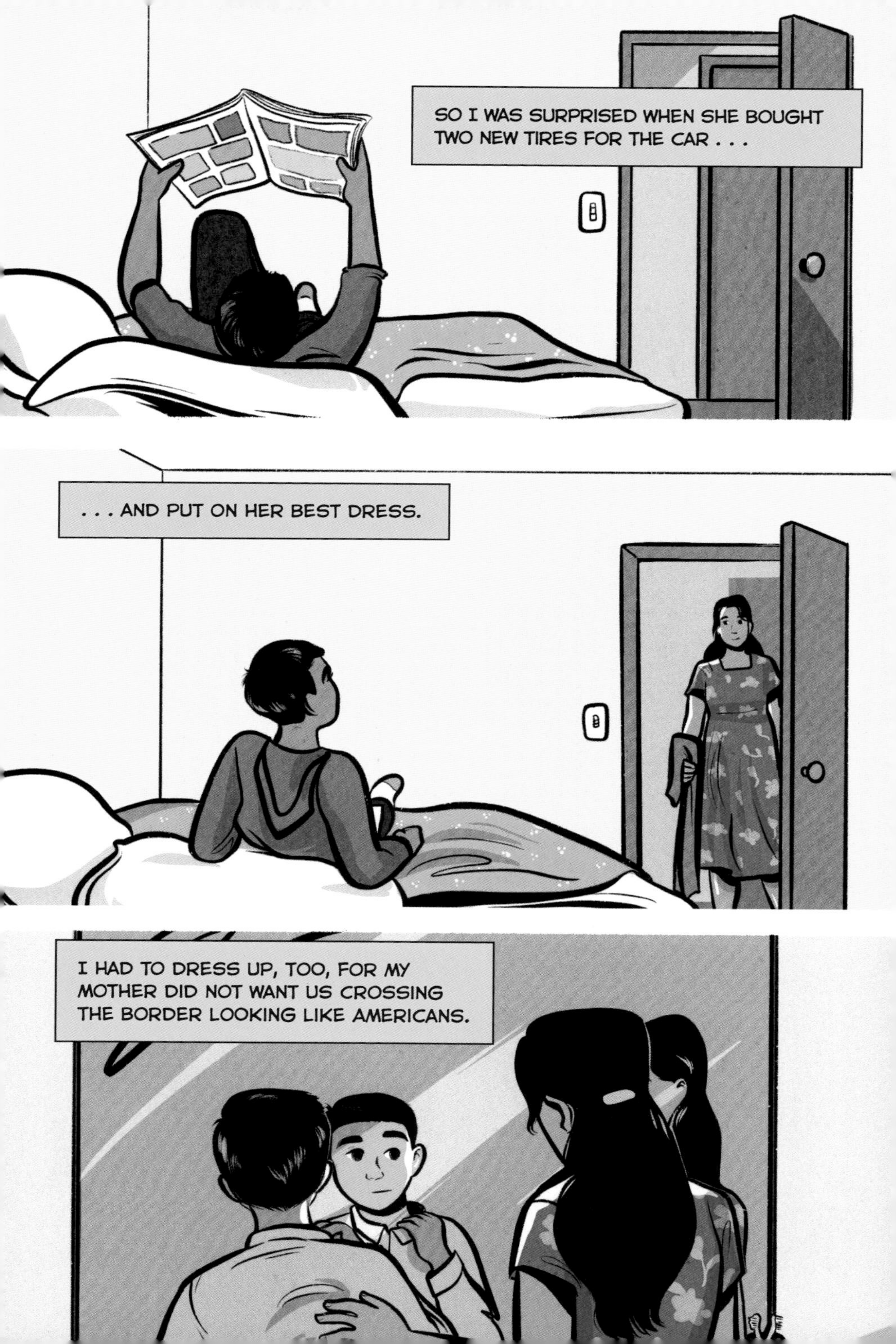
SO I WAS SURPRISED WHEN SHE BOUGHT TWO NEW TIRES FOR THE CAR . . .
. . . AND PUT ON HER BEST DRESS.
I HAD TO DRESS UP, TOO, FOR MY MOTHER DID NOT WANT US CROSSING THE BORDER LOOKING LIKE AMERICANS.

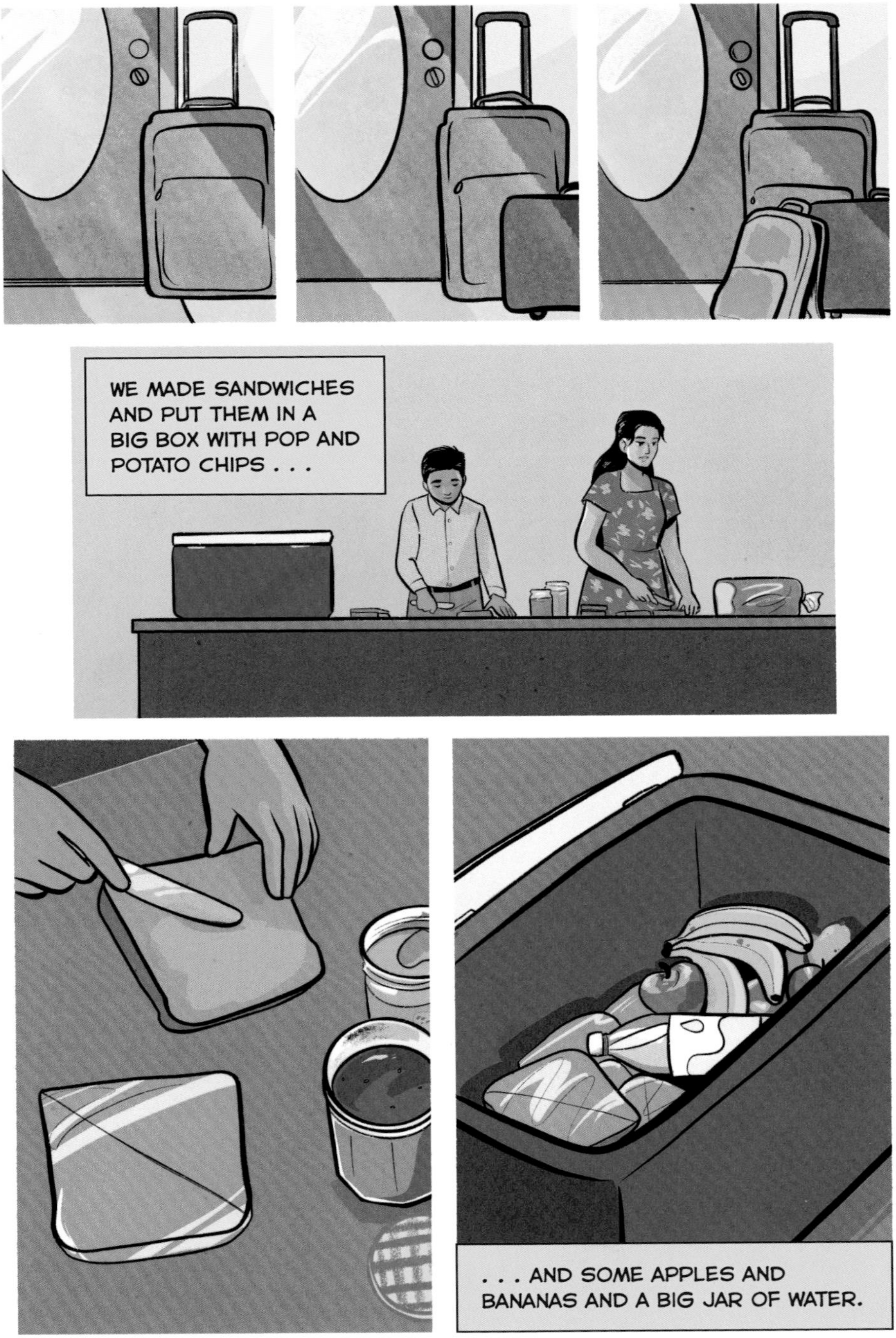
WE MADE SANDWICHES AND PUT THEM IN A BIG BOX WITH POP AND POTATO CHIPS . . .
. . . AND SOME APPLES AND BANANAS AND A BIG JAR OF WATER.

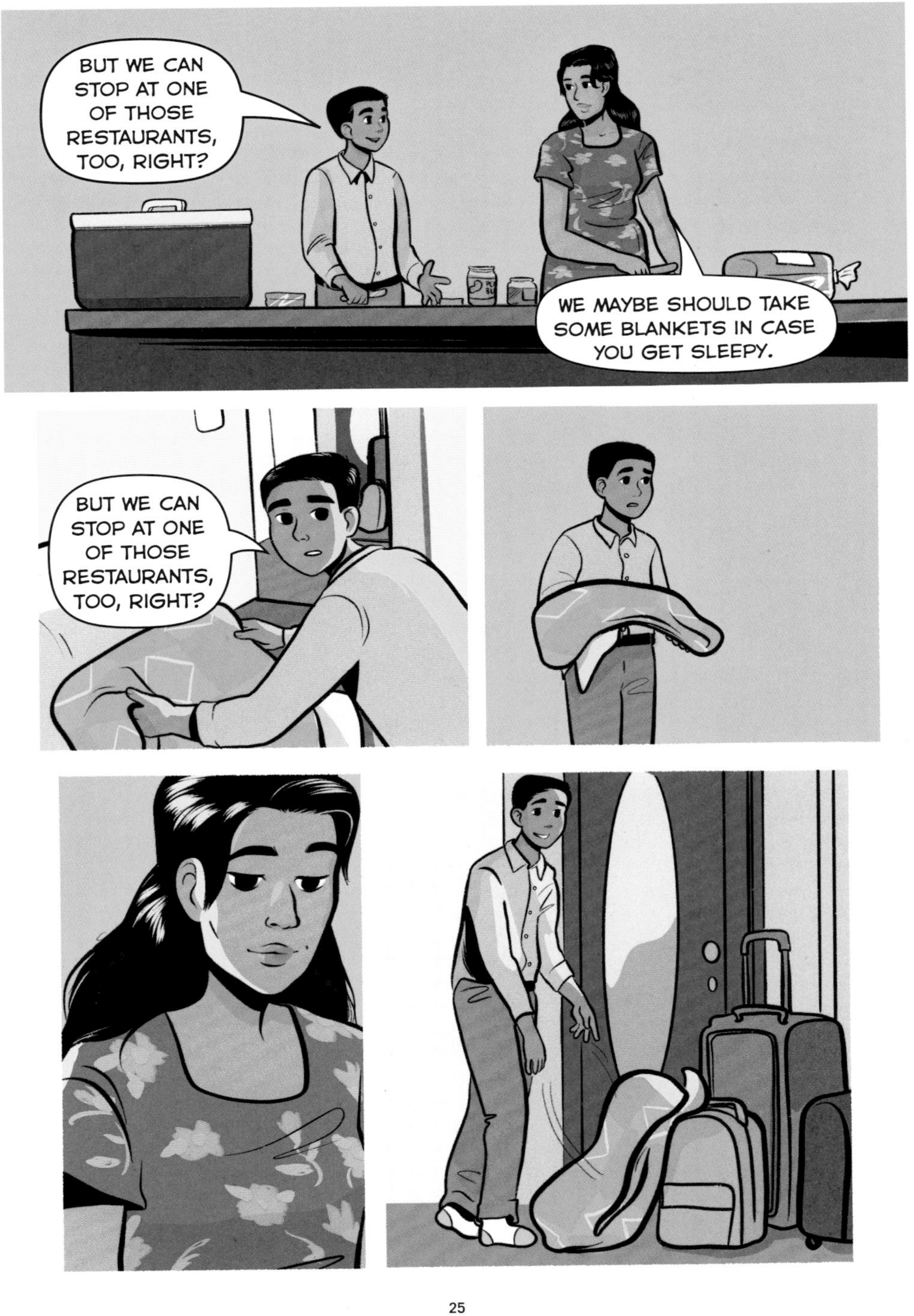
BUT WE CAN STOP AT ONE OF THOSE RESTAURANTS, TOO, RIGHT?
WE MAYBE SHOULD TAKE SOME BLANKETS IN CASE YOU GET SLEEPY.
BUT WE CAN STOP AT ONE OF THOSE RESTAURANTS, TOO, RIGHT?

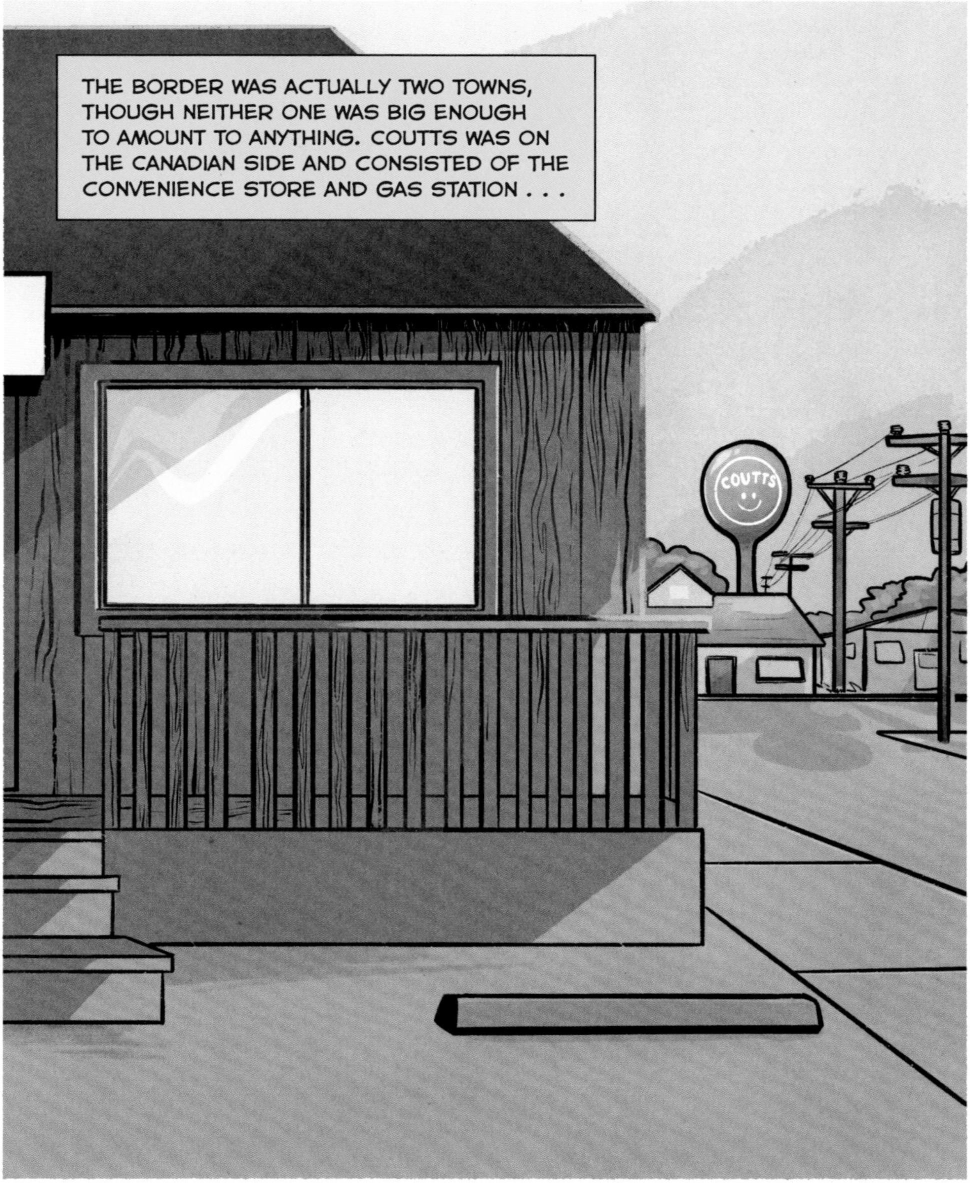
THE BORDER WAS ACTUALLY TWO TOWNS, THOUGH NEITHER ONE WAS BIG ENOUGH TO AMOUNT TO ANYTHING. COUTTS WAS ON THE CANADIAN SIDE AND CONSISTED OF THE CONVENIENCE STORE AND GAS STATION . . .
COUTTS

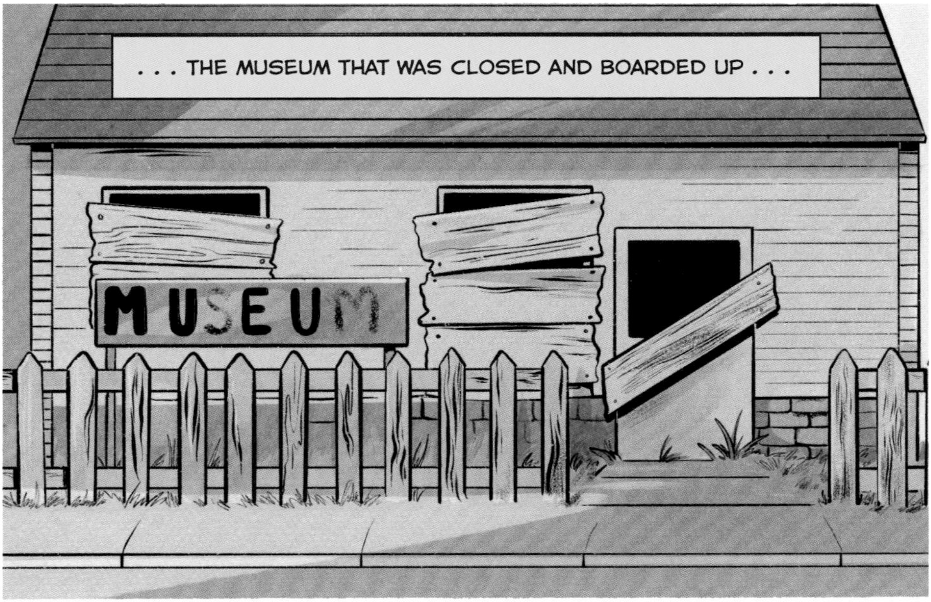
. . . THE MUSEUM THAT WAS CLOSED AND BOARDED UP . . .
MUSEUM

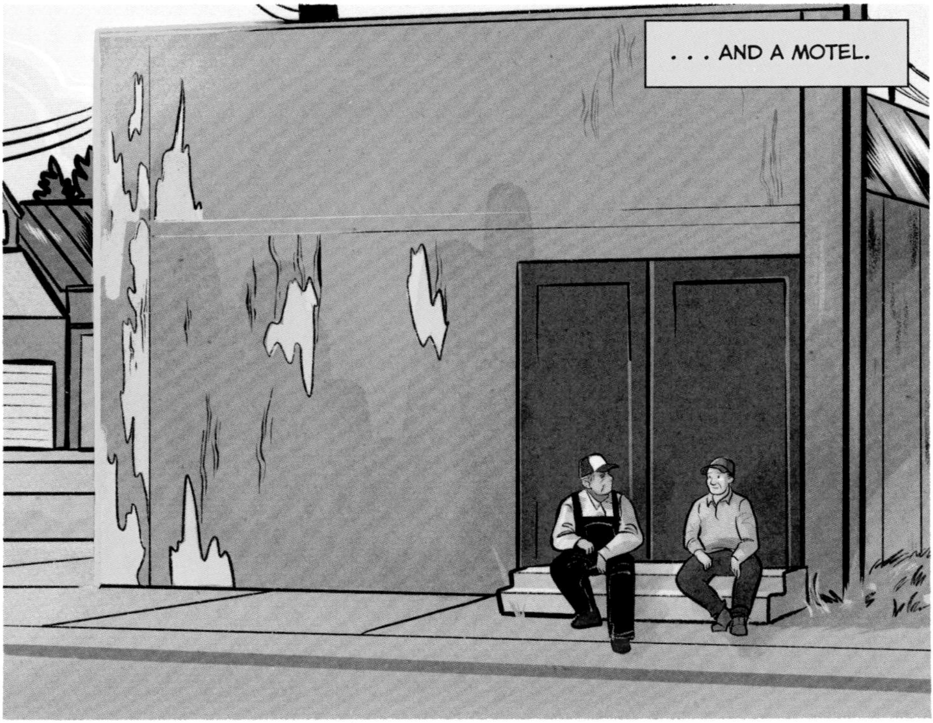
. . . AND A MOTEL.

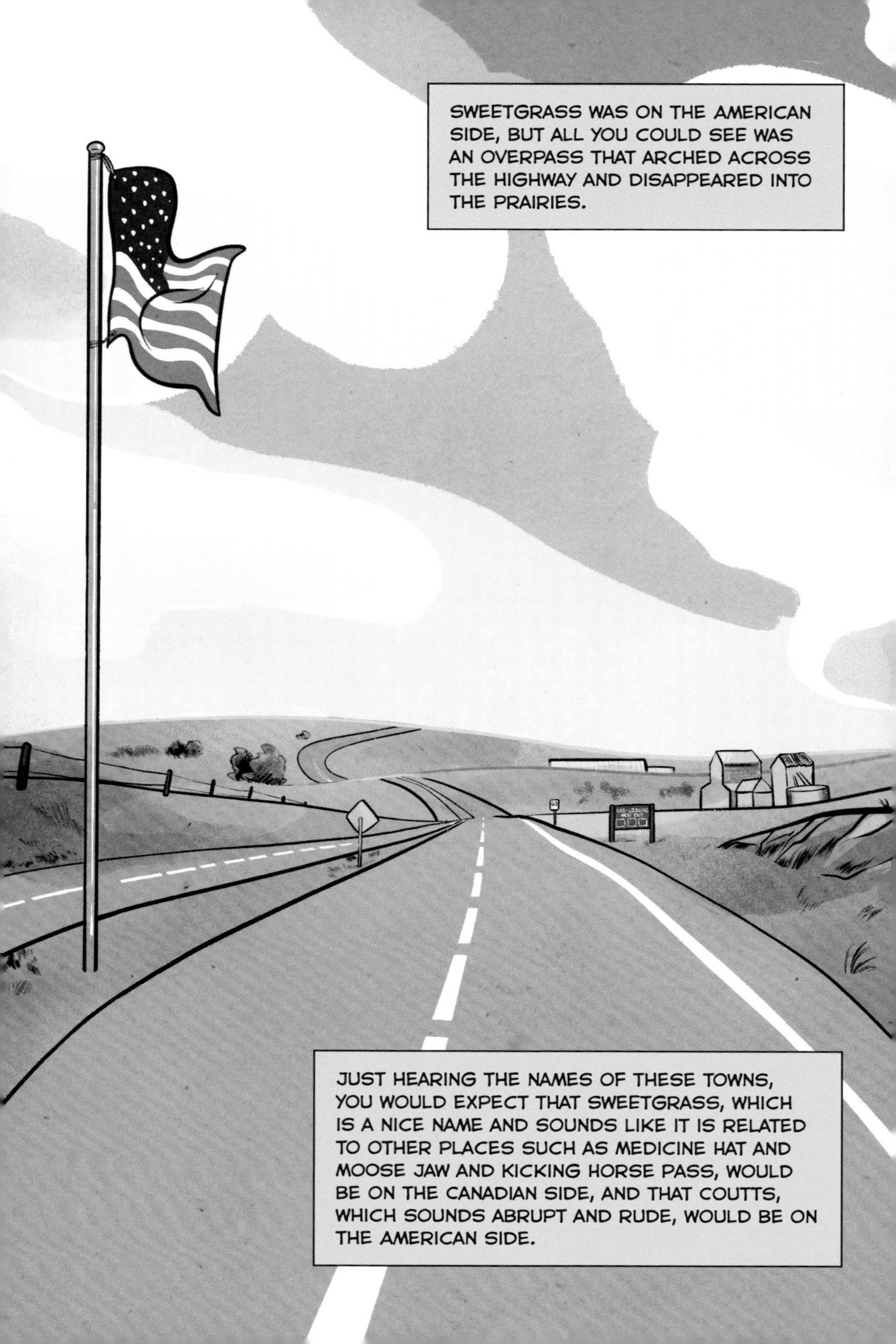
SWEETGRASS WAS ON THE AMERICAN SIDE, BUT ALL YOU COULD SEE WAS AN OVERPASS THAT ARCHED ACROSS THE HIGHWAY AND DISAPPEARED INTO THE PRAIRIES.
JUST HEARING THE NAMES OF THESE TOWNS, YOU WOULD EXPECT THAT SWEETGRASS, WHICH IS A NICE NAME AND SOUNDS LIKE IT IS RELATED TO OTHER PLACES SUCH AS MEDICINE HAT AND MOOSE JAW AND KICKING HORSE PASS, WOULD BE ON THE CANADIAN SIDE, AND THAT COUTTS, WHICH SOUNDS ABRUPT AND RUDE, WOULD BE ON THE AMERICAN SIDE.

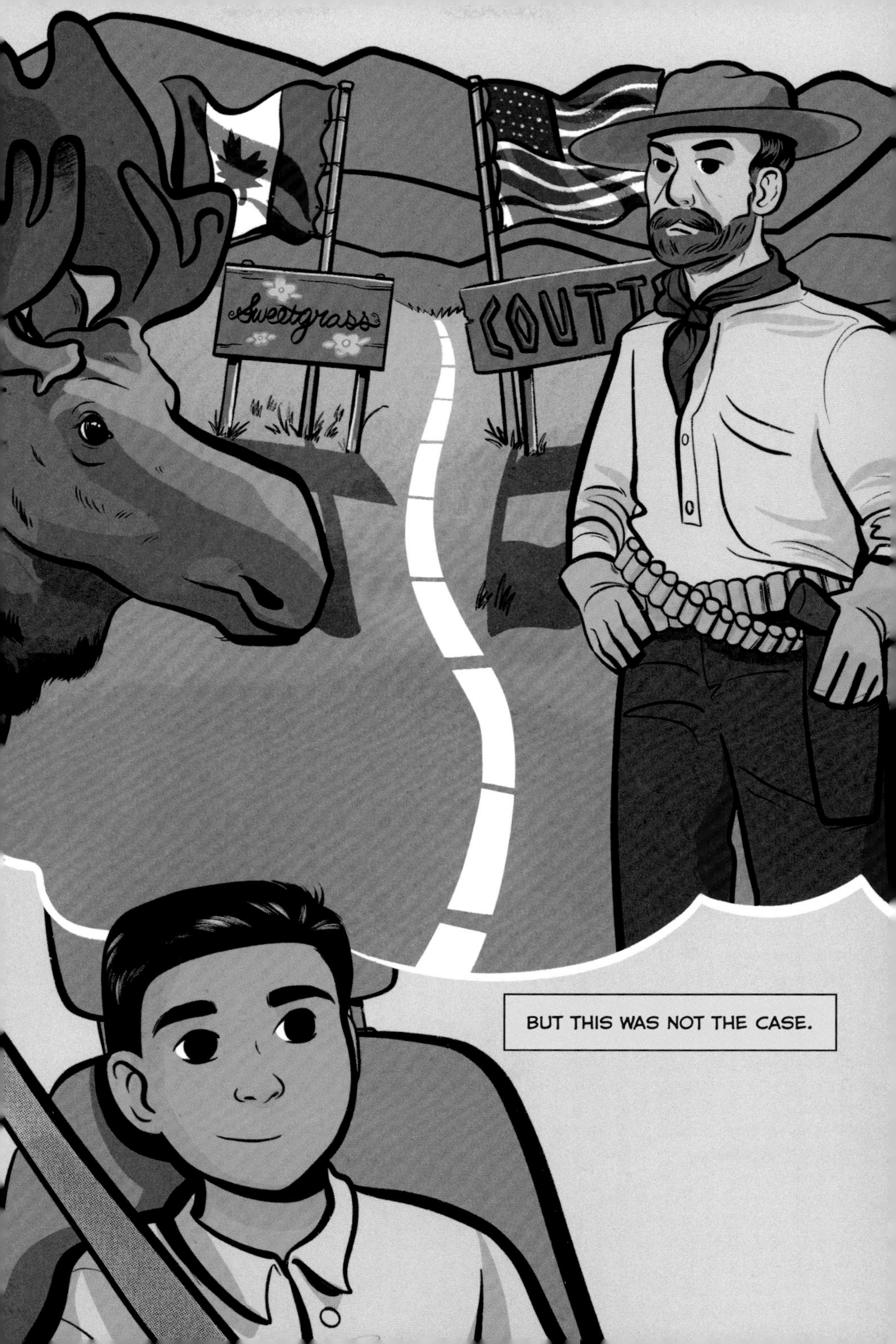
Sweetgrass
BUT THIS WAS NOT THE CASE.

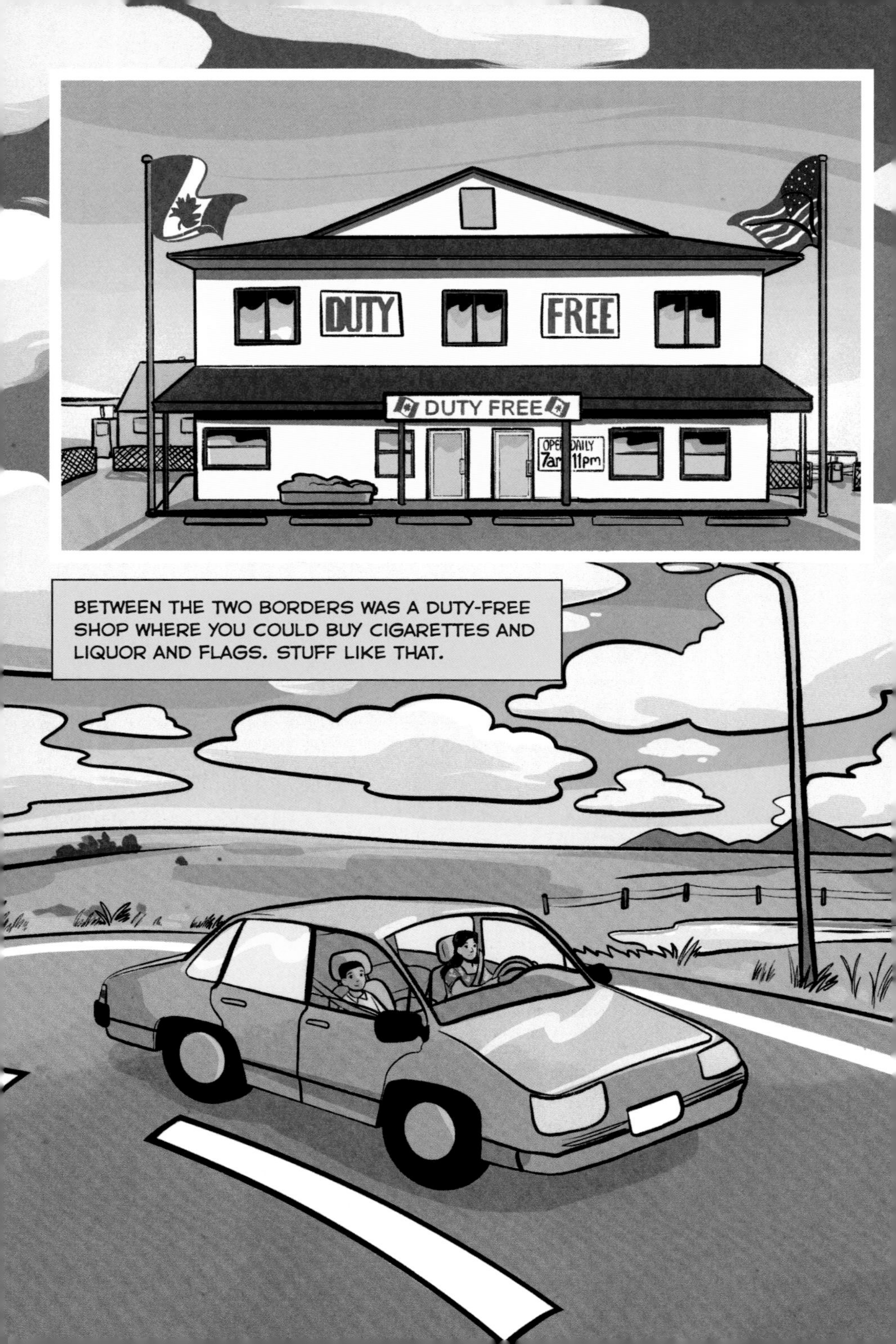
DUTY
FREE
DUTY FREE
BETWEEN THE TWO BORDERS WAS A DUTY-FREE SHOP WHERE YOU COULD BUY CIGARETTES AND LIQUOR AND FLAGS. STUFF LIKE THAT.

WE LEFT THE RESERVE IN THE MORNING AND DROVE UNTIL WE GOT TO COUTTS.

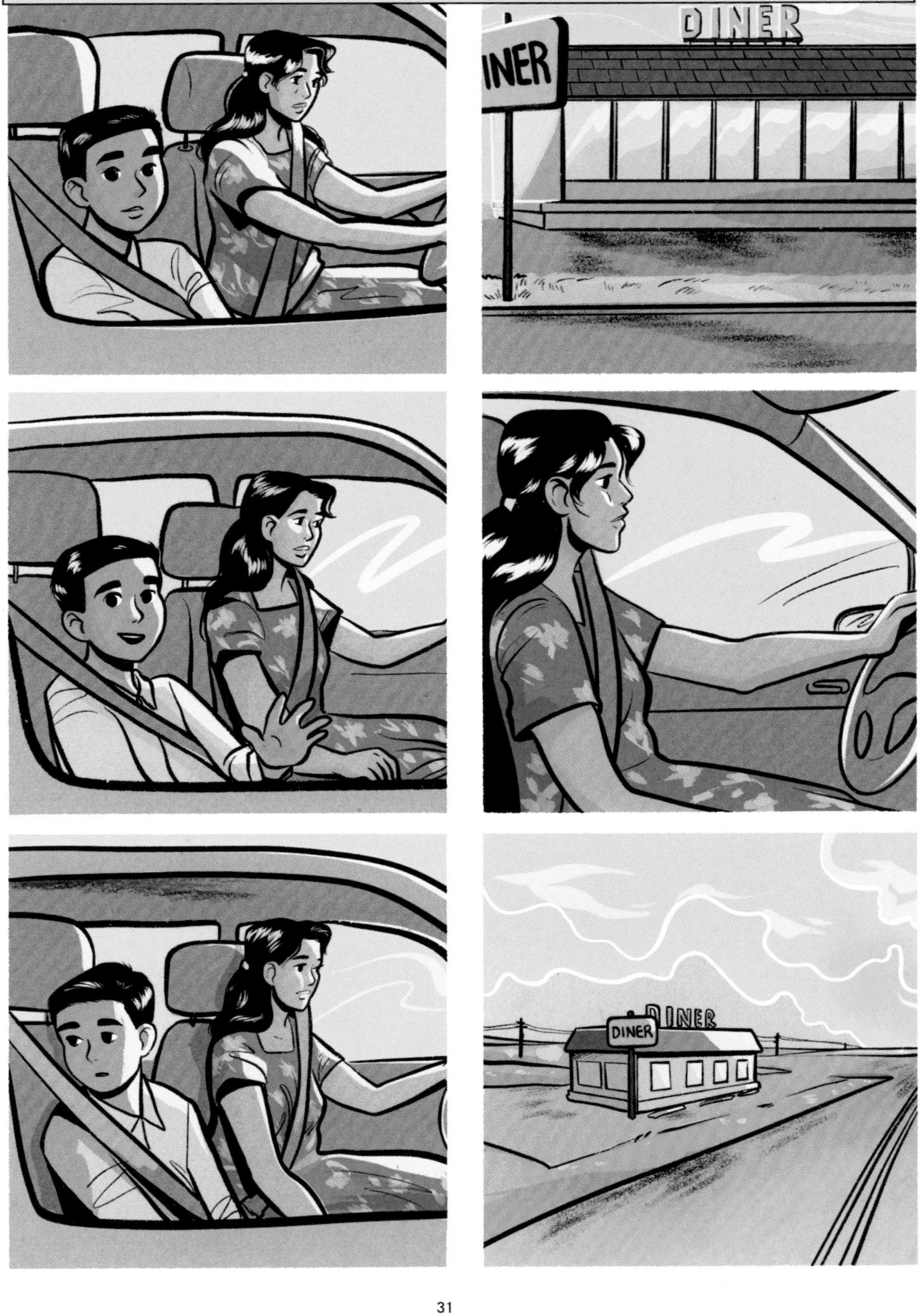
DINER
INER
DINER
DINER
DINER

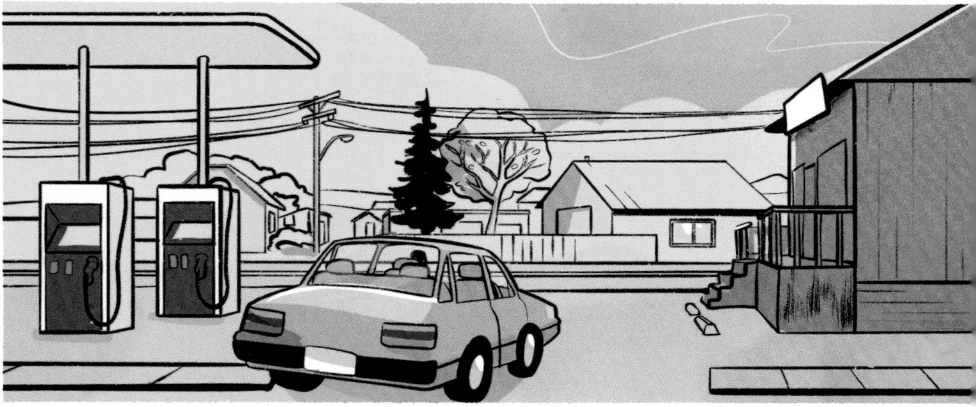

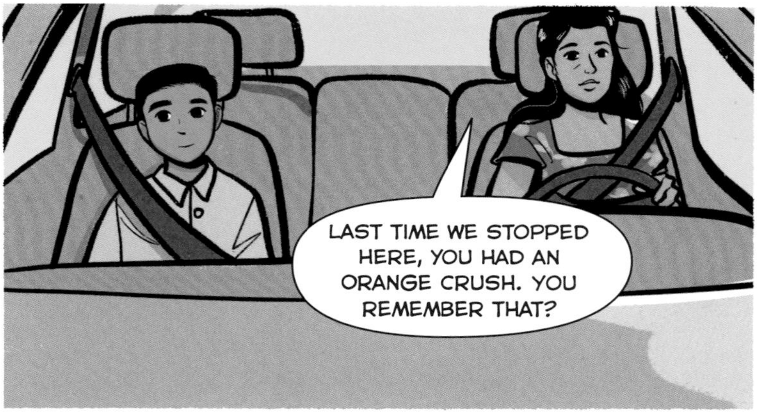
LAST TIME WE STOPPED HERE, YOU HAD AN ORANGE CRUSH. YOU REMEMBER THAT?

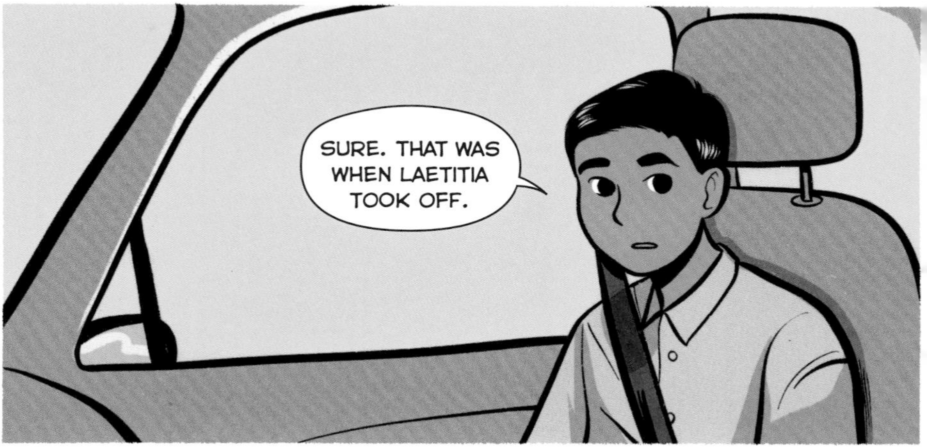
SURE. THAT WAS WHEN LAETITIA TOOK OFF.

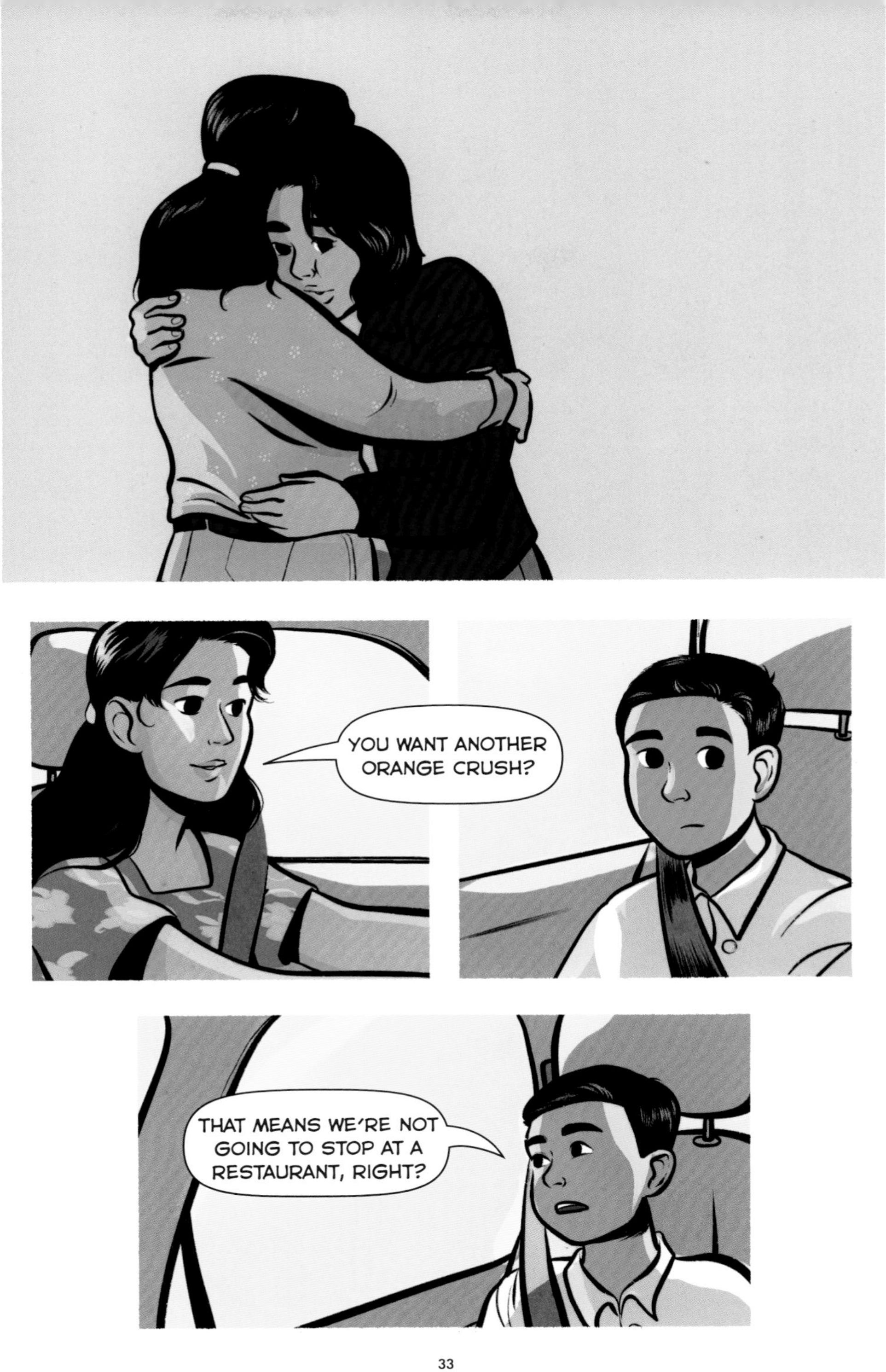
YOU WANT ANOTHER ORANGE CRUSH?
THAT MEANS WE'RE NOT GOING TO STOP AT A RESTAURANT, RIGHT?

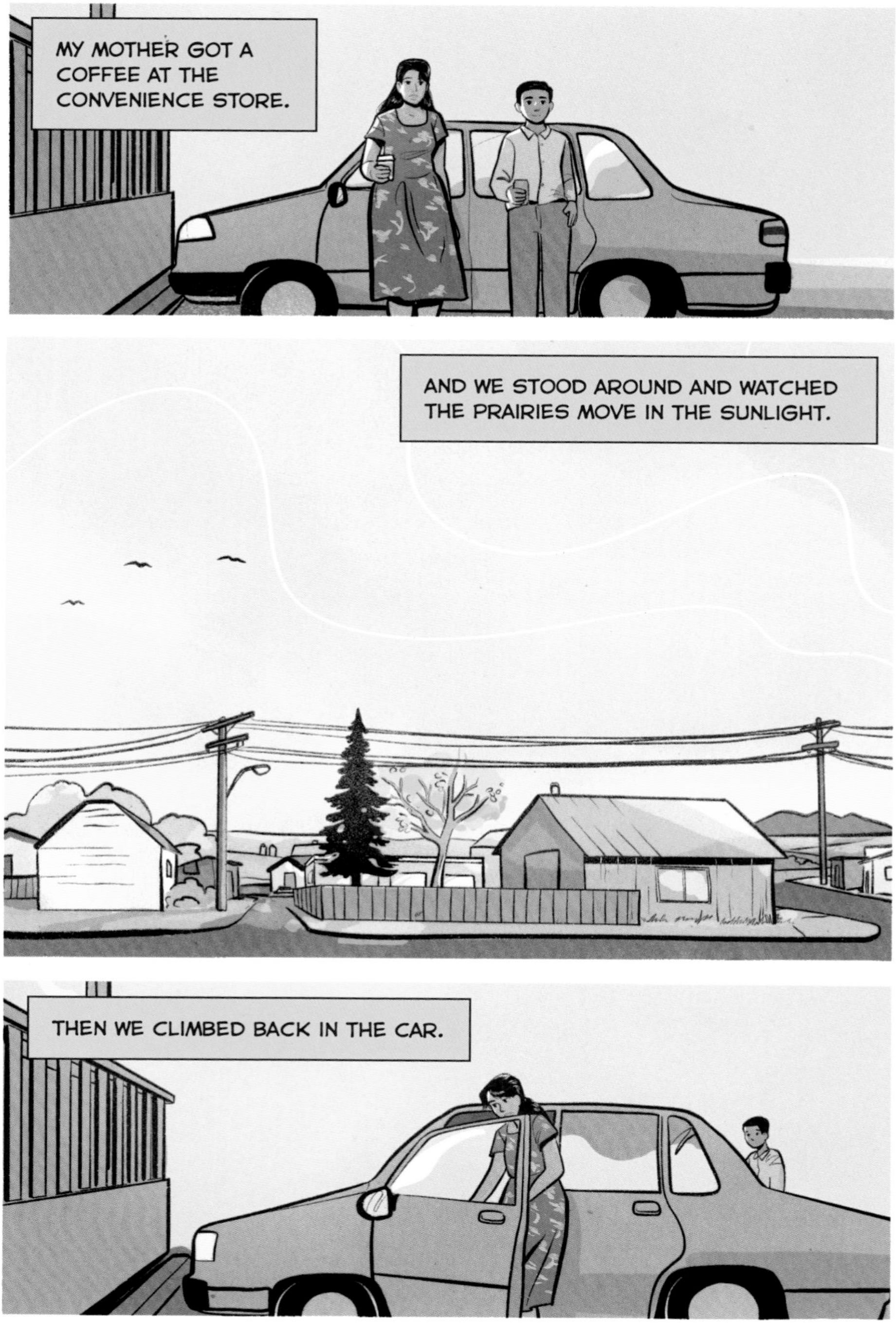
MY MOTHER GOT A COFFEE AT THE CONVENIENCE STORE.
AND WE STOOD AROUND AND WATCHED THE PRAIRIES MOVE IN THE SUNLIGHT.
THEN WE CLIMBED BACK IN THE CAR.

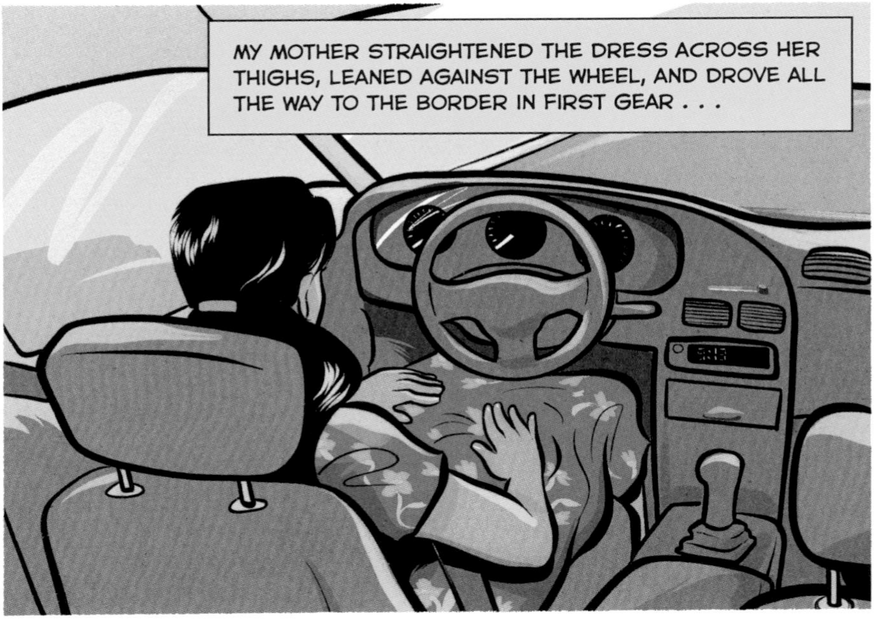
MY MOTHER STRAIGHTENED THE DRESS ACROSS HER THIGHS, LEANED AGAINST THE WHEEL, AND DROVE ALL THE WAY TO THE BORDER IN FIRST GEAR . . .

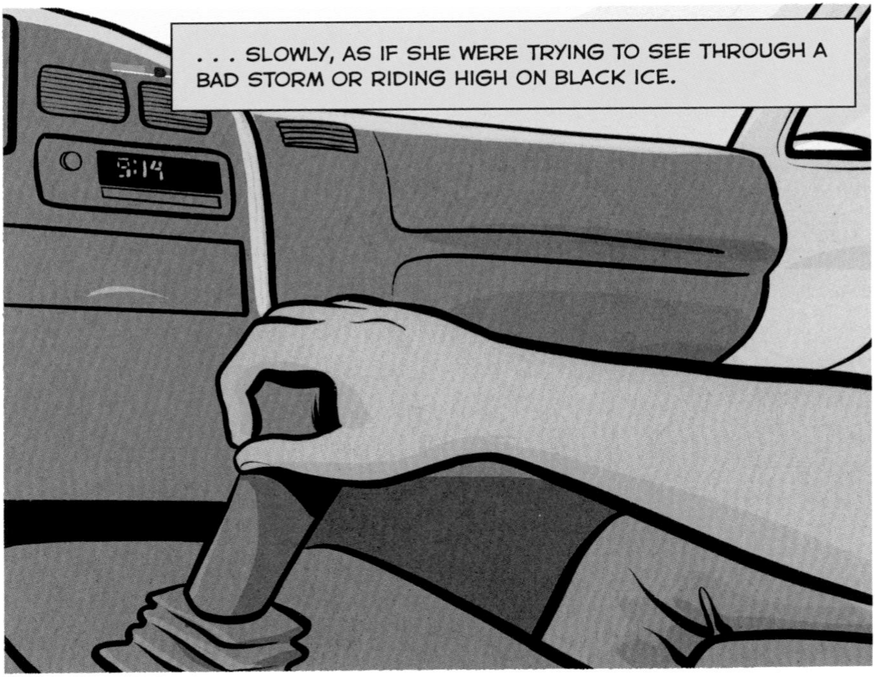
. . . SLOWLY, AS IF SHE WERE TRYING TO SEE THROUGH A BAD STORM OR RIDING HIGH ON BLACK ICE.
9:14

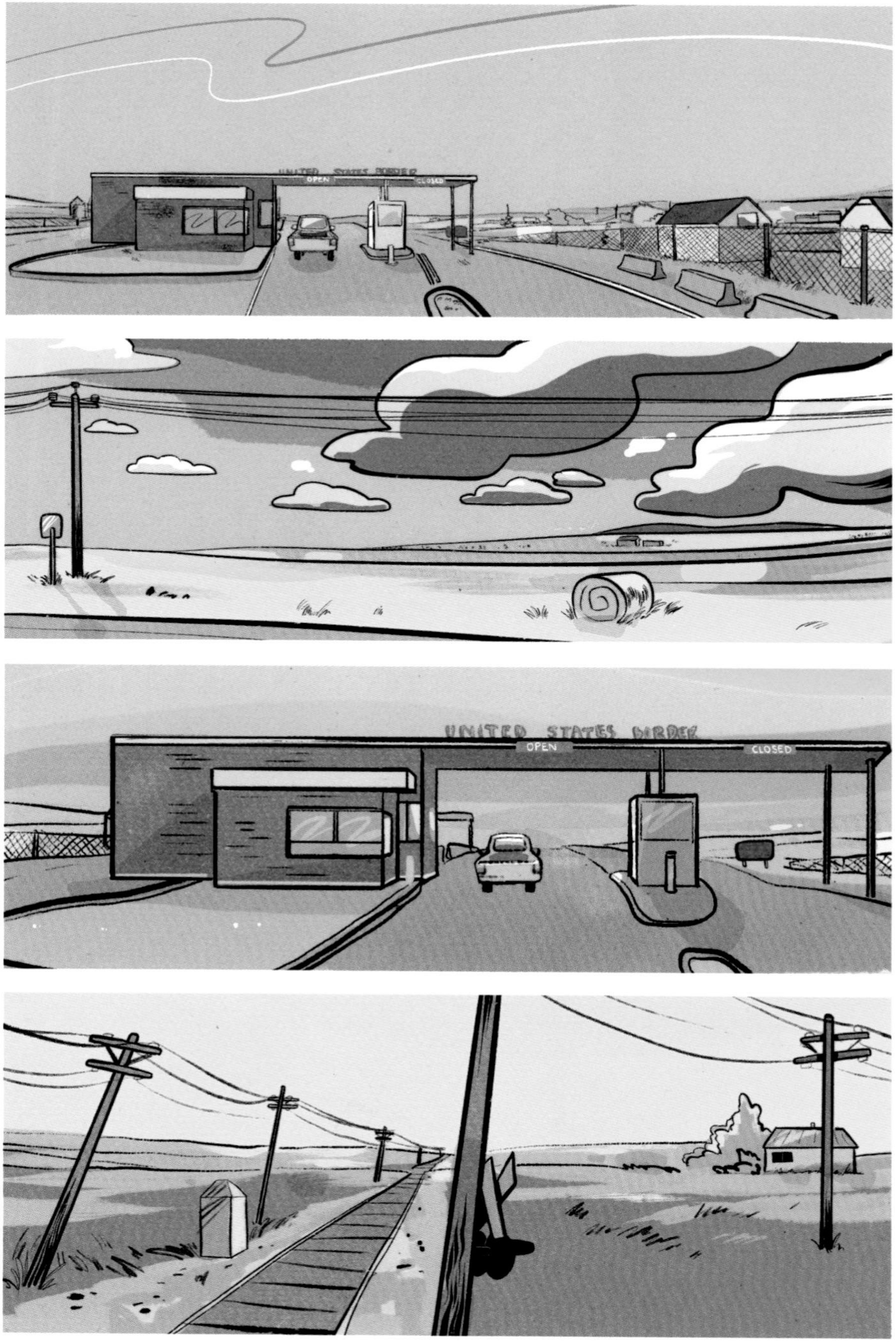
UNITED STATES BORDER
OPEN
CLOSED
UNITED STATES BORDER
OPEN
CLOSED

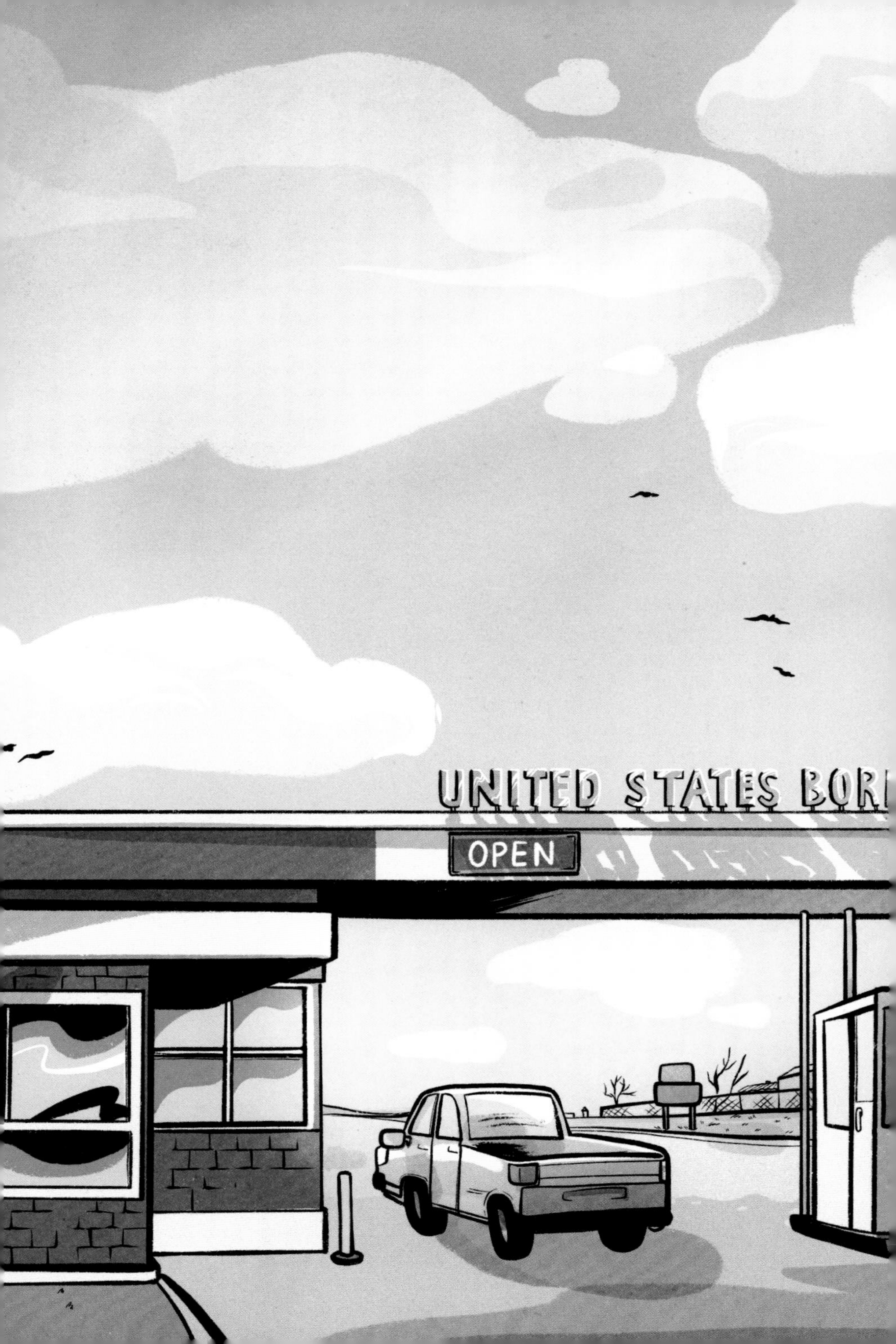
UNITED STATES BOR
OPEN

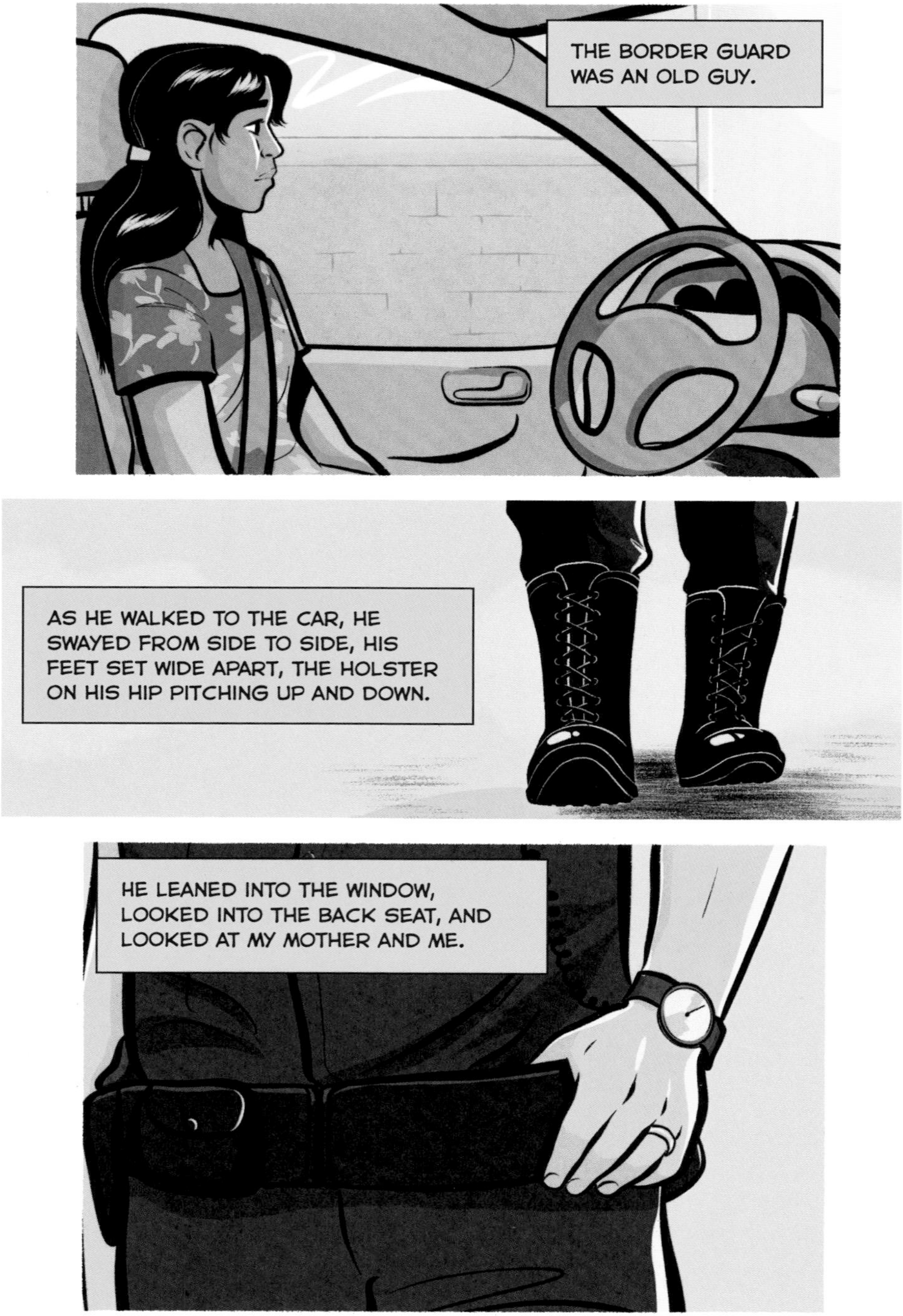
THE BORDER GUARD WAS AN OLD GUY.
AS HE WALKED TO THE CAR, HE SWAYED FROM SIDE TO SIDE, HIS FEET SET WIDE APART, THE HOLSTER ON HIS HIP PITCHING UP AND DOWN.
HE LEANED INTO THE WINDOW, LOOKED INTO THE BACK SEAT, AND LOOKED AT MY MOTHER AND ME.

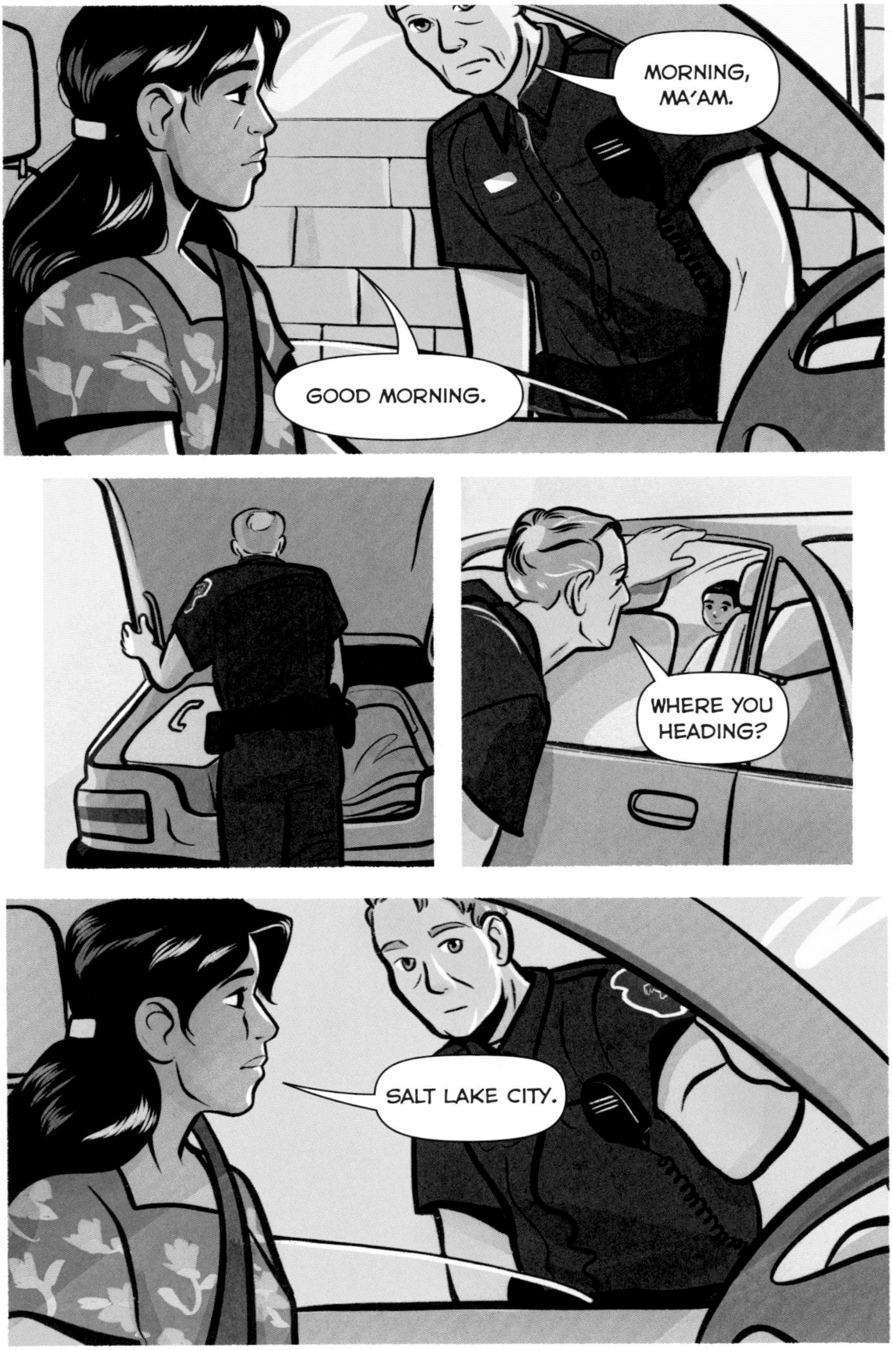
MORNING, MA'AM.
GOOD MORNING.
WHERE YOU HEADING?
SALT LAKE CITY.

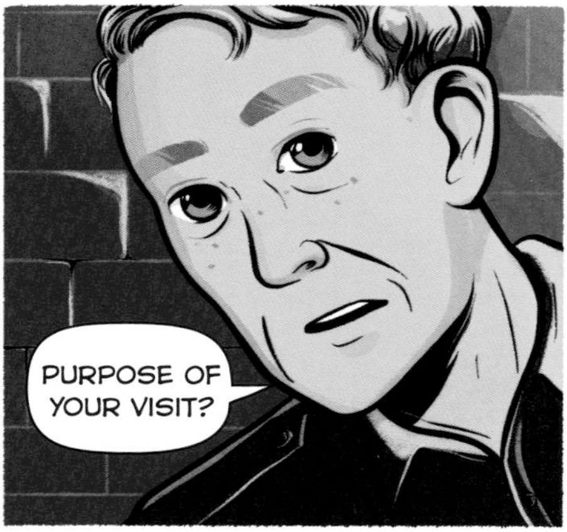
PURPOSE OF YOUR VISIT?

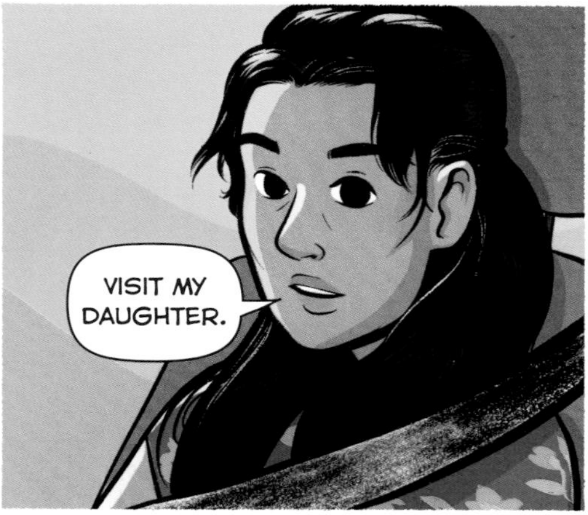
VISIT MY DAUGHTER.

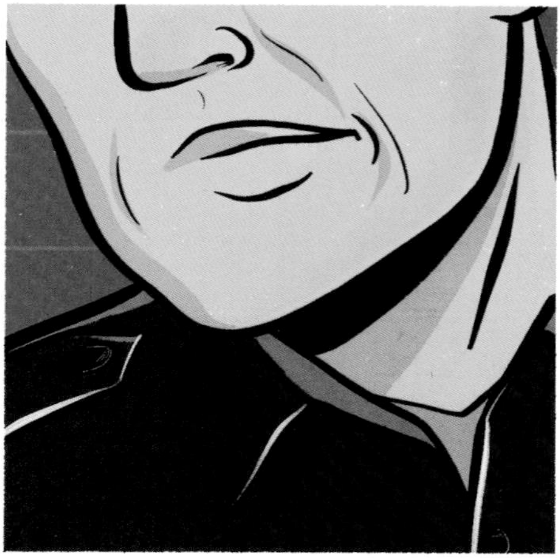

CITIZENSHIP?

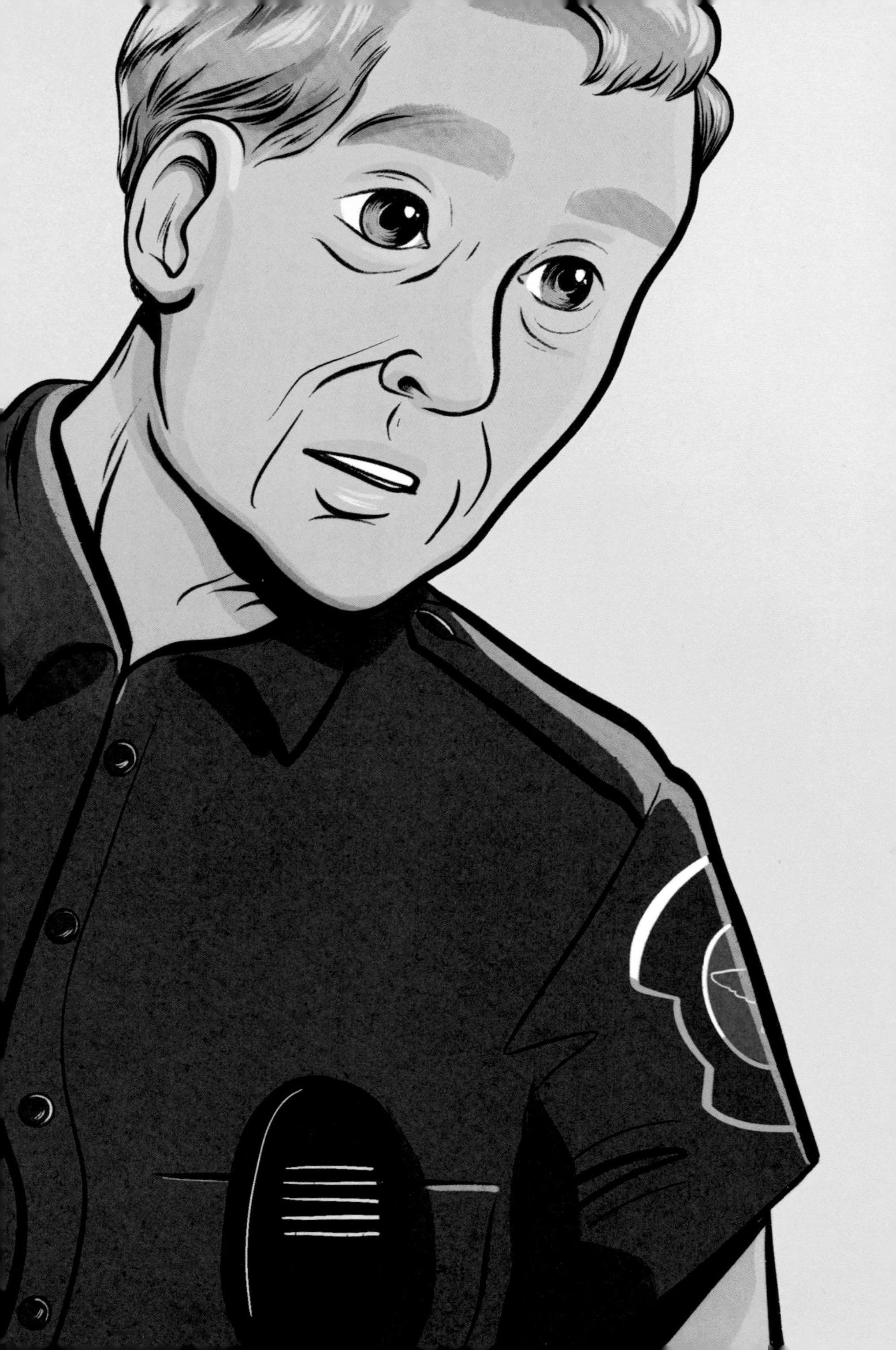

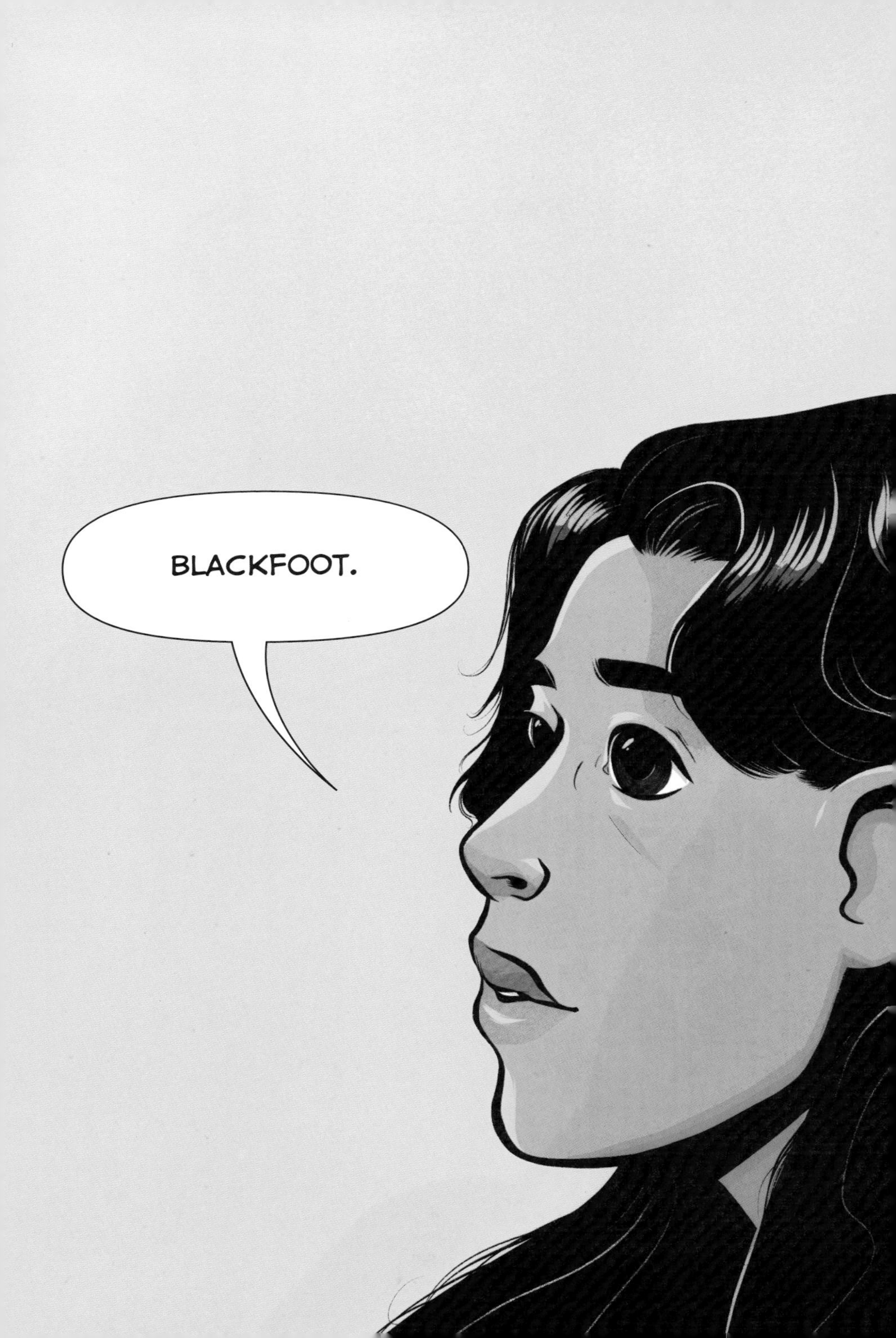
BLACKFOOT.

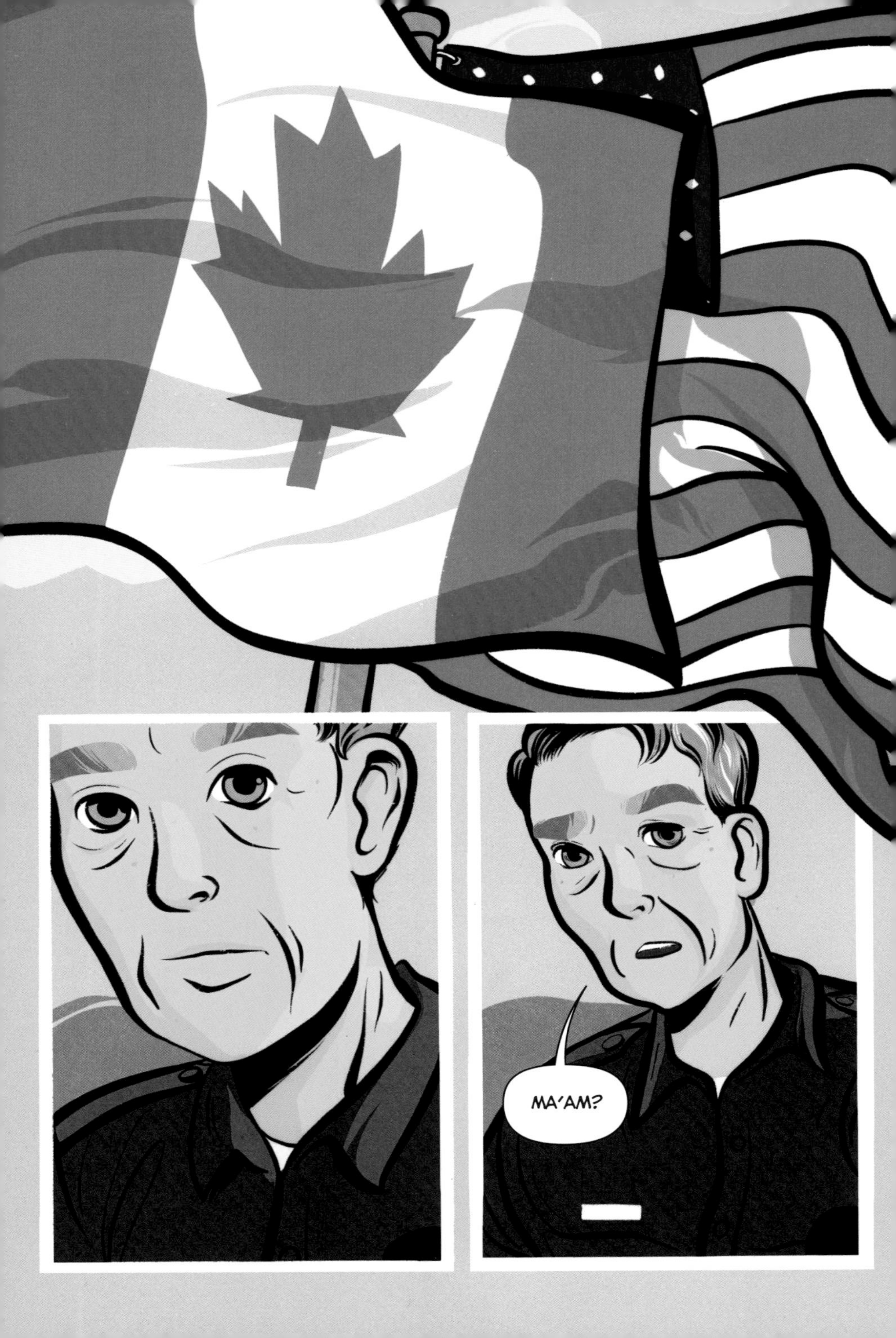
MA'AM?

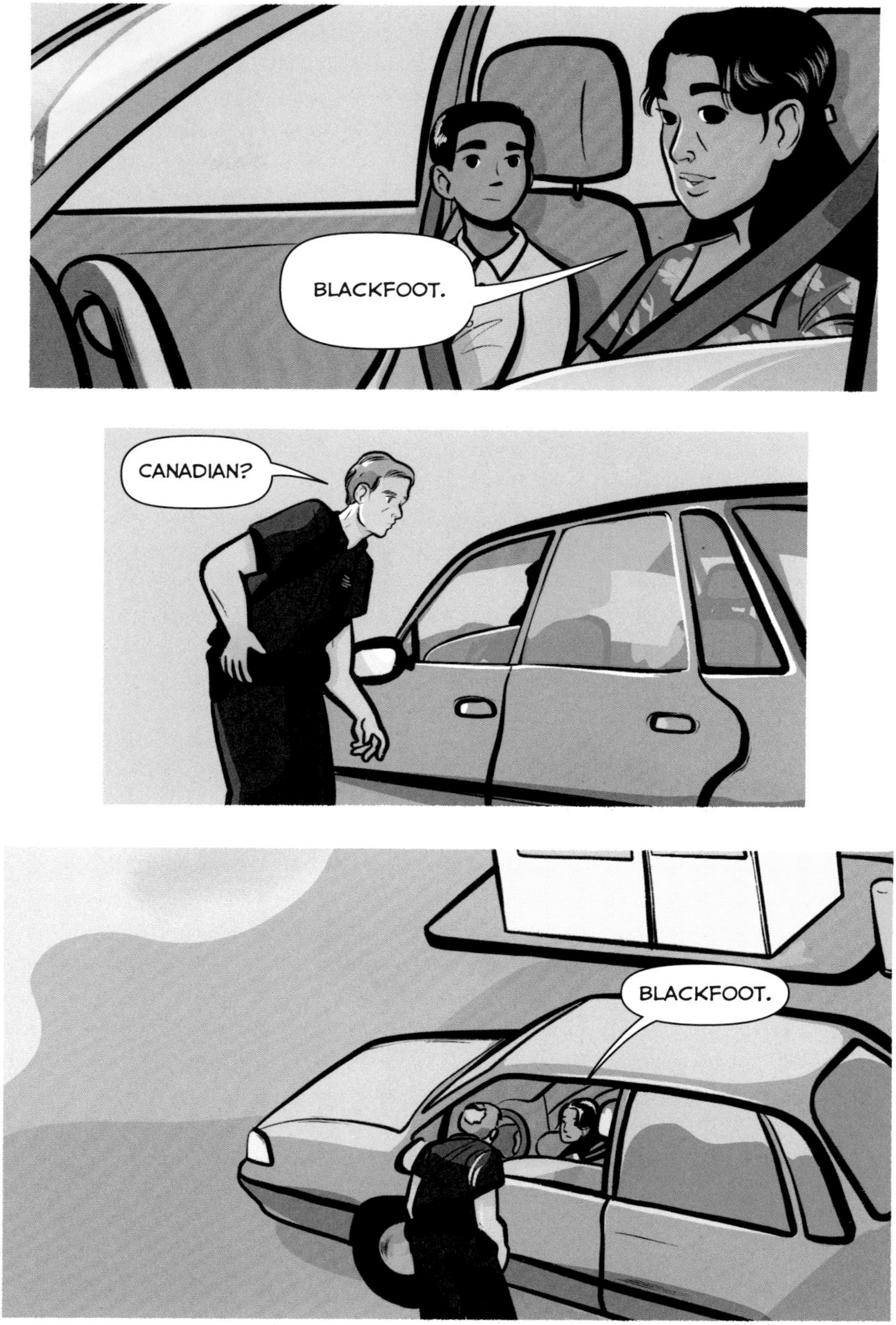
BLACKFOOT.
CANADIAN?
BLACKFOOT.

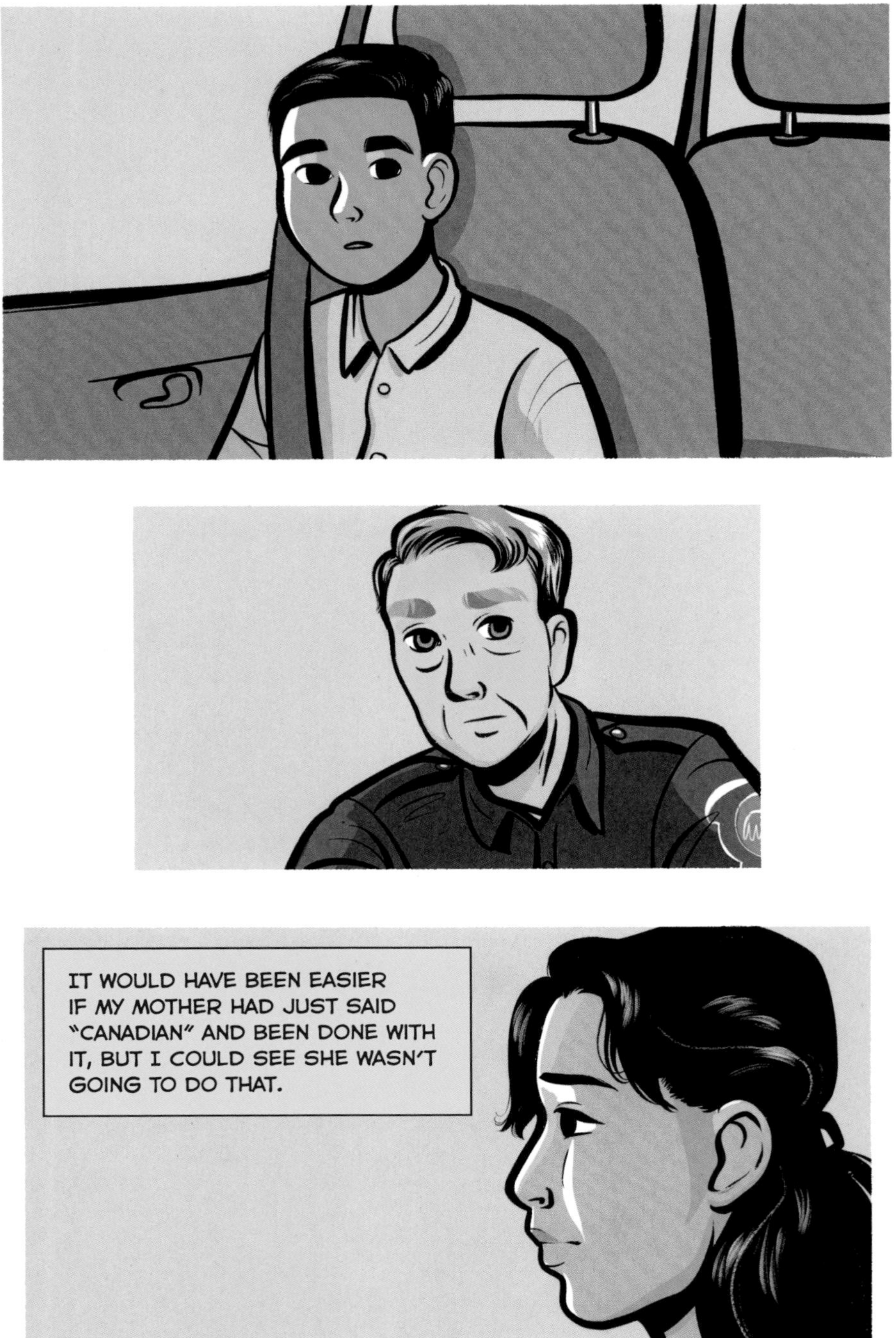
IT WOULD HAVE BEEN EASIER IF MY MOTHER HAD JUST SAID "CANADIAN" AND BEEN DONE WITH IT, BUT I COULD SEE SHE WASN'T GOING TO DO THAT.

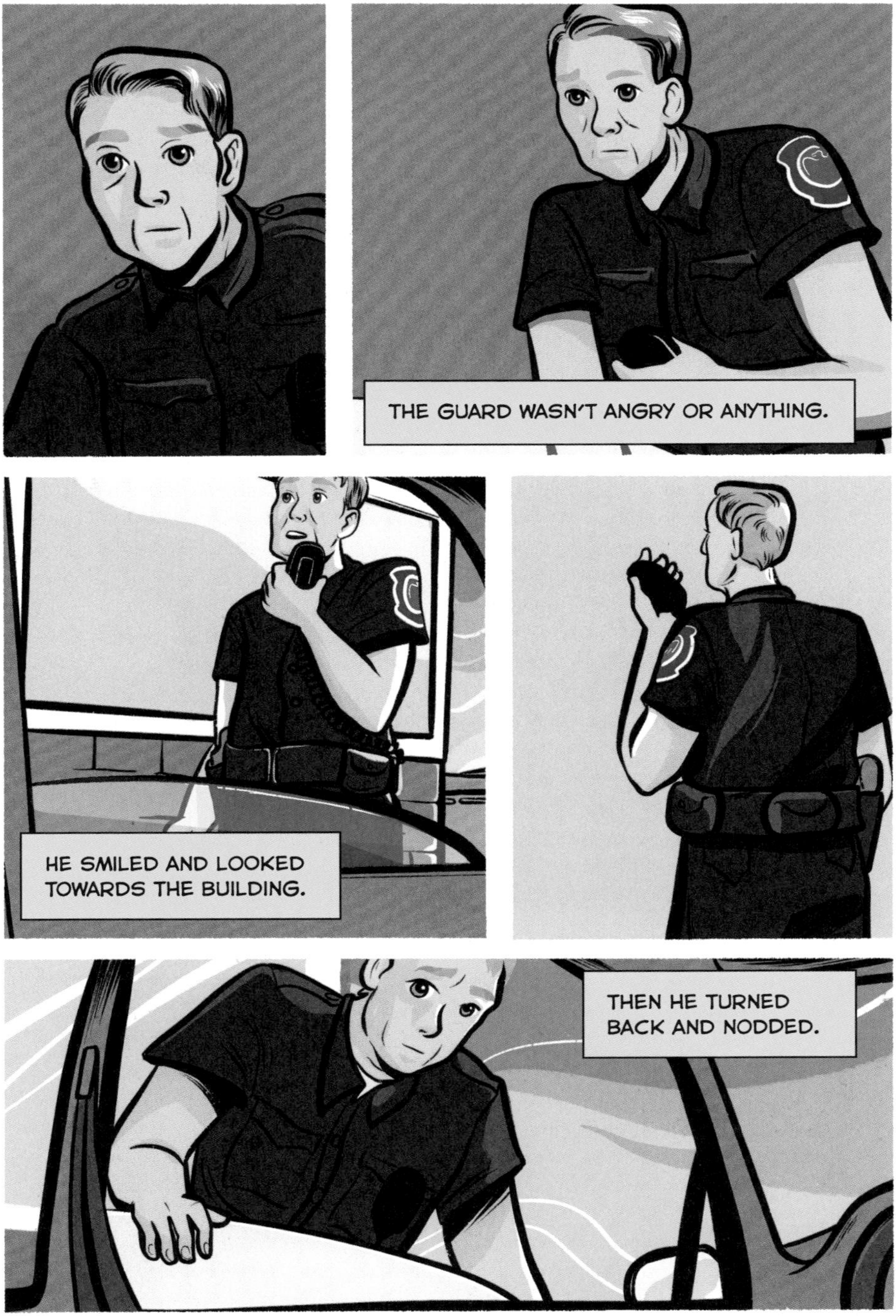
THE GUARD WASN'T ANGRY OR ANYTHING.
HE SMILED AND LOOKED TOWARDS THE BUILDING.
THEN HE TURNED BACK AND NODDED.

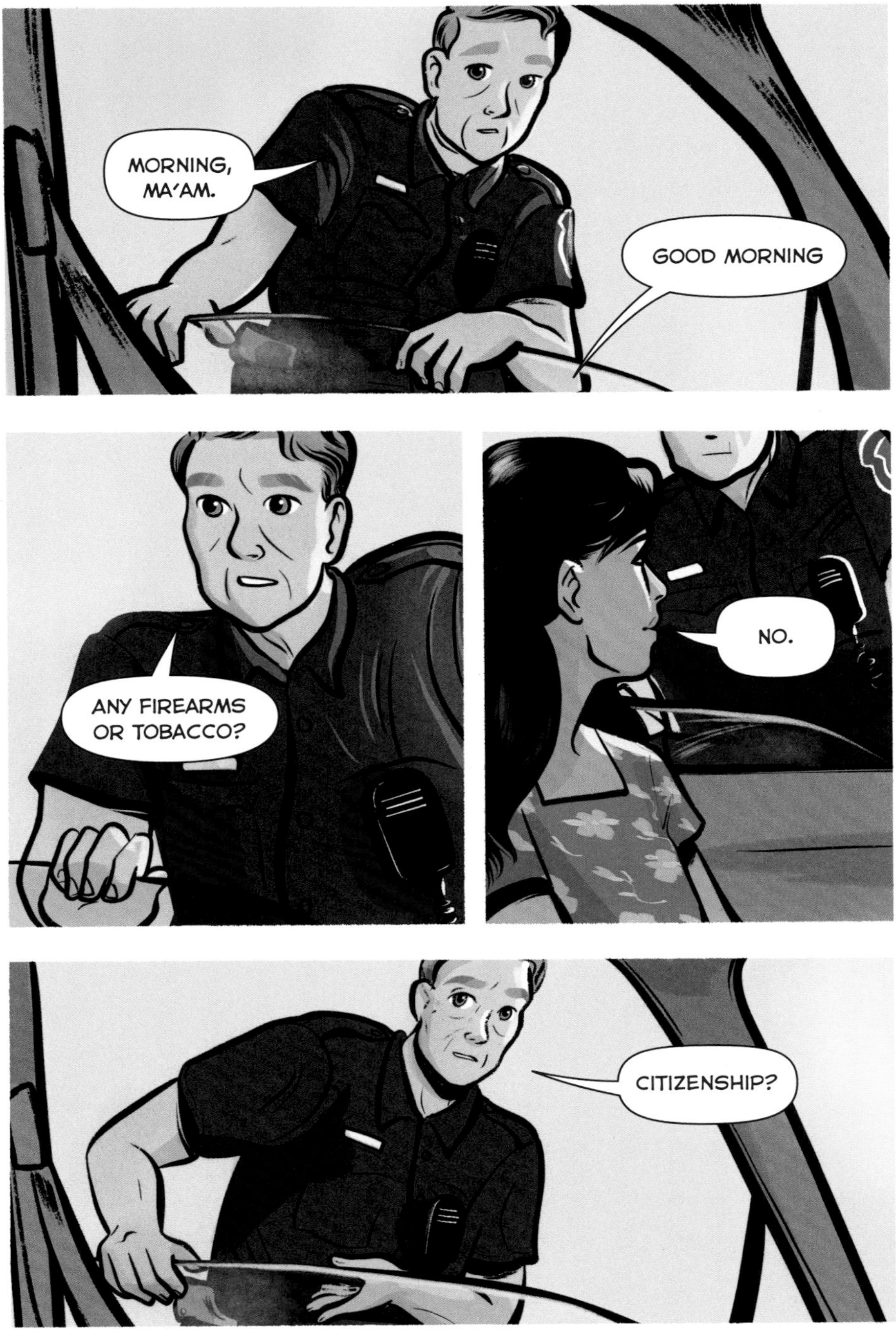
MORNING, MA'AM.
GOOD MORNING
ANY FIREARMS OR TOBACCO?
NO.
CITIZENSHIP?

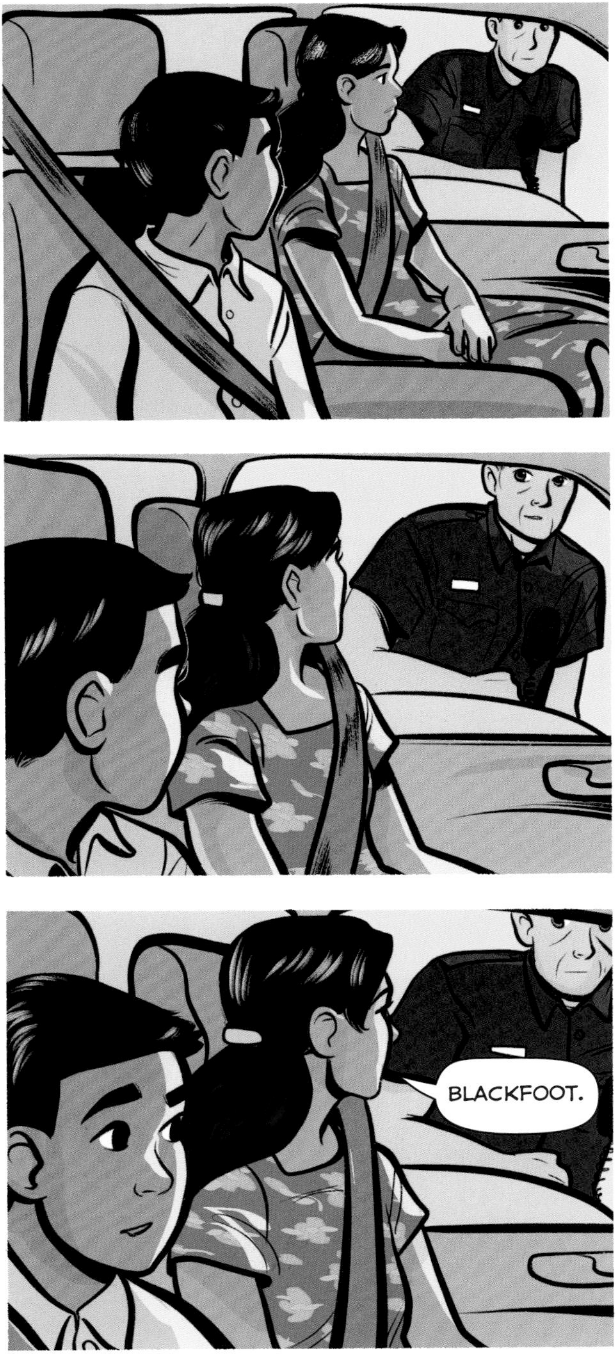
BLACKFOOT.

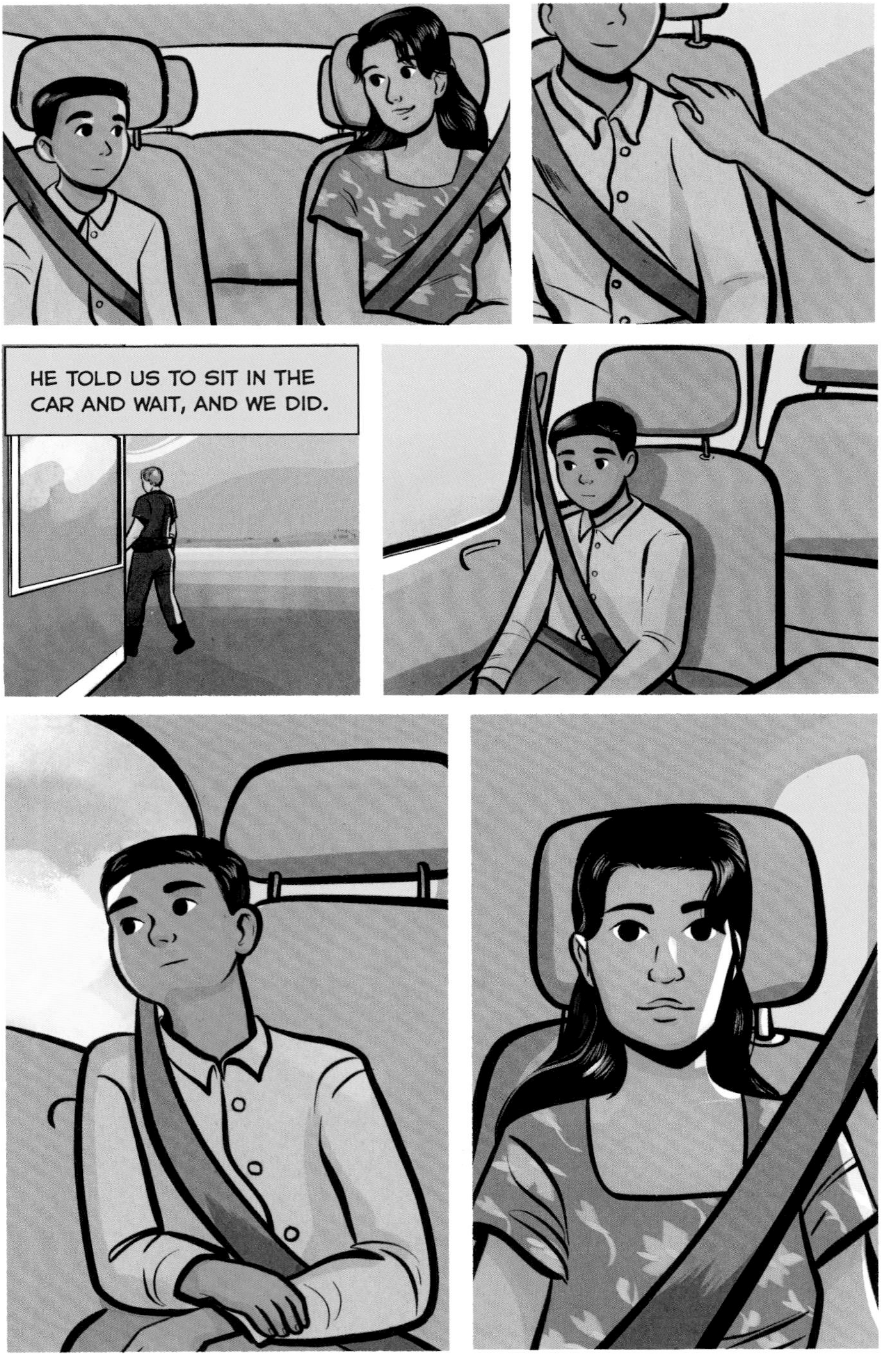
HE TOLD US TO SIT IN THE CAR AND WAIT, AND WE DID.

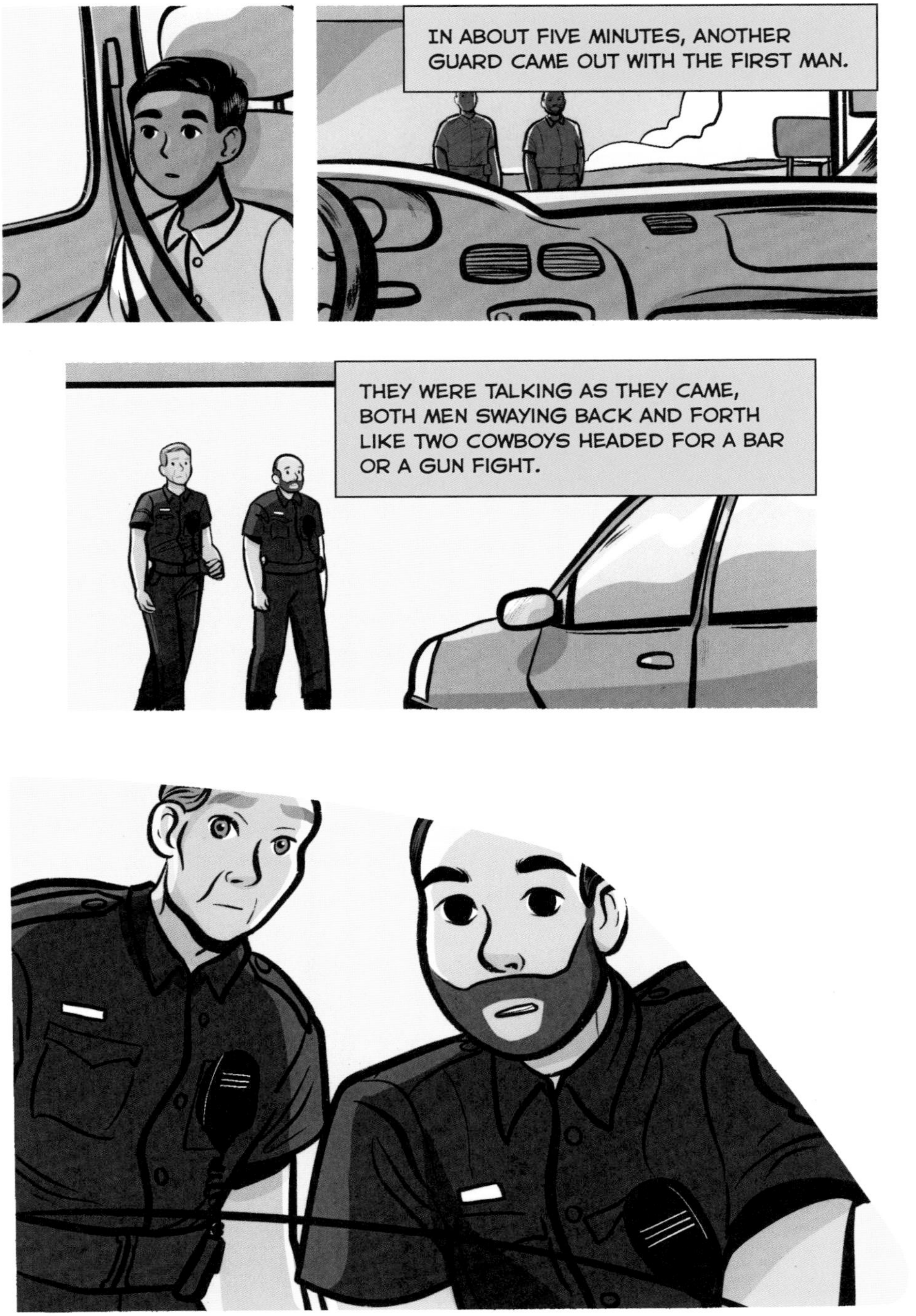
IN ABOUT FIVE MINUTES, ANOTHER GUARD CAME OUT WITH THE FIRST MAN.
THEY WERE TALKING AS THEY CAME, BOTH MEN SWAYING BACK AND FORTH LIKE TWO COWBOYS HEADED FOR A BAR OR A GUN FIGHT.

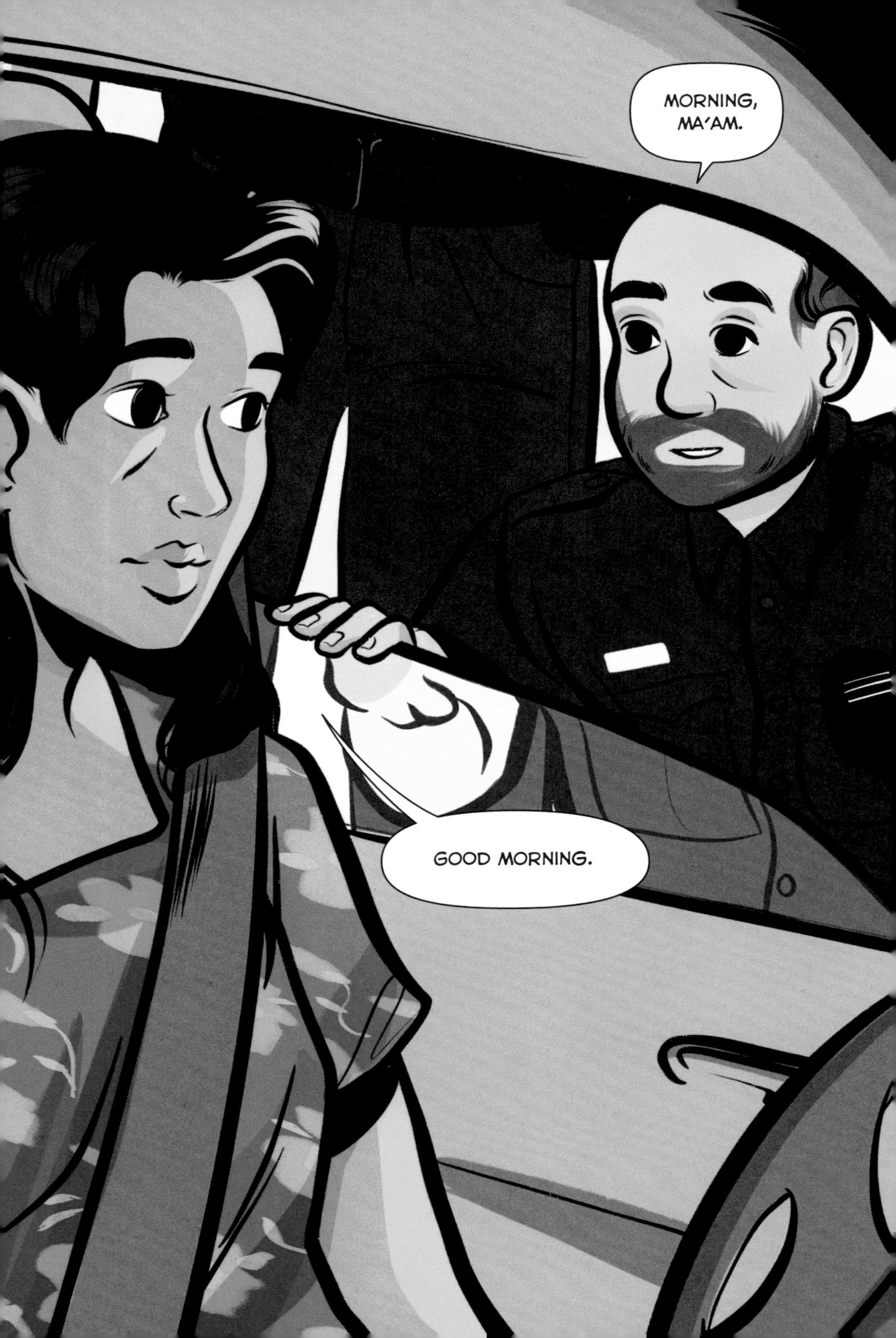
MORNING, MA'AM.
GOOD MORNING.

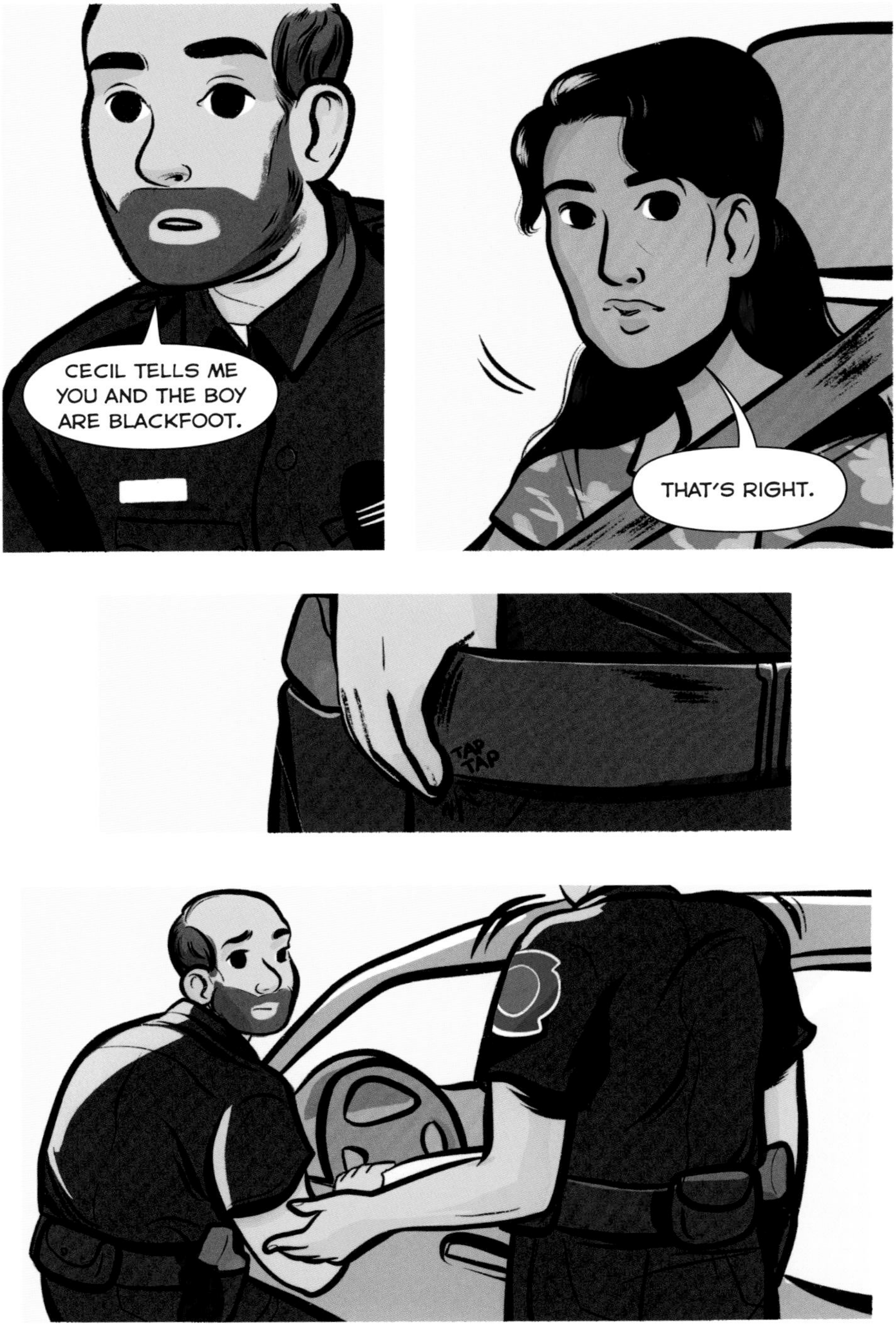
CECIL TELLS ME YOU AND THE BOY ARE BLACKFOOT.
THAT'S RIGHT.
TAP TAP

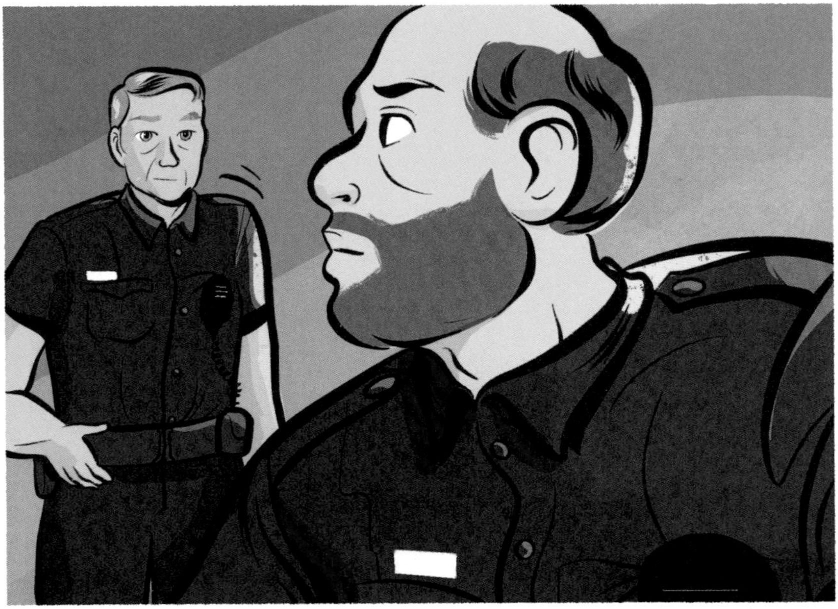

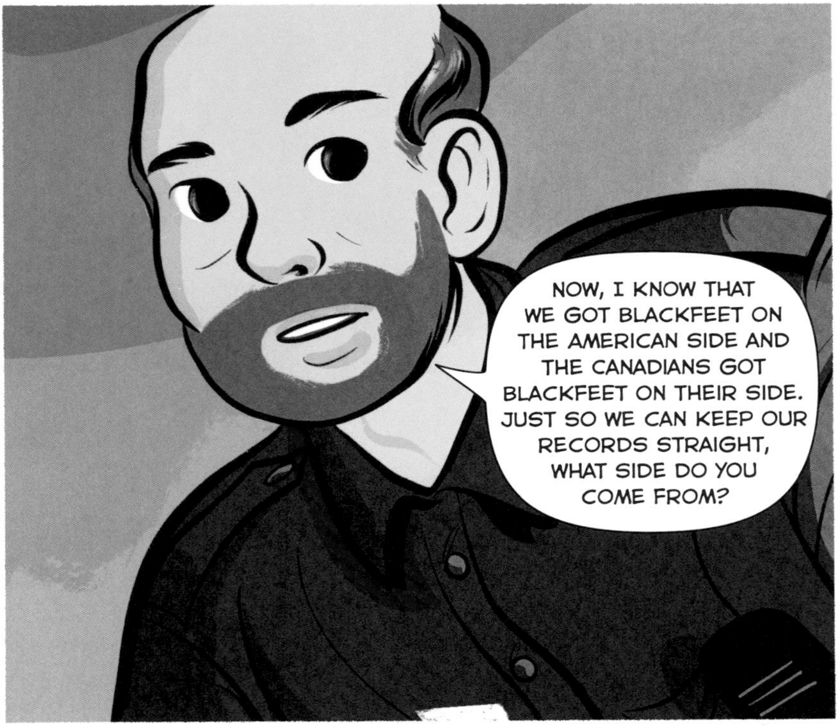
NOW, I KNOW THAT WE GOT BLACKFEET ON THE AMERICAN SIDE AND THE CANADIANS GOT BLACKFEET ON THEIR SIDE. JUST SO WE CAN KEEP OUR RECORDS STRAIGHT, WHAT SIDE DO YOU COME FROM?

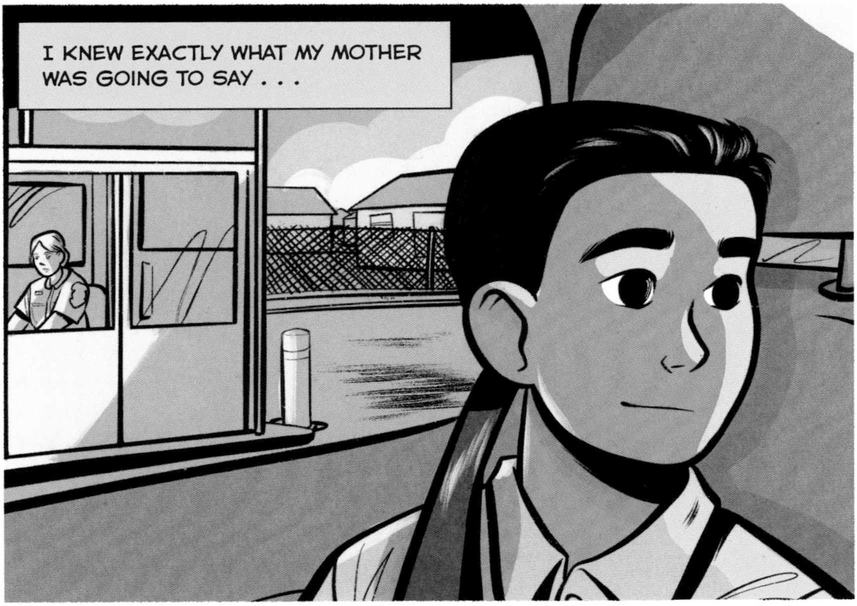
I KNEW EXACTLY WHAT MY MOTHER WAS GOING TO SAY . . .

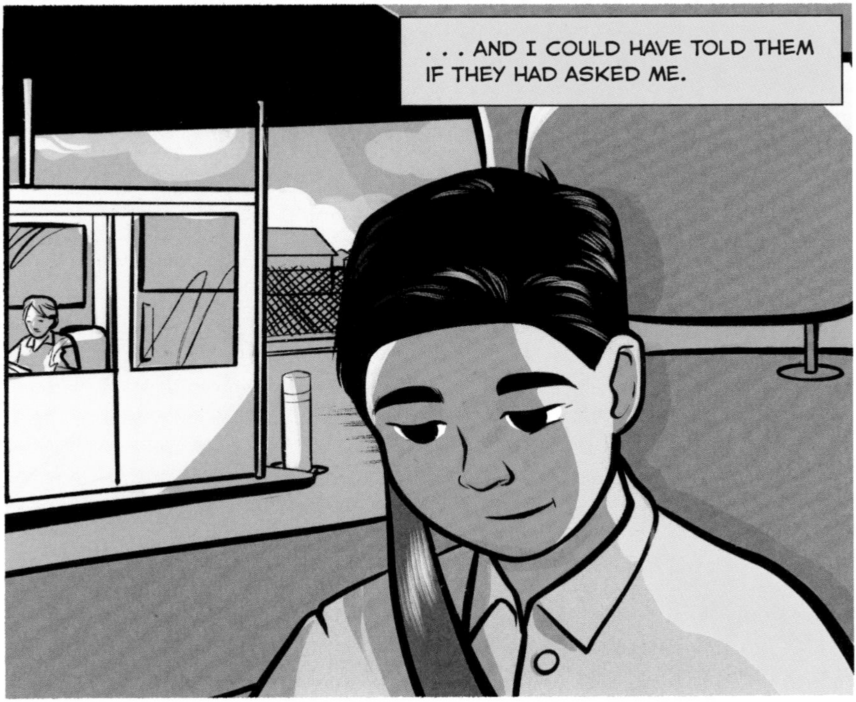
. . . AND I COULD HAVE TOLD THEM IF THEY HAD ASKED ME.

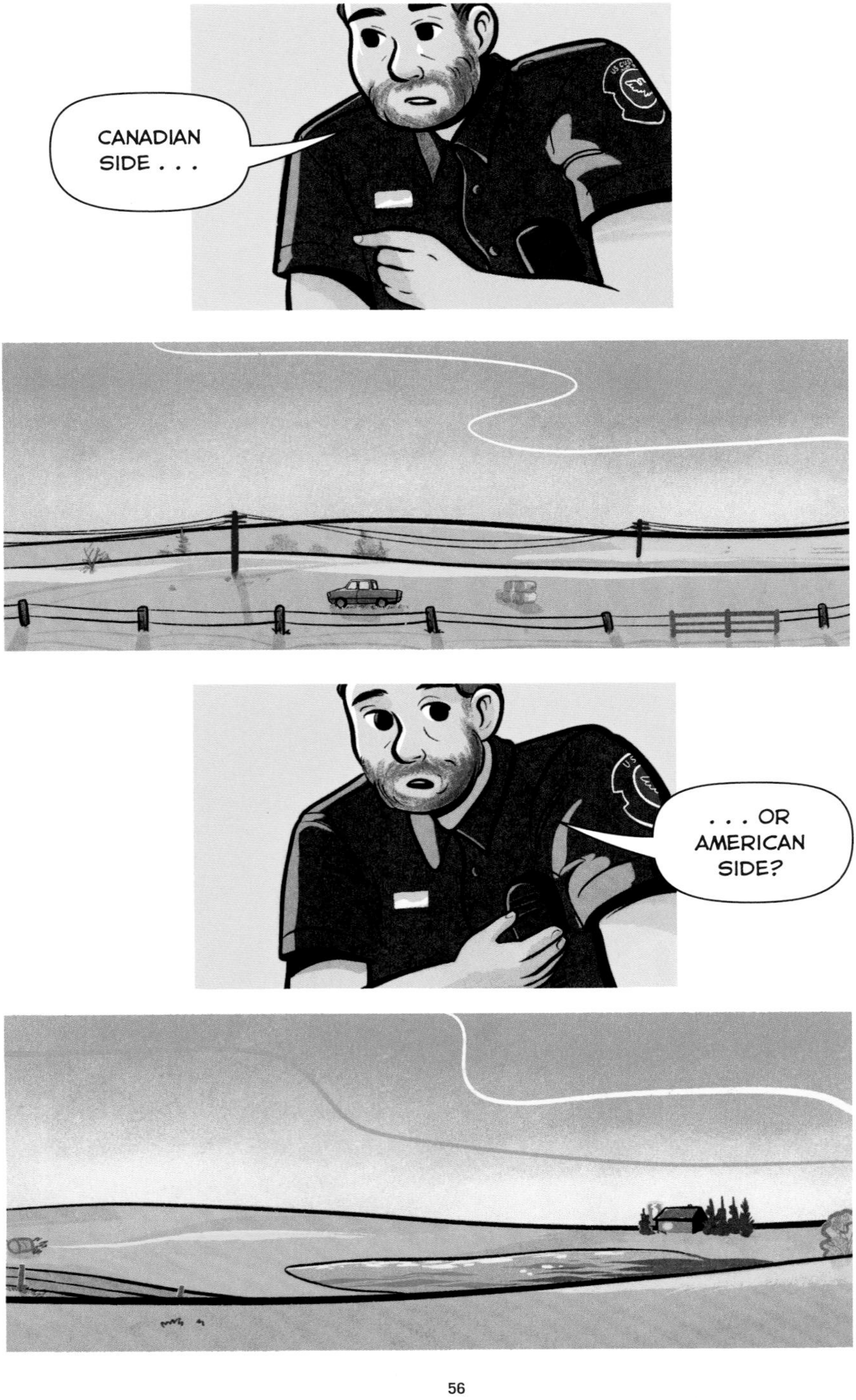
CANADIAN SIDE . . .
. . . OR AMERICAN SIDE?

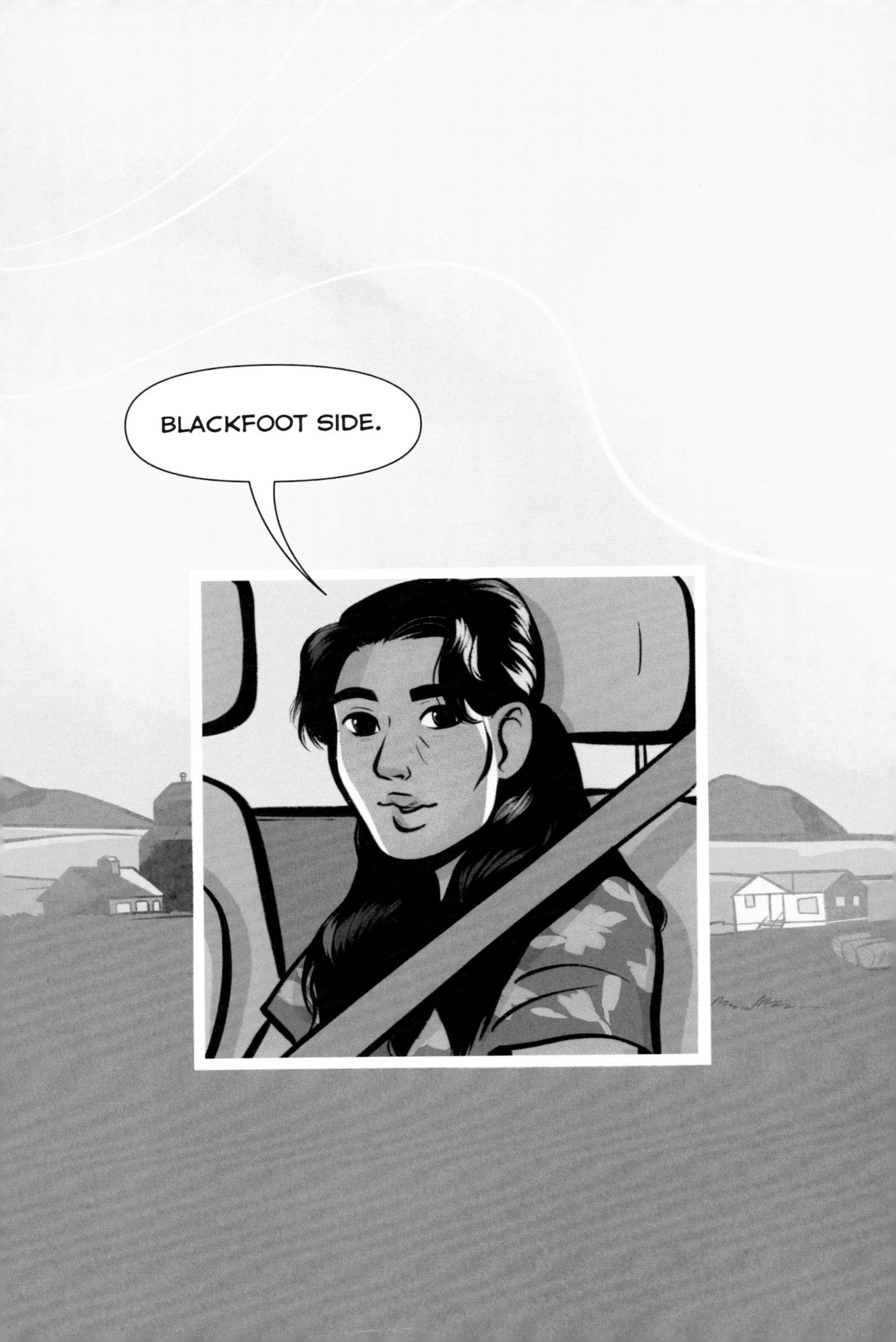
BLACKFOOT SIDE.

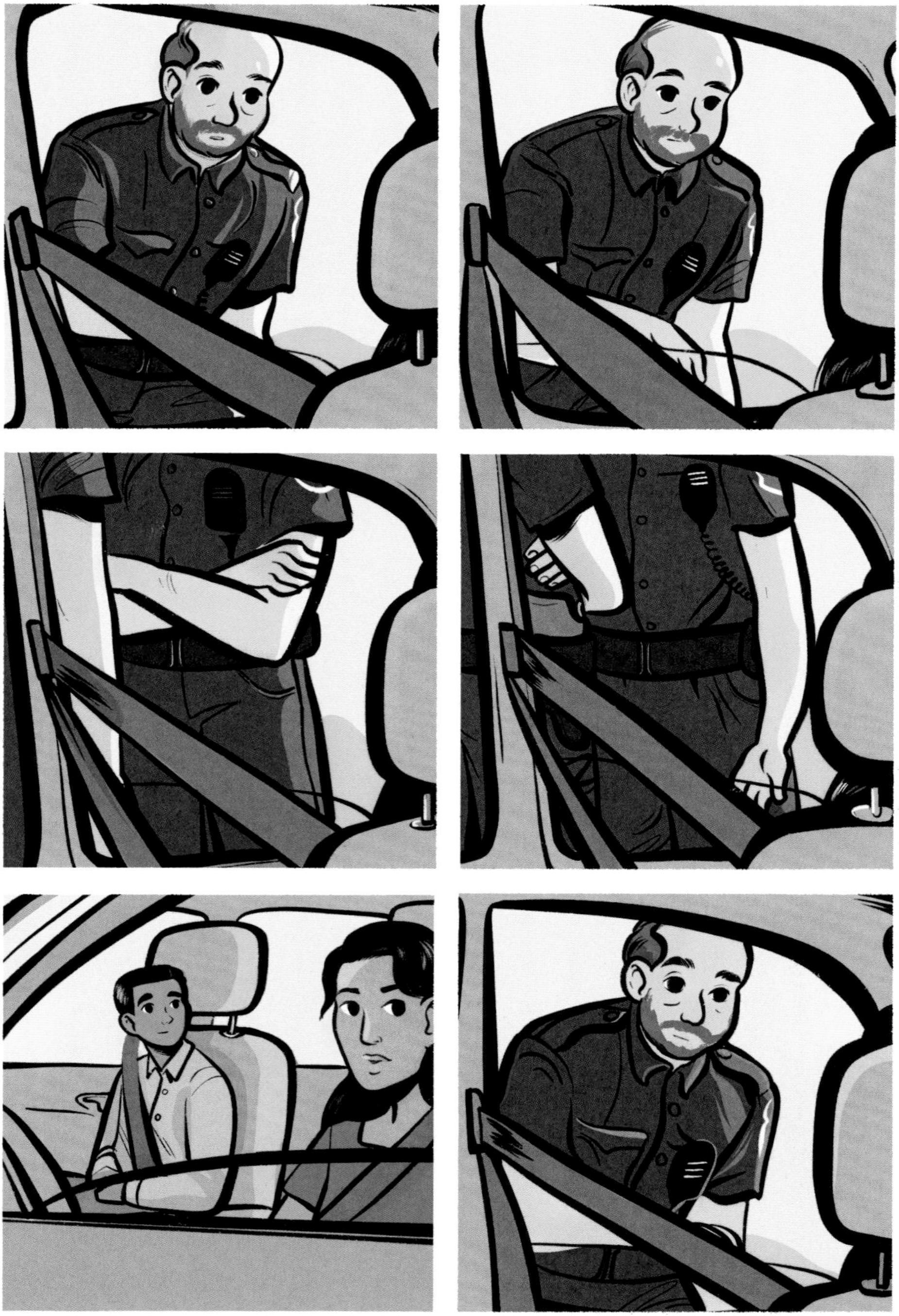

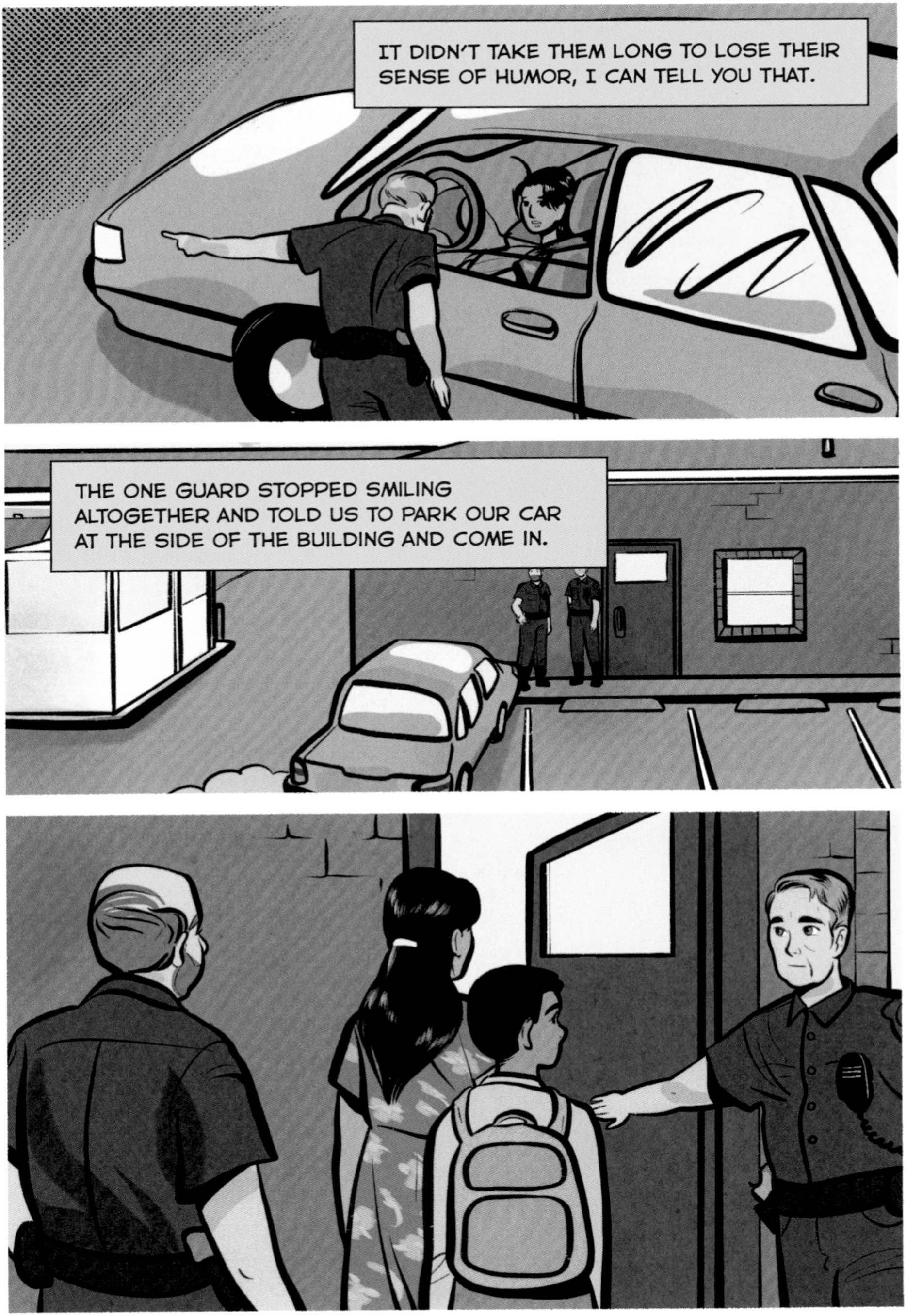
IT DIDN'T TAKE THEM LONG TO LOSE THEIR SENSE OF HUMOR, I CAN TELL YOU THAT.
THE ONE GUARD STOPPED SMILING ALTOGETHER AND TOLD US TO PARK OUR CAR AT THE SIDE OF THE BUILDING AND COME IN.

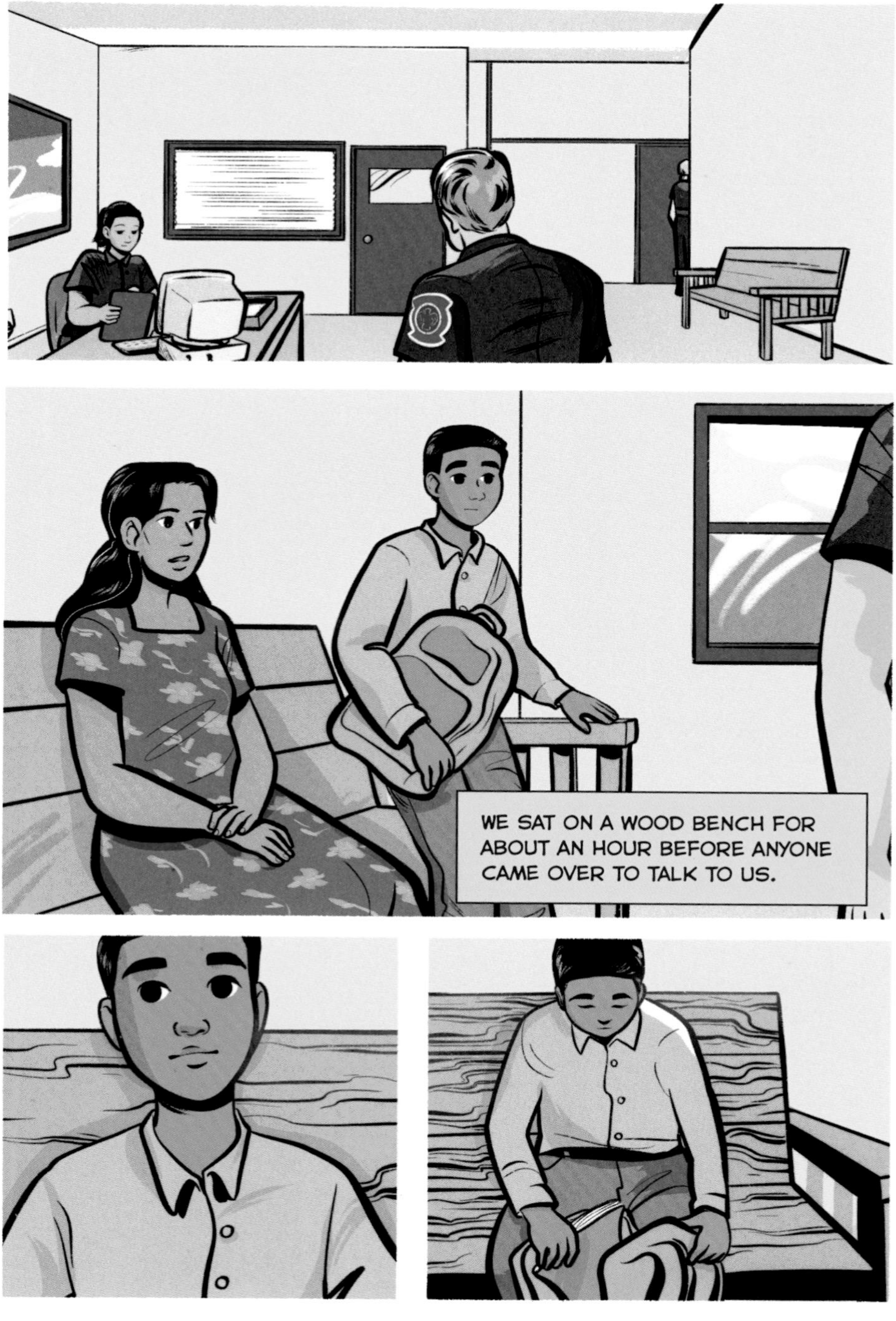
WE SAT ON A WOOD BENCH FOR ABOUT AN HOUR BEFORE ANYONE CAME OVER TO TALK TO US.

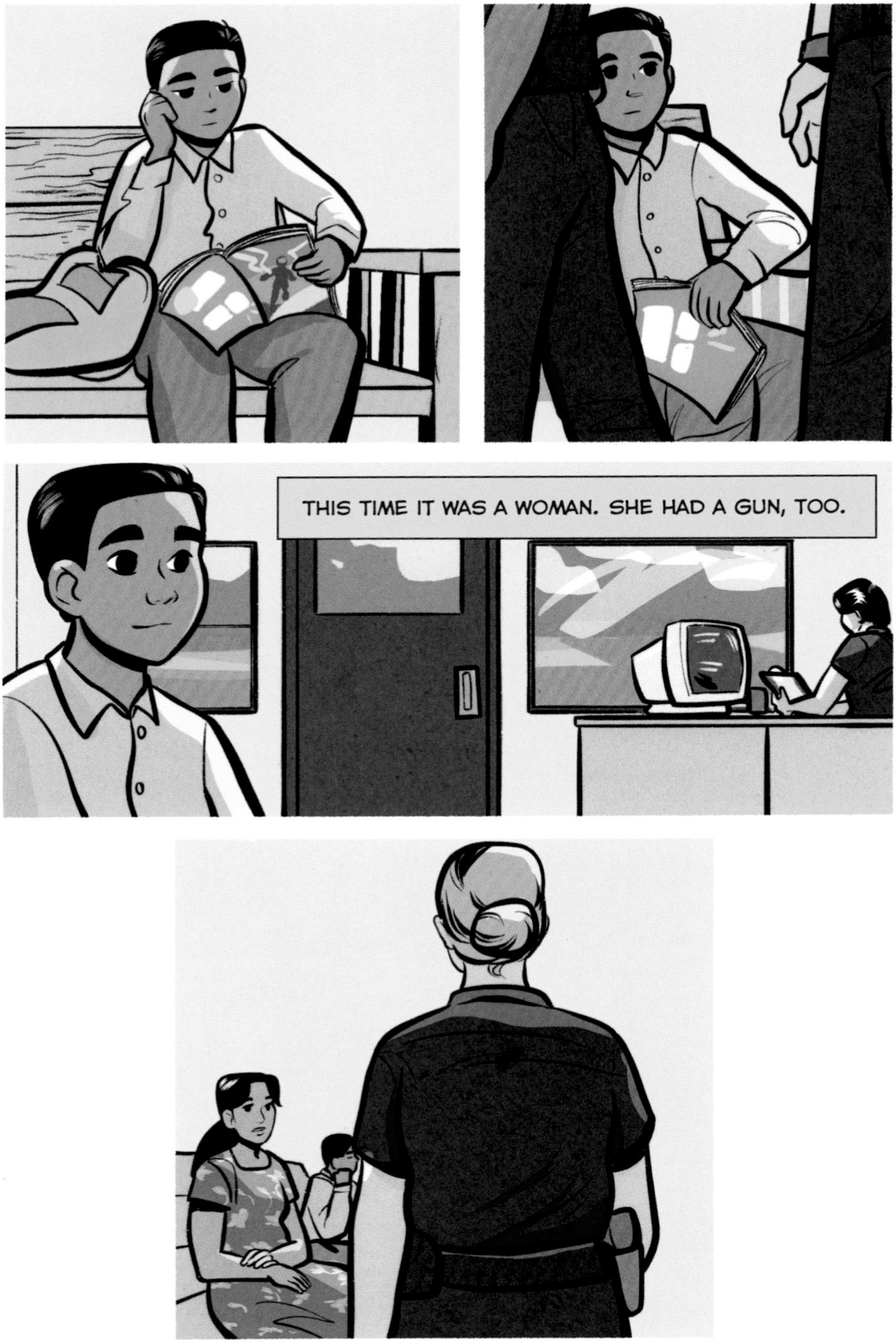
THIS TIME IT WAS A WOMAN. SHE HAD A GUN, TOO.

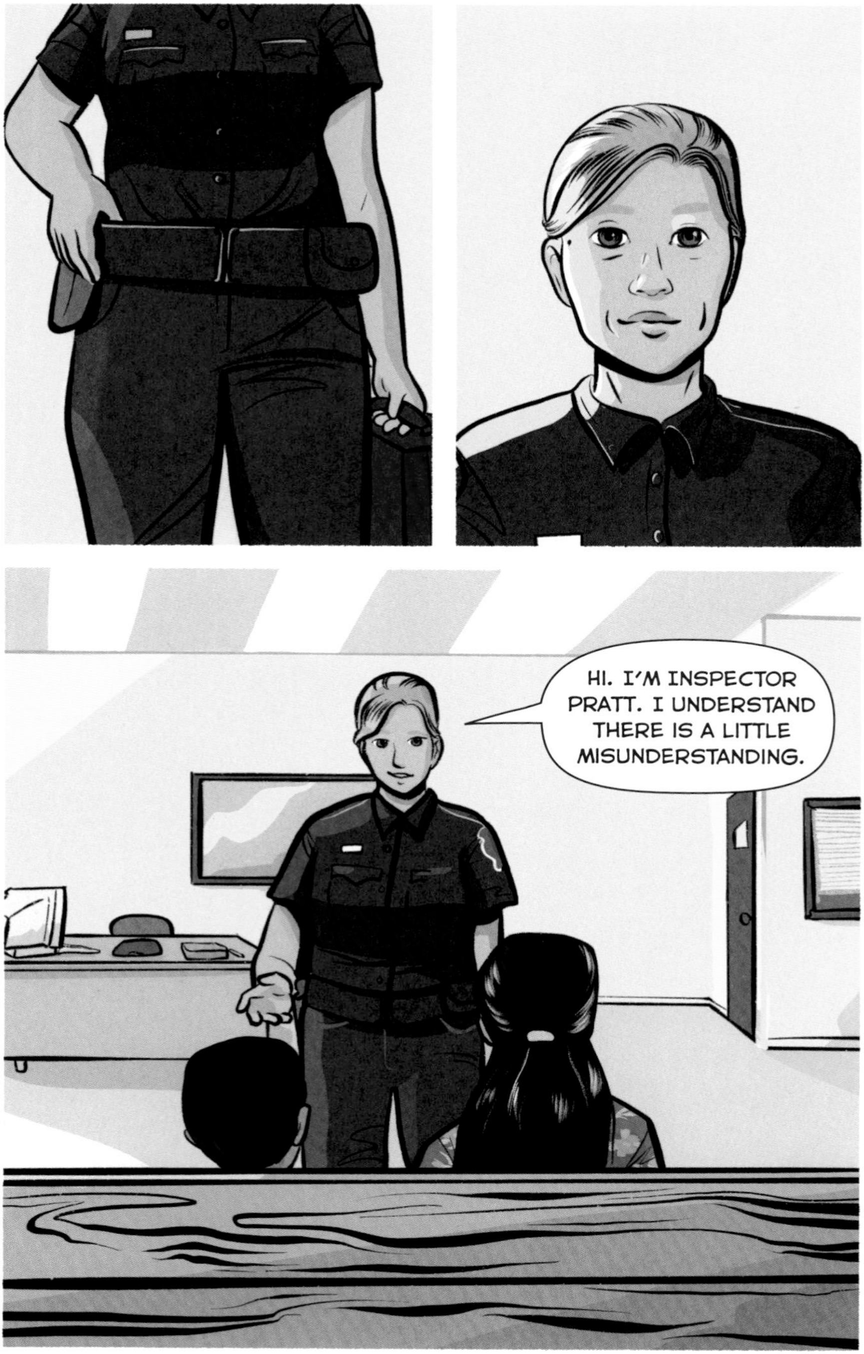
HI. I'M INSPECTOR PRATT. I UNDERSTAND THERE IS A LITTLE MISUNDERSTANDING.

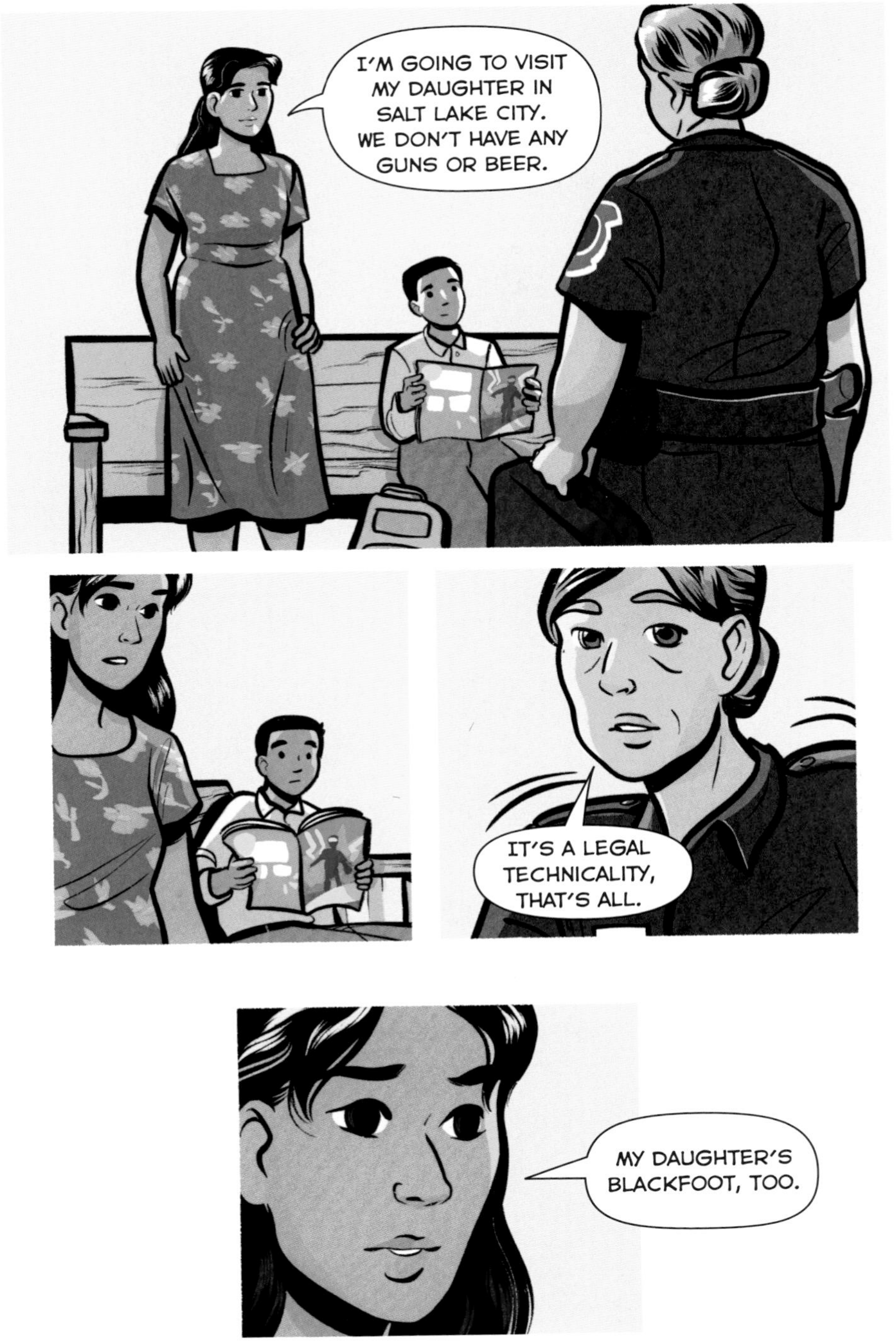
I'M GOING TO VISIT MY DAUGHTER IN SALT LAKE CITY. WE DON'T HAVE ANY GUNS OR BEER.
IT'S A LEGAL TECHNICALITY, THAT'S ALL.
MY DAUGHTER'S BLACKFOOT, TOO.

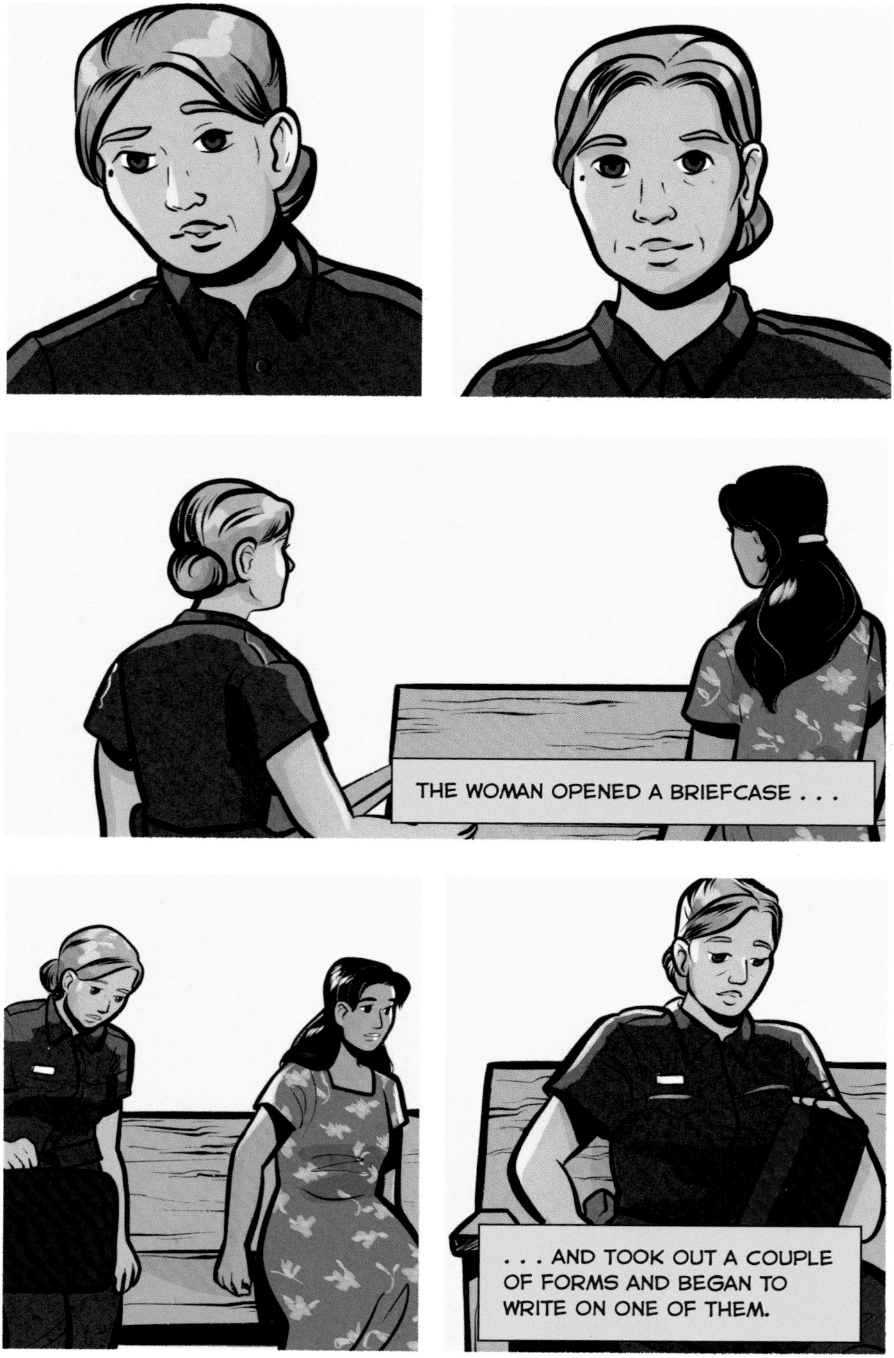
THE WOMAN OPENED A BRIEFCASE . . .
. . . AND TOOK OUT A COUPLE OF FORMS AND BEGAN TO WRITE ON ONE OF THEM.

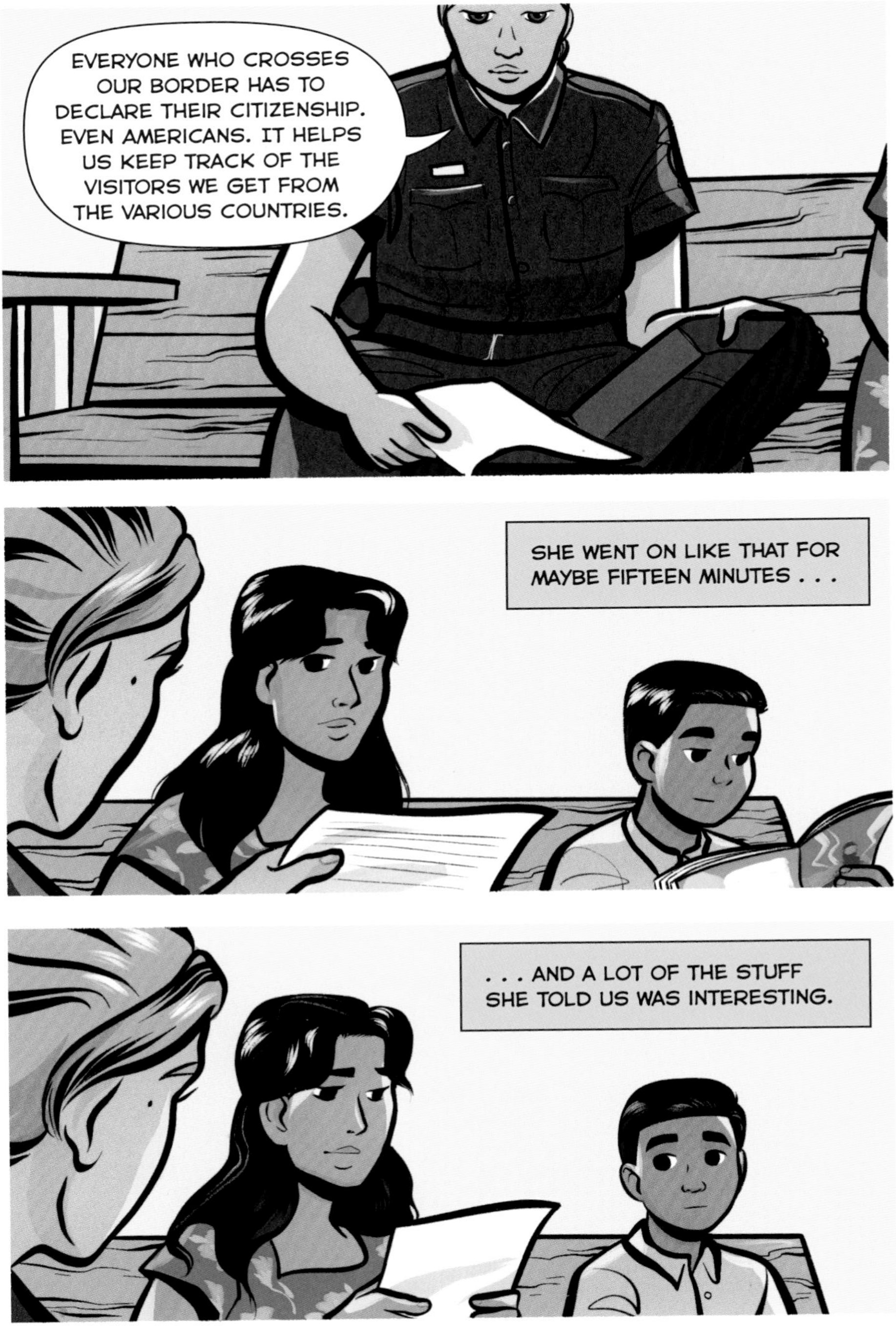
EVERYONE WHO CROSSES OUR BORDER HAS TO DECLARE THEIR CITIZENSHIP. EVEN AMERICANS. IT HELPS US KEEP TRACK OF THE VISITORS WE GET FROM THE VARIOUS COUNTRIES.
SHE WENT ON LIKE THAT FOR MAYBE FIFTEEN MINUTES . . .
. . . AND A LOT OF THE STUFF SHE TOLD US WAS INTERESTING.

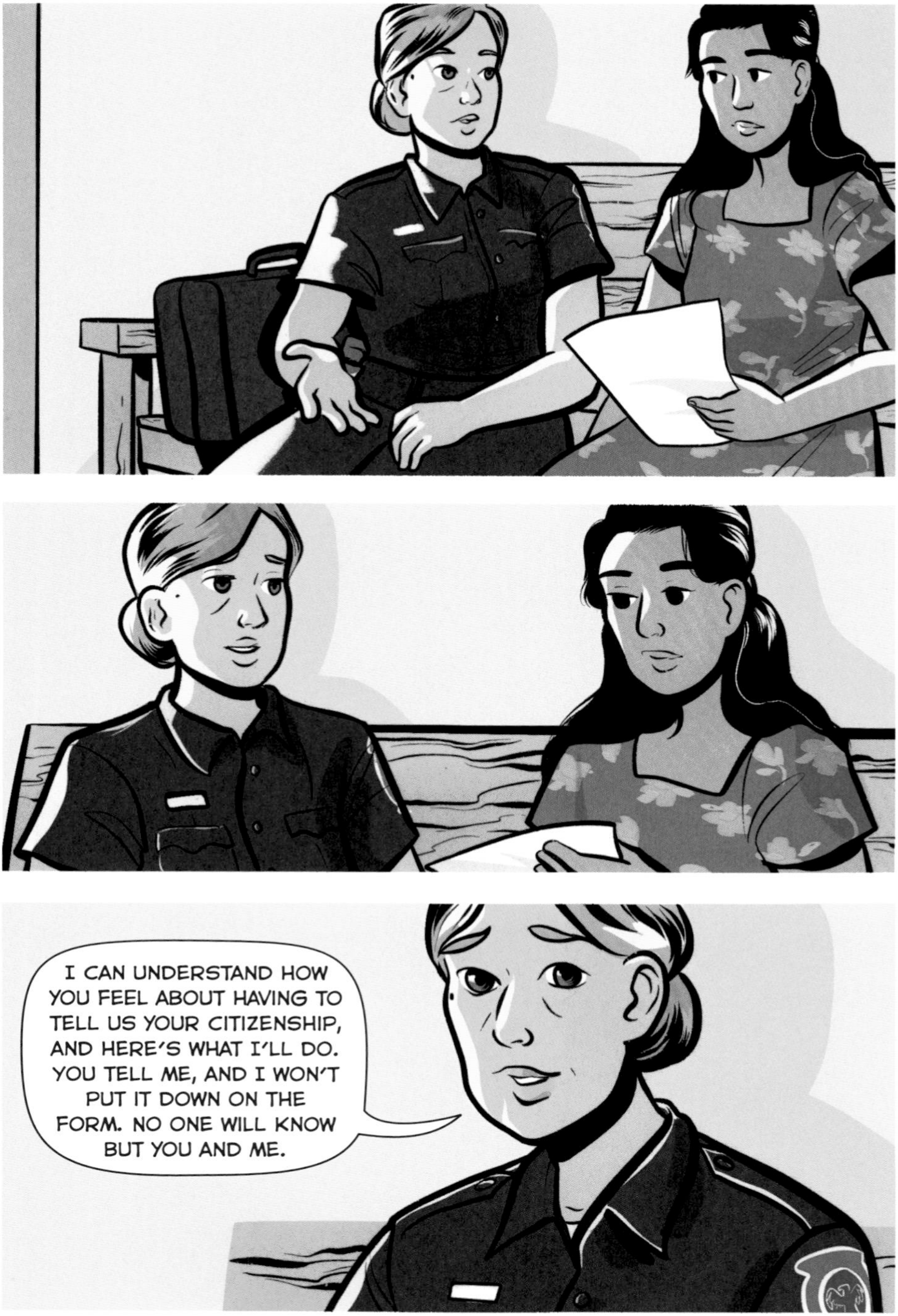
I CAN UNDERSTAND HOW YOU FEEL ABOUT HAVING TO TELL US YOUR CITIZENSHIP, AND HERE'S WHAT I'LL DO. YOU TELL ME, AND I WON'T PUT IT DOWN ON THE FORM. NO ONE WILL KNOW BUT YOU AND ME.

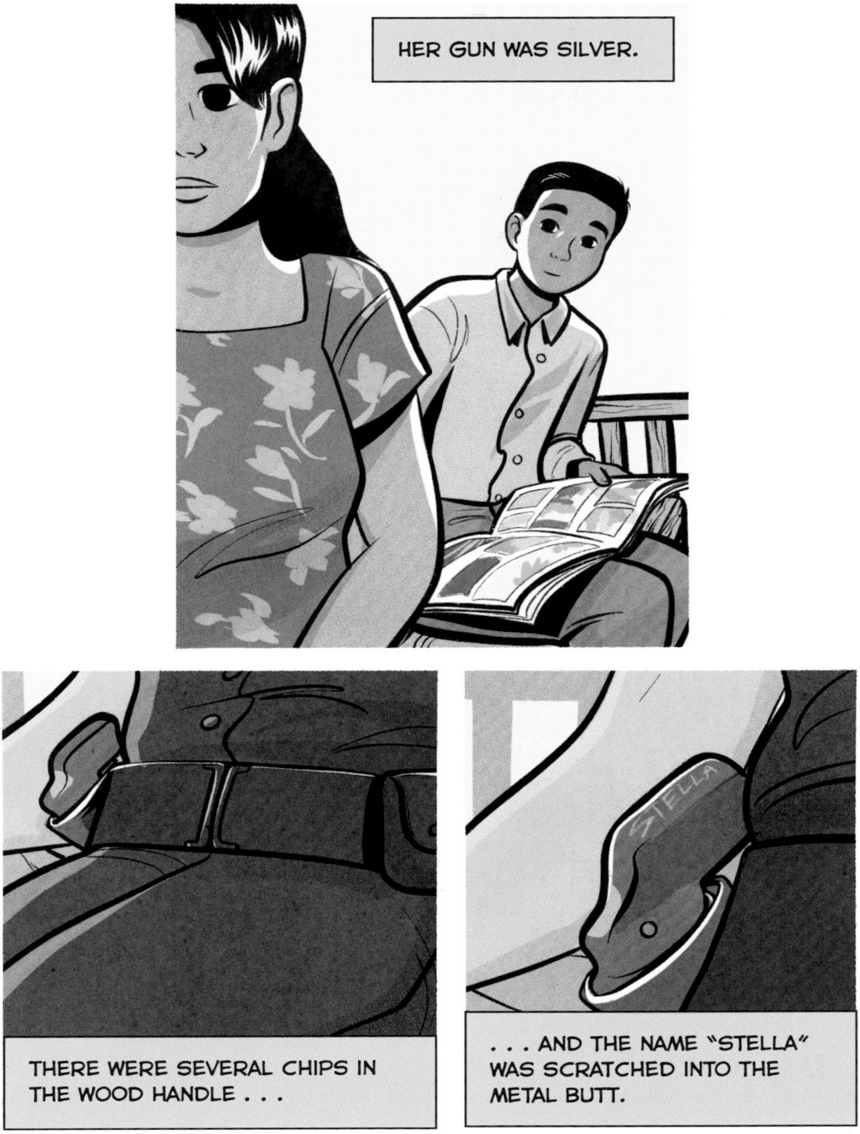
HER GUN WAS SILVER.
THERE WERE SEVERAL CHIPS IN THE WOOD HANDLE . . .
. . . AND THE NAME "STELLA" WAS SCRATCHED INTO THE METAL BUTT.
STELLA

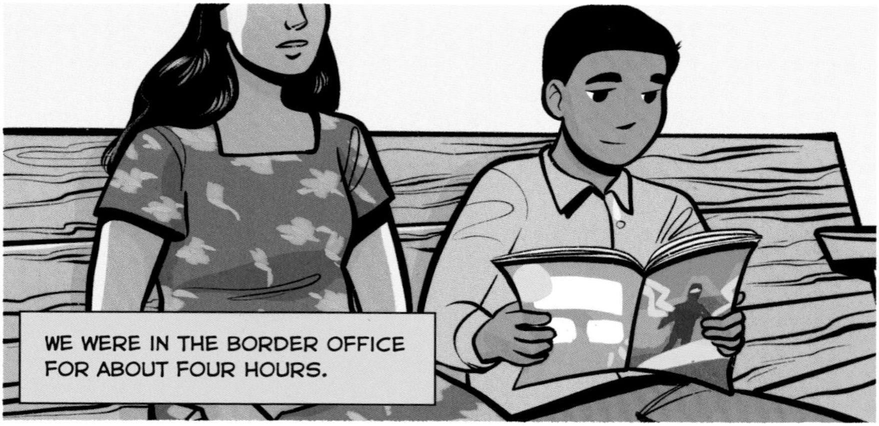
WE WERE IN THE BORDER OFFICE FOR ABOUT FOUR HOURS.

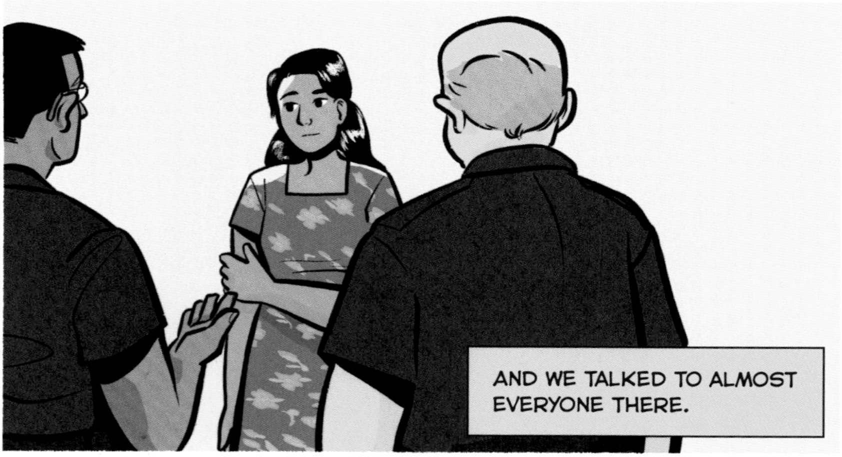
AND WE TALKED TO ALMOST EVERYONE THERE.

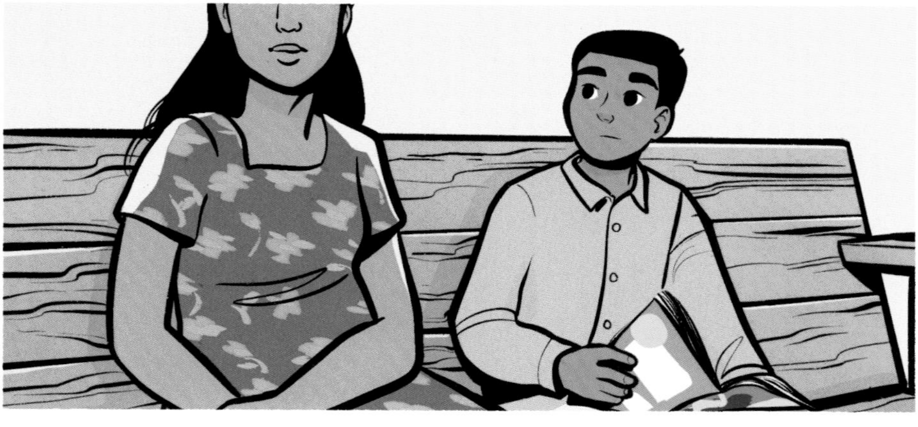

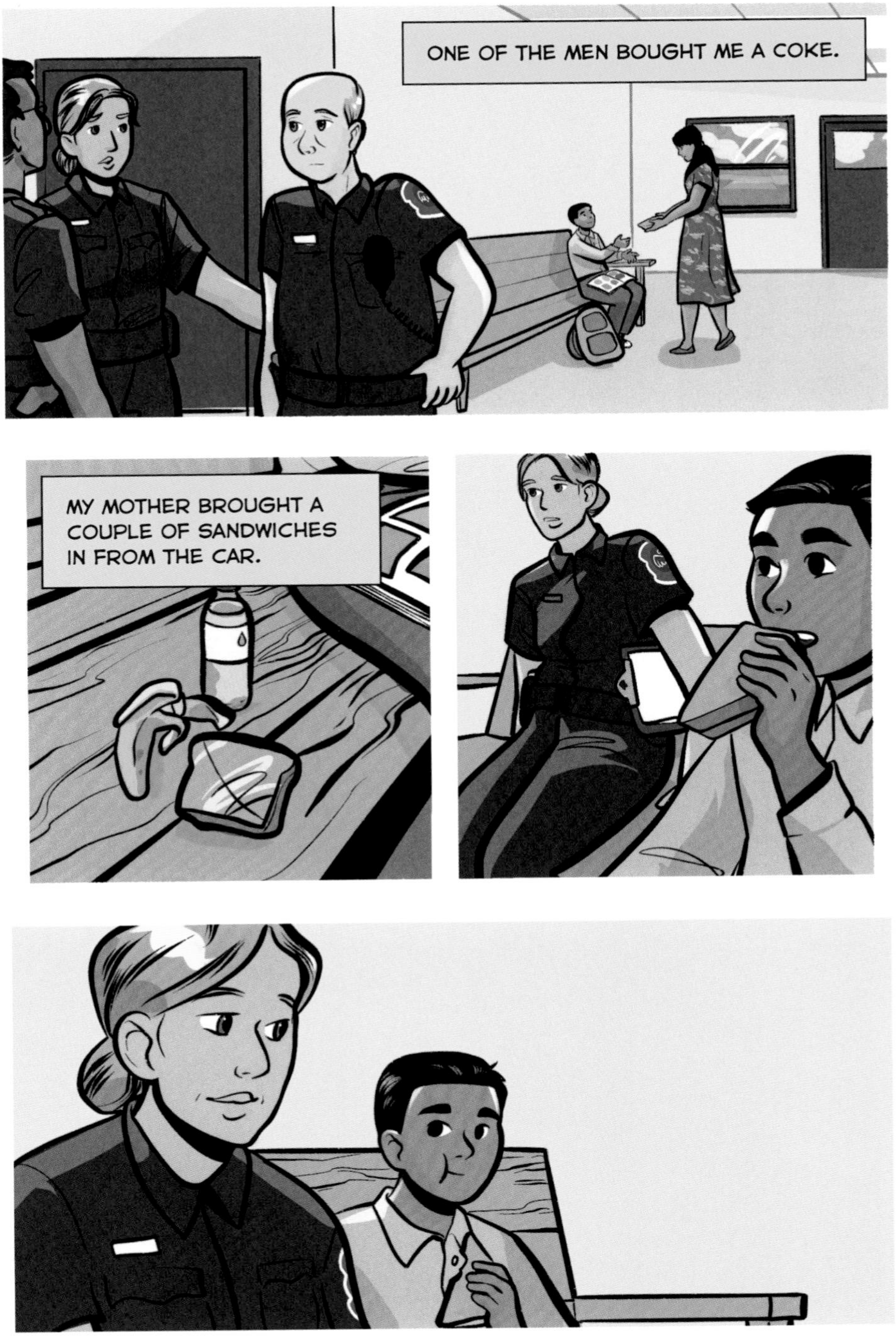
ONE OF THE MEN BOUGHT ME A COKE.
MY MOTHER BROUGHT A COUPLE OF SANDWICHES IN FROM THE CAR.

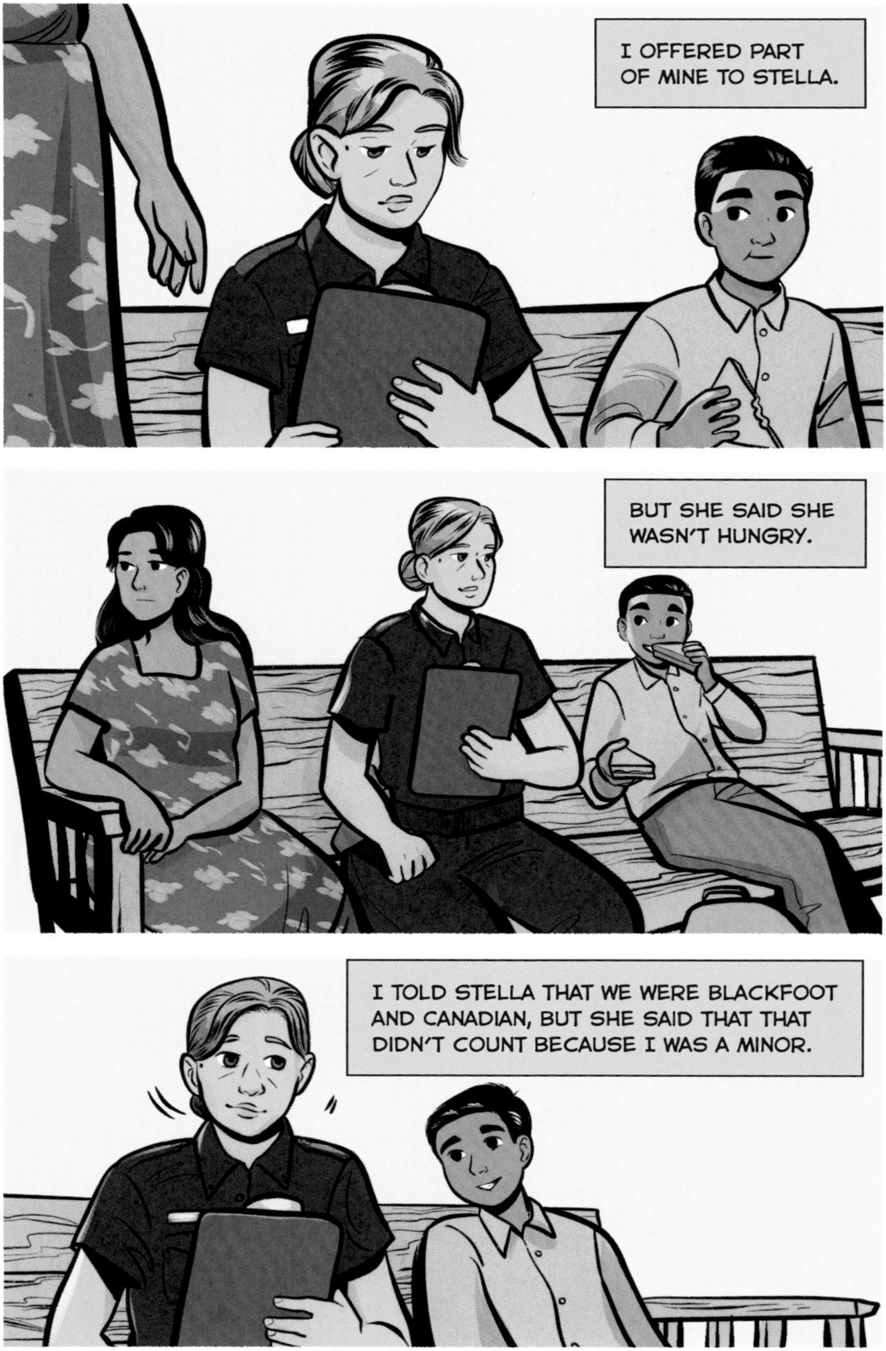

I OFFERED PART OF MINE TO STELLA.
BUT SHE SAID SHE WASN'T HUNGRY.
I TOLD STELLA THAT WE WERE BLACKFOOT AND CANADIAN, BUT SHE SAID THAT THAT DIDN'T COUNT BECAUSE I WAS A MINOR.

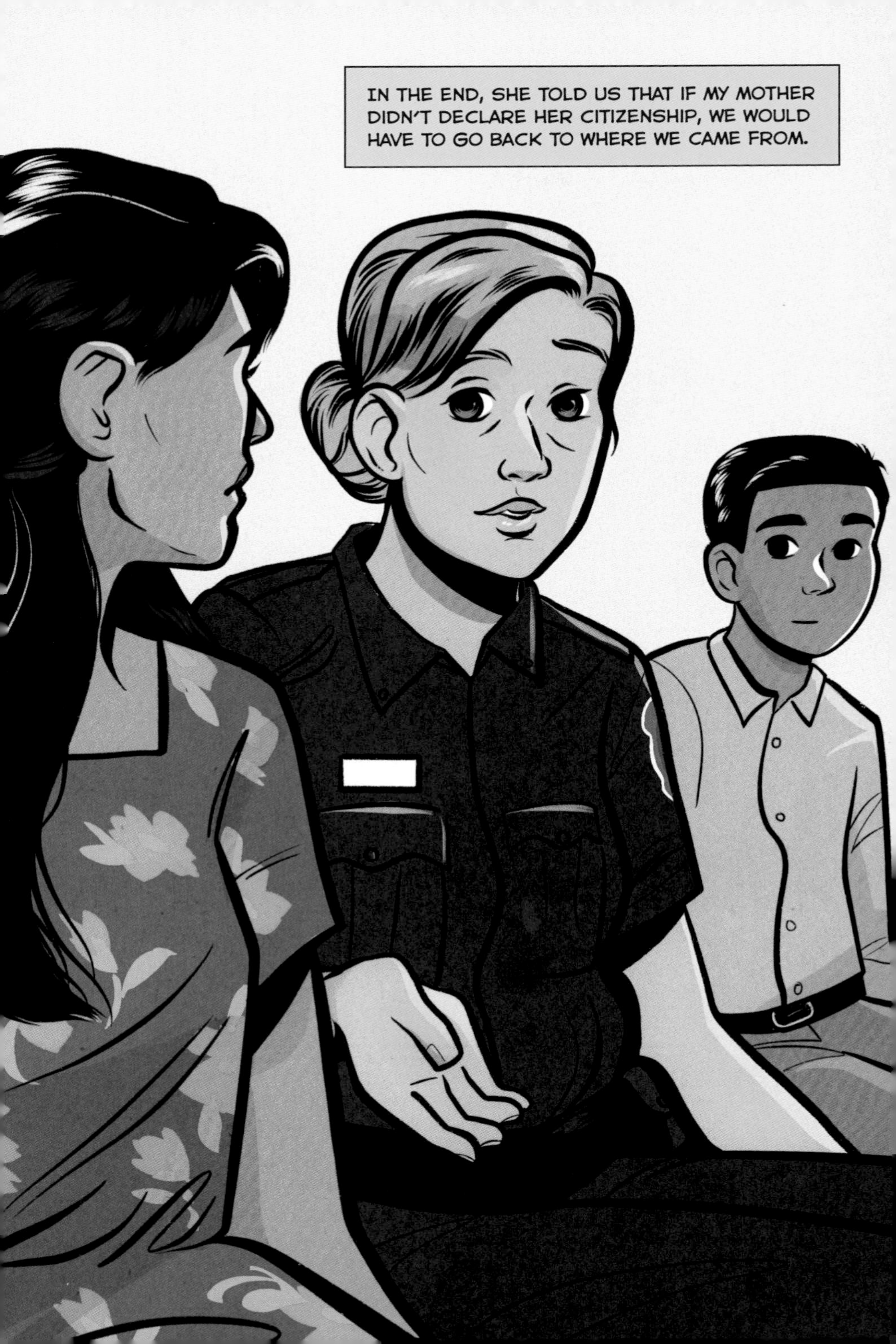
IN THE END, SHE TOLD US THAT IF MY MOTHER DIDN'T DECLARE HER CITIZENSHIP, WE WOULD HAVE TO GO BACK TO WHERE WE CAME FROM.

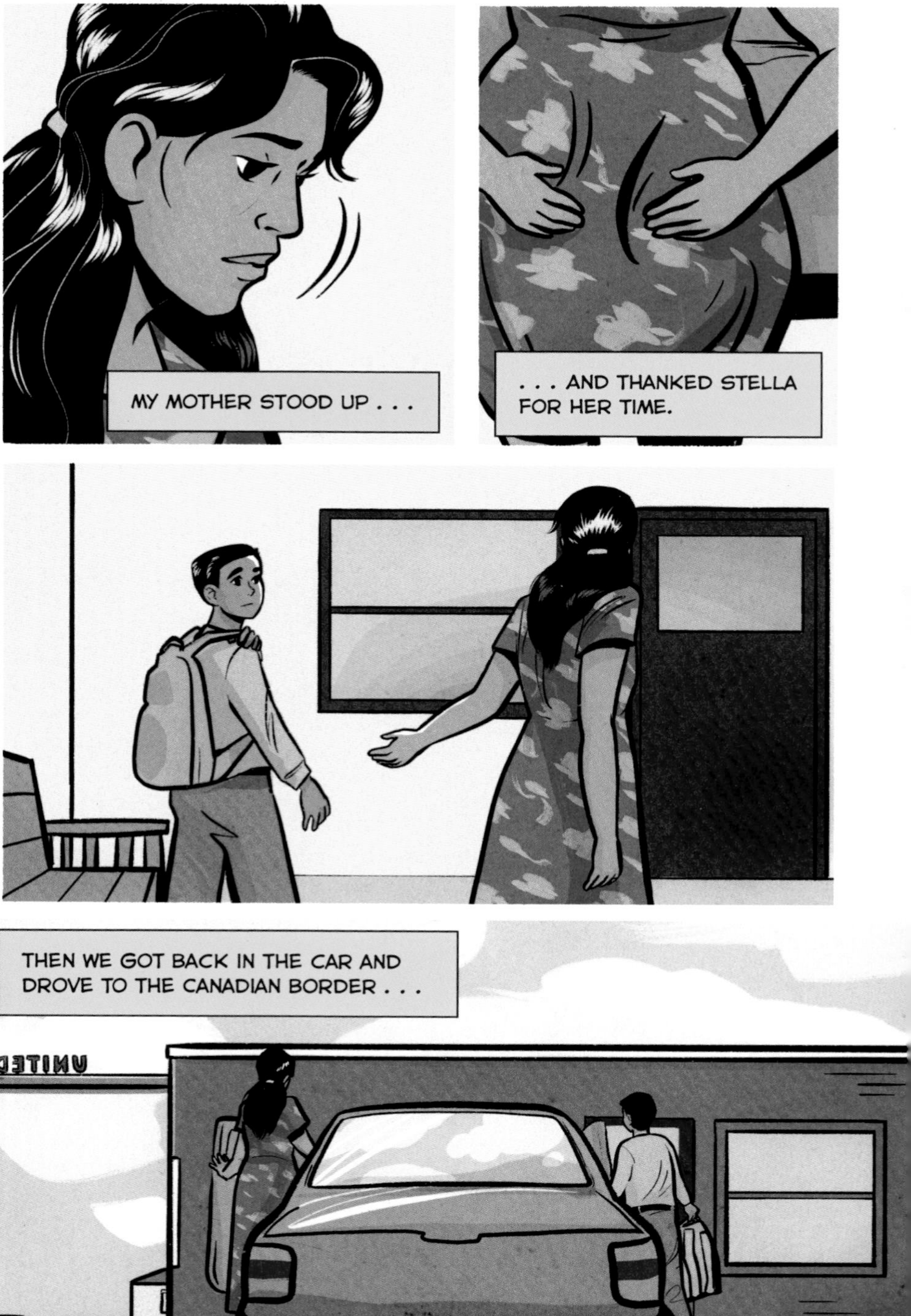
MY MOTHER STOOD UP . . .
. . . AND THANKED STELLA FOR HER TIME.
THEN WE GOT BACK IN THE CAR AND DROVE TO THE CANADIAN BORDER . . .

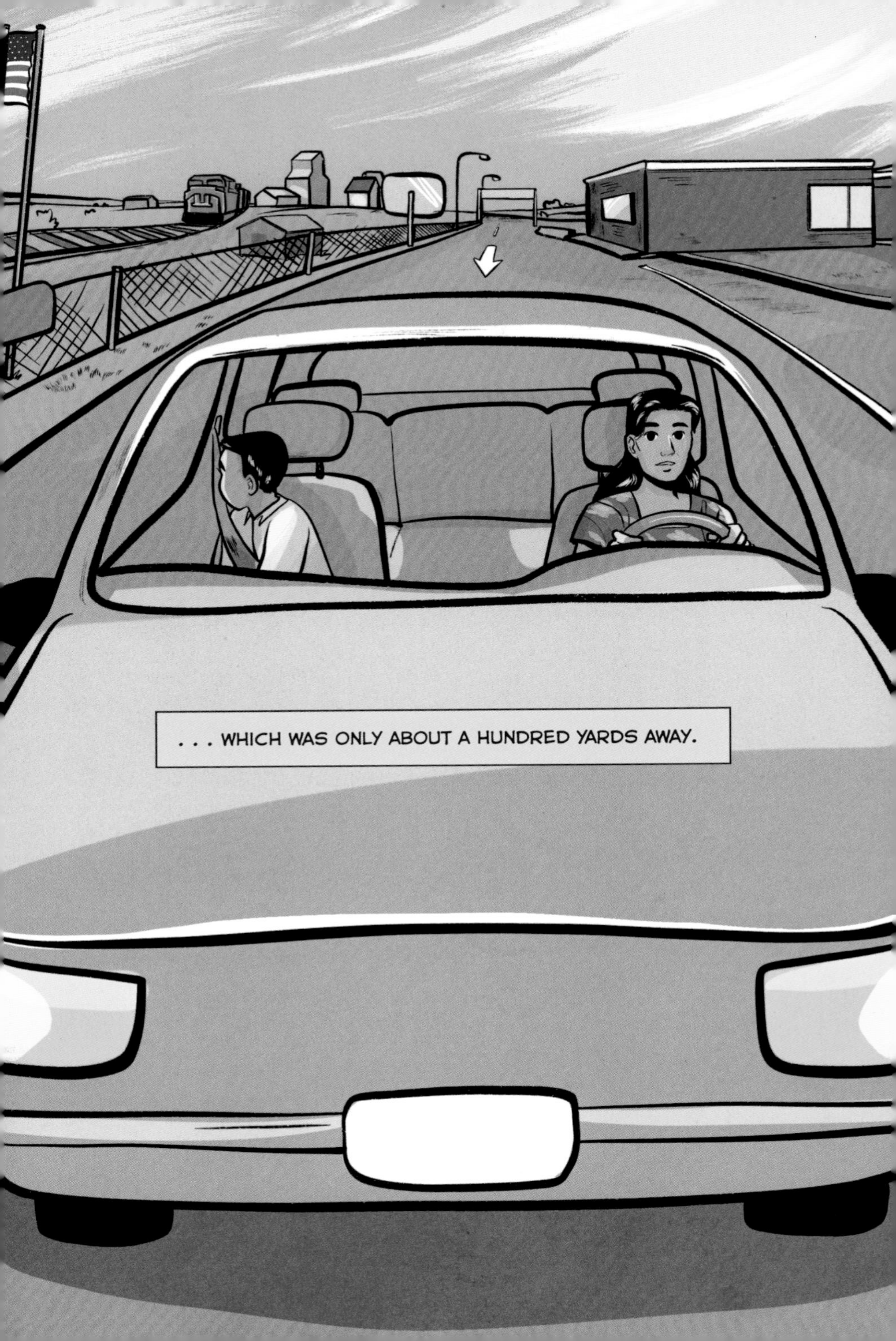
. . . WHICH WAS ONLY ABOUT A HUNDRED YARDS AWAY.

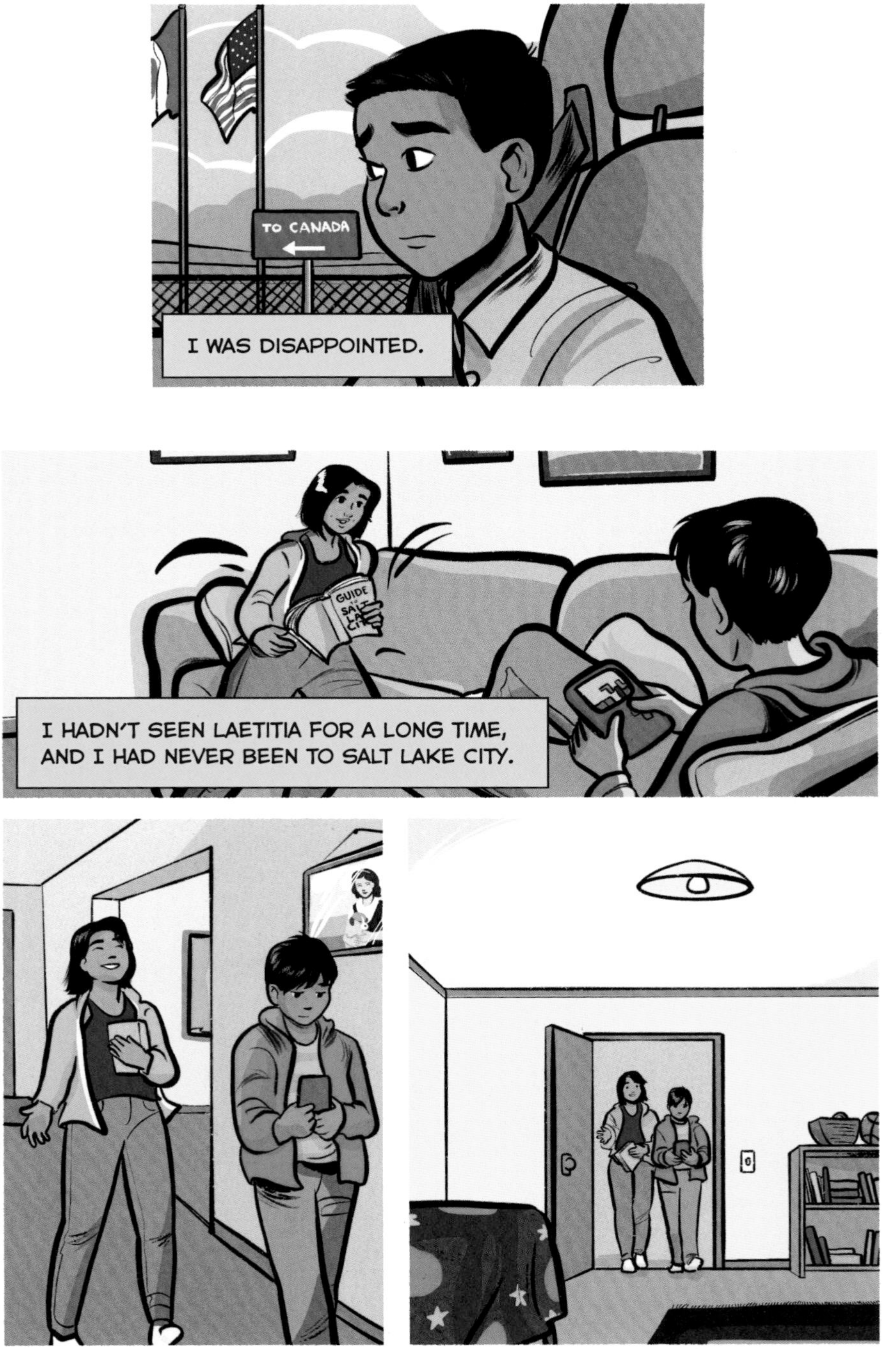
TO CANADA
I WAS DISAPPOINTED.
GUIDE
I HADN'T SEEN LAETITIA FOR A LONG TIME, AND I HAD NEVER BEEN TO SALT LAKE CITY.

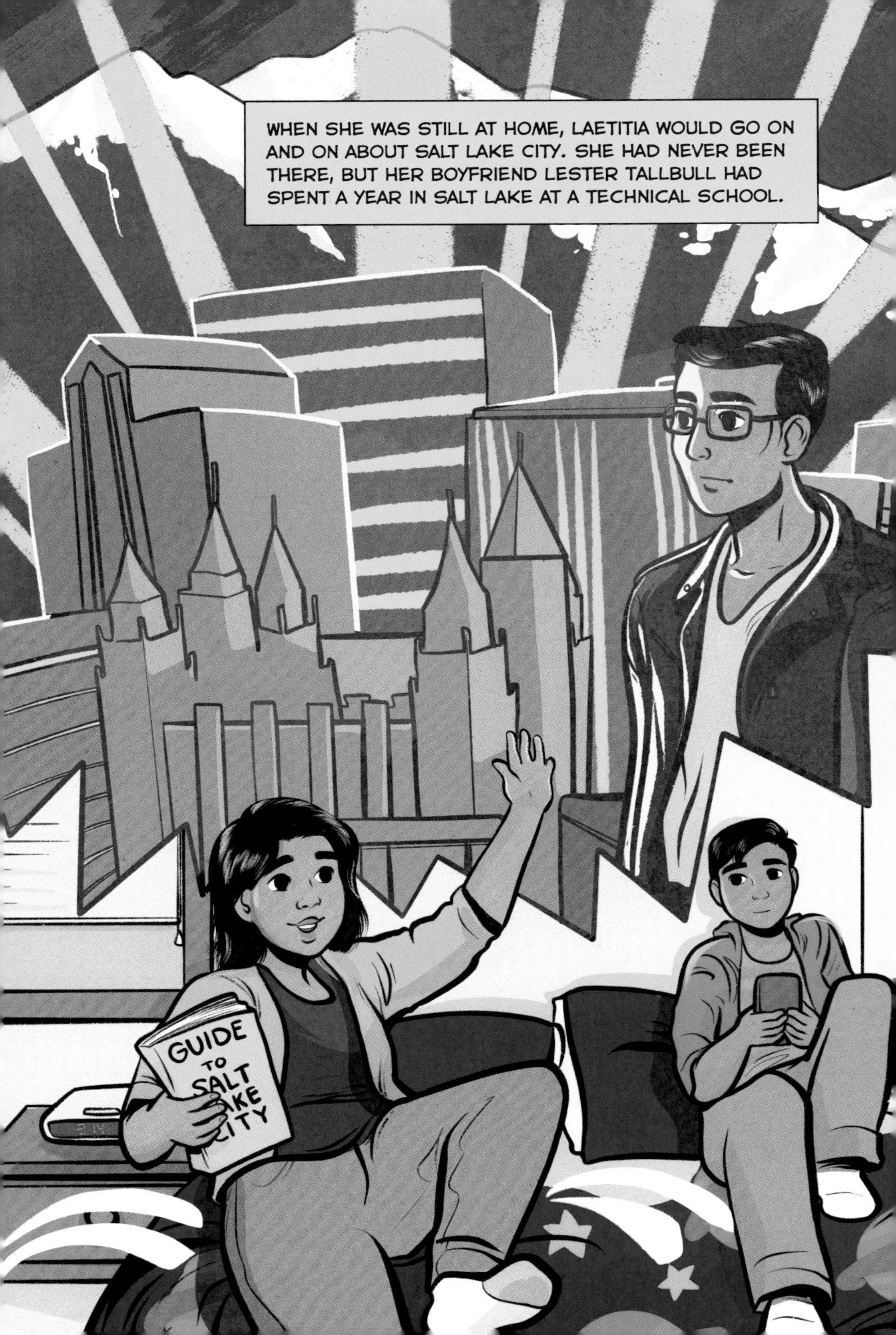
WHEN SHE WAS STILL AT HOME, LAETITIA WOULD GO ON AND ON ABOUT SALT LAKE CITY. SHE HAD NEVER BEEN THERE, BUT HER BOYFRIEND LESTER TALLBULL HAD SPENT A YEAR IN SALT LAKE AT A TECHNICAL SCHOOL.
GUIDE TO SALT LAKE CITY

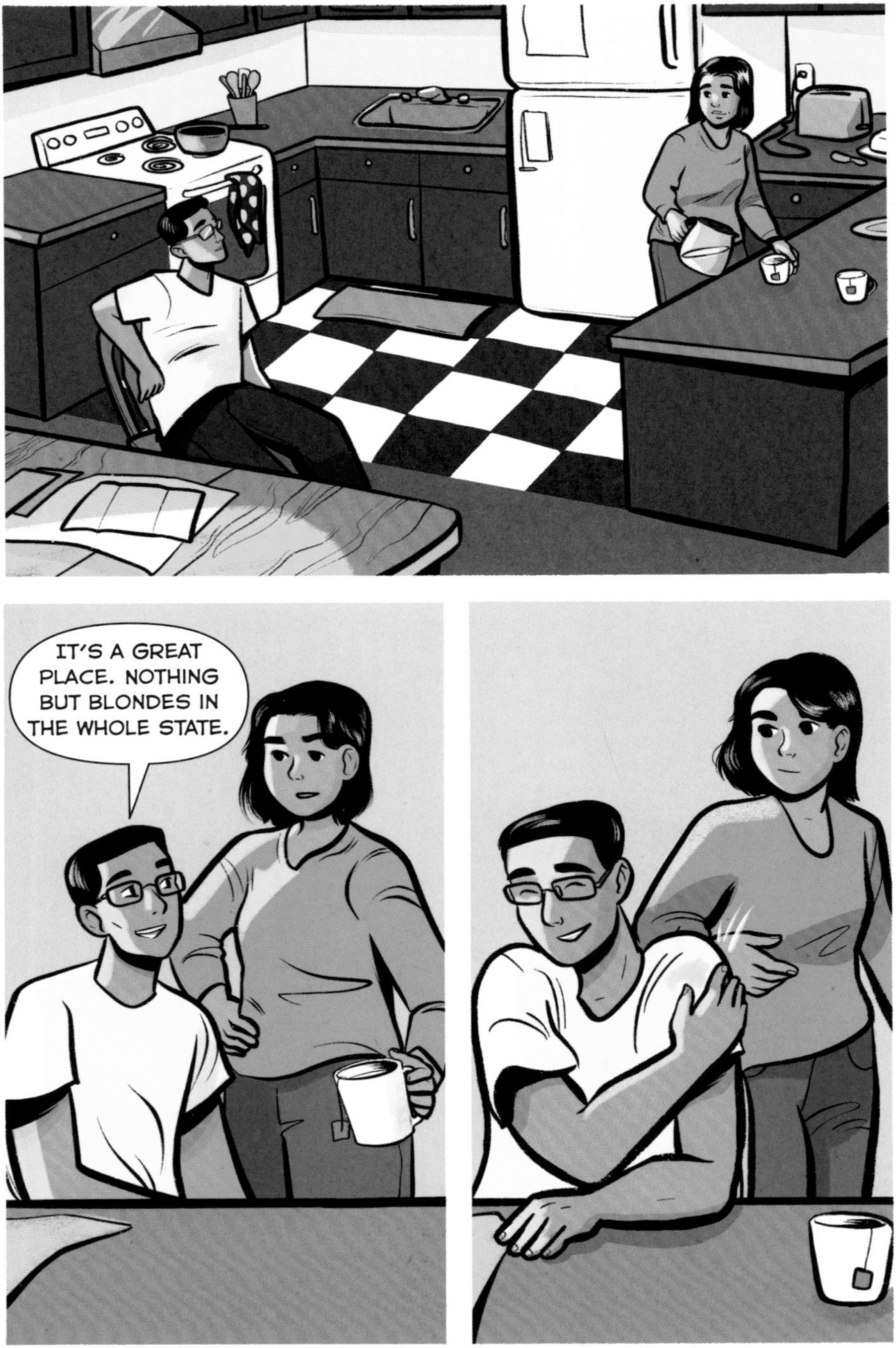
IT'S A GREAT PLACE. NOTHING BUT BLONDES IN THE WHOLE STATE.

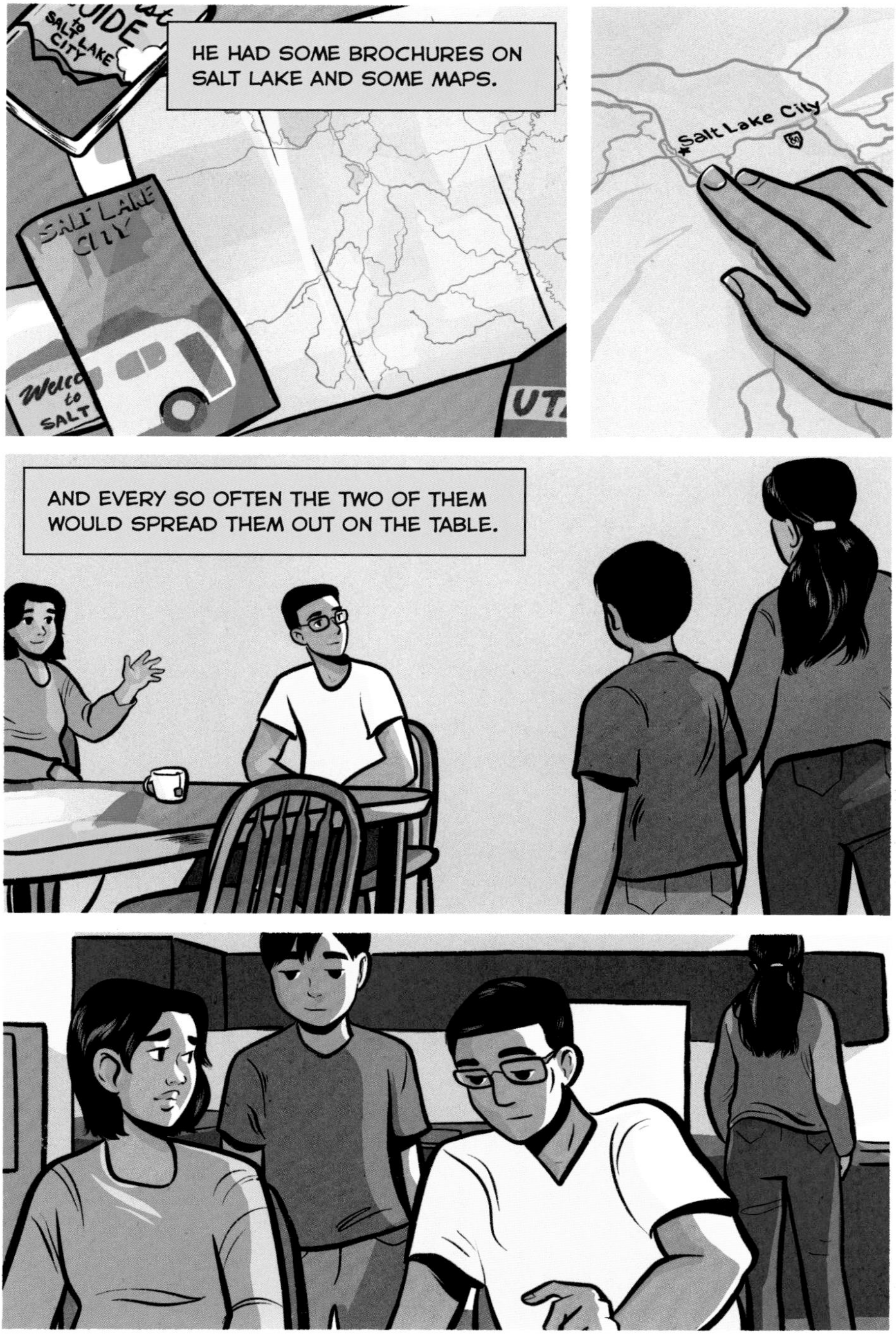
HE HAD SOME BROCHURES ON SALT LAKE AND SOME MAPS.
SALT LAKE CITY
Salt Lake City
AND EVERY SO OFTEN THE TWO OF THEM WOULD SPREAD THEM OUT ON THE TABLE.

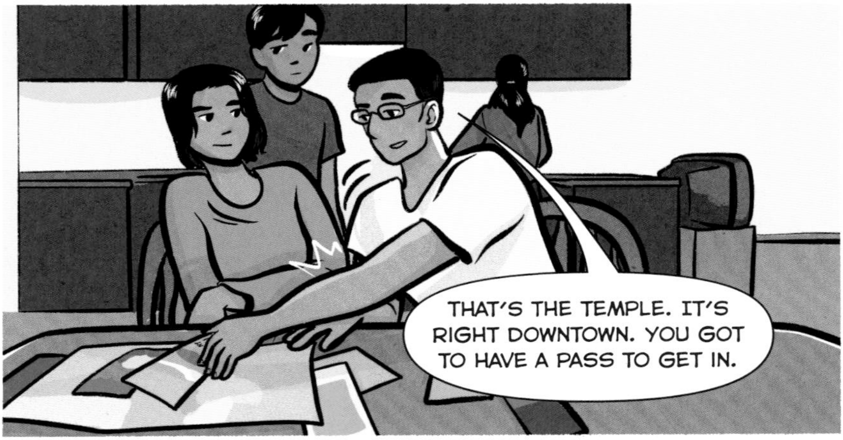
THAT'S THE TEMPLE. IT'S RIGHT DOWNTOWN. YOU GOT TO HAVE A PASS TO GET IN.

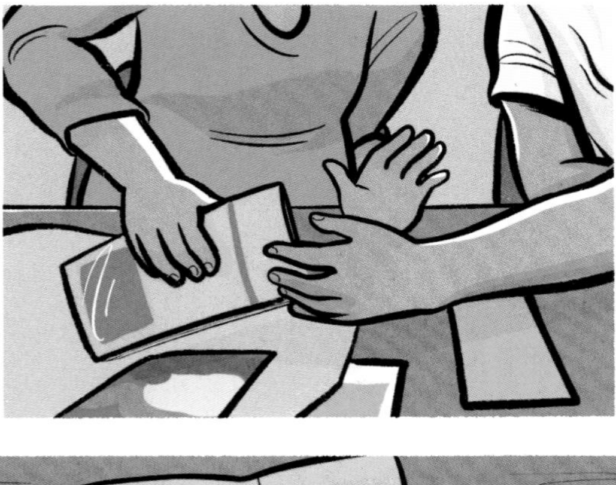

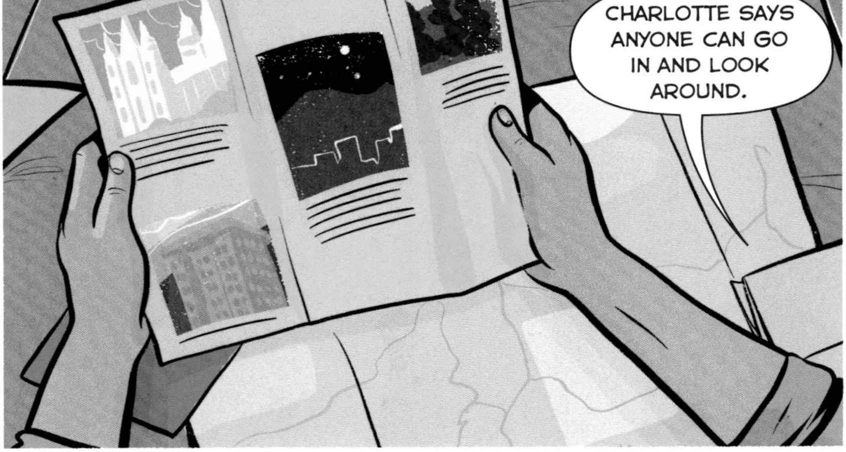
CHARLOTTE SAYS ANYONE CAN GO IN AND LOOK AROUND.

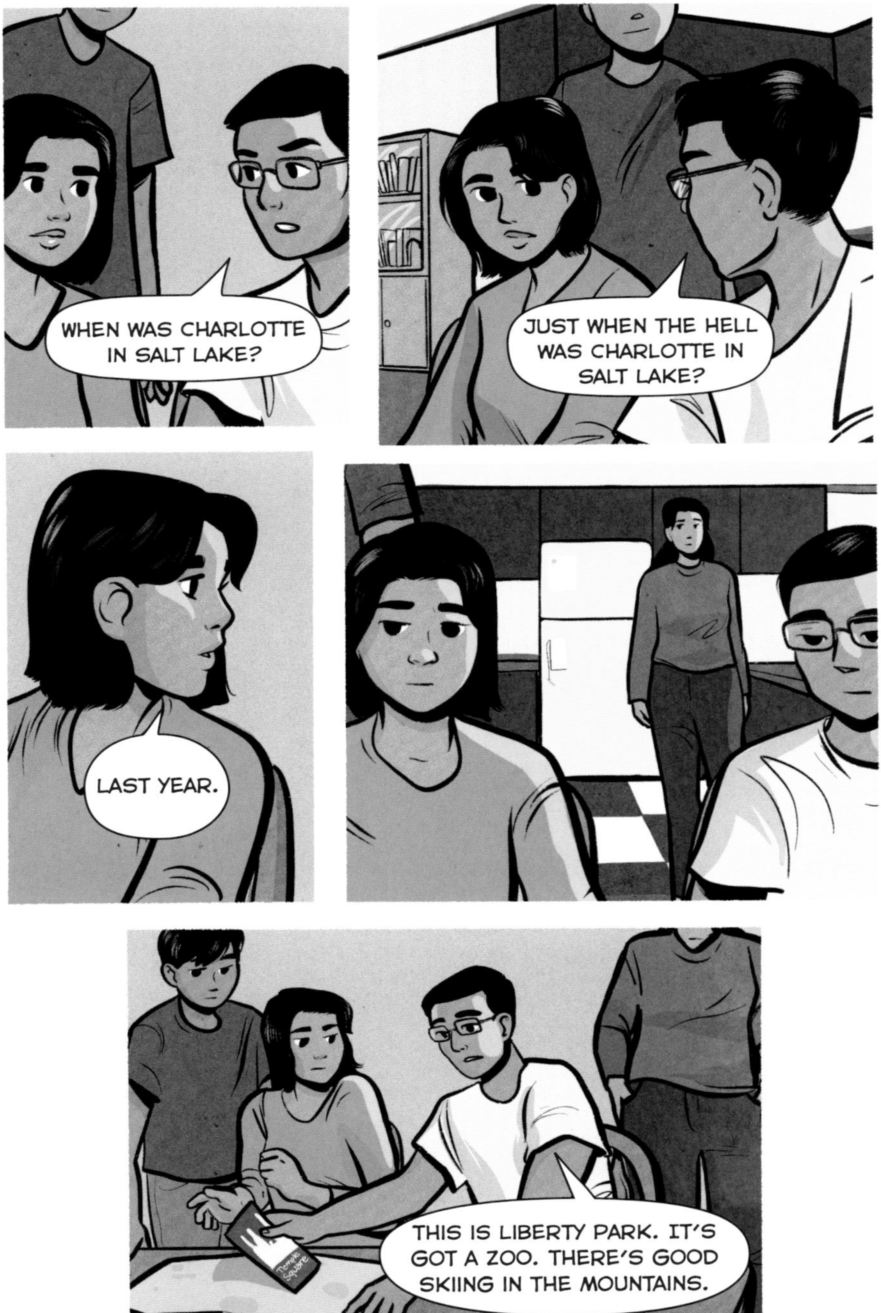
WHEN WAS CHARLOTTE IN SALT LAKE?
JUST WHEN THE HELL WAS CHARLOTTE IN SALT LAKE?
LAST YEAR.
Temple Square
THIS IS LIBERTY PARK. IT'S GOT A ZOO. THERE'S GOOD SKIING IN THE MOUNTAINS.

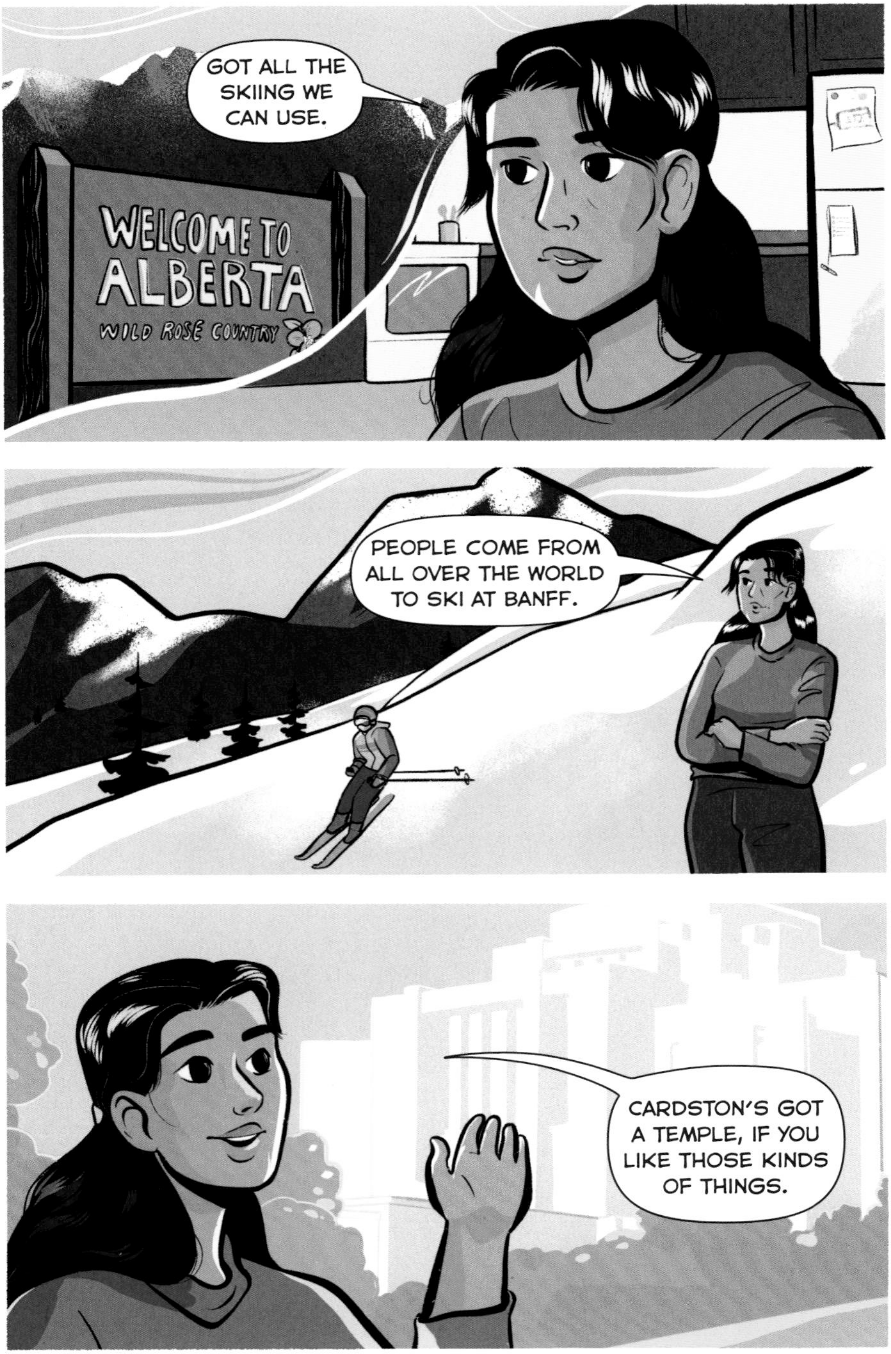
GOT ALL THE SKIING WE CAN USE.
WELCOME TO ALBERTA
WILD ROSE COUNTRY
PEOPLE COME FROM ALL OVER THE WORLD TO SKI AT BANFF.
CARDSTON'S GOT A TEMPLE, IF YOU LIKE THOSE KINDS OF THINGS.

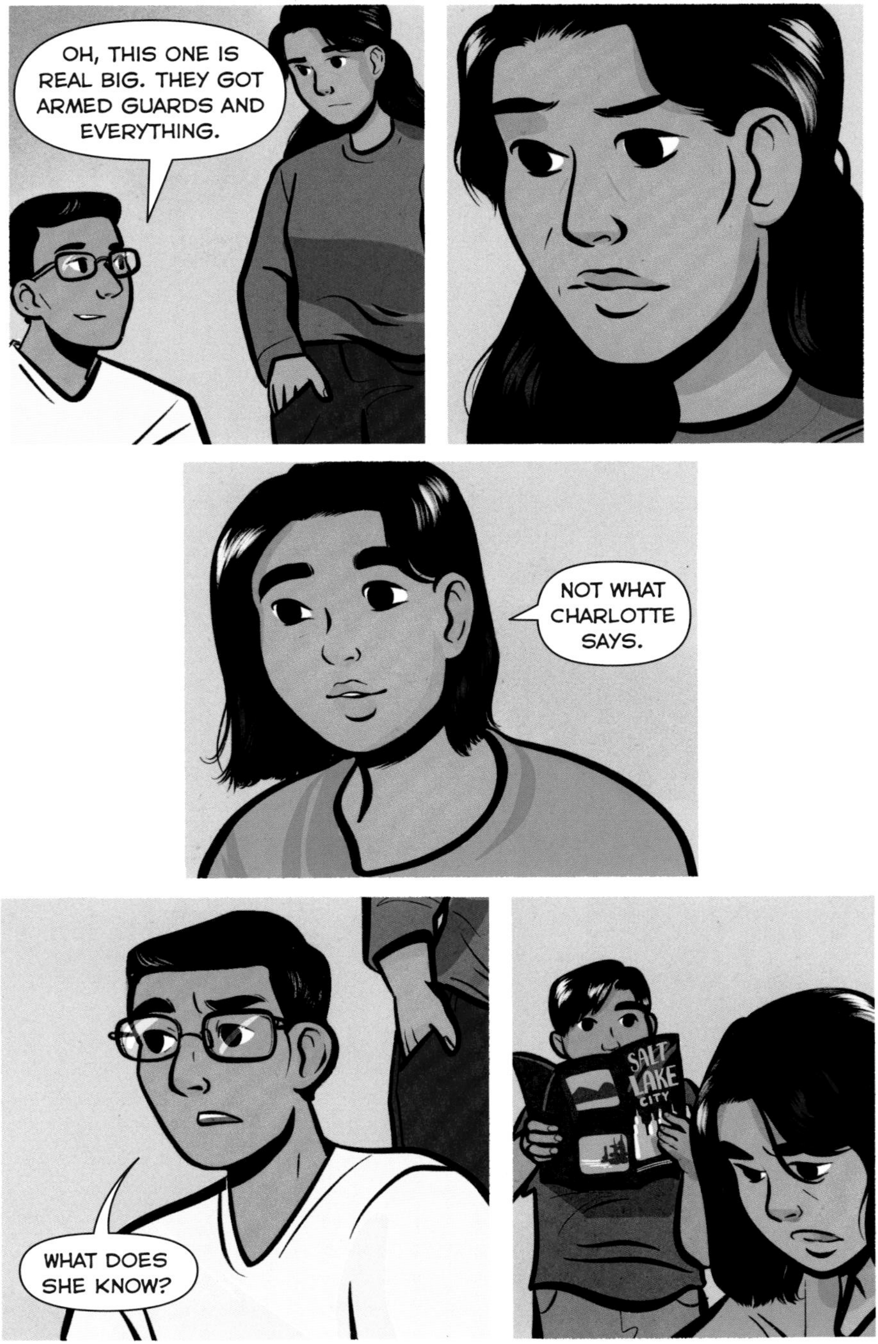
OH, THIS ONE IS REAL BIG. THEY GOT ARMED GUARDS AND EVERYTHING.
NOT WHAT CHARLOTTE SAYS.
WHAT DOES SHE KNOW?
SALT LAKE CITY

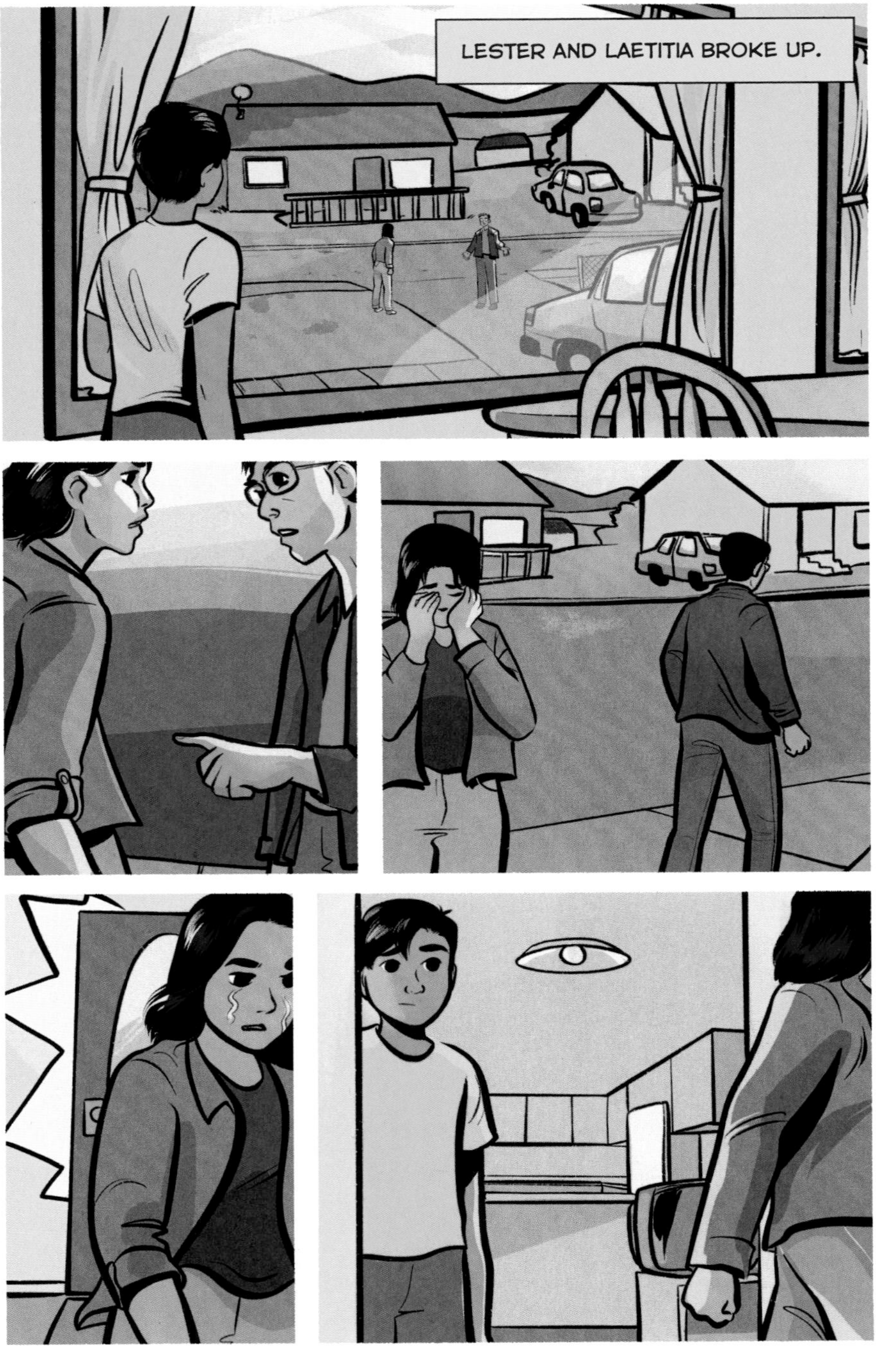
LESTER AND LAETITIA BROKE UP.

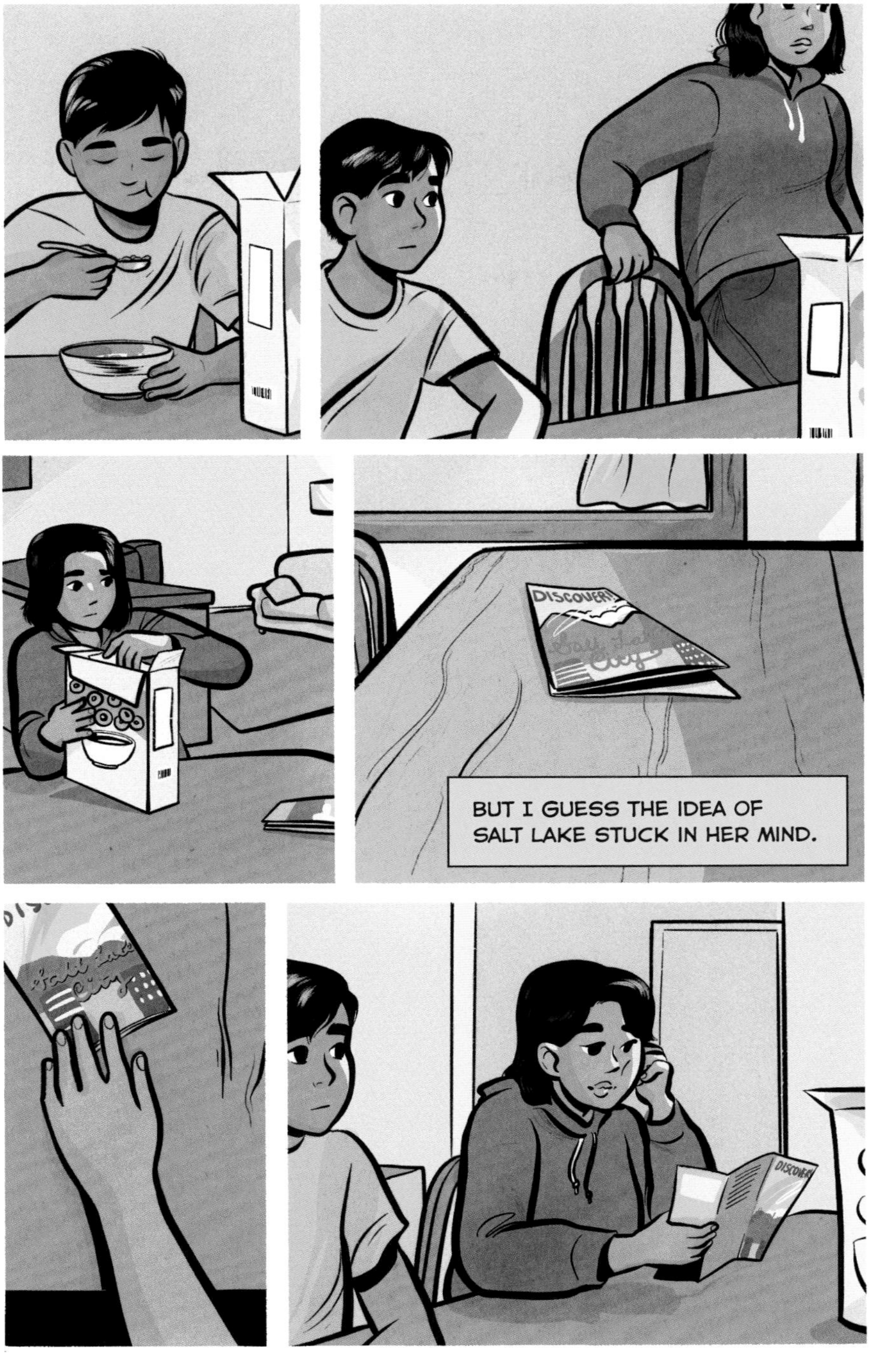
DISCOVER!
Salt Lake City
BUT I GUESS THE IDEA OF SALT LAKE STUCK IN HER MIND.
Salt Lake City
DISCOVER!

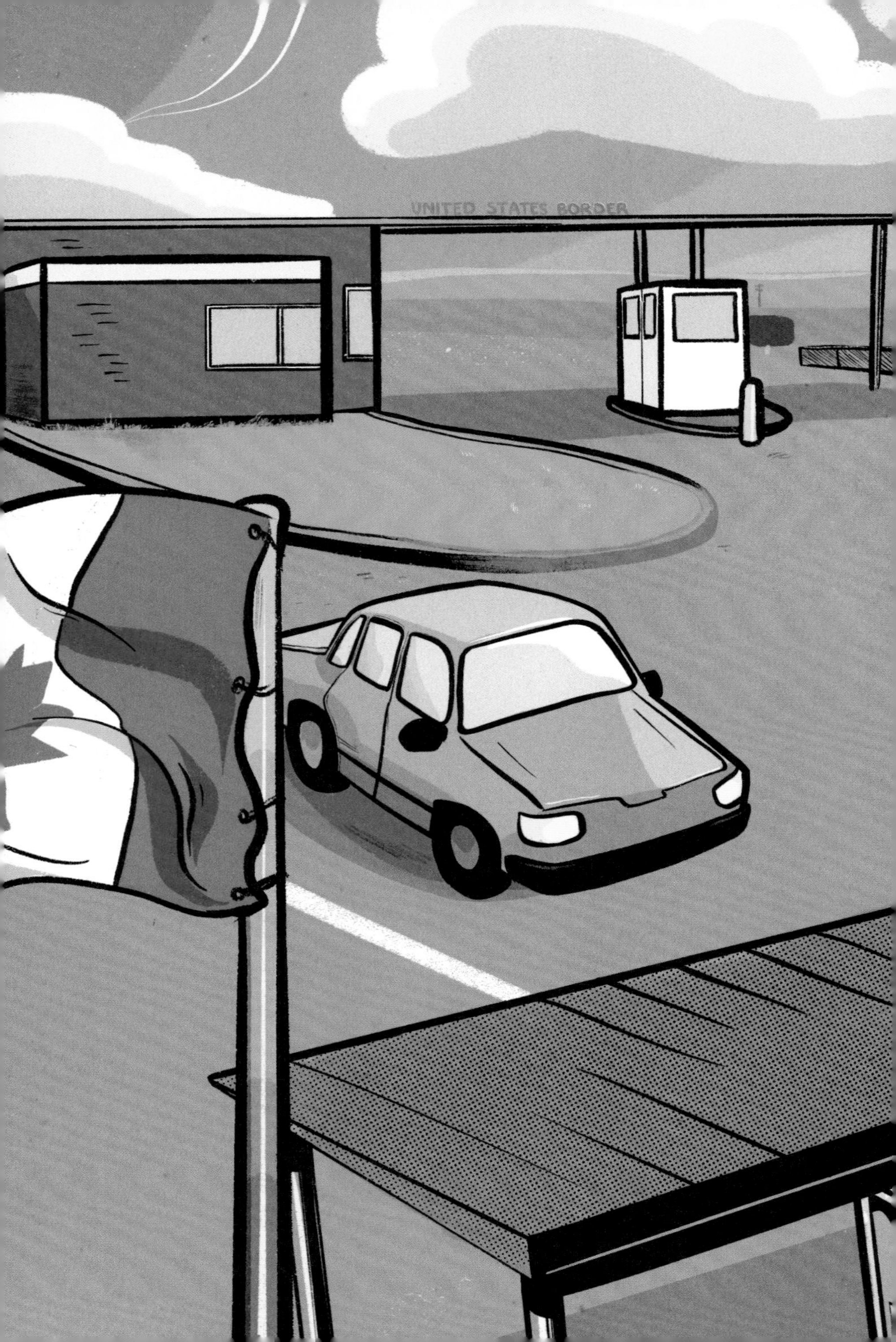
UNITED STATES BORDER

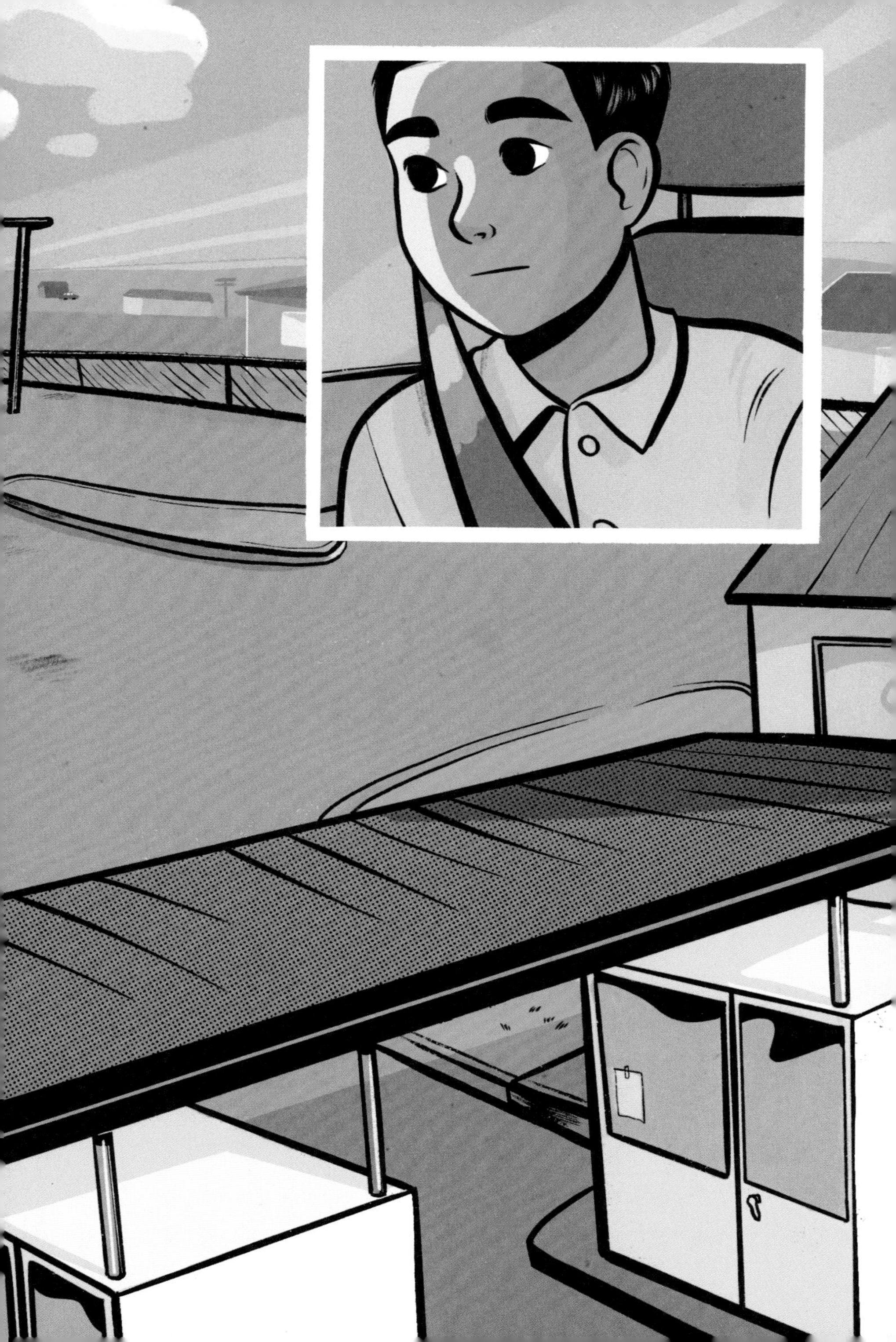

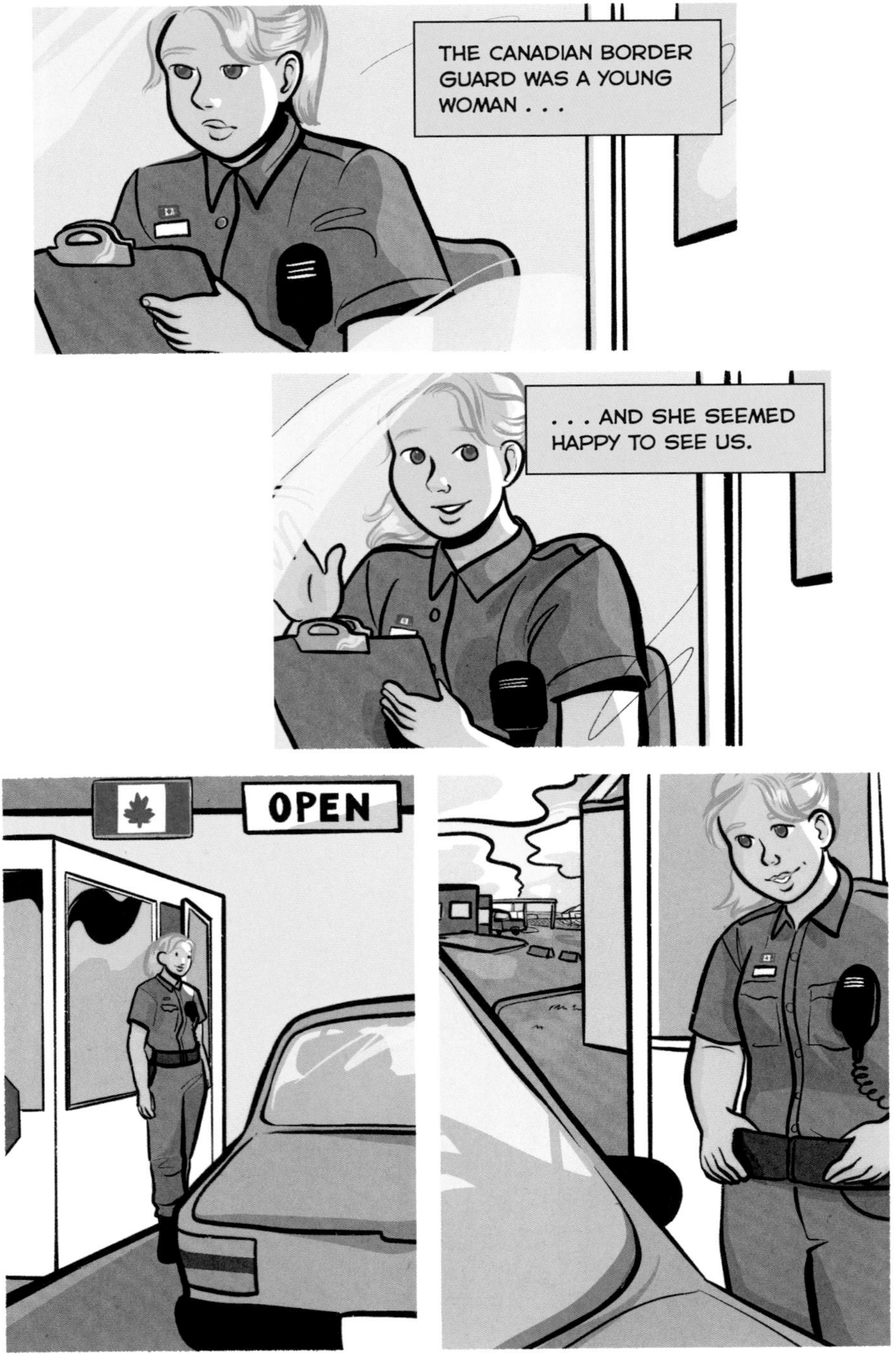
THE CANADIAN BORDER GUARD WAS A YOUNG WOMAN . . .
. . . AND SHE SEEMED HAPPY TO SEE US.
OPEN

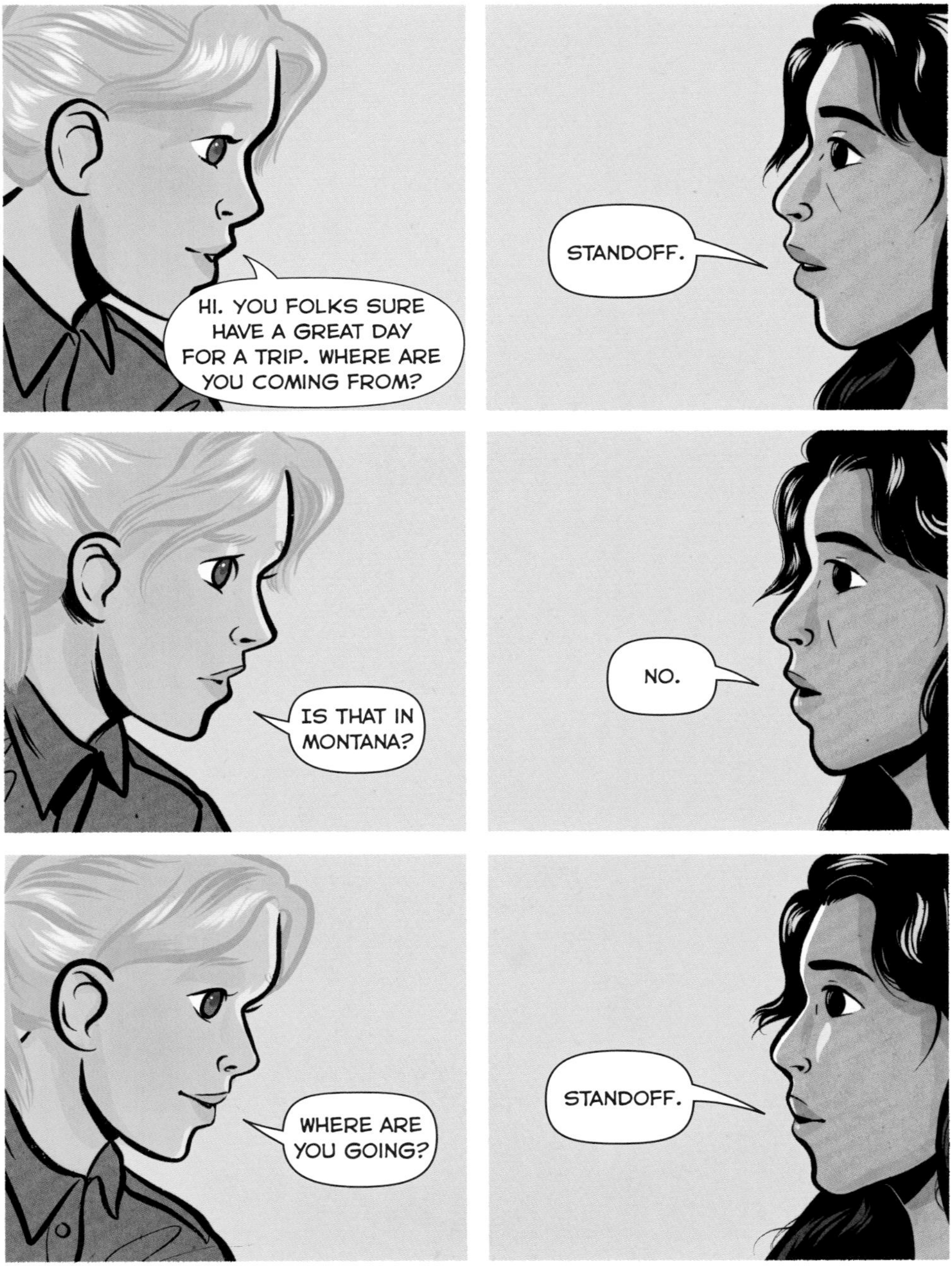
HI. YOU FOLKS SURE HAVE A GREAT DAY FOR A TRIP. WHERE ARE YOU COMING FROM?
STANDOFF.
IS THAT IN MONTANA?
NO.
WHERE ARE YOU GOING?
STANDOFF.

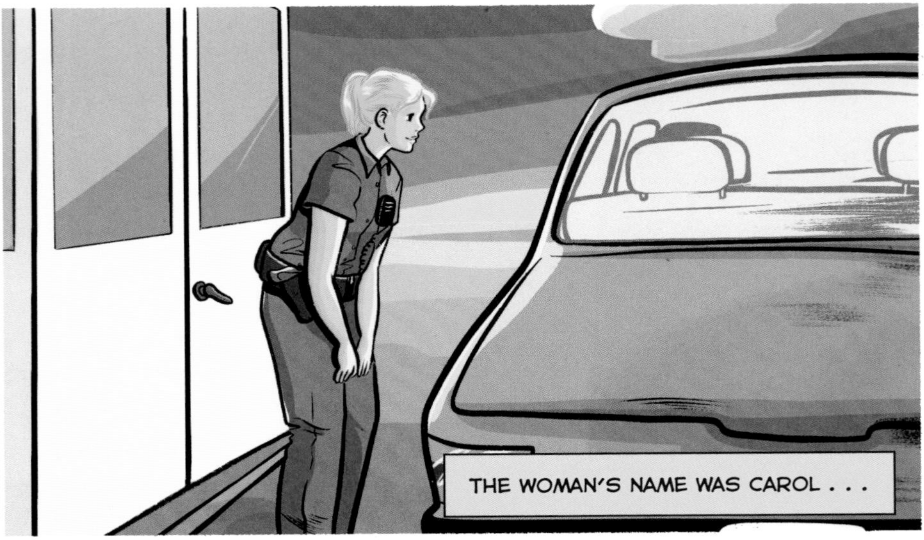

THE WOMAN'S NAME WAS CAROL . . .

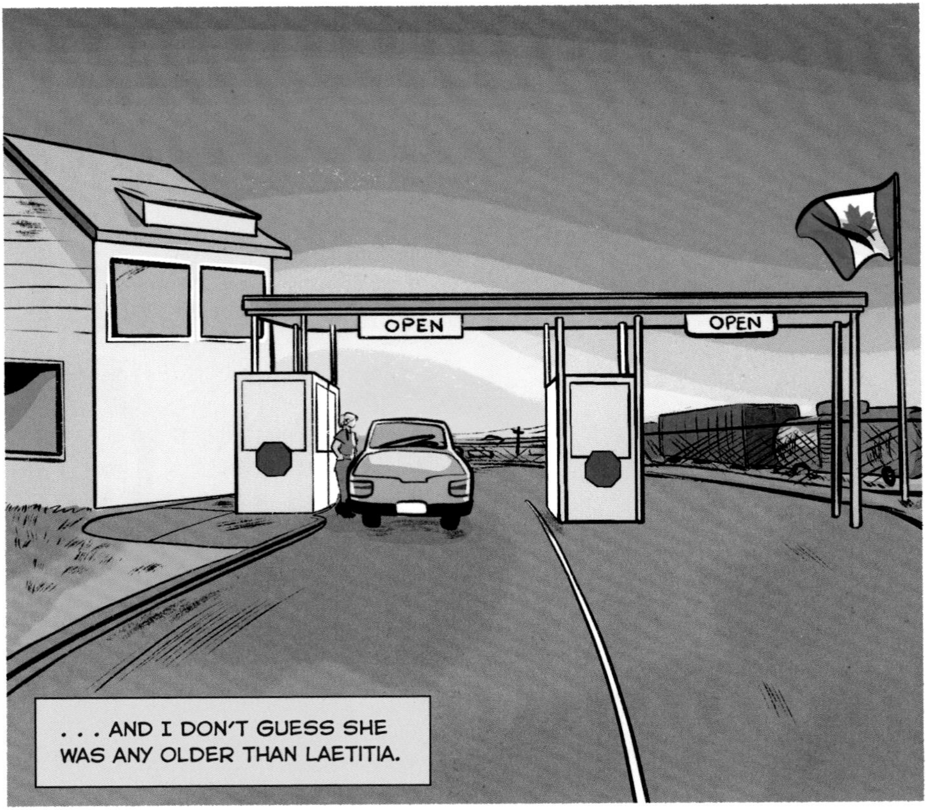

OPEN
OPEN
. . . AND I DON'T GUESS SHE WAS ANY OLDER THAN LAETITIA.

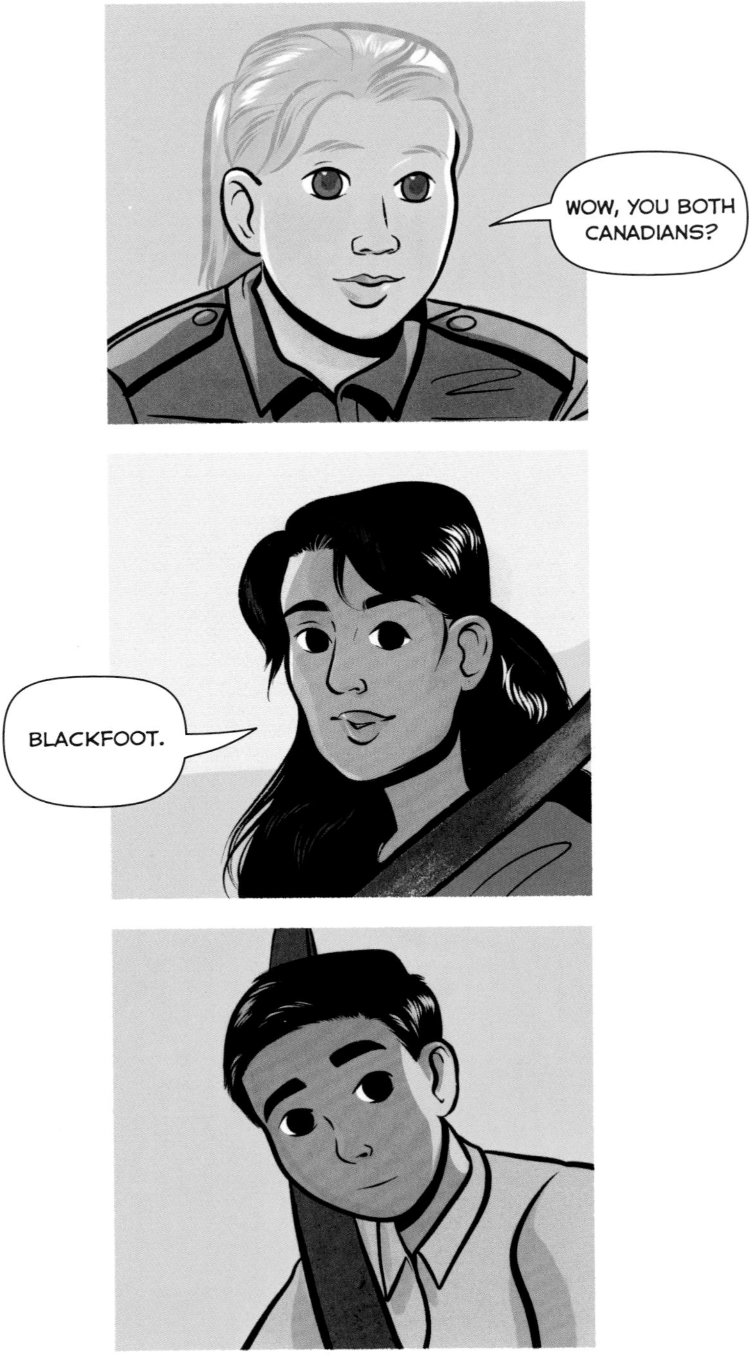
WOW, YOU BOTH CANADIANS?
BLACKFOOT.

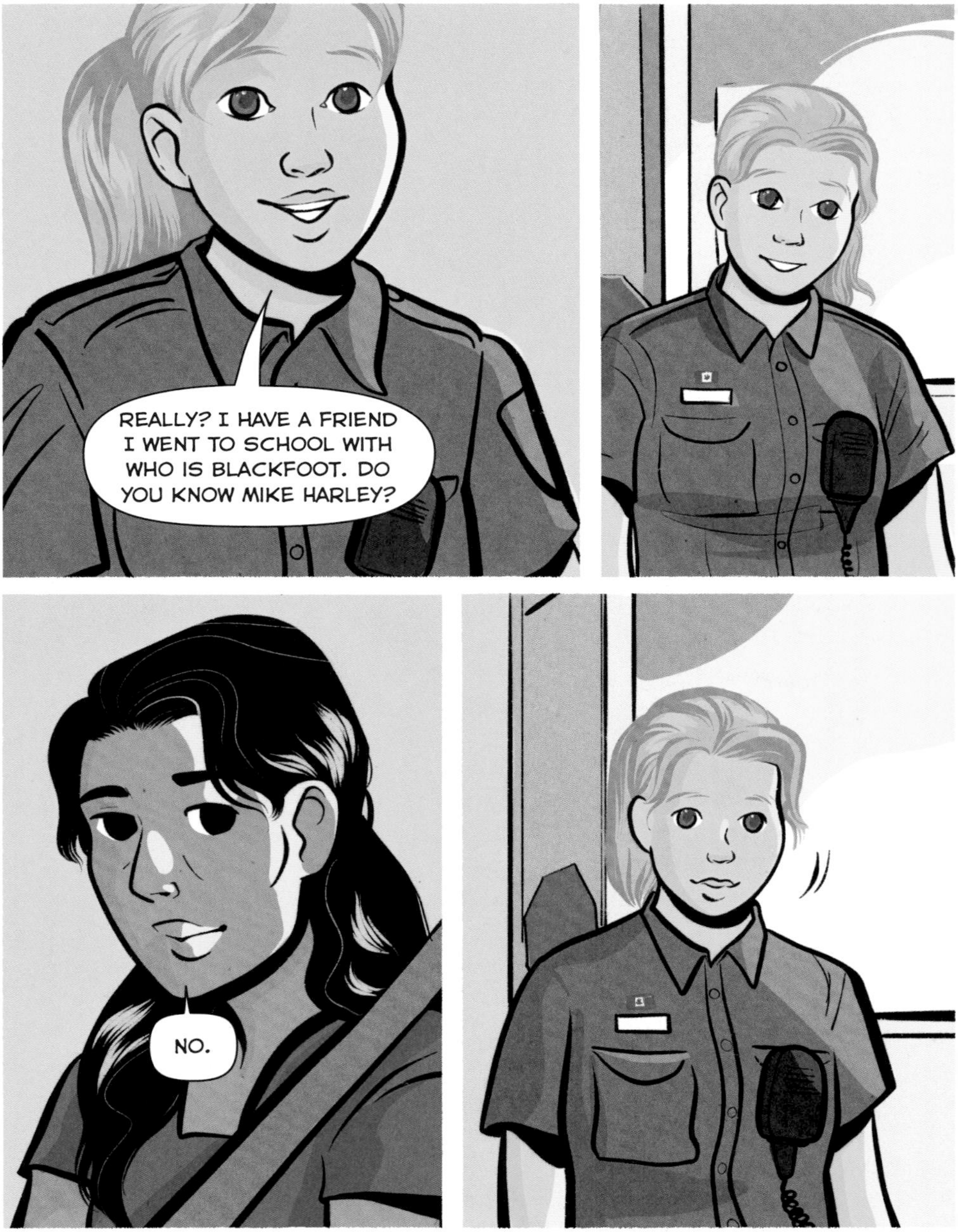
REALLY? I HAVE A FRIEND I WENT TO SCHOOL WITH WHO IS BLACKFOOT. DO YOU KNOW MIKE HARLEY?
NO.

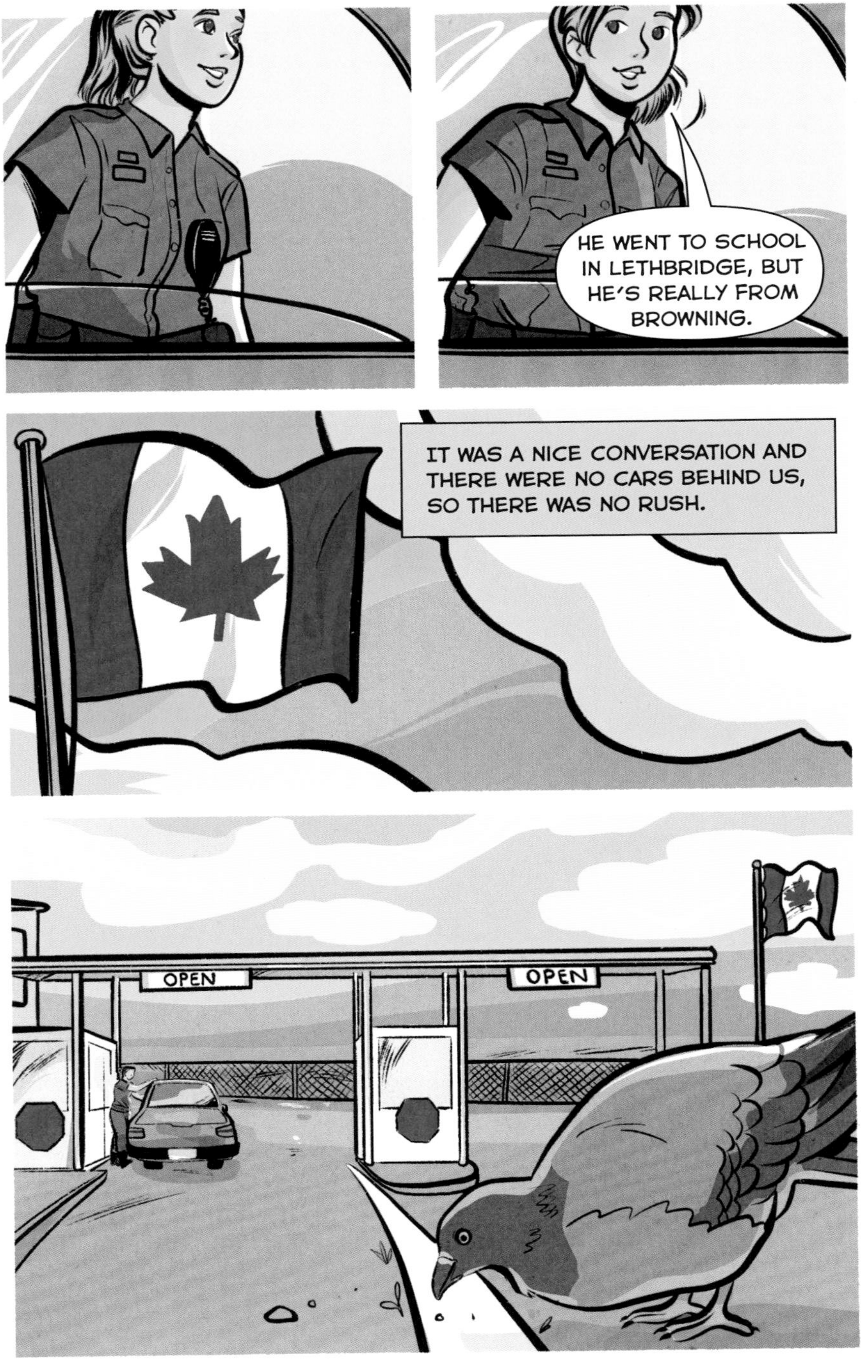
HE WENT TO SCHOOL IN LETHBRIDGE, BUT HE'S REALLY FROM BROWNING.
IT WAS A NICE CONVERSATION AND THERE WERE NO CARS BEHIND US, SO THERE WAS NO RUSH.
OPEN
OPEN

ECONDARY
NSPECTION
RETURN TO
U.S.
YOU'RE NOT BRINGING ANY LIQUOR BACK, ARE YOU?
NO.
Prohibited Items:
Animal and fish products, fresh fruit and vegetables
Weapons
Live bait
Illegal drugs
ANY CIGARETTES OR PLANTS OR STUFF LIKE THAT?
NO.

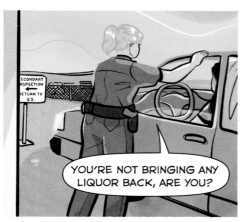

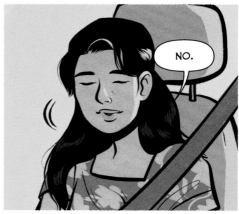

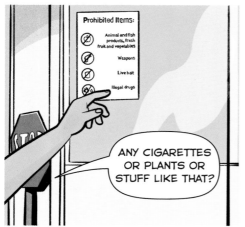

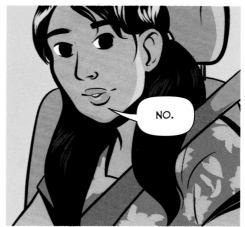

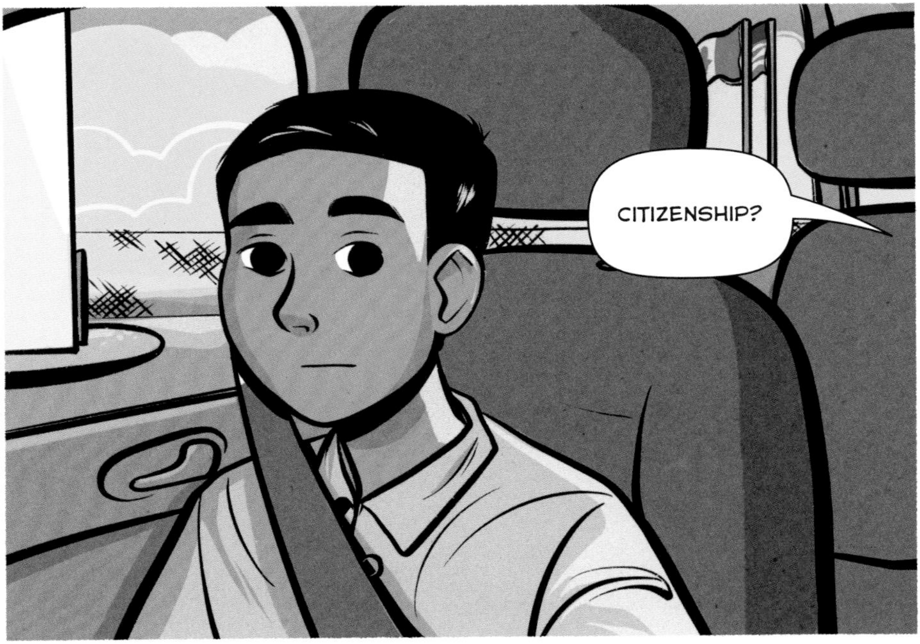
CITIZENSHIP?

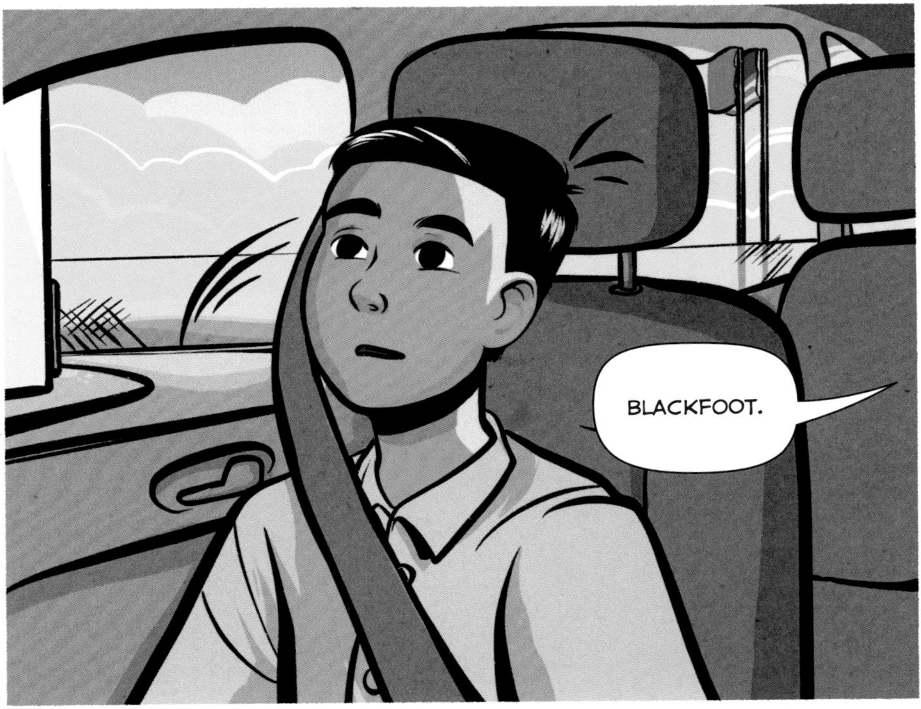
BLACKFOOT.

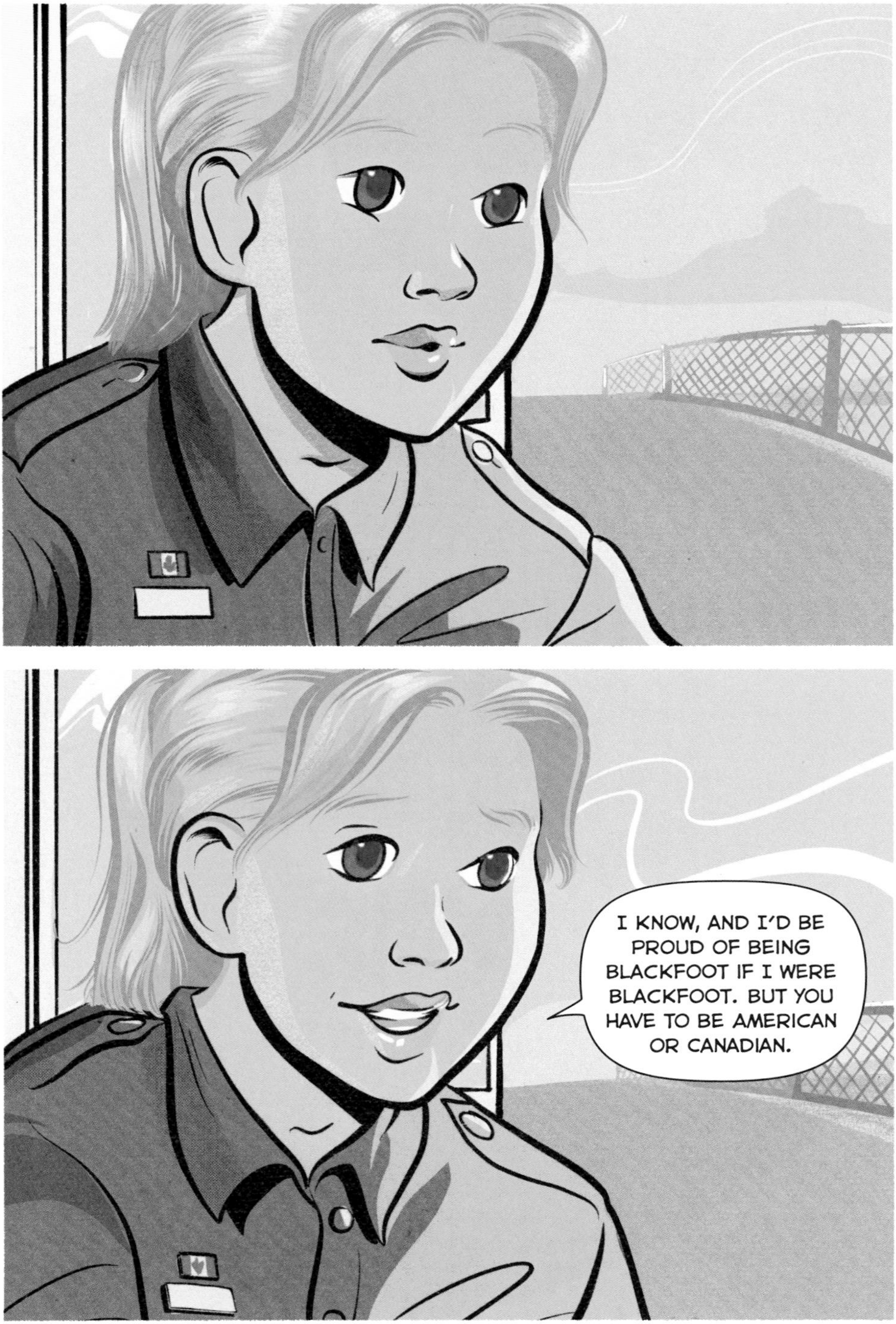
I KNOW, AND I'D BE PROUD OF BEING BLACKFOOT IF I WERE BLACKFOOT. BUT YOU HAVE TO BE AMERICAN OR CANADIAN.

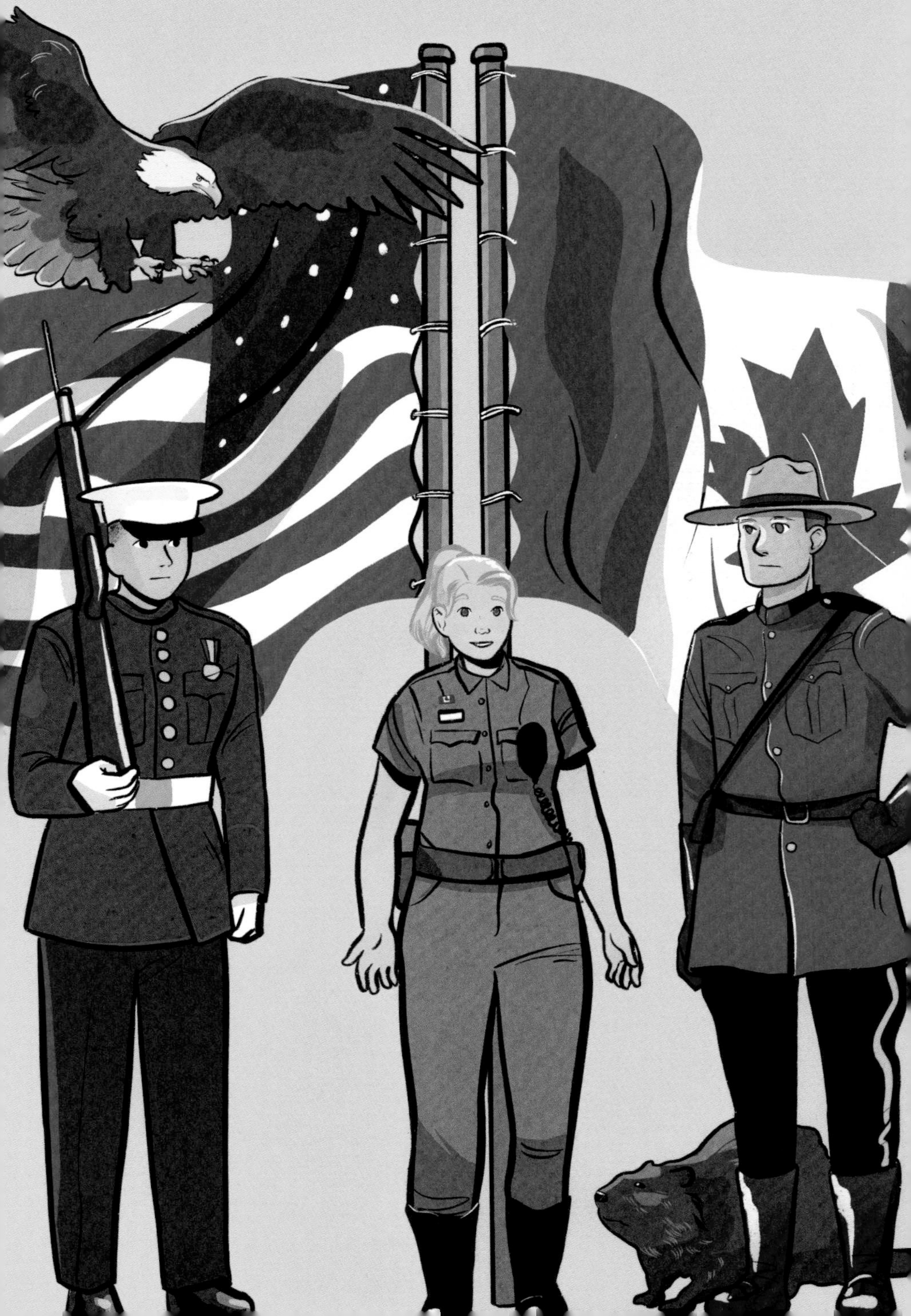

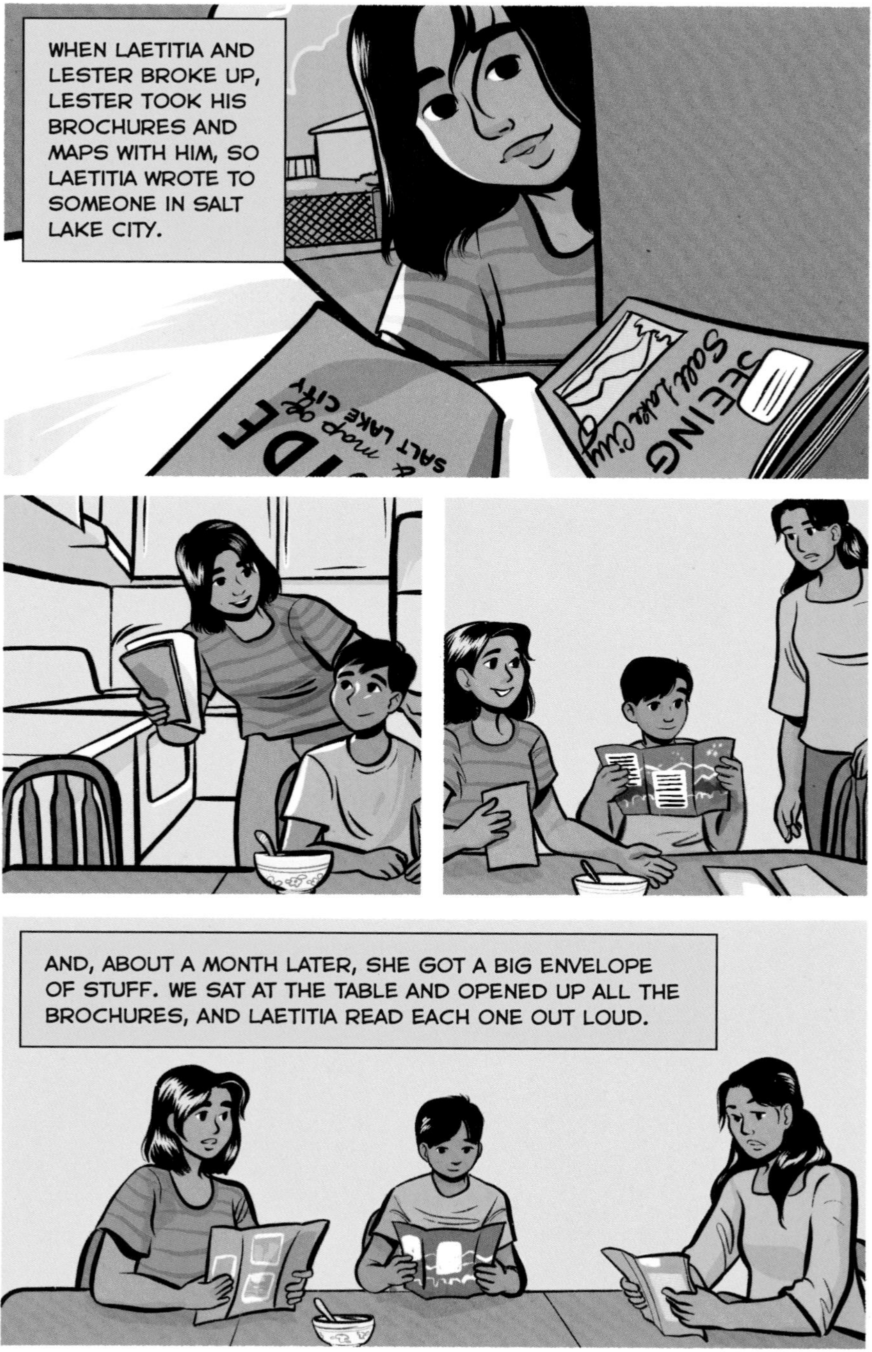
WHEN LAETITIA AND LESTER BROKE UP, LESTER TOOK HIS BROCHURES AND MAPS WITH HIM, SO LAETITIA WROTE TO SOMEONE IN SALT LAKE CITY.
SEEING Salt Lake City
AND, ABOUT A MONTH LATER, SHE GOT A BIG ENVELOPE OF STUFF. WE SAT AT THE TABLE AND OPENED UP ALL THE BROCHURES, AND LAETITIA READ EACH ONE OUT LOUD.

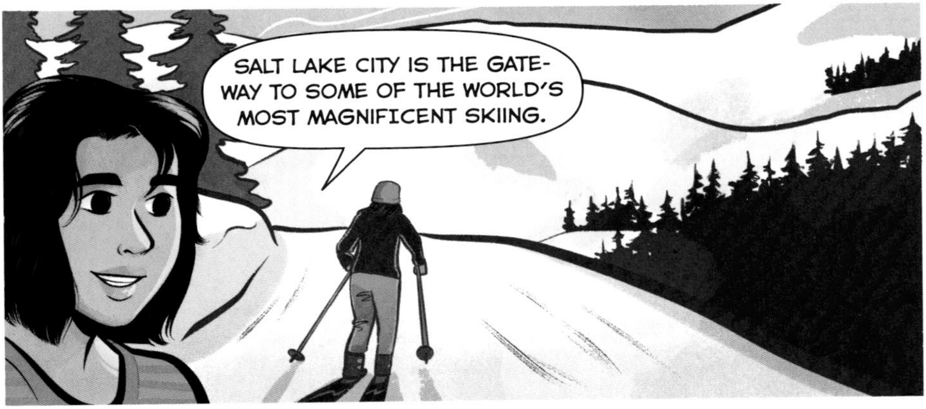
SALT LAKE CITY IS THE GATE-WAY TO SOME OF THE WORLD'S MOST MAGNIFICENT SKIING.

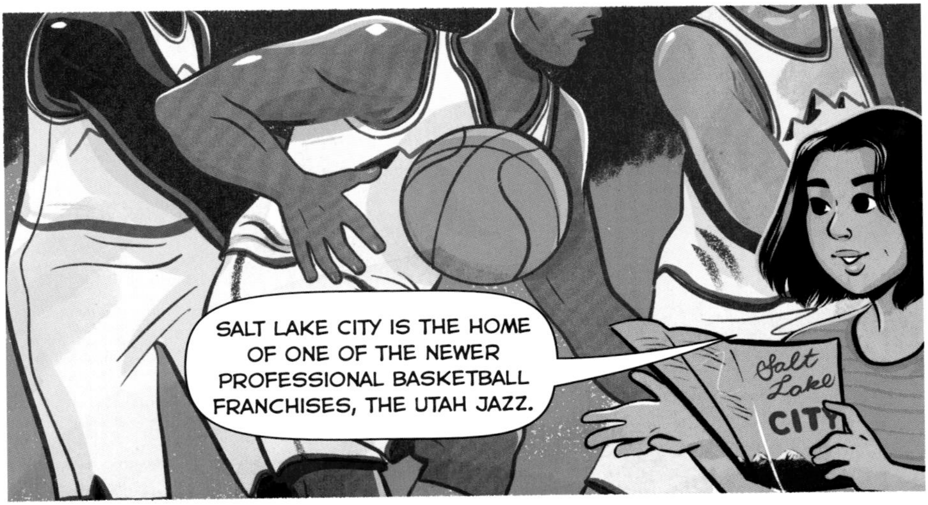
SALT LAKE CITY IS THE HOME OF ONE OF THE NEWER PROFESSIONAL BASKETBALL FRANCHISES, THE UTAH JAZZ.
Salt Lake CITY

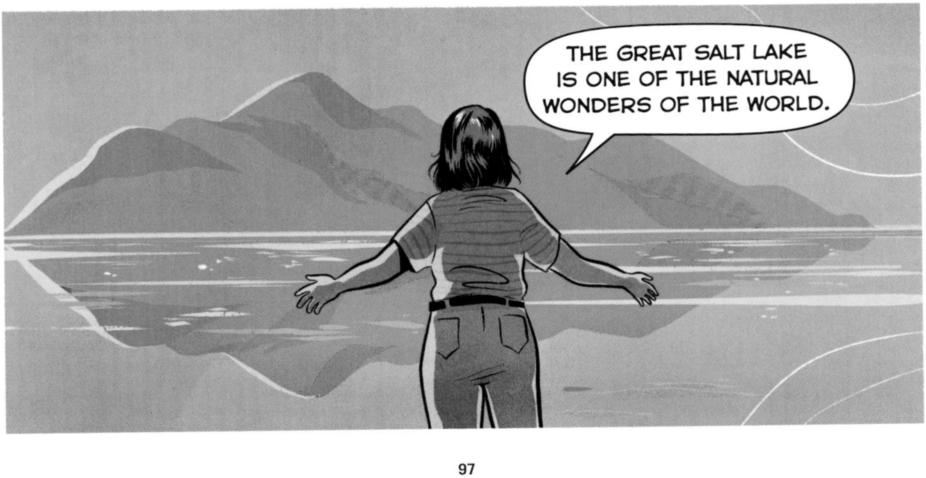
THE GREAT SALT LAKE IS ONE OF THE NATURAL WONDERS OF THE WORLD.

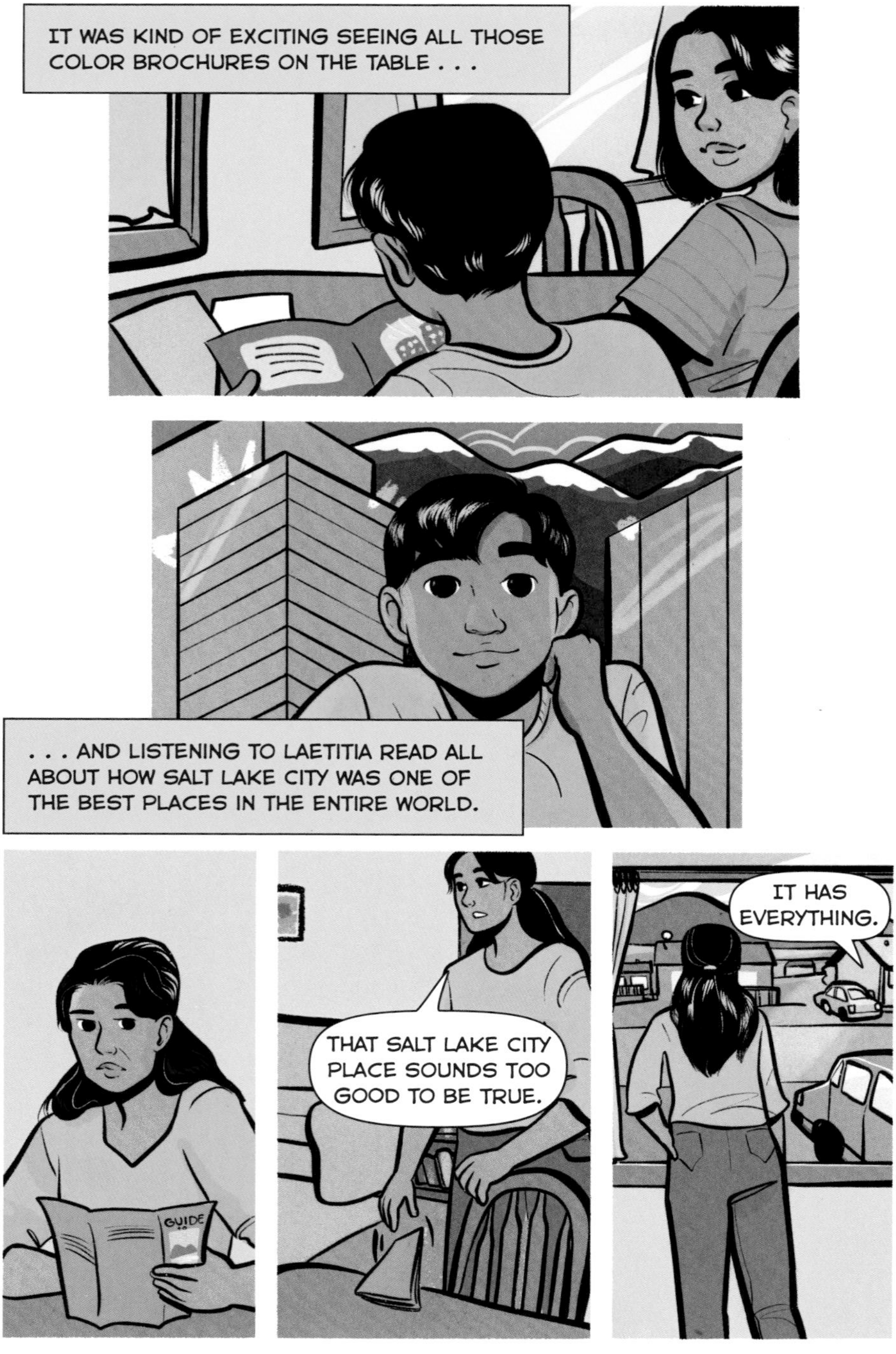
IT WAS KIND OF EXCITING SEEING ALL THOSE COLOR BROCHURES ON THE TABLE . . .
. . . AND LISTENING TO LAETITIA READ ALL ABOUT HOW SALT LAKE CITY WAS ONE OF THE BEST PLACES IN THE ENTIRE WORLD.
GUIDE
THAT SALT LAKE CITY PLACE SOUNDS TOO GOOD TO BE TRUE.
IT HAS EVERYTHING.

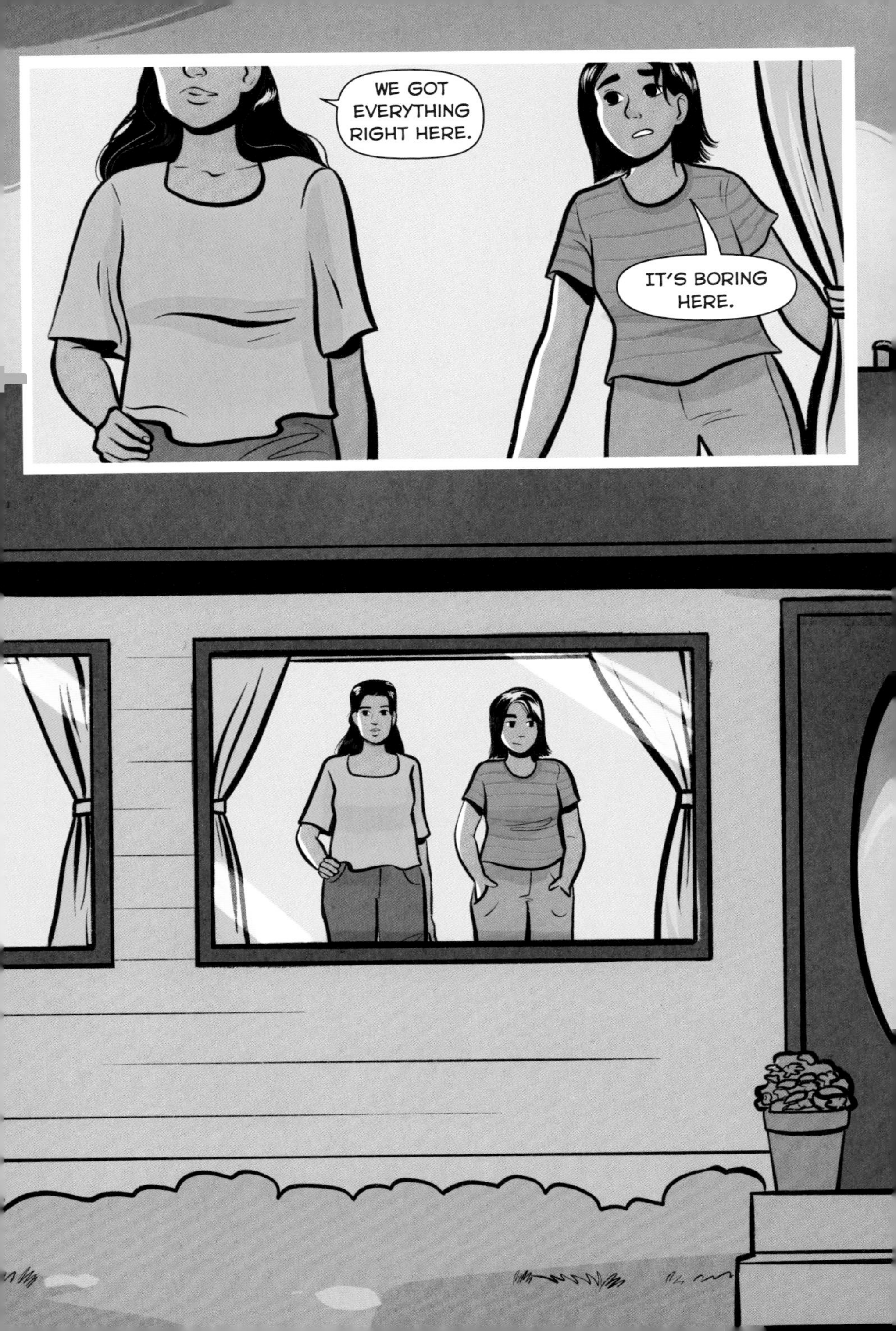
WE GOT EVERYTHING RIGHT HERE.
IT'S BORING HERE.

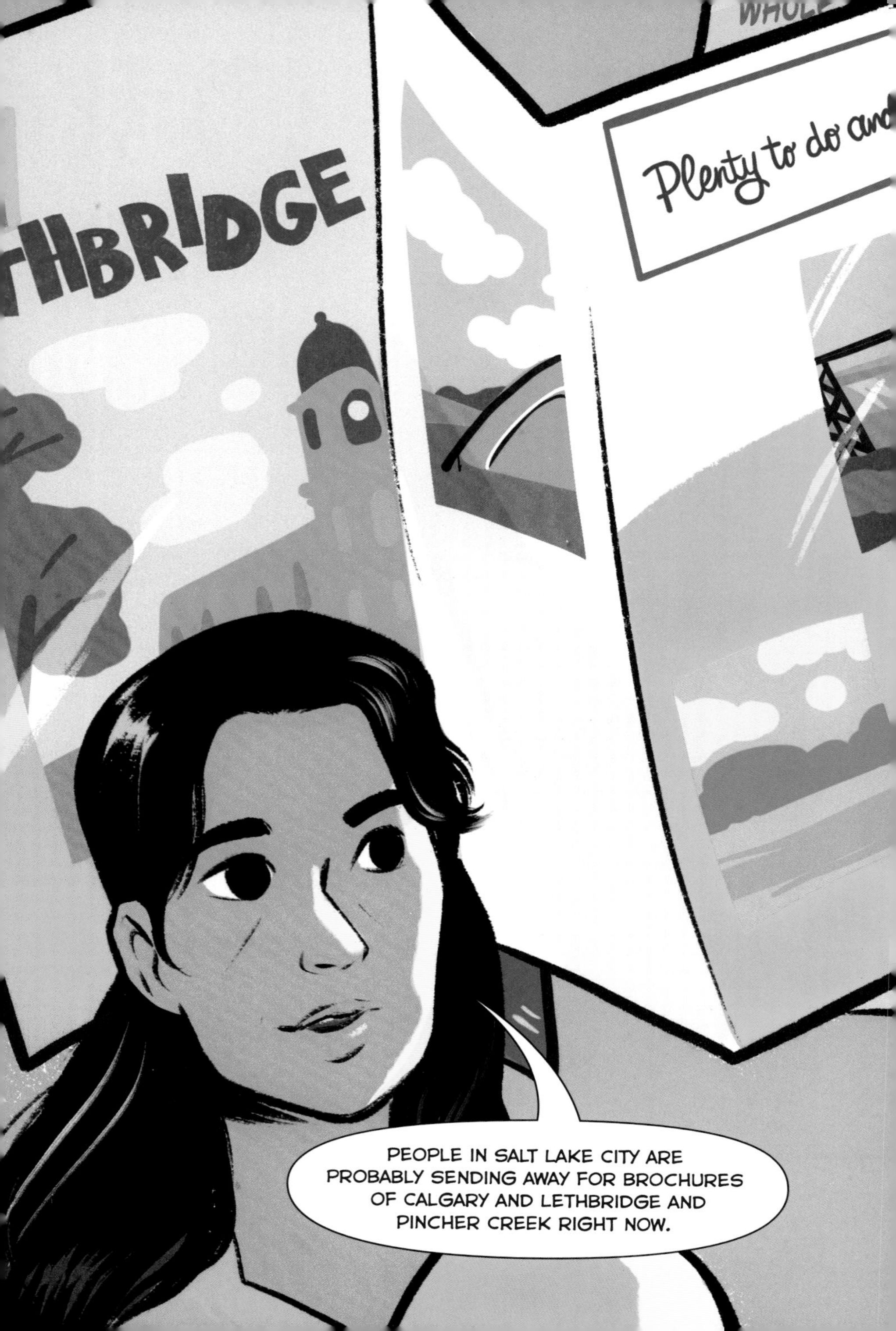
WHOL
THBRIDGE
Plenty to do and
PEOPLE IN SALT LAKE CITY ARE PROBABLY SENDING AWAY FOR BROCHURES OF CALGARY AND LETHBRIDGE AND PINCHER CREEK RIGHT NOW.

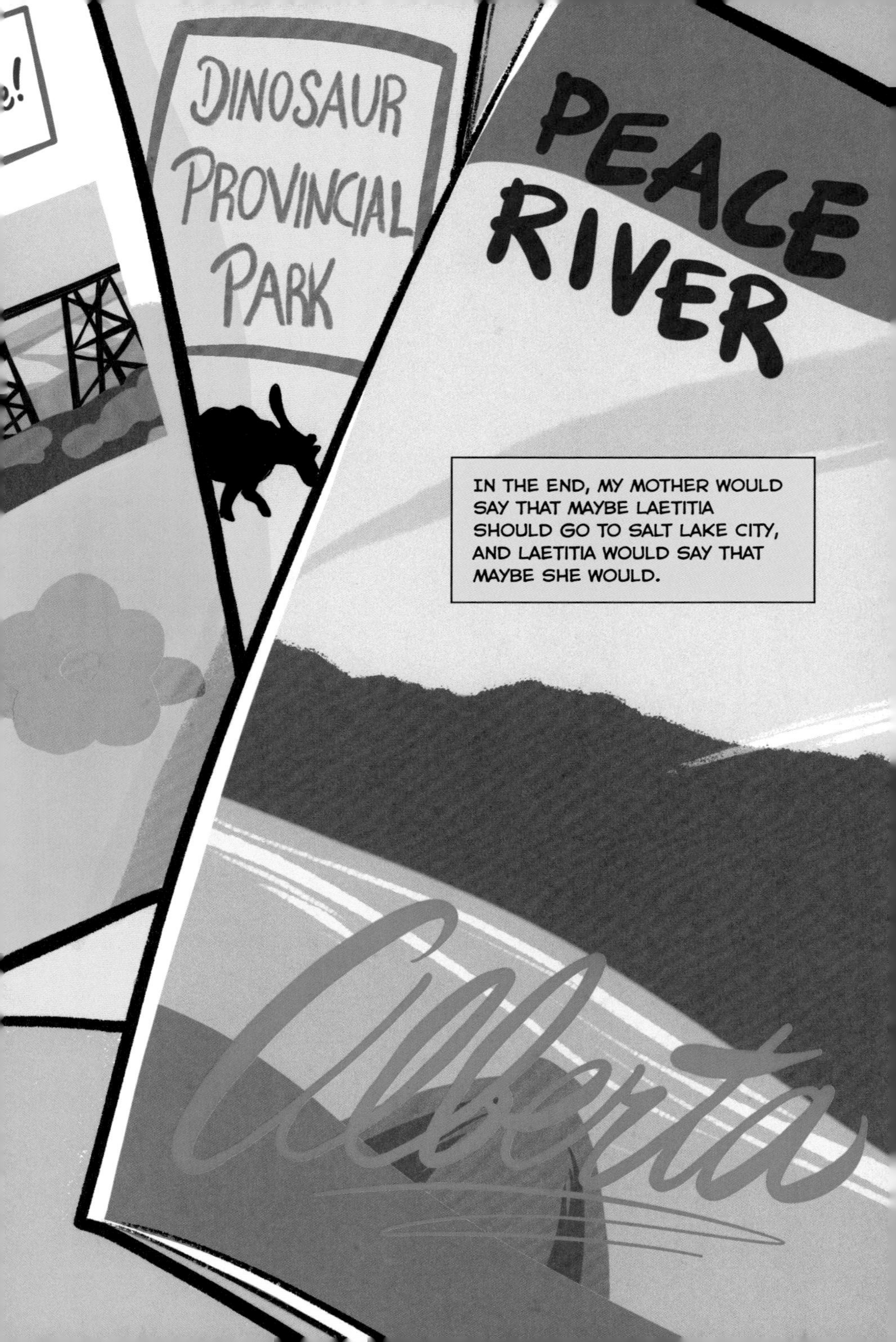
DINOSAUR PROVINCIAL PARK
PEACE RIVER
IN THE END, MY MOTHER WOULD SAY THAT MAYBE LAETITIA SHOULD GO TO SALT LAKE CITY, AND LAETITIA WOULD SAY THAT MAYBE SHE WOULD.
Alberta

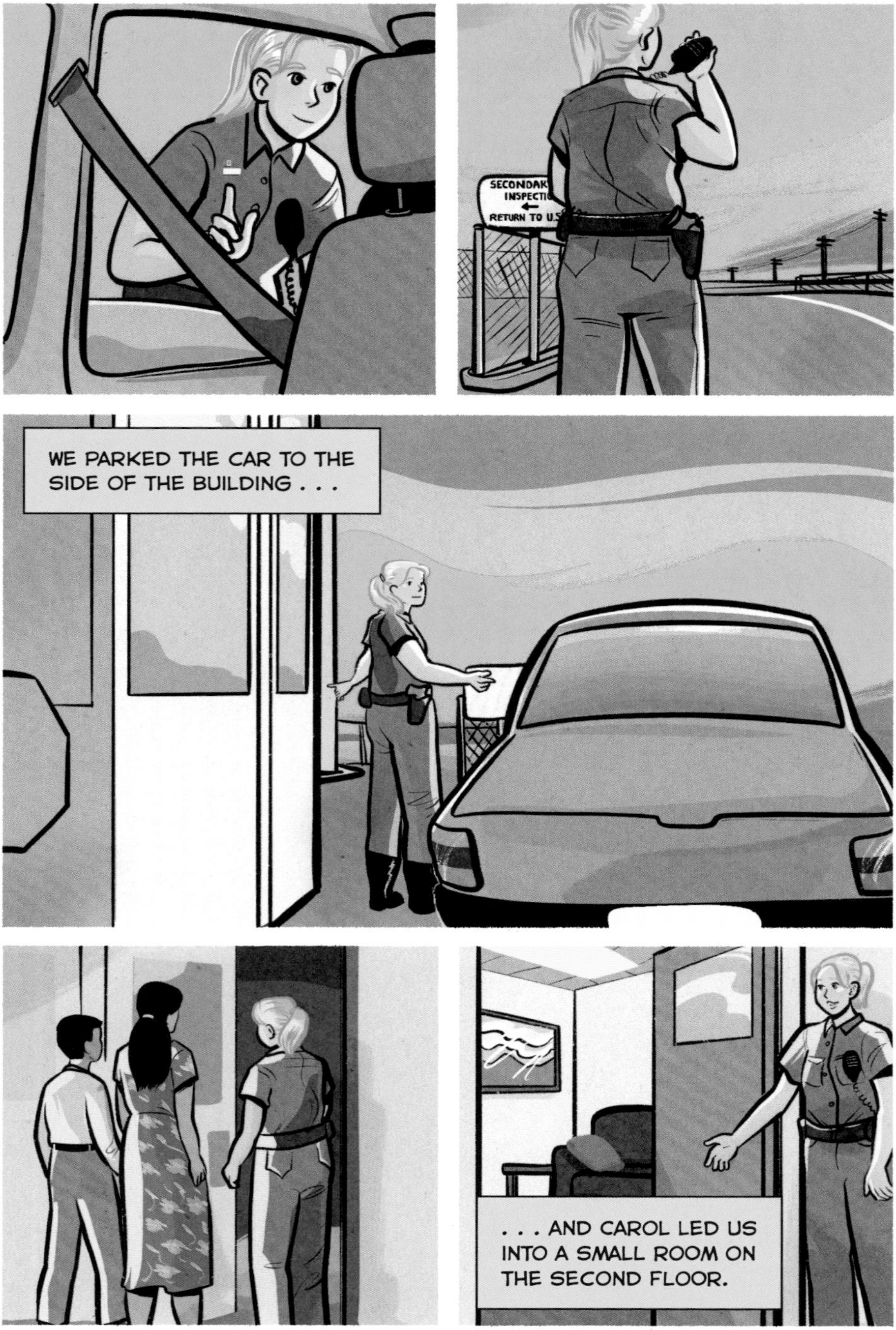
WE PARKED THE CAR TO THE SIDE OF THE BUILDING . . .
. . . AND CAROL LED US INTO A SMALL ROOM ON THE SECOND FLOOR.

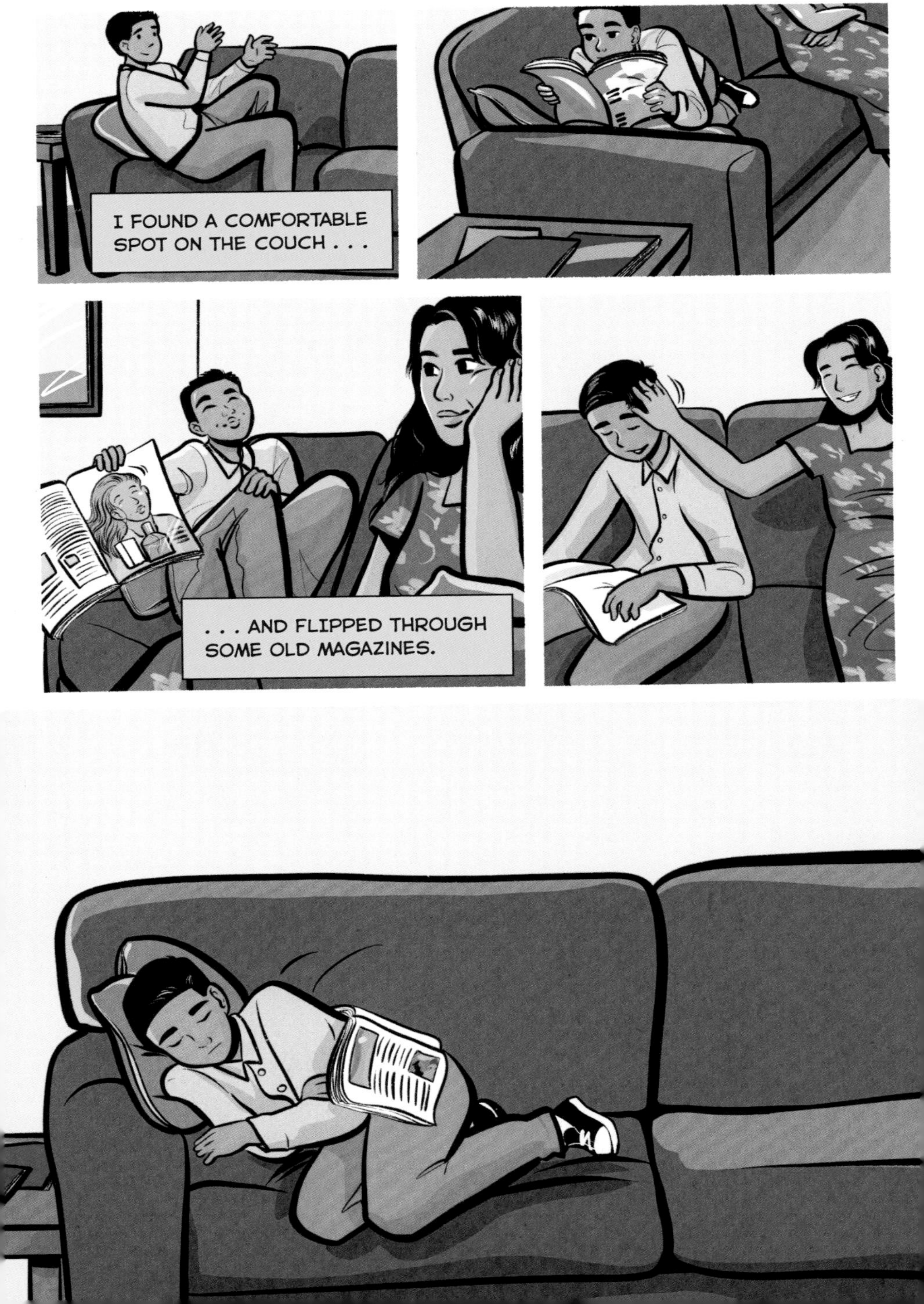
I FOUND A COMFORTABLE SPOT ON THE COUCH . . .
. . . AND FLIPPED THROUGH SOME OLD MAGAZINES.

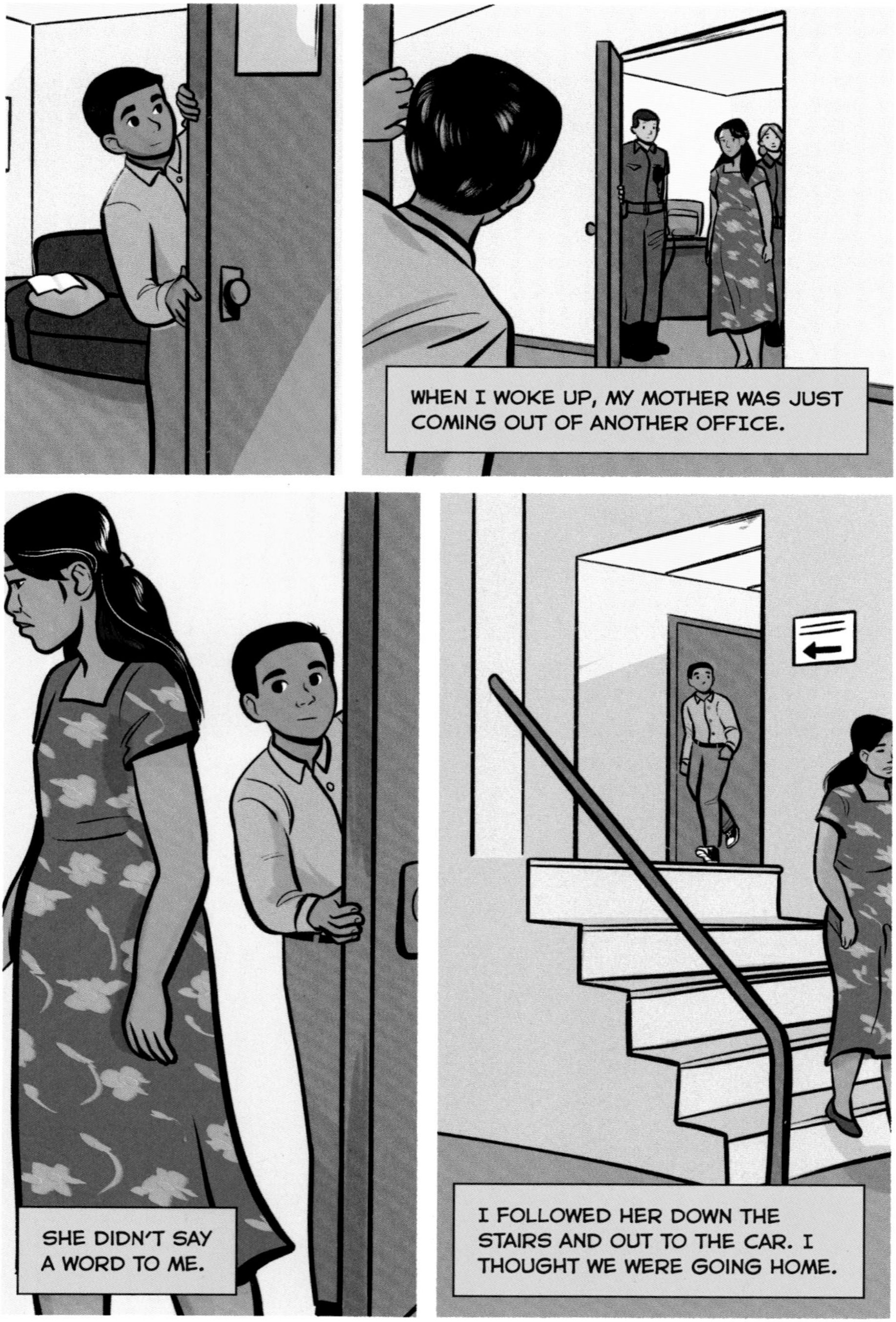
WHEN I WOKE UP, MY MOTHER WAS JUST COMING OUT OF ANOTHER OFFICE.
SHE DIDN'T SAY A WORD TO ME.
I FOLLOWED HER DOWN THE STAIRS AND OUT TO THE CAR. I THOUGHT WE WERE GOING HOME.

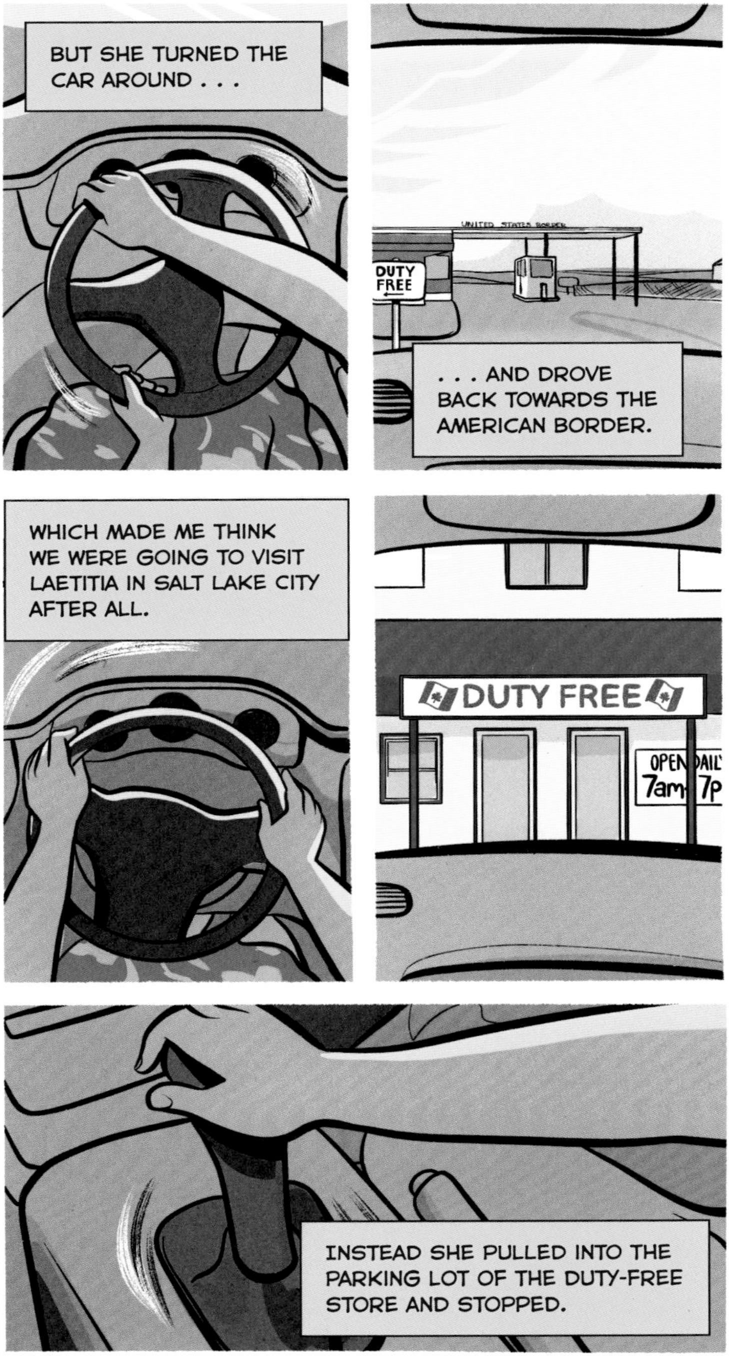
BUT SHE TURNED THE CAR AROUND . . .
UNITED STATES BORDER
DUTY FREE
. . . AND DROVE BACK TOWARDS THE AMERICAN BORDER.
WHICH MADE ME THINK WE WERE GOING TO VISIT LAETITIA IN SALT LAKE CITY AFTER ALL.
DUTY FREE
OPEN DAIL
7am 7p
INSTEAD SHE PULLED INTO THE PARKING LOT OF THE DUTY-FREE STORE AND STOPPED.

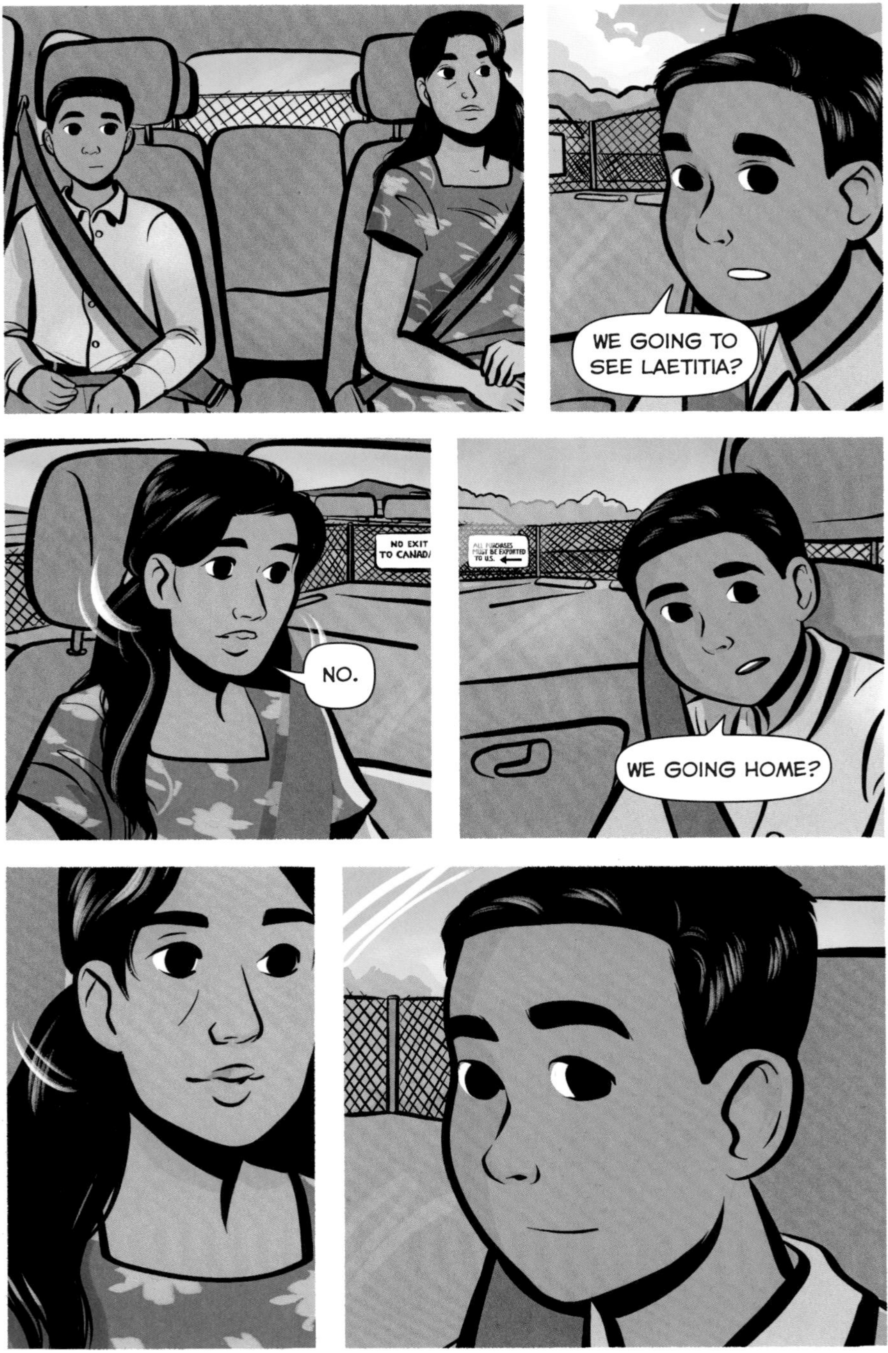
WE GOING TO SEE LAETITIA?
NO EXIT TO CANAD
NO.
ALL PURCHASES MUST BE EXPORTED TO U.S.
WE GOING HOME?

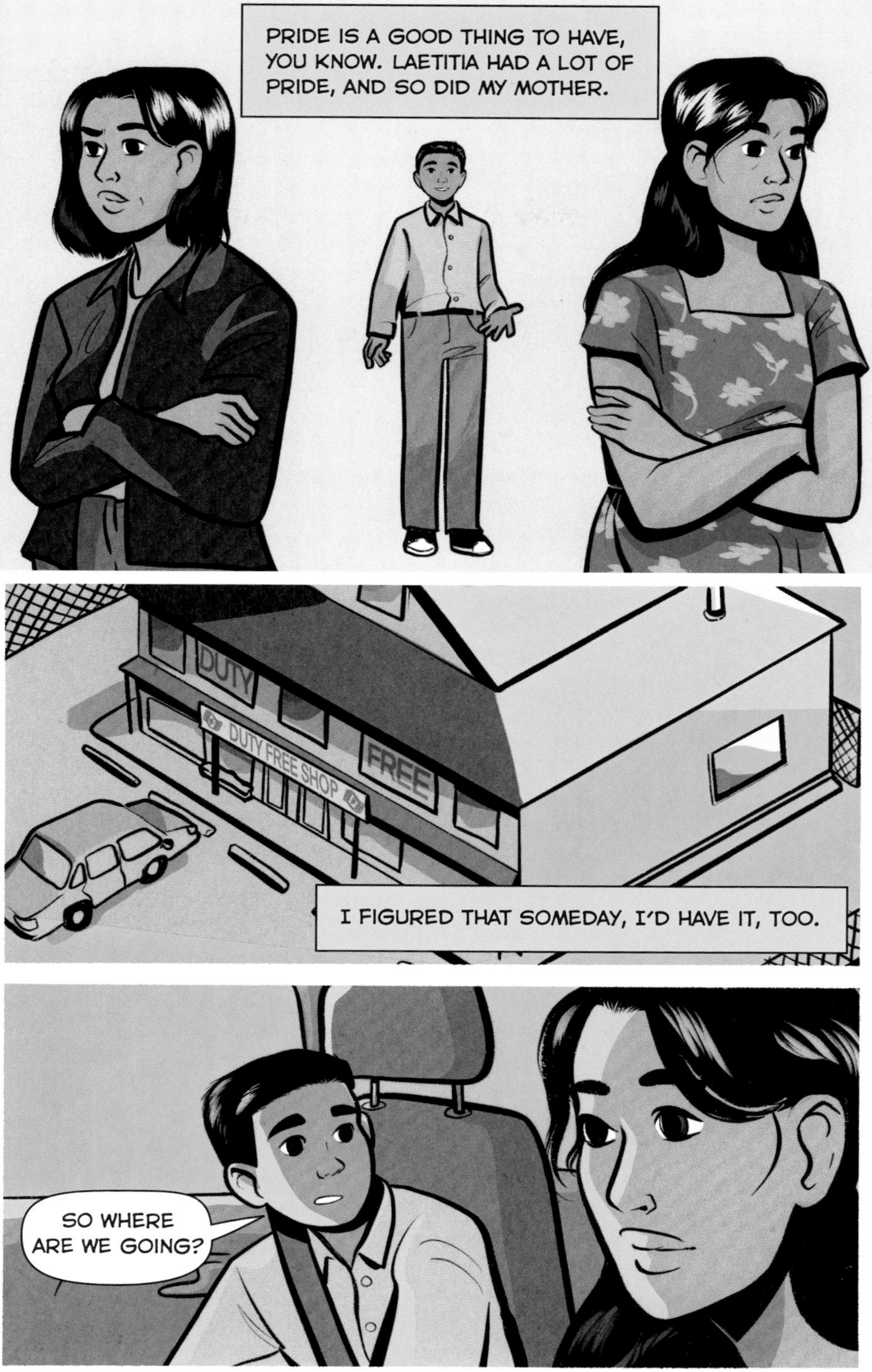
PRIDE IS A GOOD THING TO HAVE, YOU KNOW. LAETITIA HAD A LOT OF PRIDE, AND SO DID MY MOTHER.
DUTY
DUTY FREE SHOP
FREE
I FIGURED THAT SOMEDAY, I'D HAVE IT, TOO.
SO WHERE ARE WE GOING?

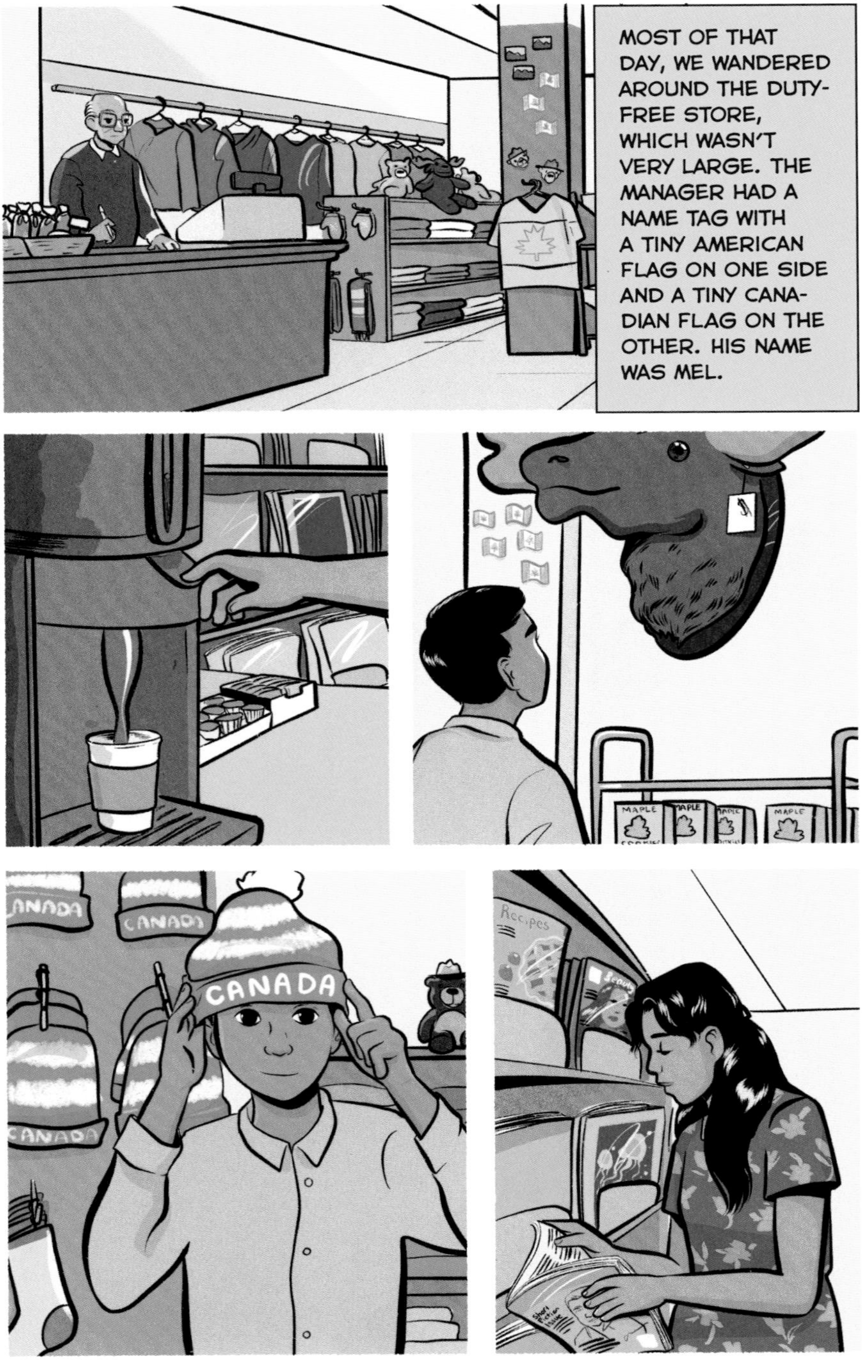
MOST OF THAT DAY, WE WANDERED AROUND THE DUTY-FREE STORE, WHICH WASN'T VERY LARGE. THE MANAGER HAD A NAME TAG WITH A TINY AMERICAN FLAG ON ONE SIDE AND A TINY CANADIAN FLAG ON THE OTHER. HIS NAME WAS MEL.
MAPLE
MAPLE
MAPLE
MAPLE
CANADA
CANADA
Recipes

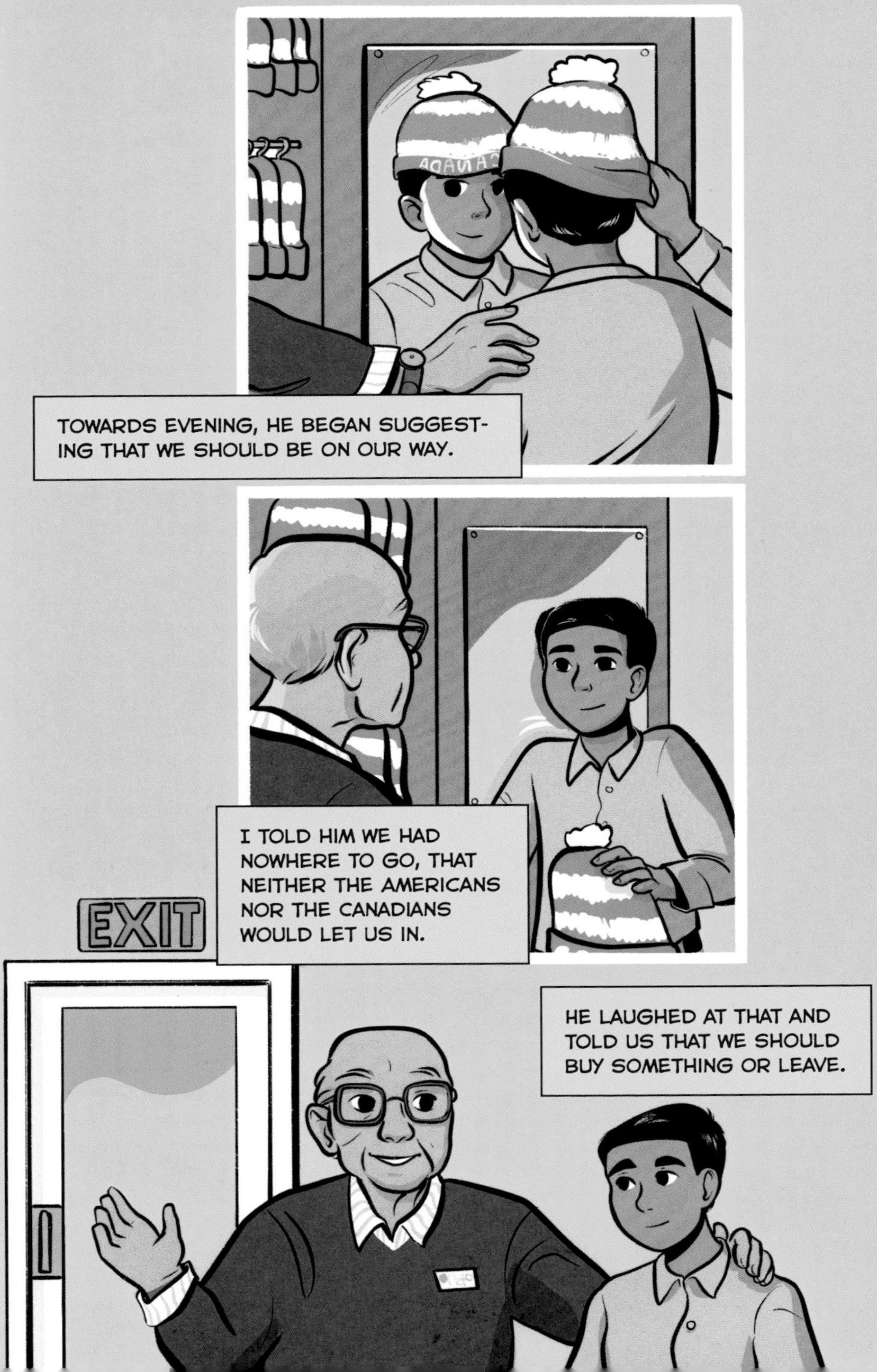
CANADA
TOWARDS EVENING, HE BEGAN SUGGESTING THAT WE SHOULD BE ON OUR WAY.
I TOLD HIM WE HAD NOWHERE TO GO, THAT NEITHER THE AMERICANS NOR THE CANADIANS WOULD LET US IN.
EXIT
HE LAUGHED AT THAT AND TOLD US THAT WE SHOULD BUY SOMETHING OR LEAVE.

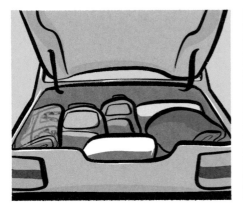

THE CAR WAS NOT VERY COMFORTABLE, BUT WE DID HAVE ALL THAT FOOD.

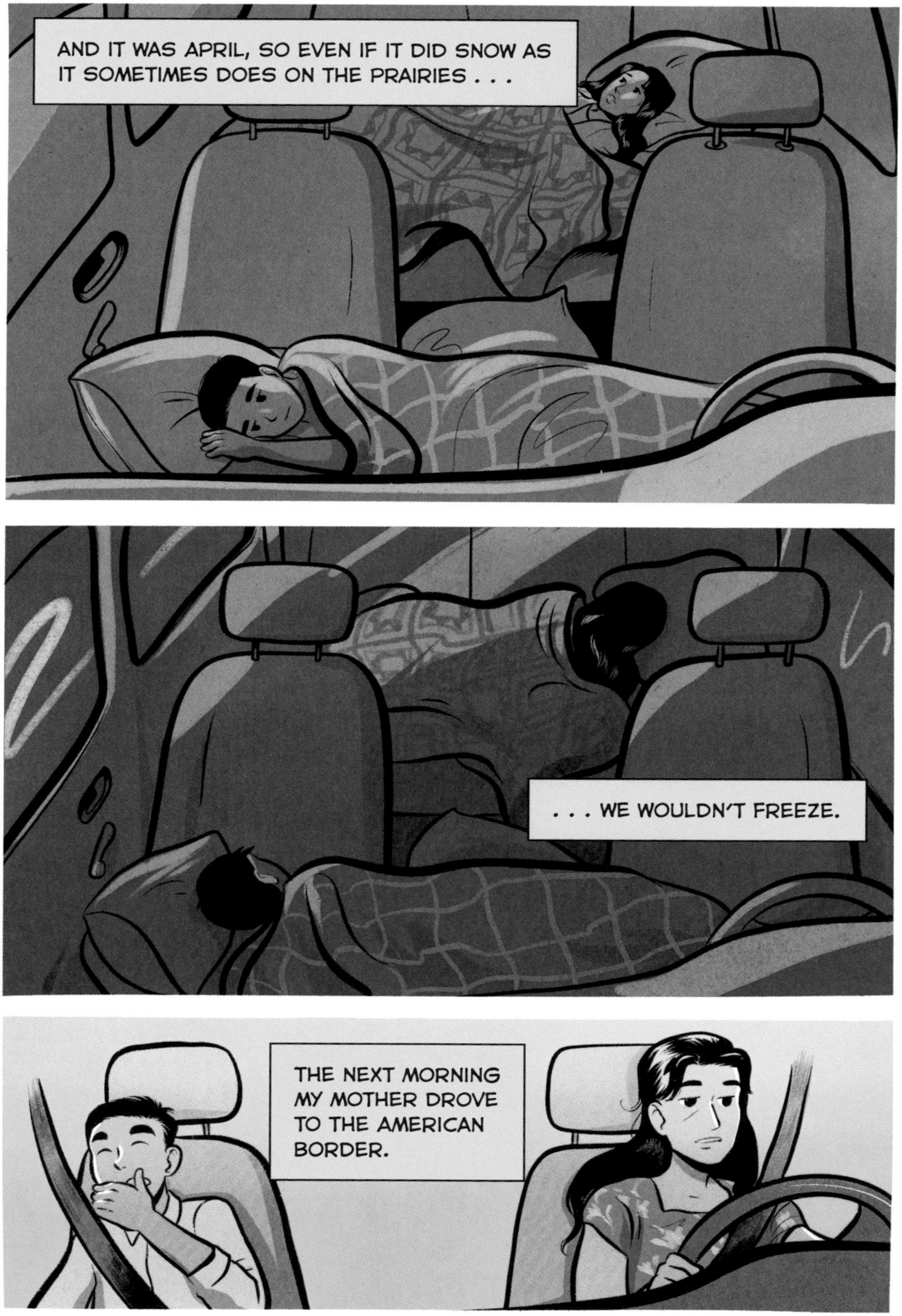
AND IT WAS APRIL, SO EVEN IF IT DID SNOW AS IT SOMETIMES DOES ON THE PRAIRIES . . .
. . . WE WOULDN'T FREEZE.
THE NEXT MORNING MY MOTHER DROVE TO THE AMERICAN BORDER.

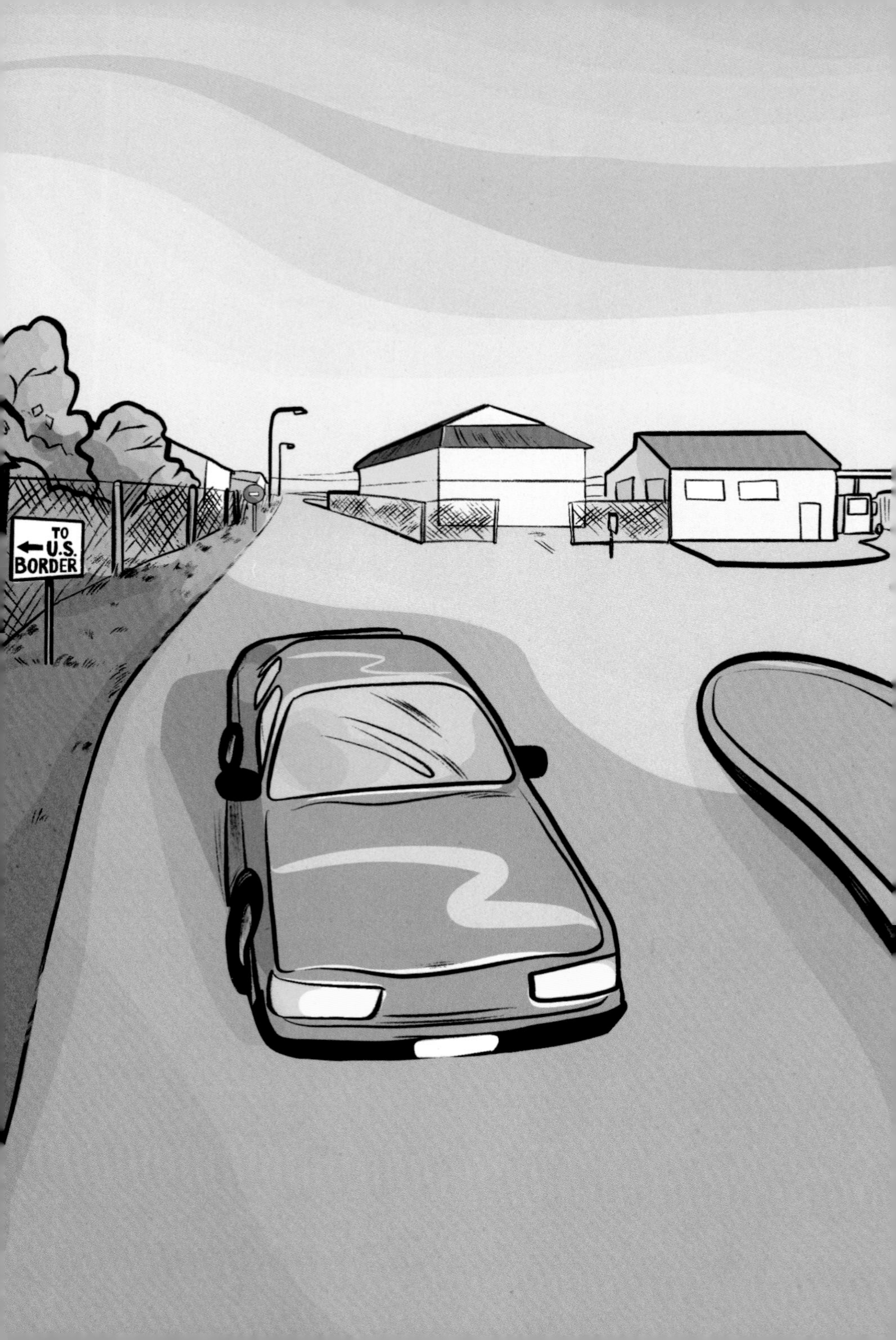
TO
U.S.
BORDER

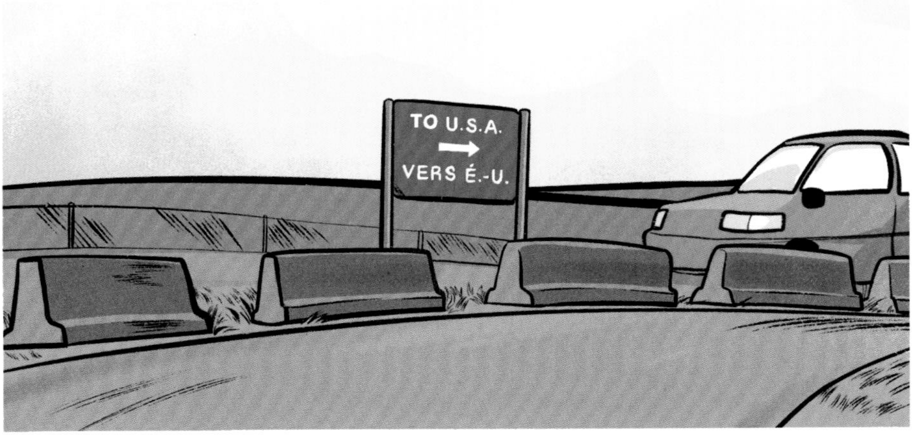
TO U.S.A.
VERS É.-U.

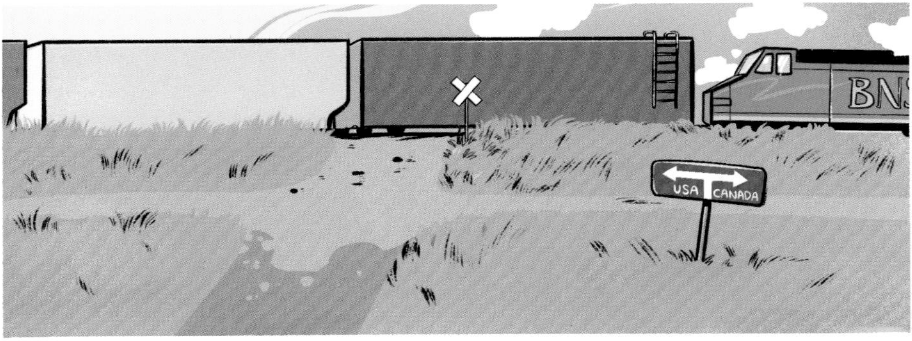
USA
CANADA

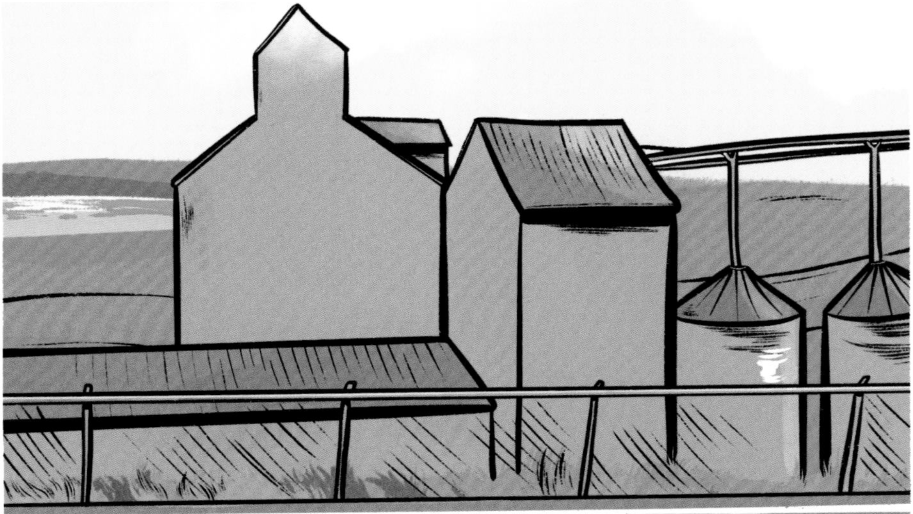

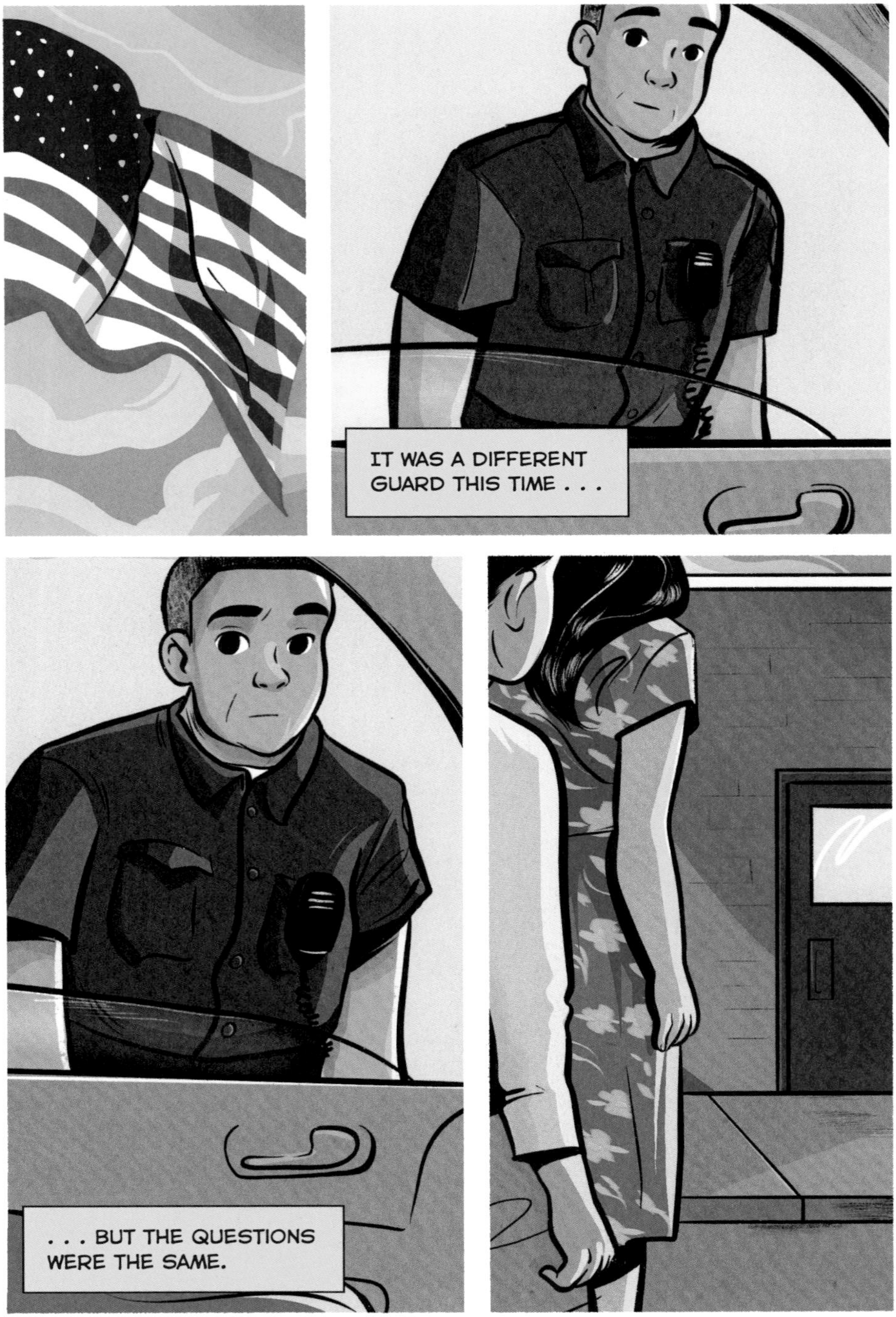
IT WAS A DIFFERENT GUARD THIS TIME . . .
. . . BUT THE QUESTIONS WERE THE SAME.

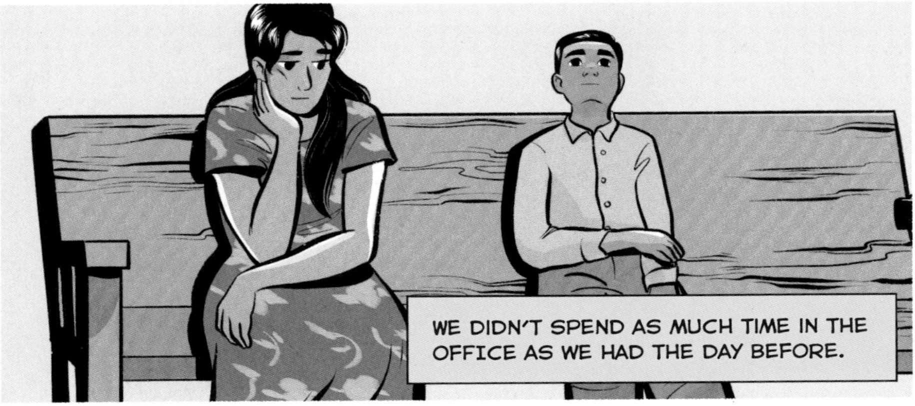
WE DIDN'T SPEND AS MUCH TIME IN THE OFFICE AS WE HAD THE DAY BEFORE.

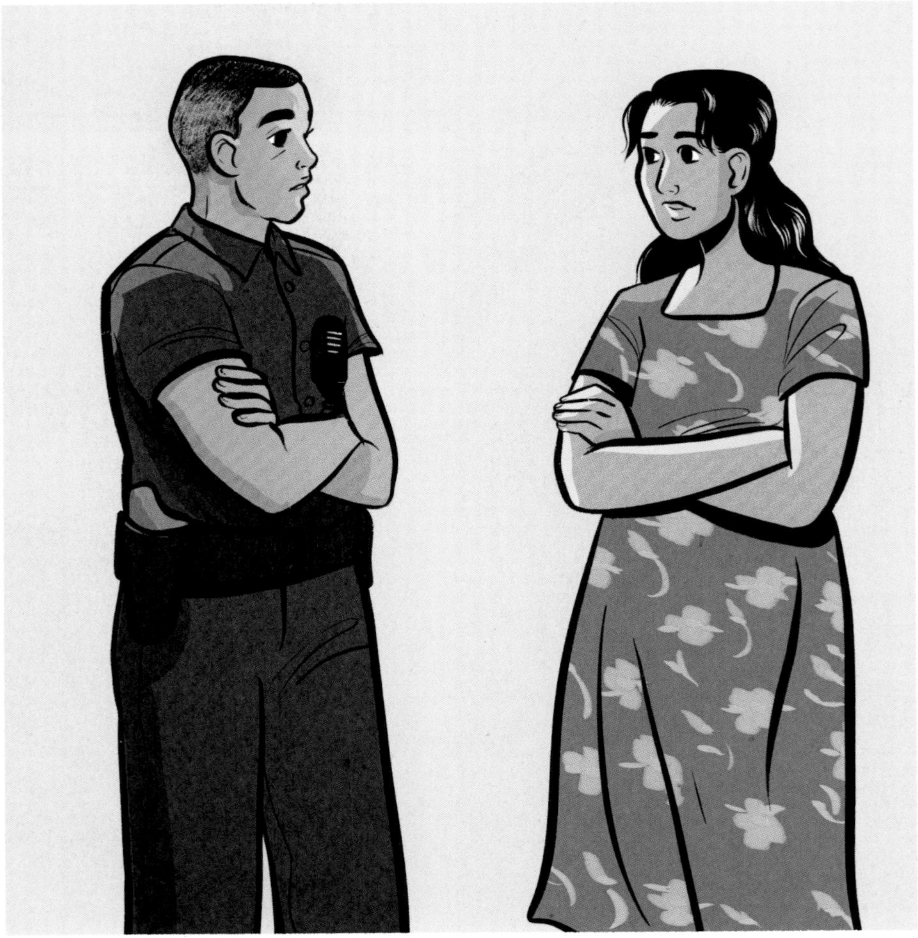

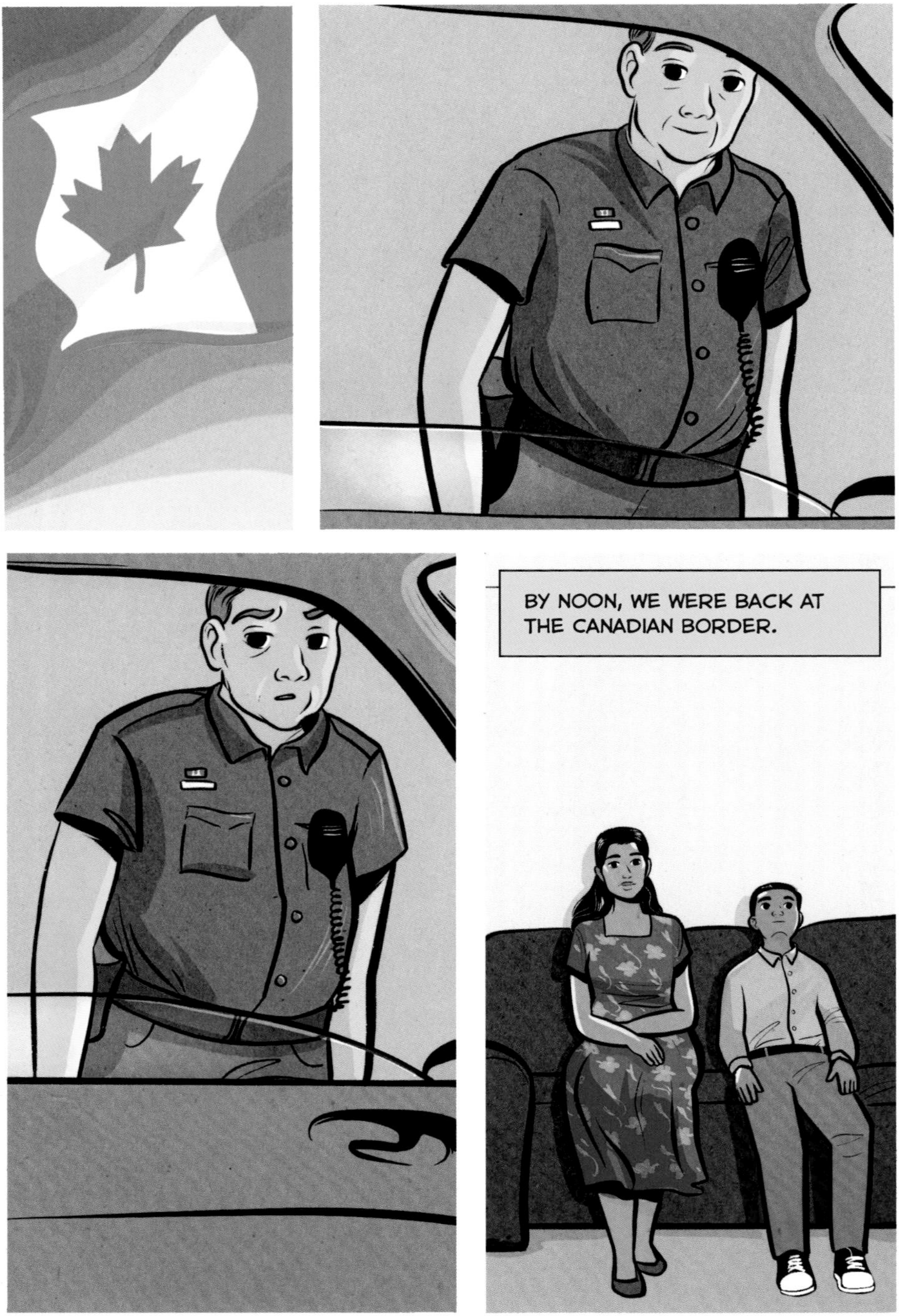
BY NOON, WE WERE BACK AT THE CANADIAN BORDER.

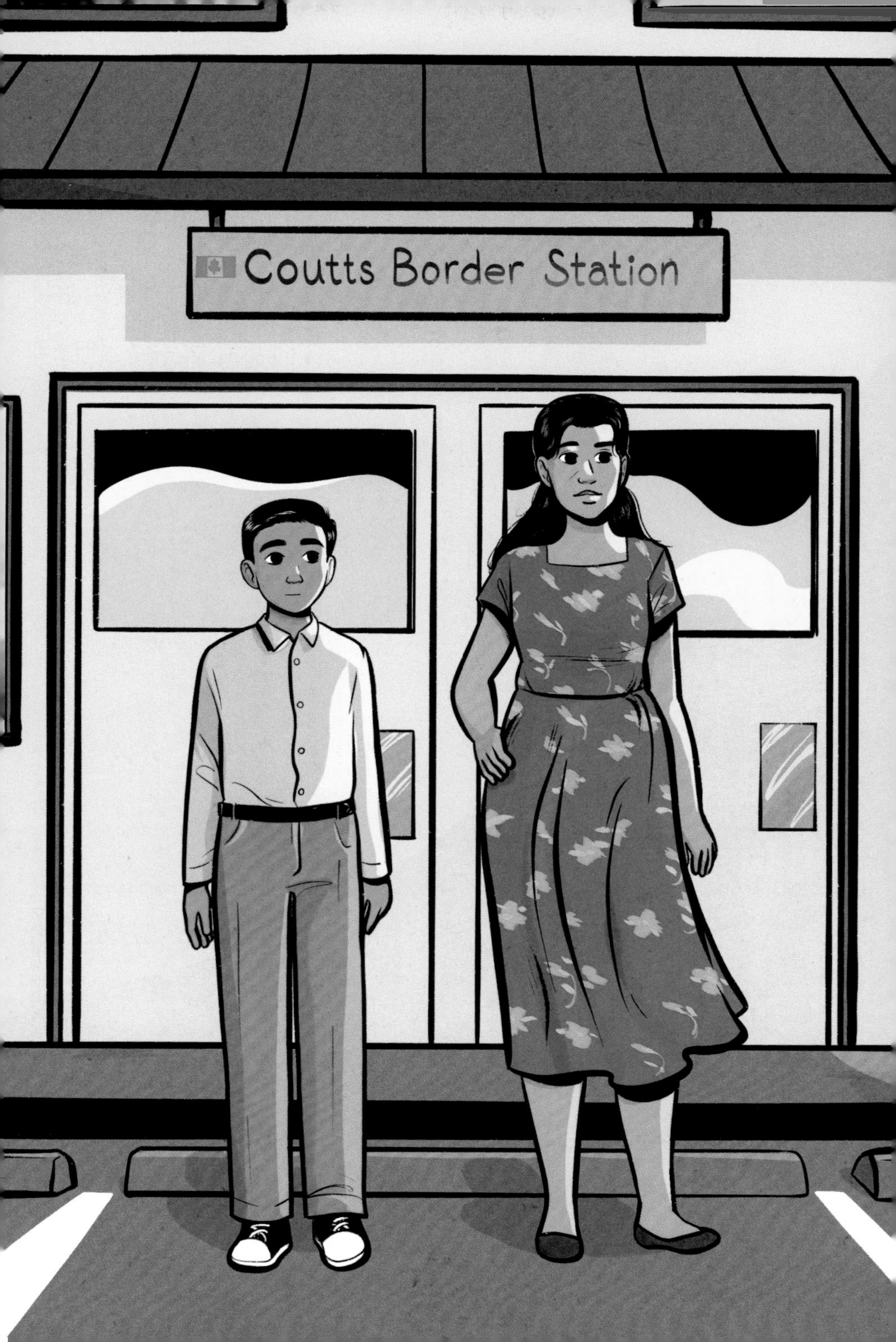
Coutts Border Station

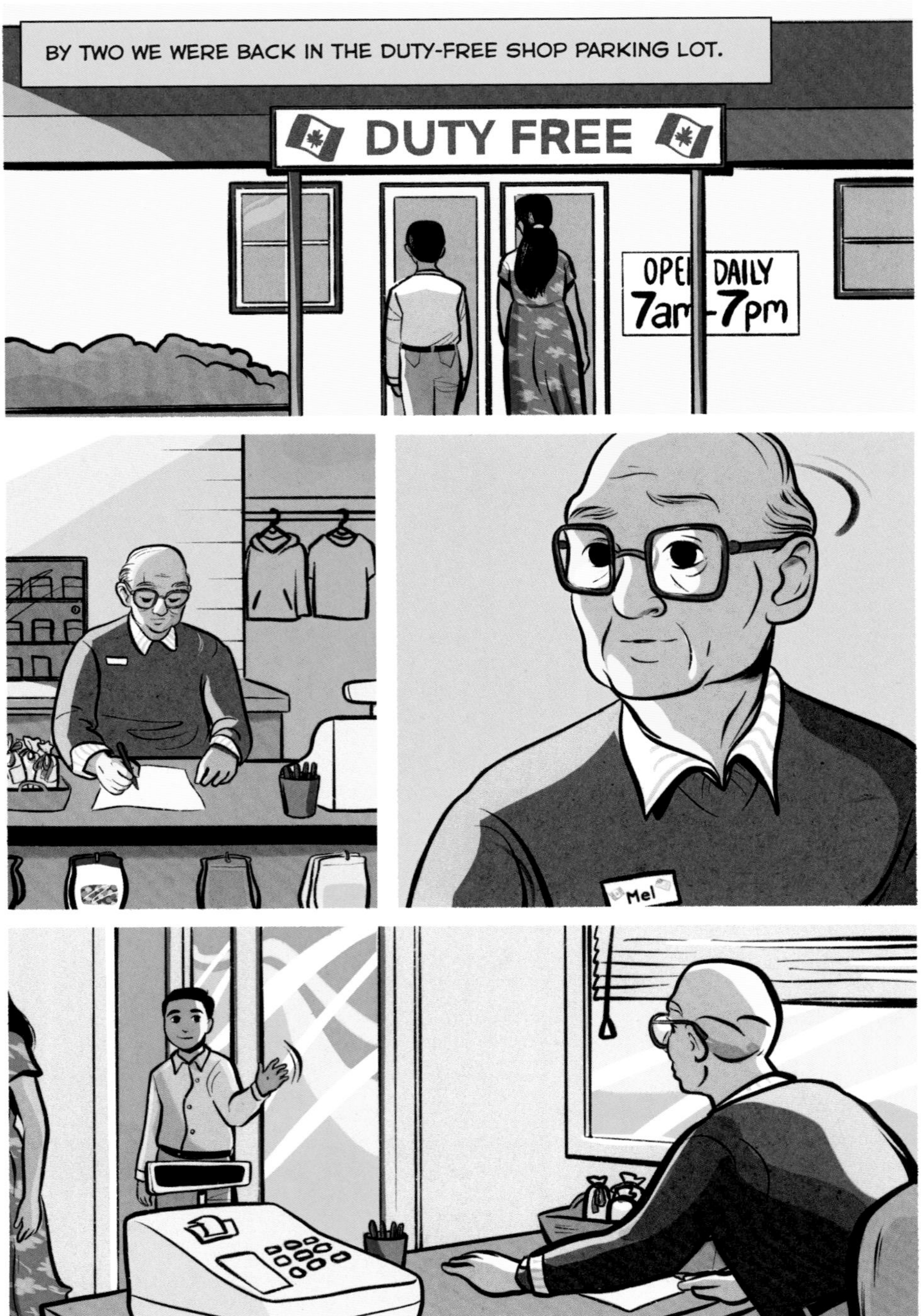
BY TWO WE WERE BACK IN THE DUTY-FREE SHOP PARKING LOT.
DUTY FREE
OPE DAILY 7am-7pm
Mel

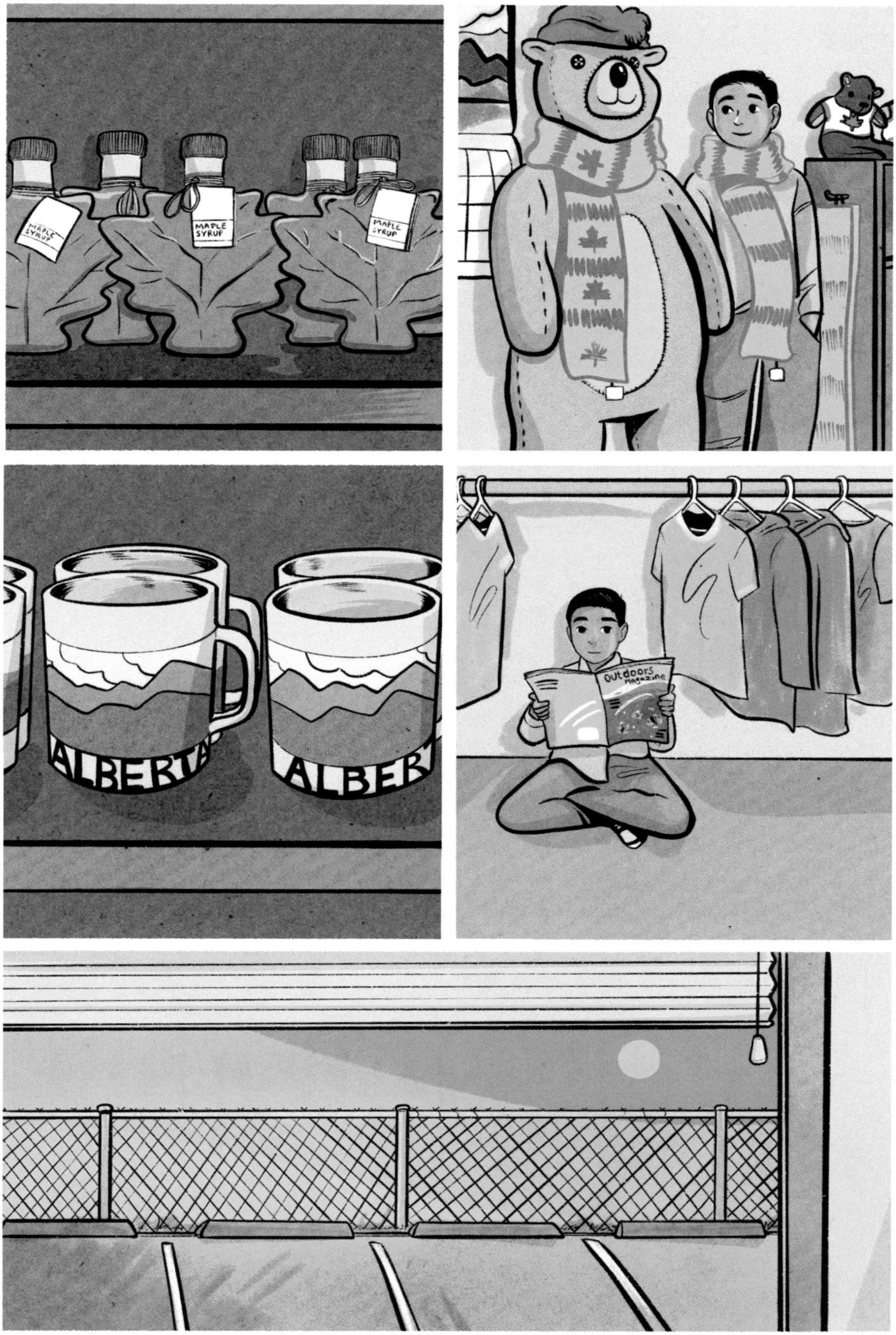
MAPLE SYRUP
MAPLE SYRUP
MAPLE SYRUP
ALBERTA
ALBER
Outdoors Magazine

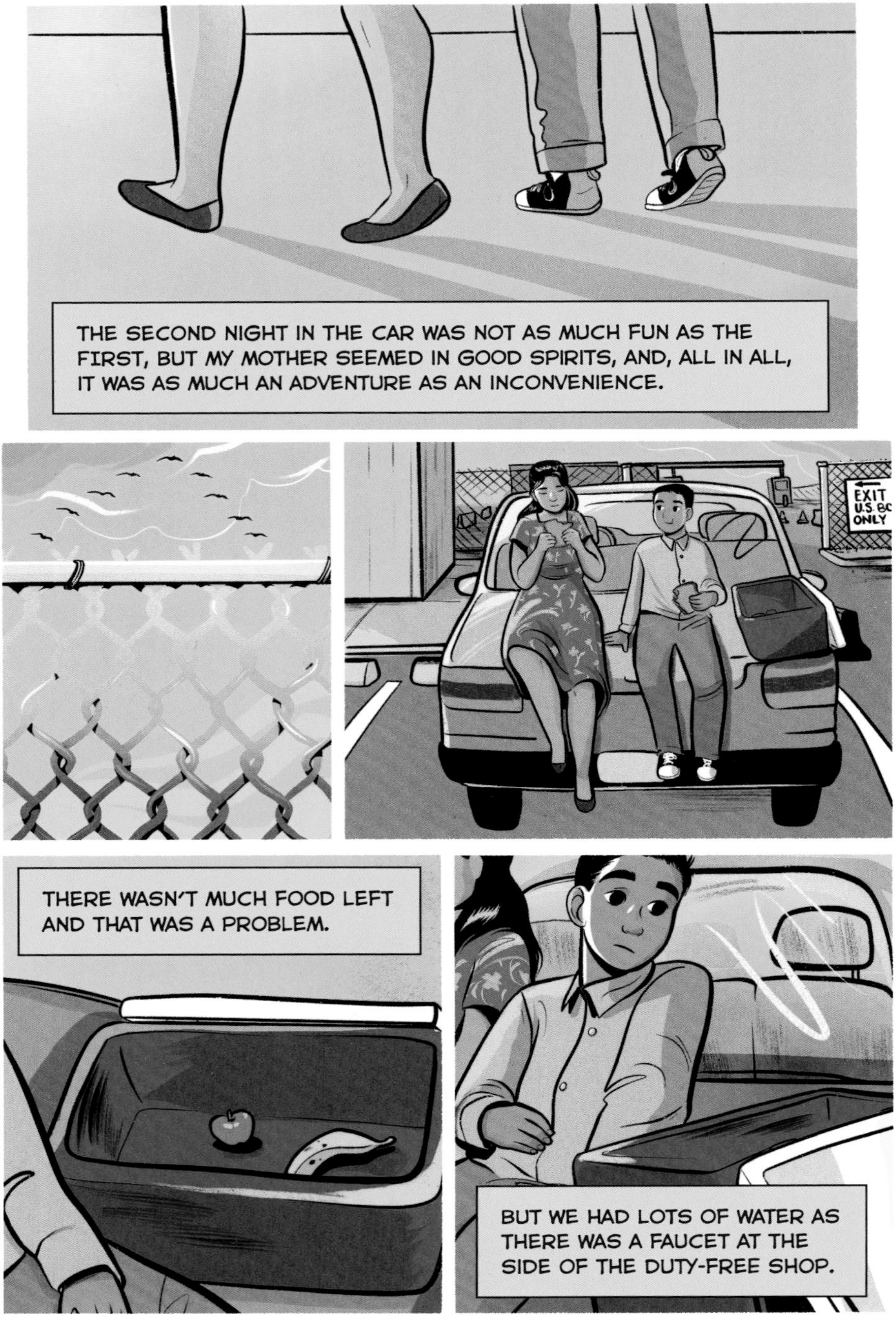
THE SECOND NIGHT IN THE CAR WAS NOT AS MUCH FUN AS THE FIRST, BUT MY MOTHER SEEMED IN GOOD SPIRITS, AND, ALL IN ALL, IT WAS AS MUCH AN ADVENTURE AS AN INCONVENIENCE.
EXIT
ONLY
THERE WASN'T MUCH FOOD LEFT AND THAT WAS A PROBLEM.
BUT WE HAD LOTS OF WATER AS THERE WAS A FAUCET AT THE SIDE OF THE DUTY-FREE SHOP.

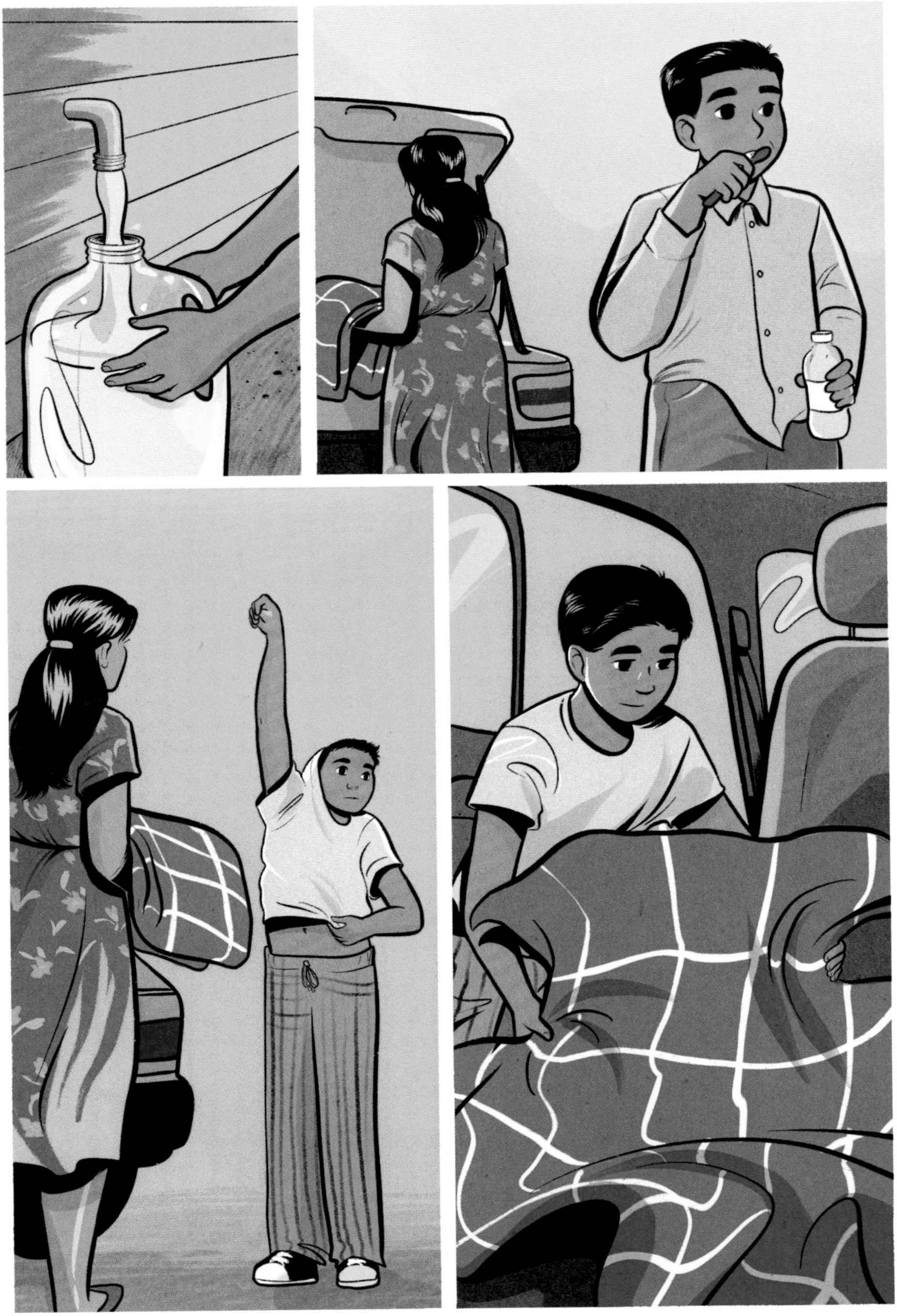

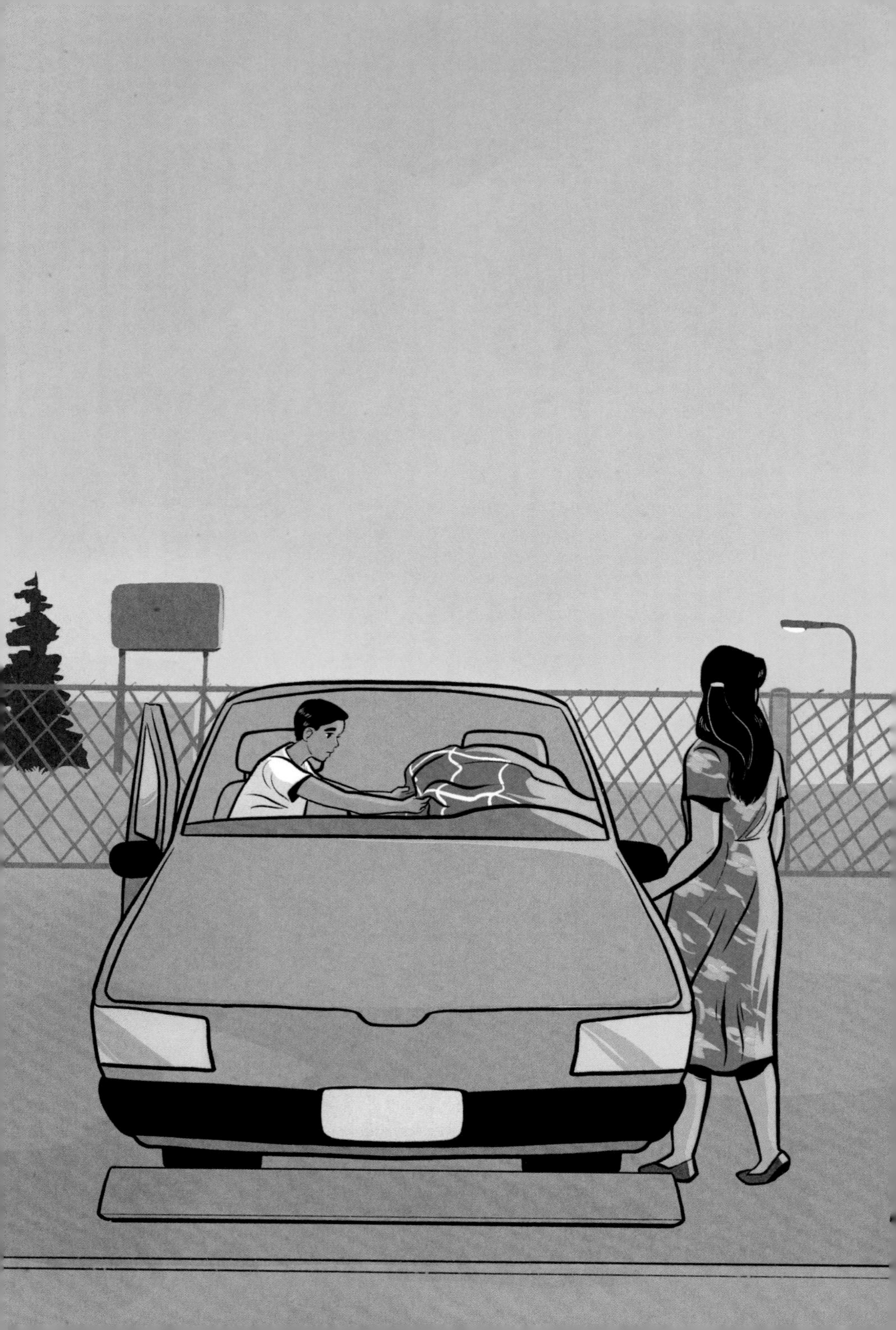

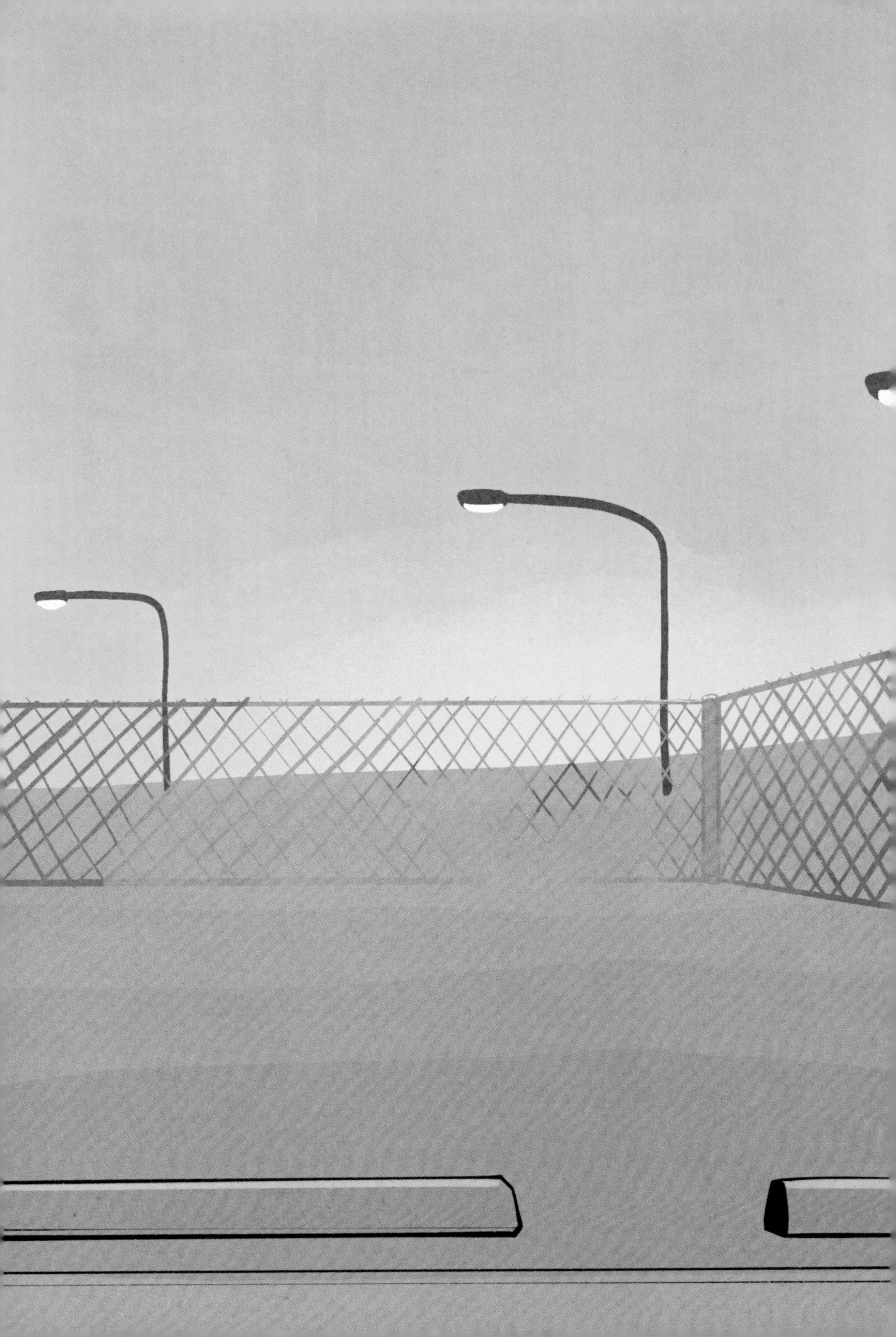

ONE SUNDAY, LAETITIA AND I WERE WATCHING TELEVISION. MOM WAS OVER AT MRS. MANYFINGERS'S.

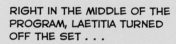

RIGHT IN THE MIDDLE OF THE PROGRAM, LAETITIA TURNED OFF THE SET . . .

. . . AND SAID SHE WAS GOING TO SALT LAKE CITY, THAT LIFE AROUND HERE WAS TOO BORING.

I HAD WANTED TO SEE THE REST OF THE PROGRAM.

AND REALLY DIDN'T CARE IF LAETITIA WENT TO SALT LAKE CITY OR NOT.

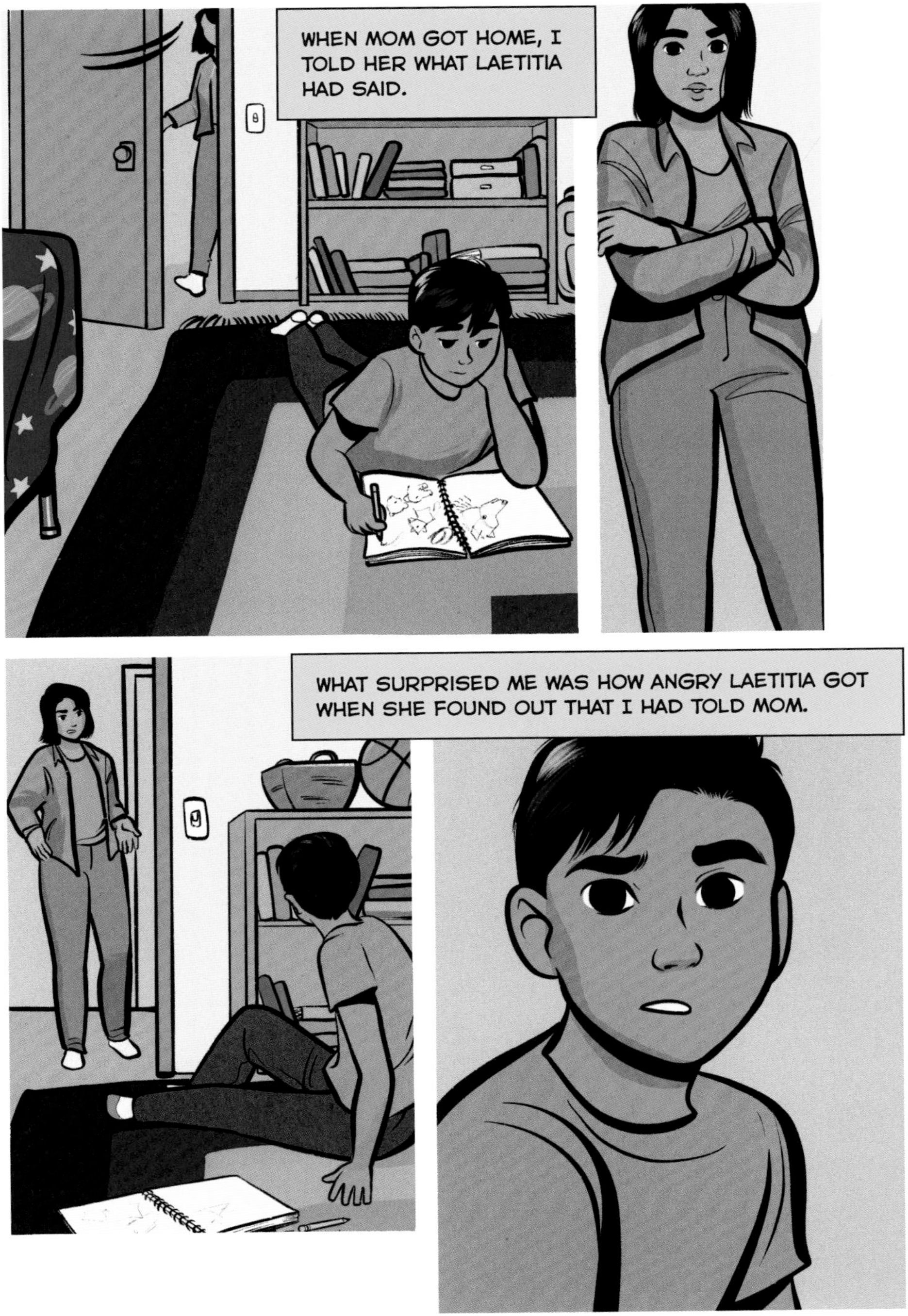
WHEN MOM GOT HOME, I TOLD HER WHAT LAETITIA HAD SAID.
WHAT SURPRISED ME WAS HOW ANGRY LAETITIA GOT WHEN SHE FOUND OUT THAT I HAD TOLD MOM.

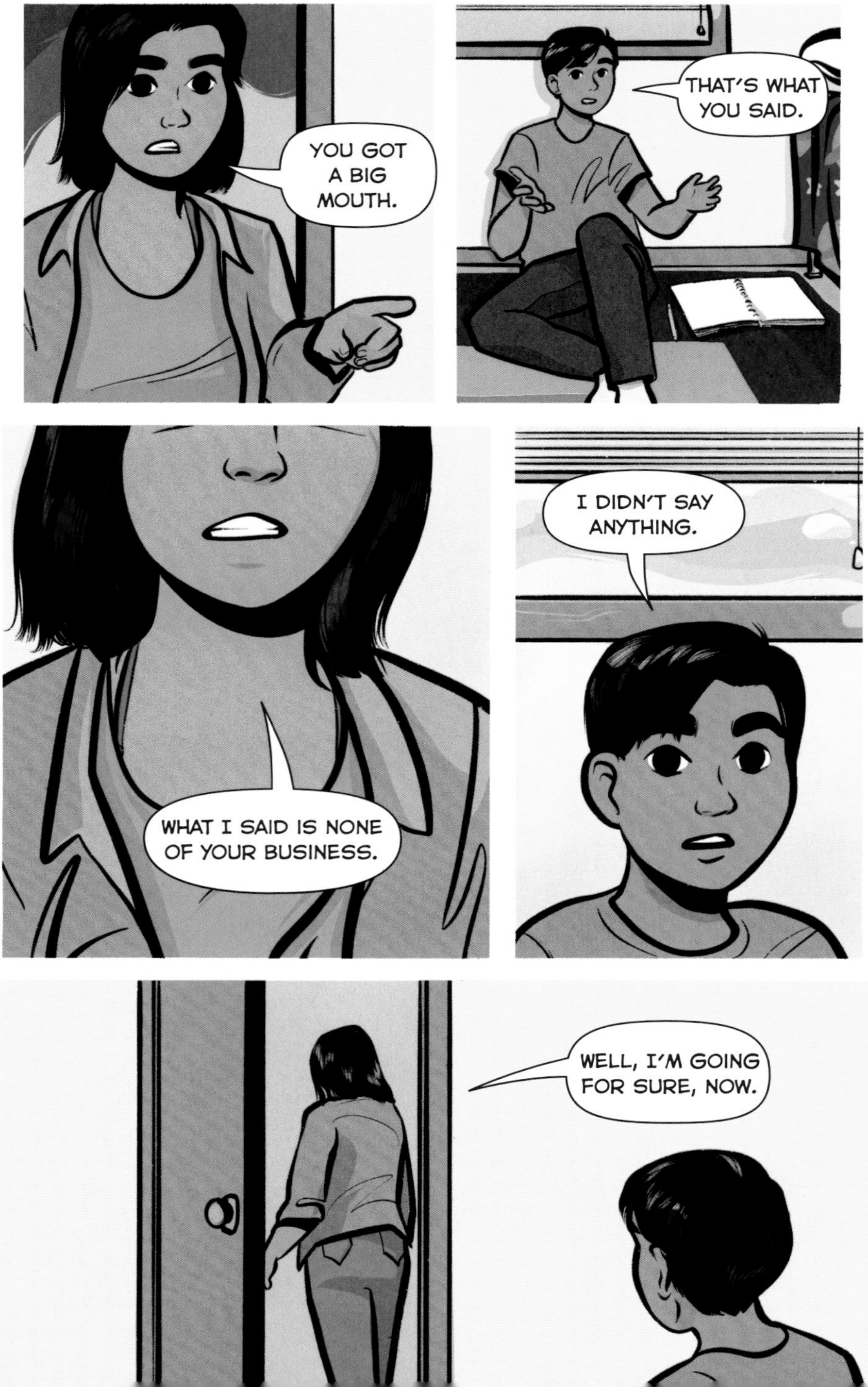
YOU GOT A BIG MOUTH.
THAT'S WHAT YOU SAID.
WHAT I SAID IS NONE OF YOUR BUSINESS.
I DIDN'T SAY ANYTHING.
WELL, I'M GOING FOR SURE, NOW.

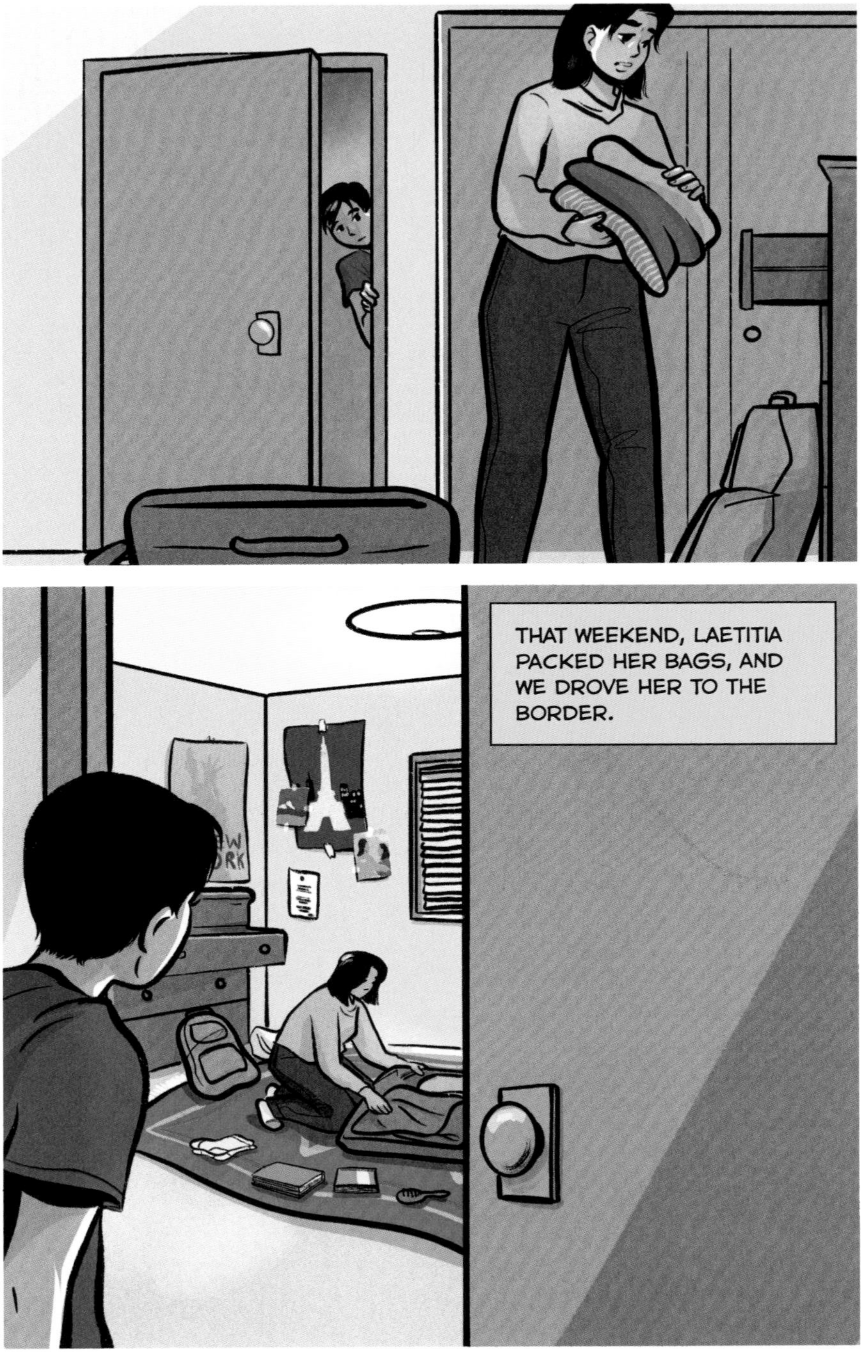
THAT WEEKEND, LAETITIA PACKED HER BAGS, AND WE DROVE HER TO THE BORDER.

MEL TURNED OUT TO BE FRIENDLY.

WHEN HE CLOSED UP FOR THE NIGHT AND FOUND US STILL PARKED IN THE LOT . . .

. . . HE CAME OVER AND ASKED US IF OUR CAR WAS BROKEN DOWN OR SOMETHING.

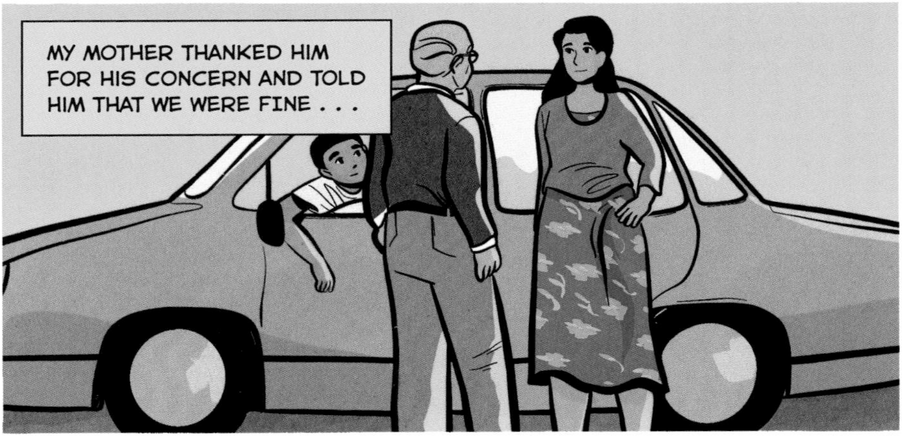
MY MOTHER THANKED HIM FOR HIS CONCERN AND TOLD HIM THAT WE WERE FINE . . .

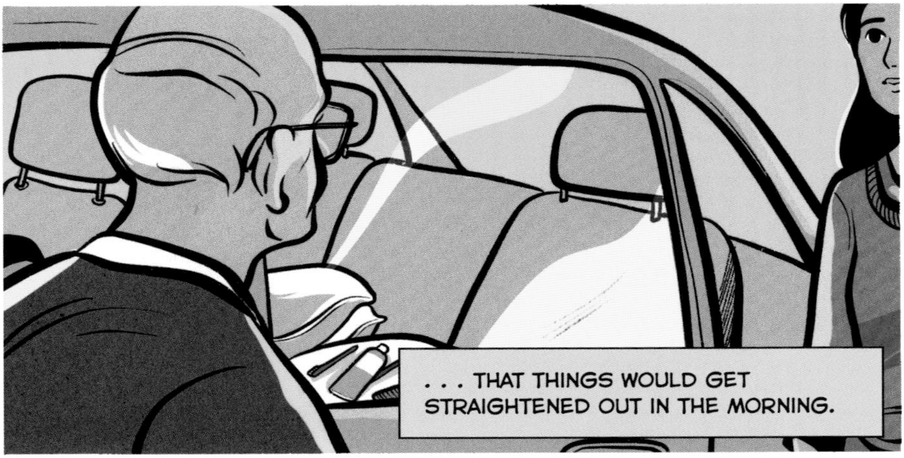
. . . THAT THINGS WOULD GET STRAIGHTENED OUT IN THE MORNING.

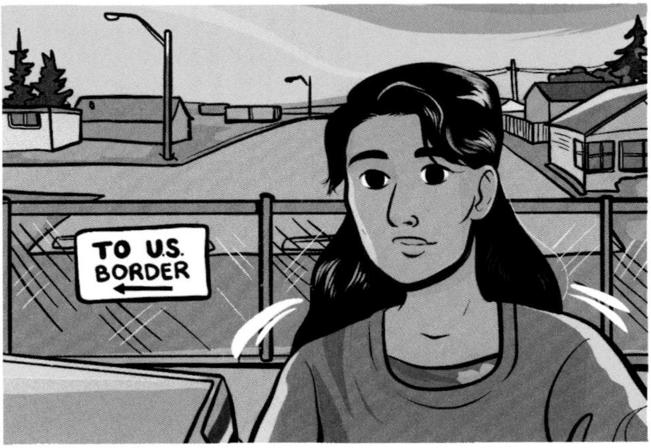
TO U.S. BORDER

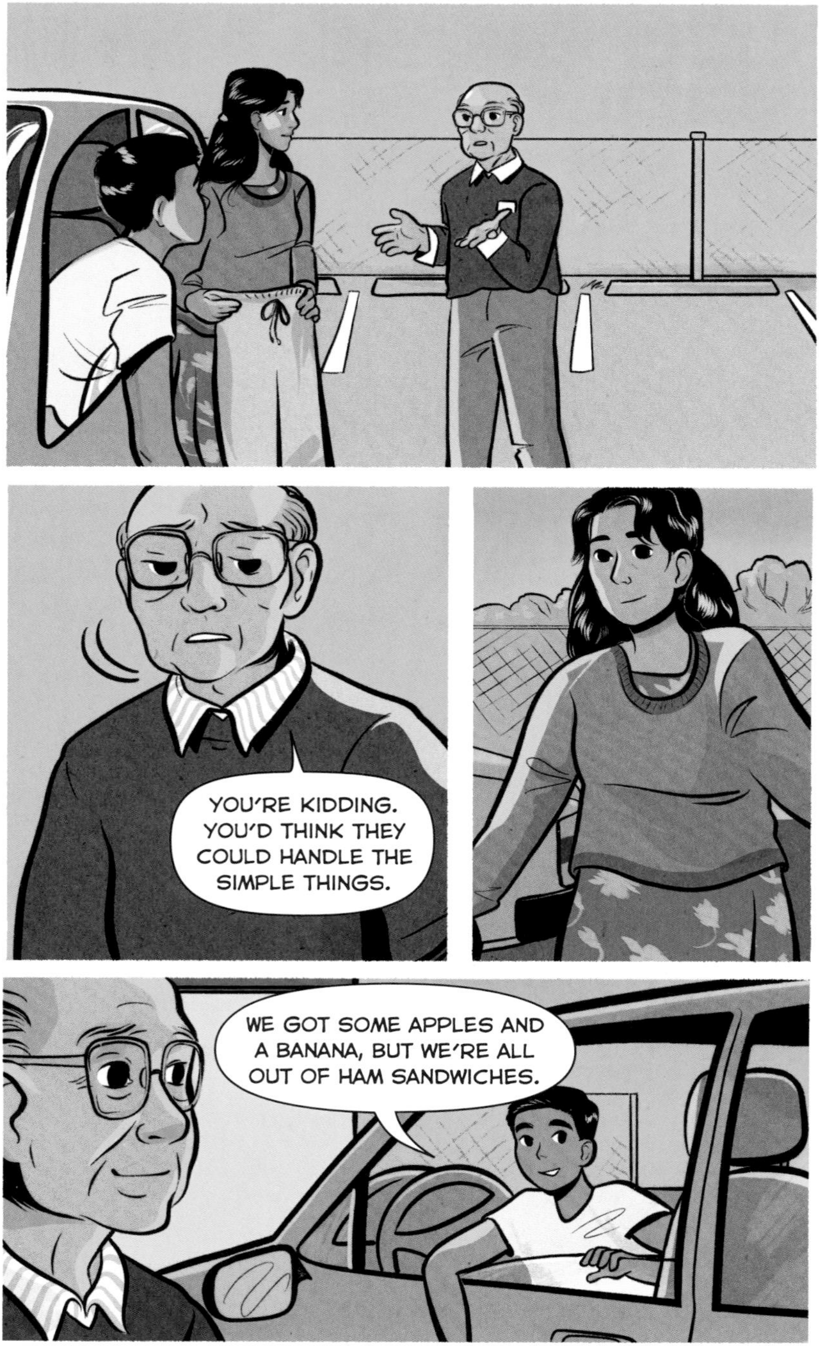
YOU'RE KIDDING. YOU'D THINK THEY COULD HANDLE THE SIMPLE THINGS.
WE GOT SOME APPLES AND A BANANA, BUT WE'RE ALL OUT OF HAM SANDWICHES.

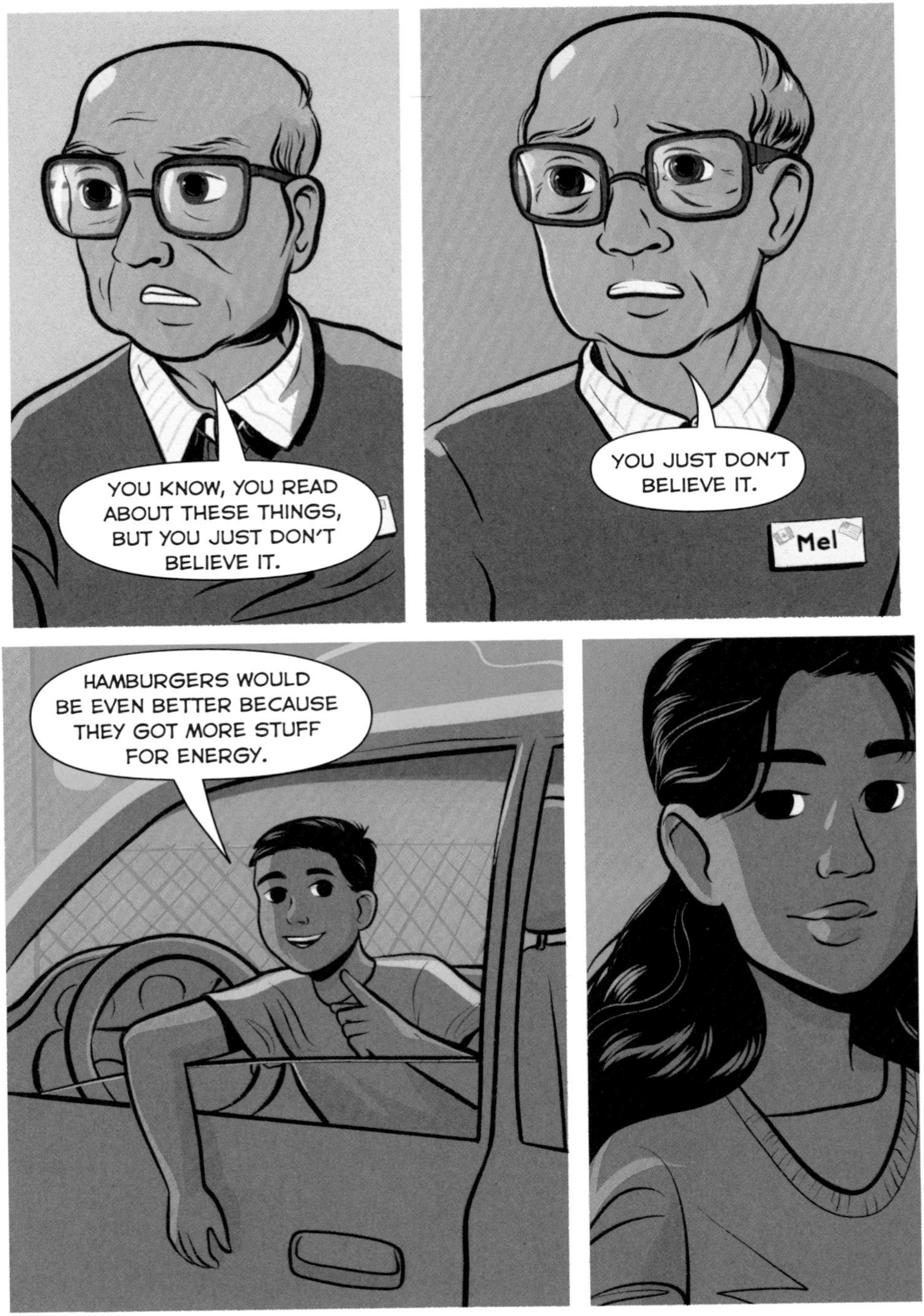
YOU KNOW, YOU READ ABOUT THESE THINGS, BUT YOU JUST DON'T BELIEVE IT.
YOU JUST DON'T BELIEVE IT.
Mel
HAMBURGERS WOULD BE EVEN BETTER BECAUSE THEY GOT MORE STUFF FOR ENERGY.

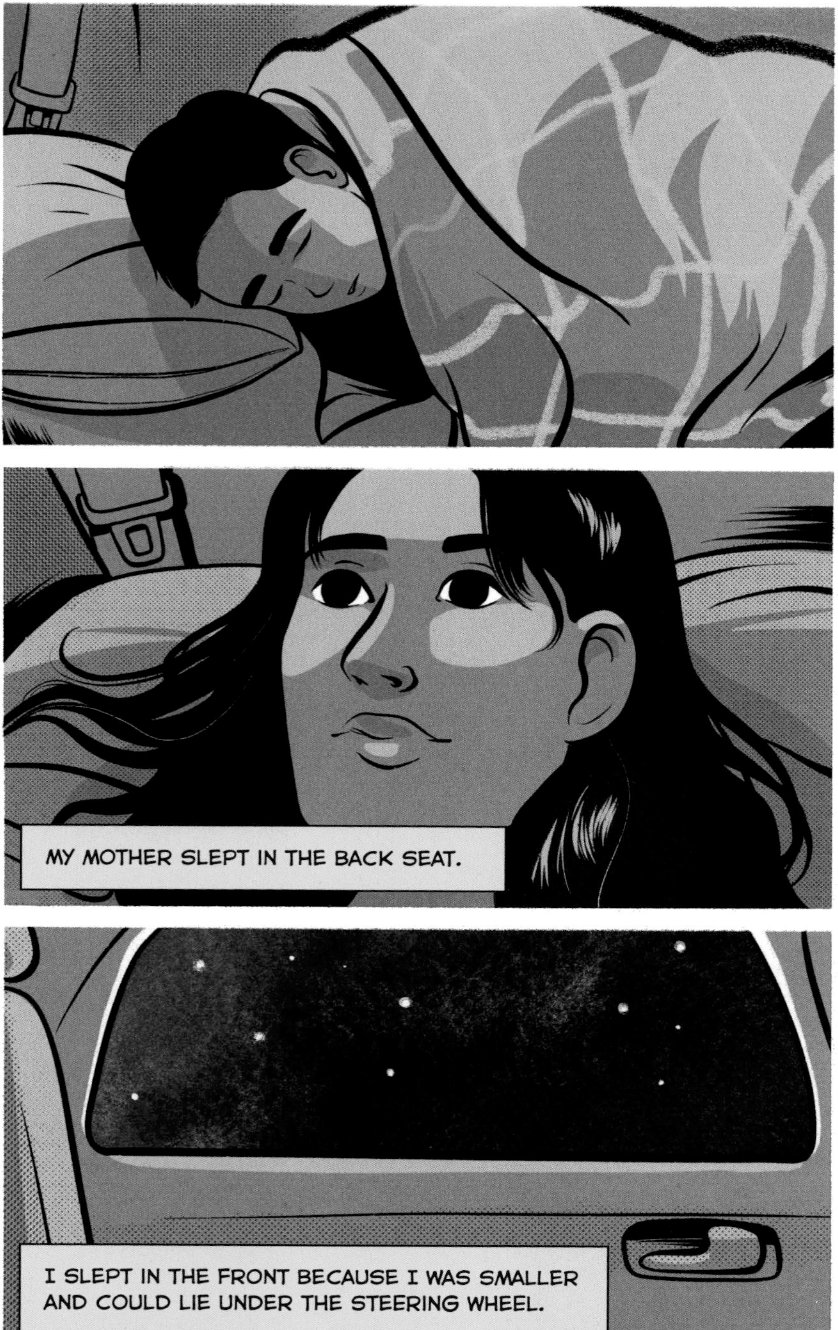
MY MOTHER SLEPT IN THE BACK SEAT.
I SLEPT IN THE FRONT BECAUSE I WAS SMALLER AND COULD LIE UNDER THE STEERING WHEEL.

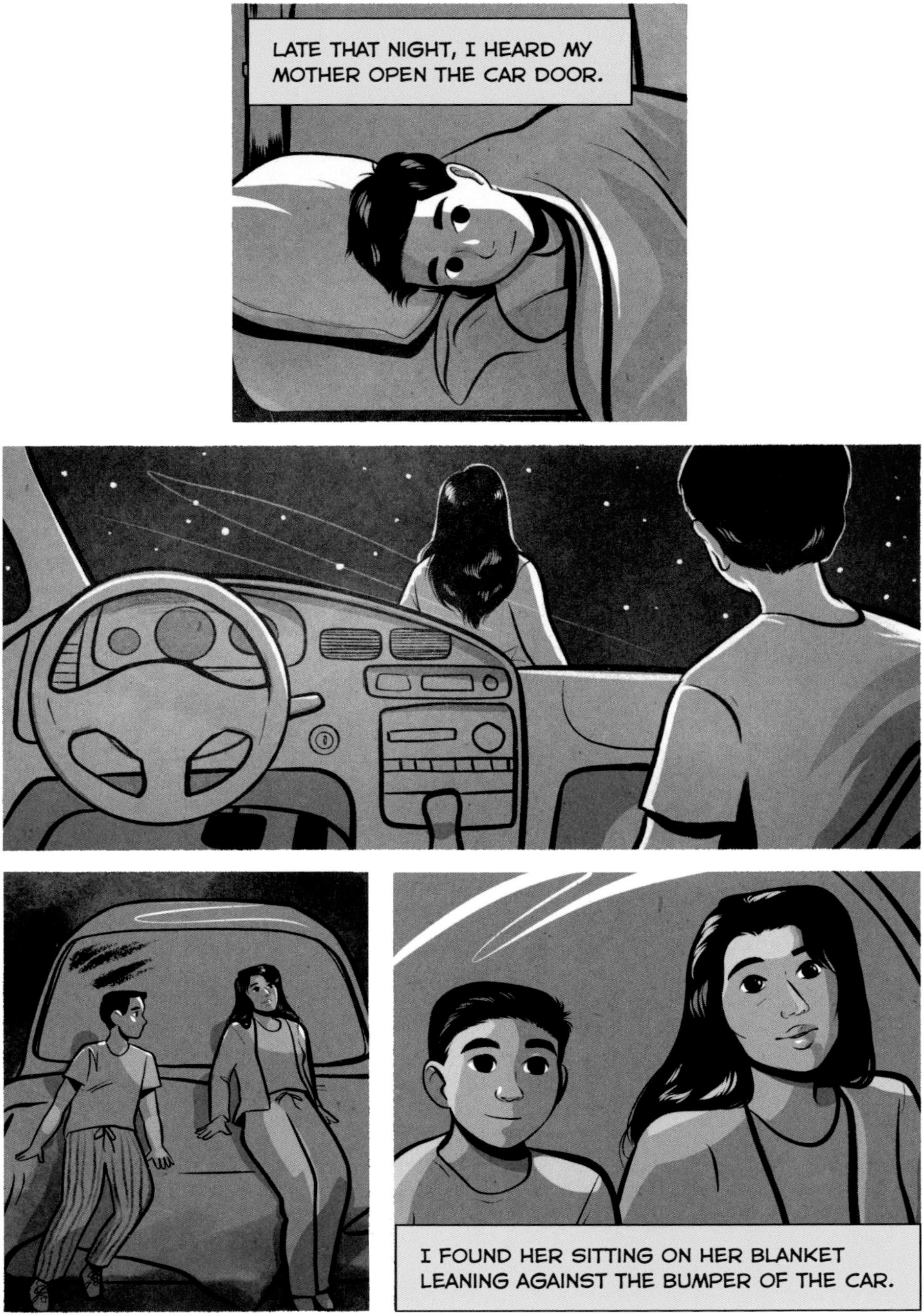
LATE THAT NIGHT, I HEARD MY MOTHER OPEN THE CAR DOOR.
I FOUND HER SITTING ON HER BLANKET LEANING AGAINST THE BUMPER OF THE CAR.

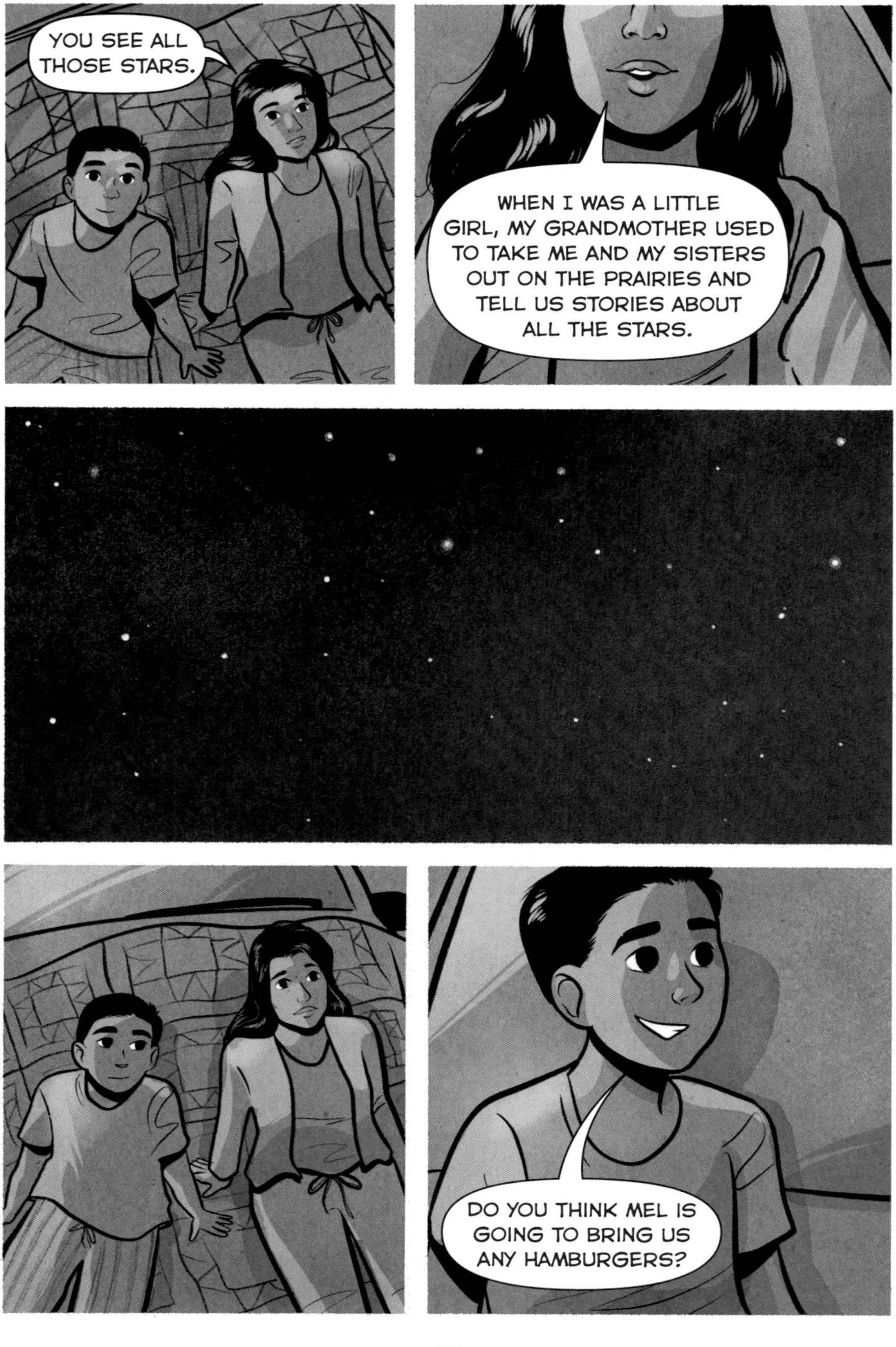
YOU SEE ALL THOSE STARS.
WHEN I WAS A LITTLE GIRL, MY GRANDMOTHER USED TO TAKE ME AND MY SISTERS OUT ON THE PRAIRIES AND TELL US STORIES ABOUT ALL THE STARS.
DO YOU THINK MEL IS GOING TO BRING US ANY HAMBURGERS?

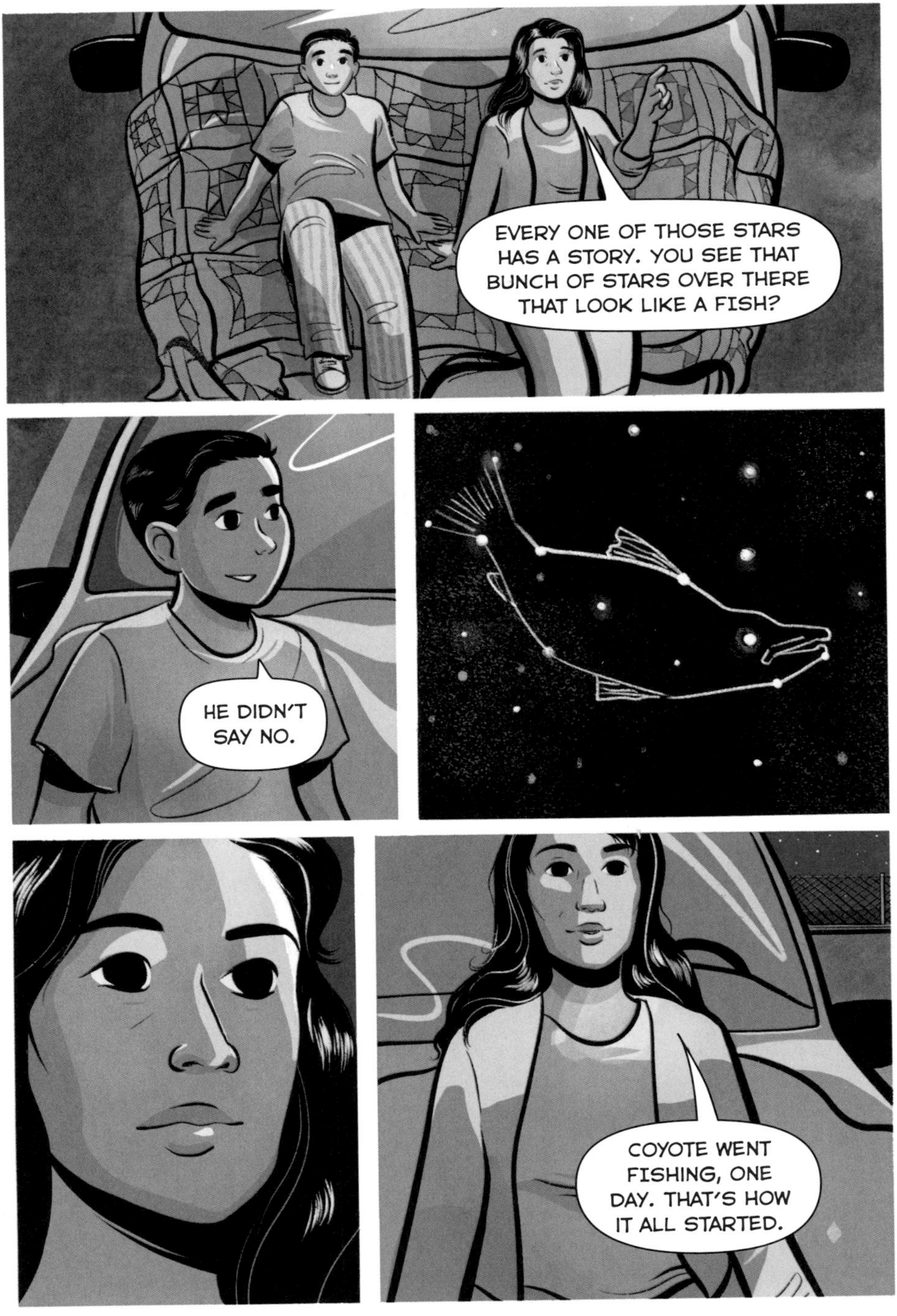
EVERY ONE OF THOSE STARS HAS A STORY. YOU SEE THAT BUNCH OF STARS OVER THERE THAT LOOK LIKE A FISH?
HE DIDN'T SAY NO.
COYOTE WENT FISHING, ONE DAY. THAT'S HOW IT ALL STARTED.

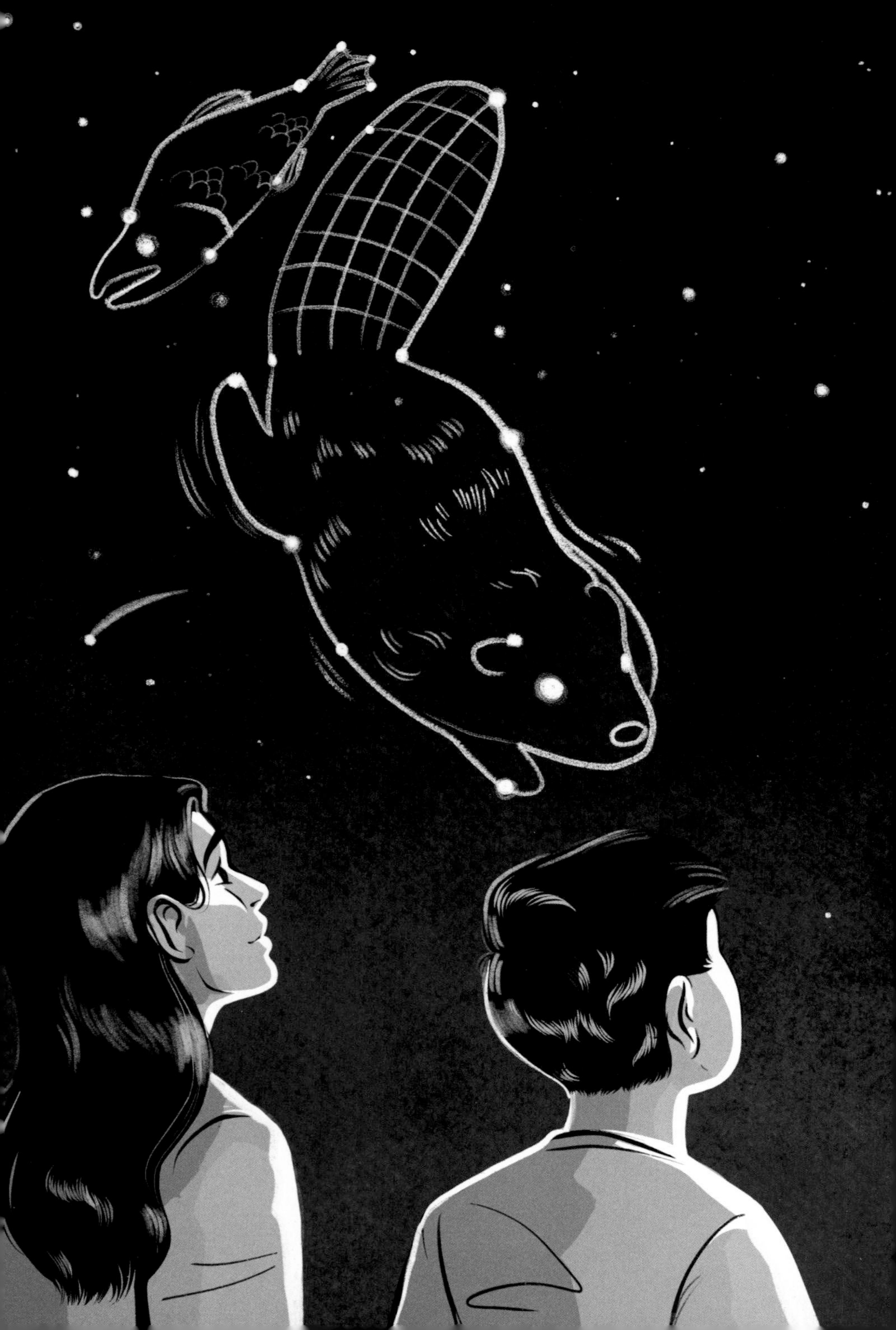

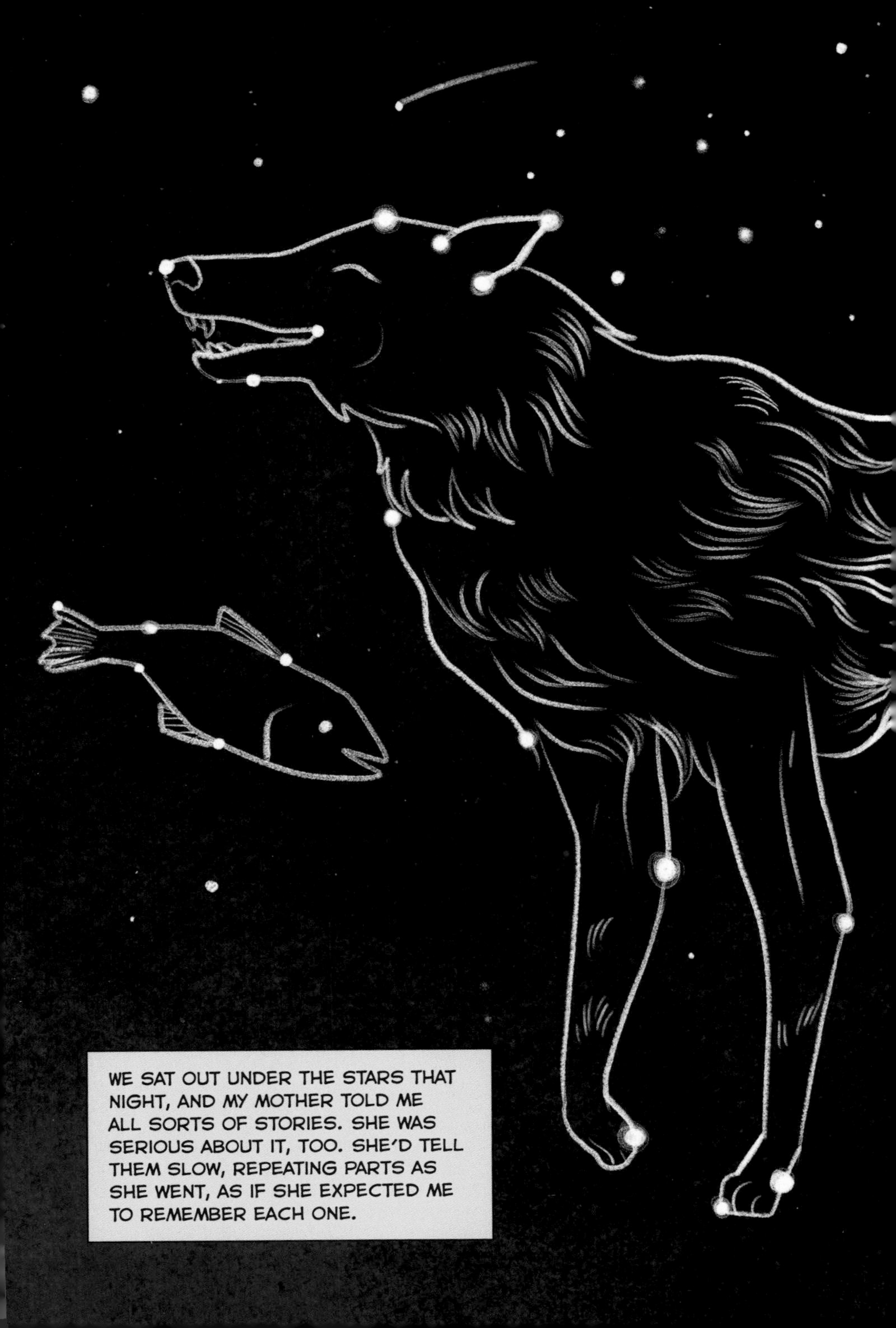
WE SAT OUT UNDER THE STARS THAT NIGHT, AND MY MOTHER TOLD ME ALL SORTS OF STORIES. SHE WAS SERIOUS ABOUT IT, TOO. SHE'D TELL THEM SLOW, REPEATING PARTS AS SHE WENT, AS IF SHE EXPECTED ME TO REMEMBER EACH ONE.

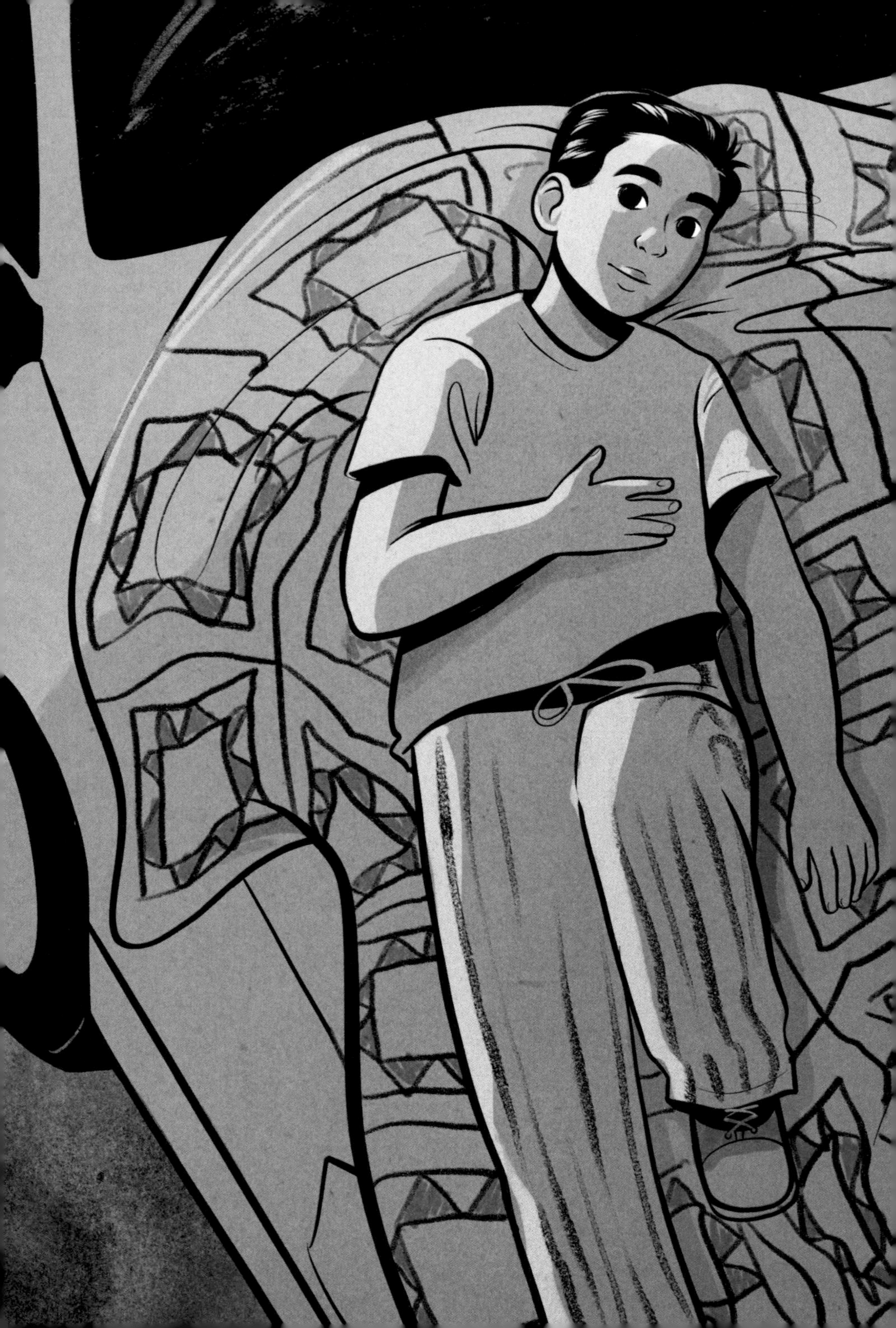

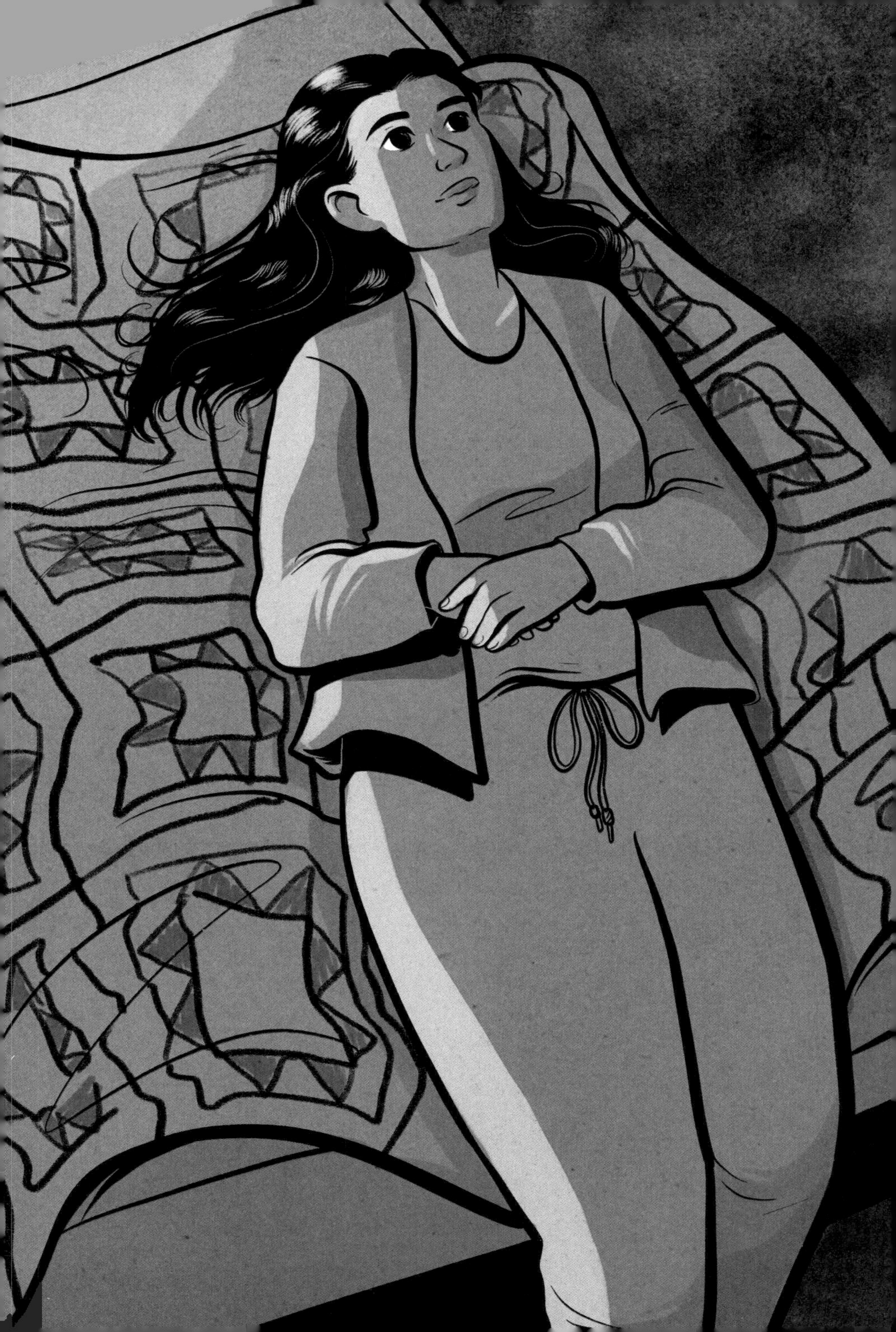

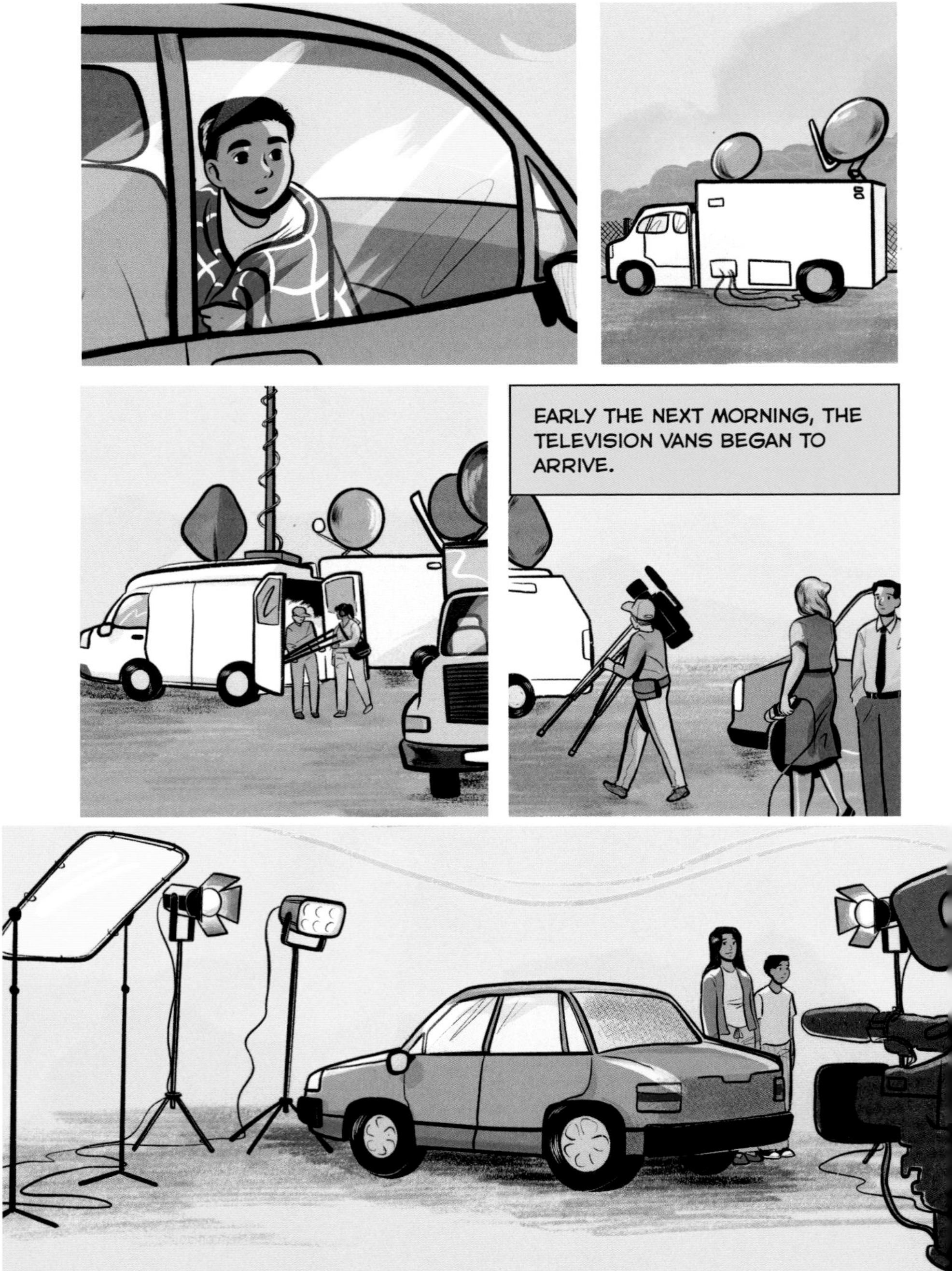
EARLY THE NEXT MORNING, THE TELEVISION VANS BEGAN TO ARRIVE.

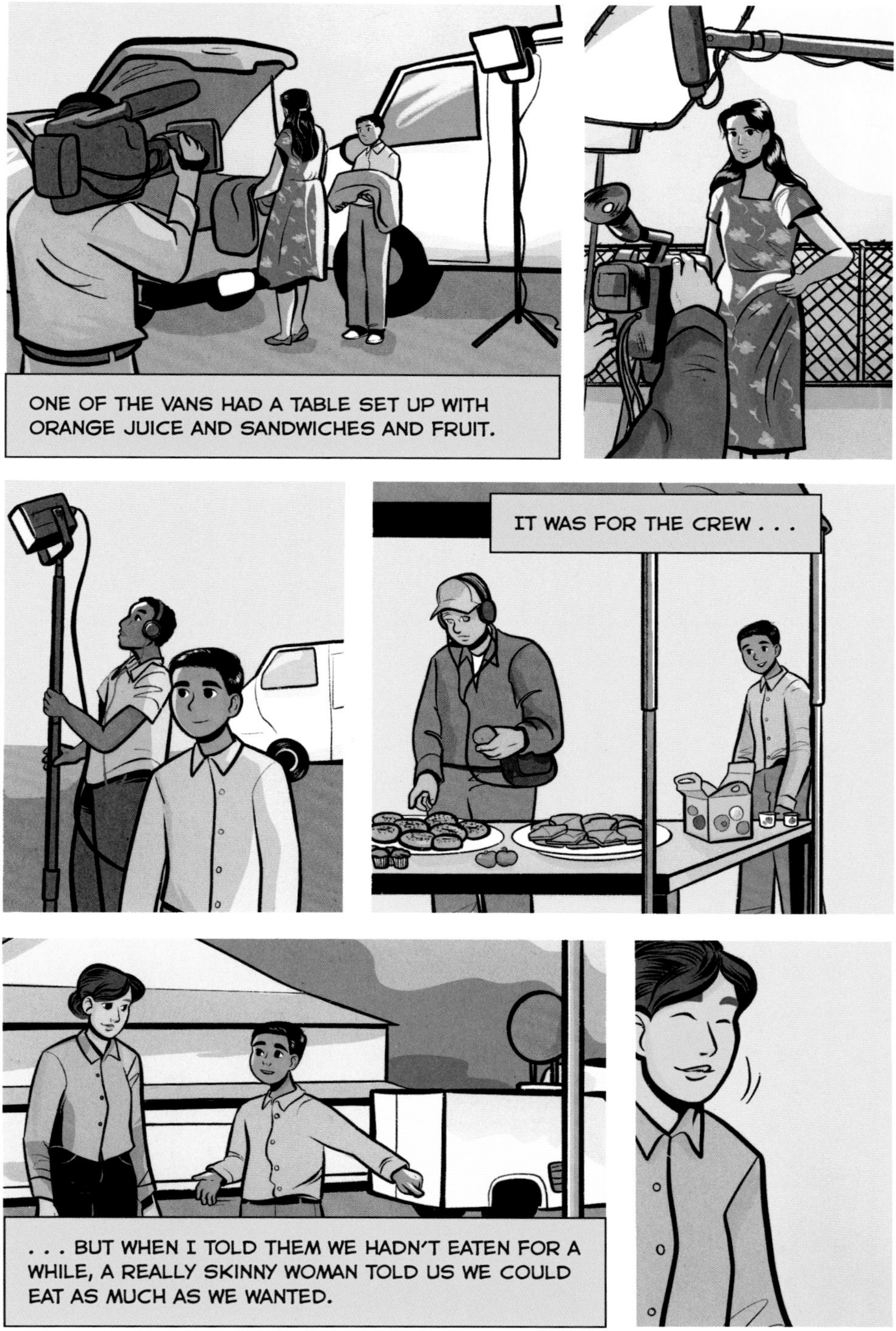
ONE OF THE VANS HAD A TABLE SET UP WITH ORANGE JUICE AND SANDWICHES AND FRUIT.
IT WAS FOR THE CREW . . .
. . . BUT WHEN I TOLD THEM WE HADN'T EATEN FOR A WHILE, A REALLY SKINNY WOMAN TOLD US WE COULD EAT AS MUCH AS WE WANTED.

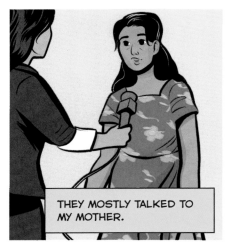

THEY MOSTLY TALKED TO MY MOTHER.

EVERY SO OFTEN ONE OF THE REPORTERS WOULD COME OVER . . .

. . . AND ASK ME QUESTIONS ABOUT HOW IT FELT TO BE AN INDIAN WITHOUT A COUNTRY.

I TOLD THEM WE HAD A NICE HOUSE ON THE RESERVE . . .

. . . AND THAT MY COUSINS HAD A COUPLE OF HORSES WE RODE WHEN WE WENT FISHING.

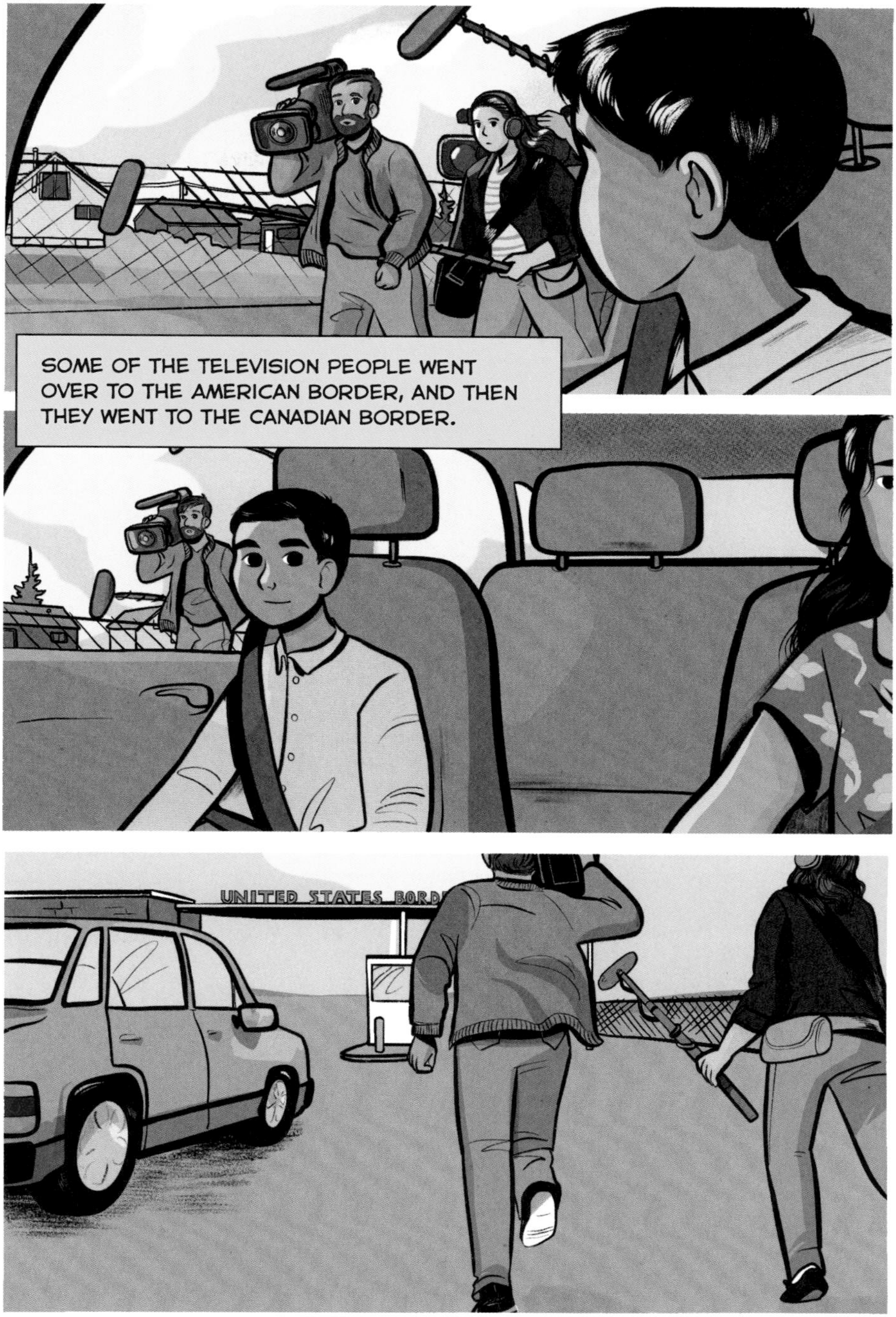
SOME OF THE TELEVISION PEOPLE WENT OVER TO THE AMERICAN BORDER, AND THEN THEY WENT TO THE CANADIAN BORDER.
UNITED STATES

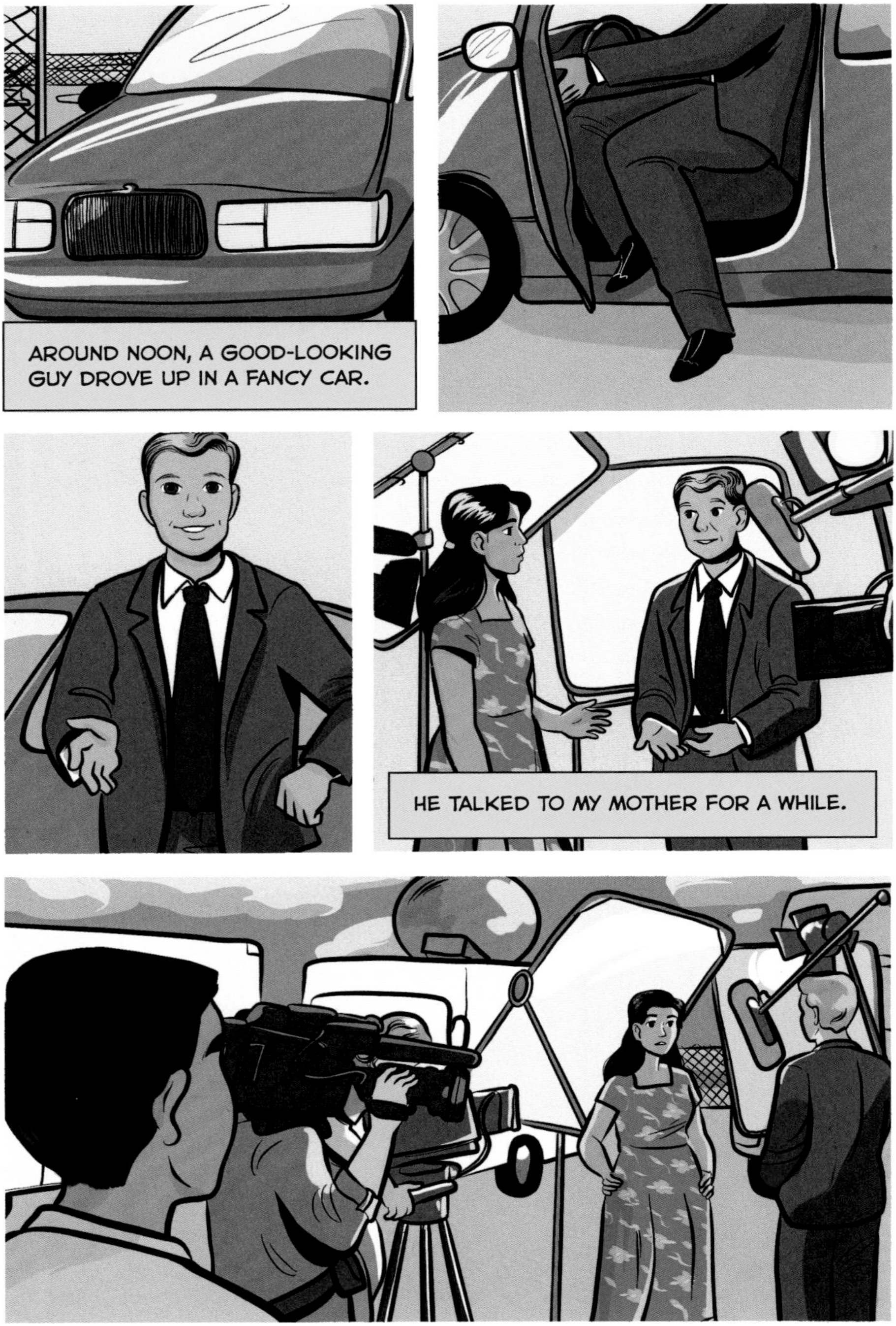
AROUND NOON, A GOOD-LOOKING GUY DROVE UP IN A FANCY CAR.
HE TALKED TO MY MOTHER FOR A WHILE.

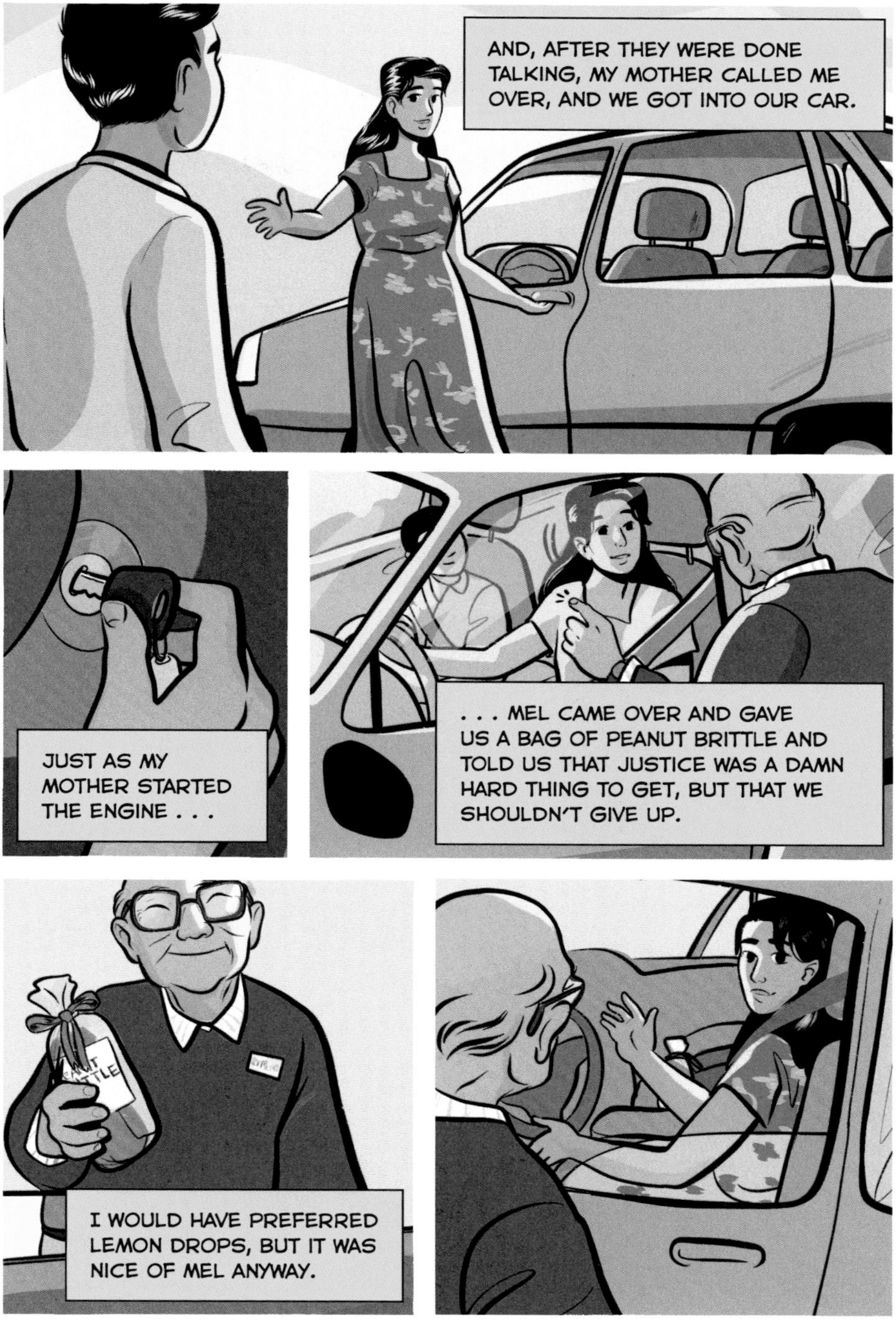
AND, AFTER THEY WERE DONE TALKING, MY MOTHER CALLED ME OVER, AND WE GOT INTO OUR CAR.
JUST AS MY MOTHER STARTED THE ENGINE . . .
. . . MEL CAME OVER AND GAVE US A BAG OF PEANUT BRITTLE AND TOLD US THAT JUSTICE WAS A DAMN HARD THING TO GET, BUT THAT WE SHOULDN'T GIVE UP.
I WOULD HAVE PREFERRED LEMON DROPS, BUT IT WAS NICE OF MEL ANYWAY.

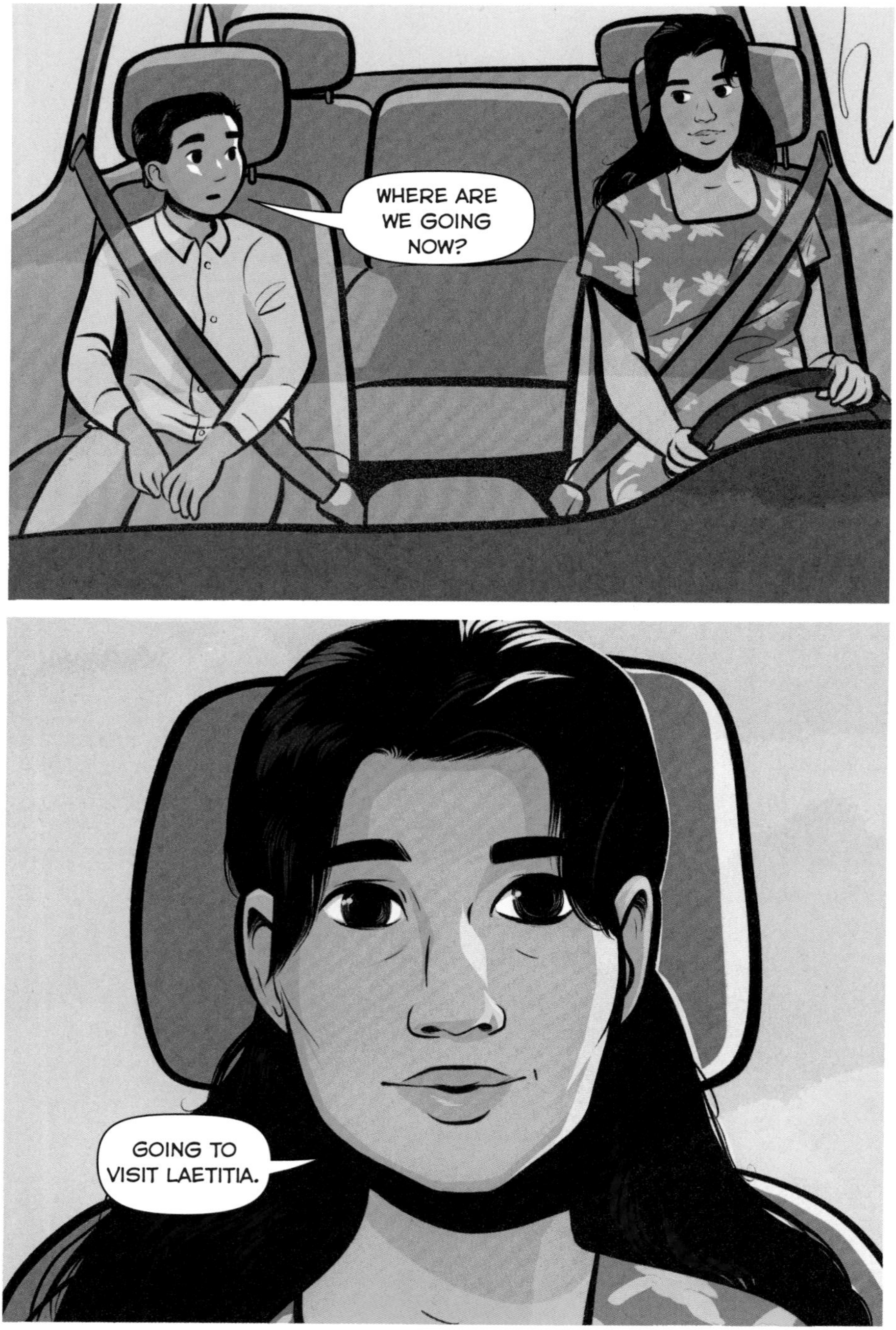
WHERE ARE WE GOING NOW?
GOING TO VISIT LAETITIA.

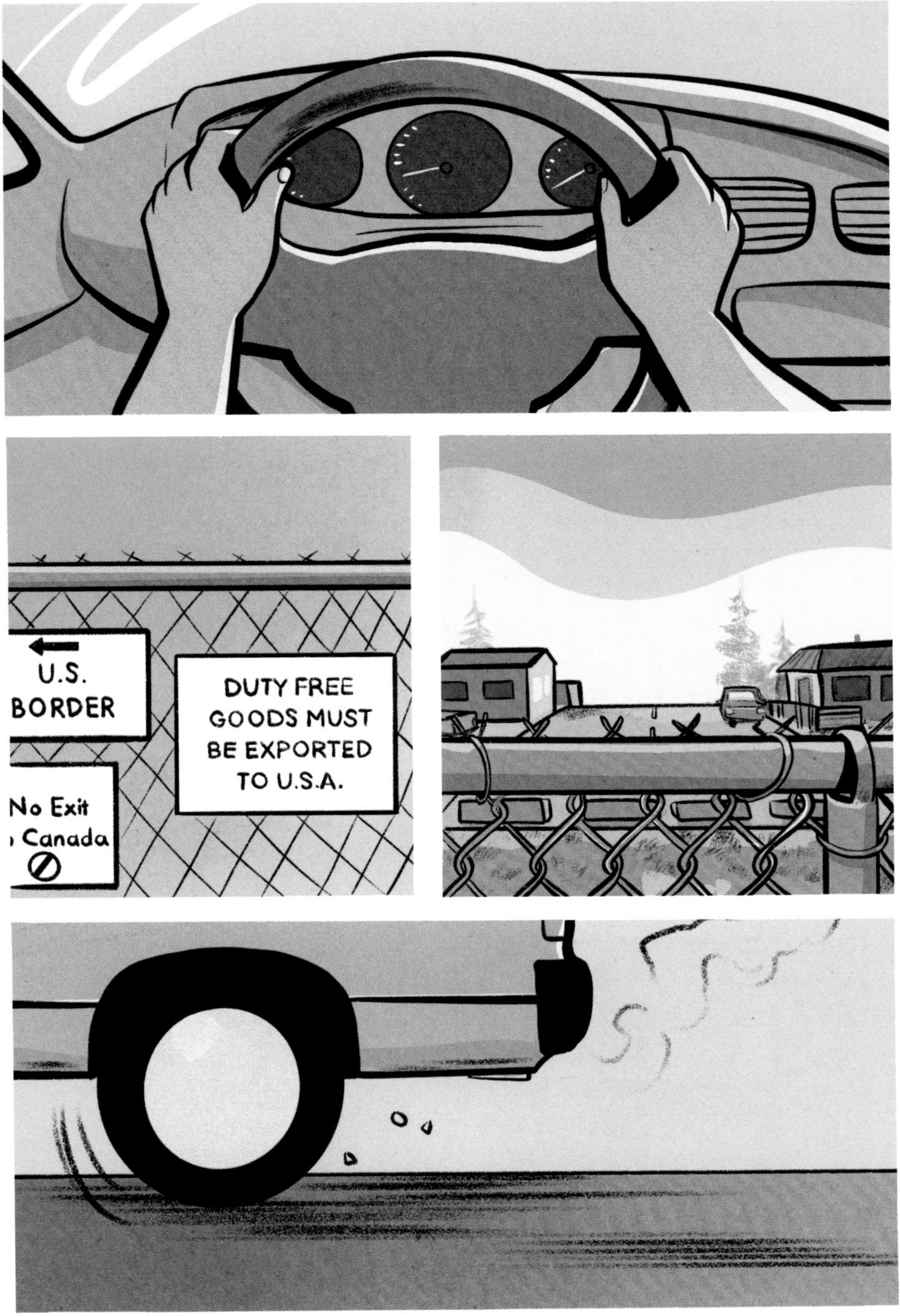
U.S.
BORDER
No Exit
Canada
DUTY FREE
GOODS MUST
BE EXPORTED
TO U.S.A.

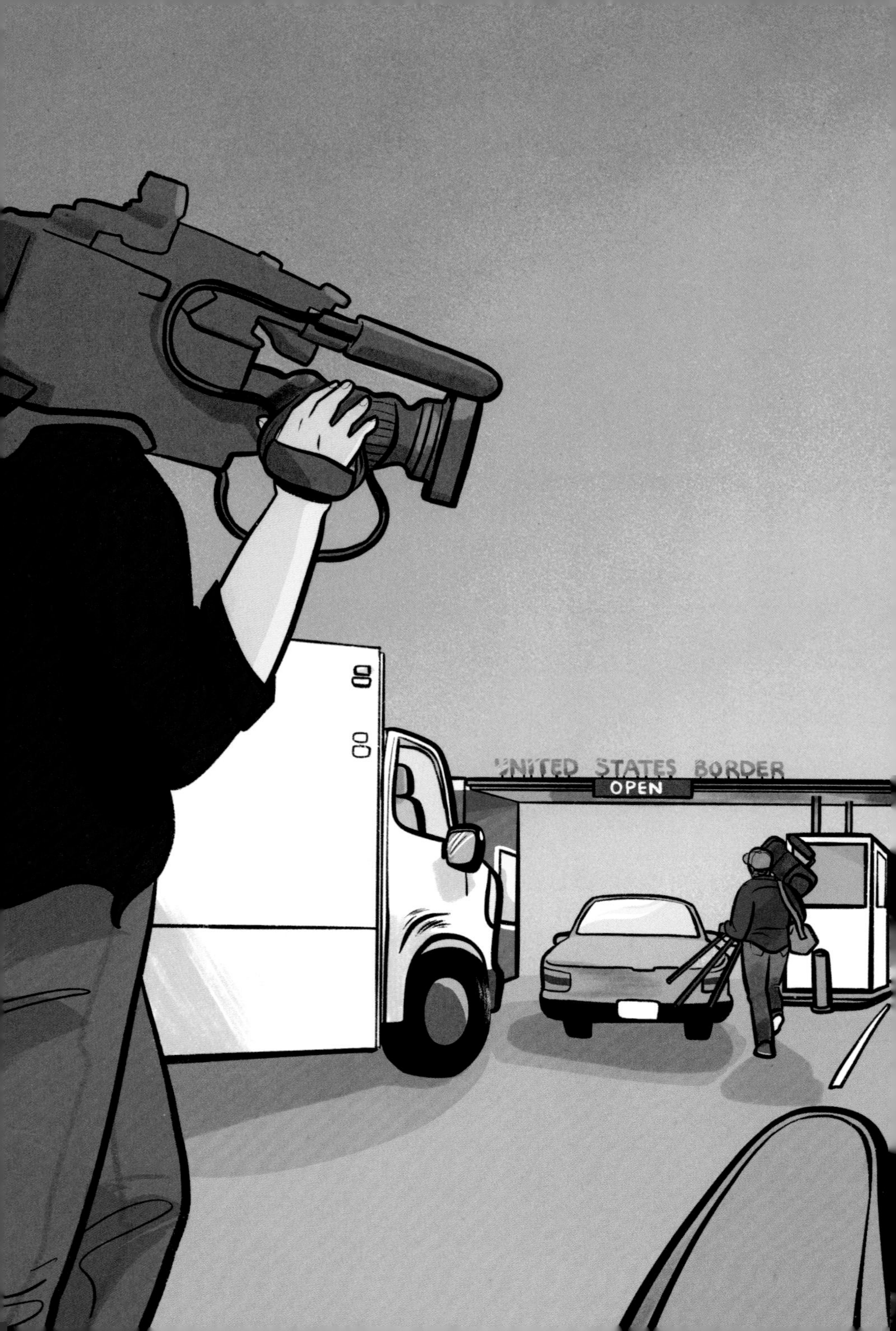
UNITED STATES BORDER
OPEN

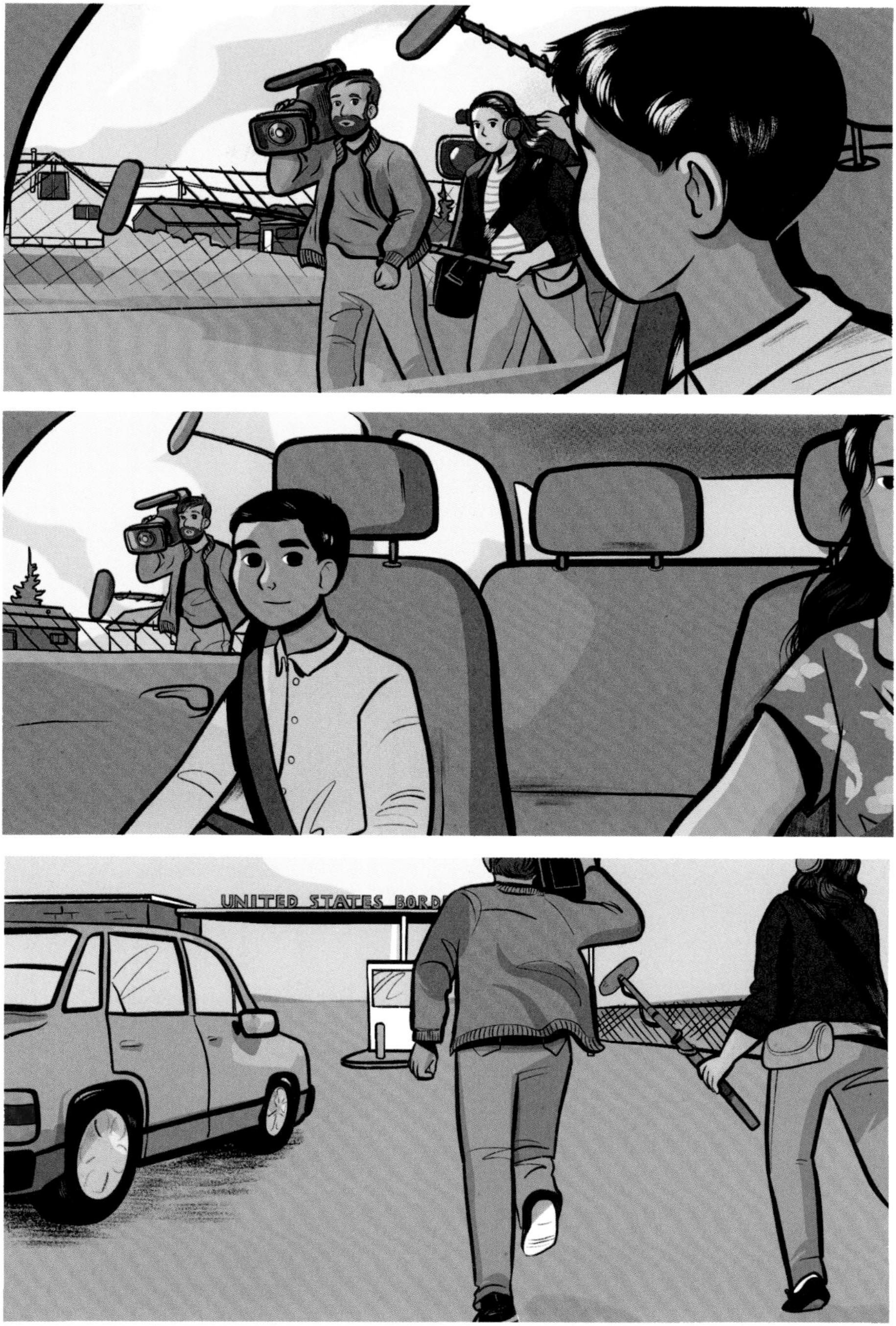
UNITED STATES BORD

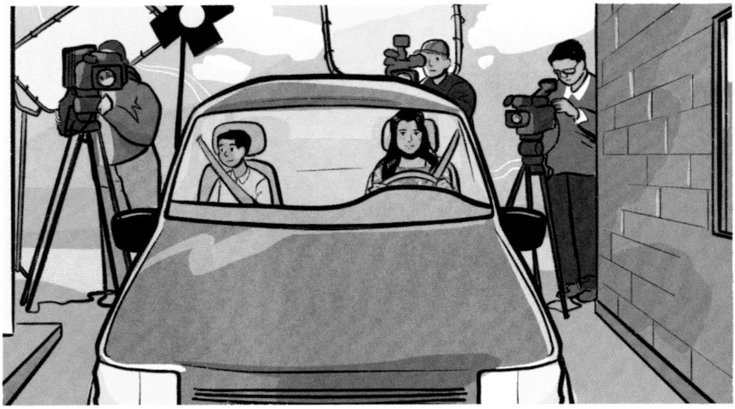

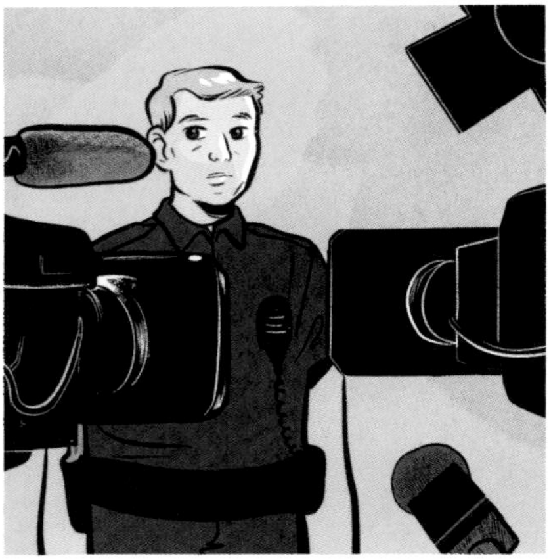

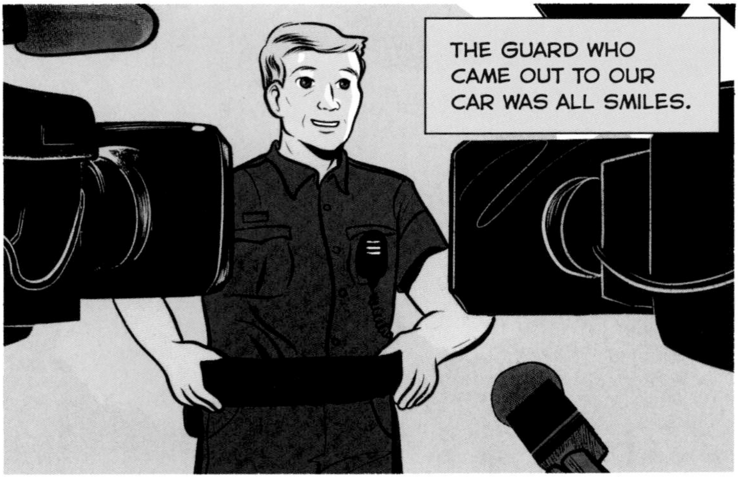
THE GUARD WHO CAME OUT TO OUR CAR WAS ALL SMILES.

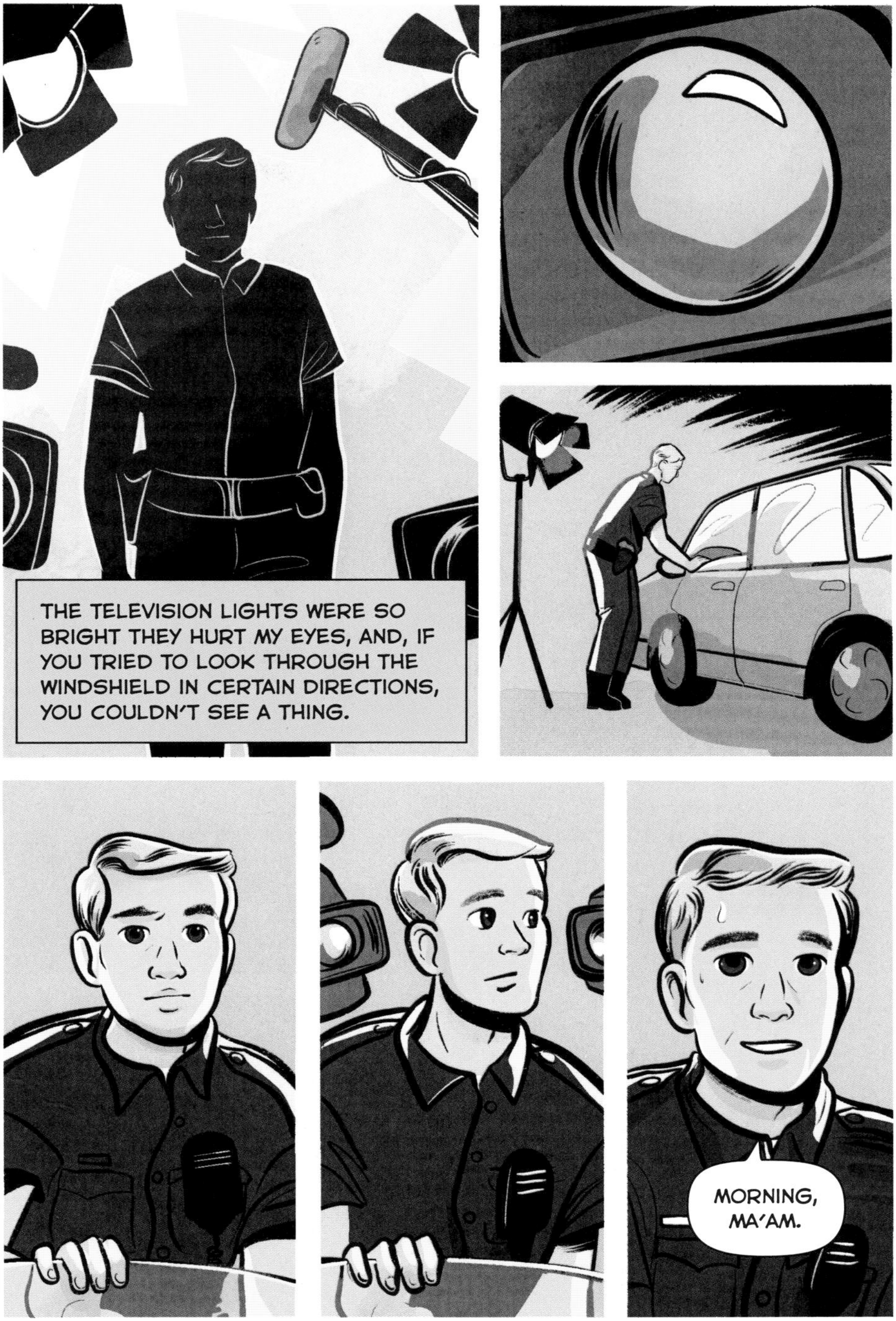
THE TELEVISION LIGHTS WERE SO BRIGHT THEY HURT MY EYES, AND, IF YOU TRIED TO LOOK THROUGH THE WINDSHIELD IN CERTAIN DIRECTIONS, YOU COULDN'T SEE A THING.
MORNING, MA'AM.

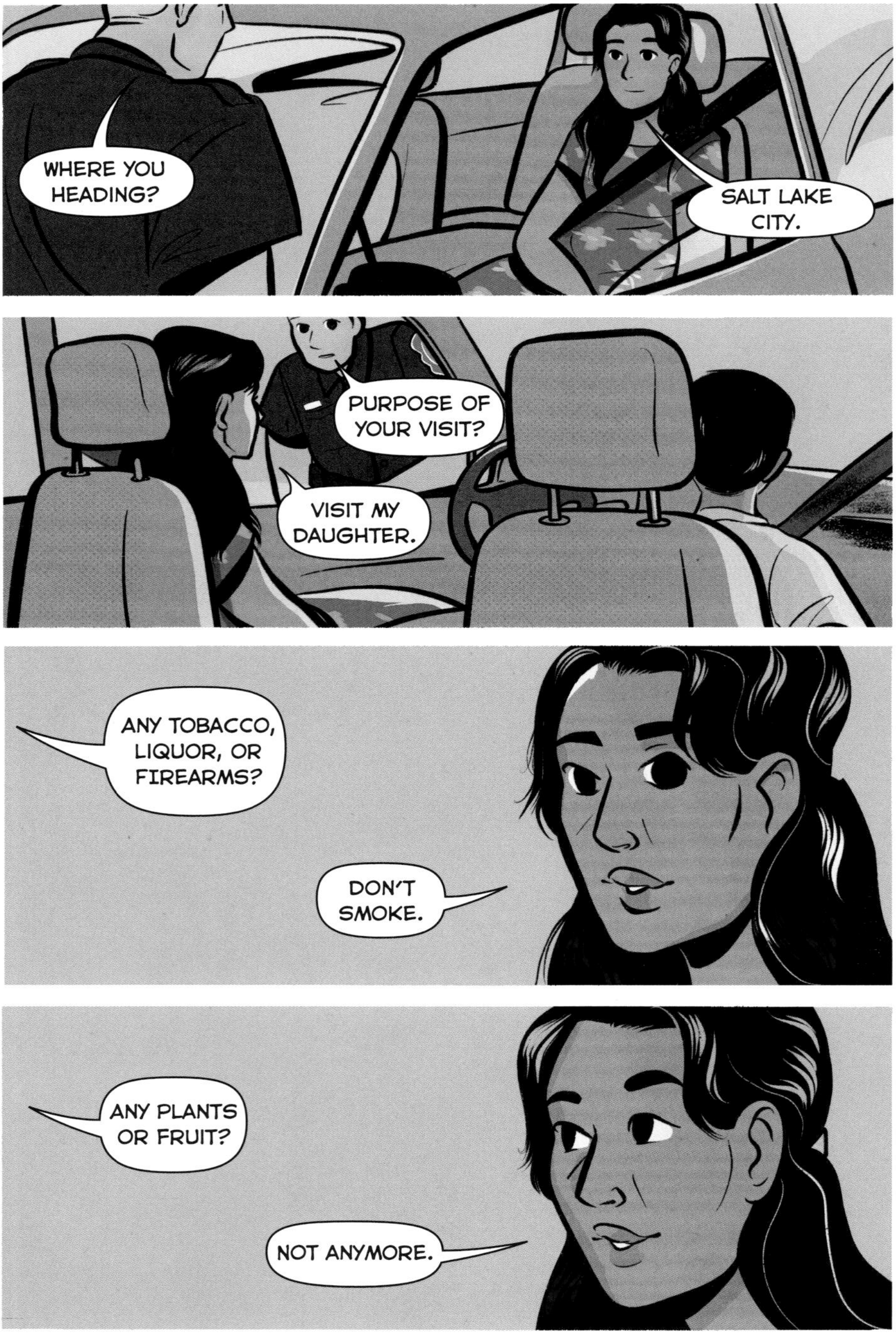
WHERE YOU HEADING?
SALT LAKE CITY.
PURPOSE OF YOUR VISIT?
VISIT MY DAUGHTER.
ANY TOBACCO, LIQUOR, OR FIREARMS?
DON'T SMOKE.
ANY PLANTS OR FRUIT?
NOT ANYMORE.

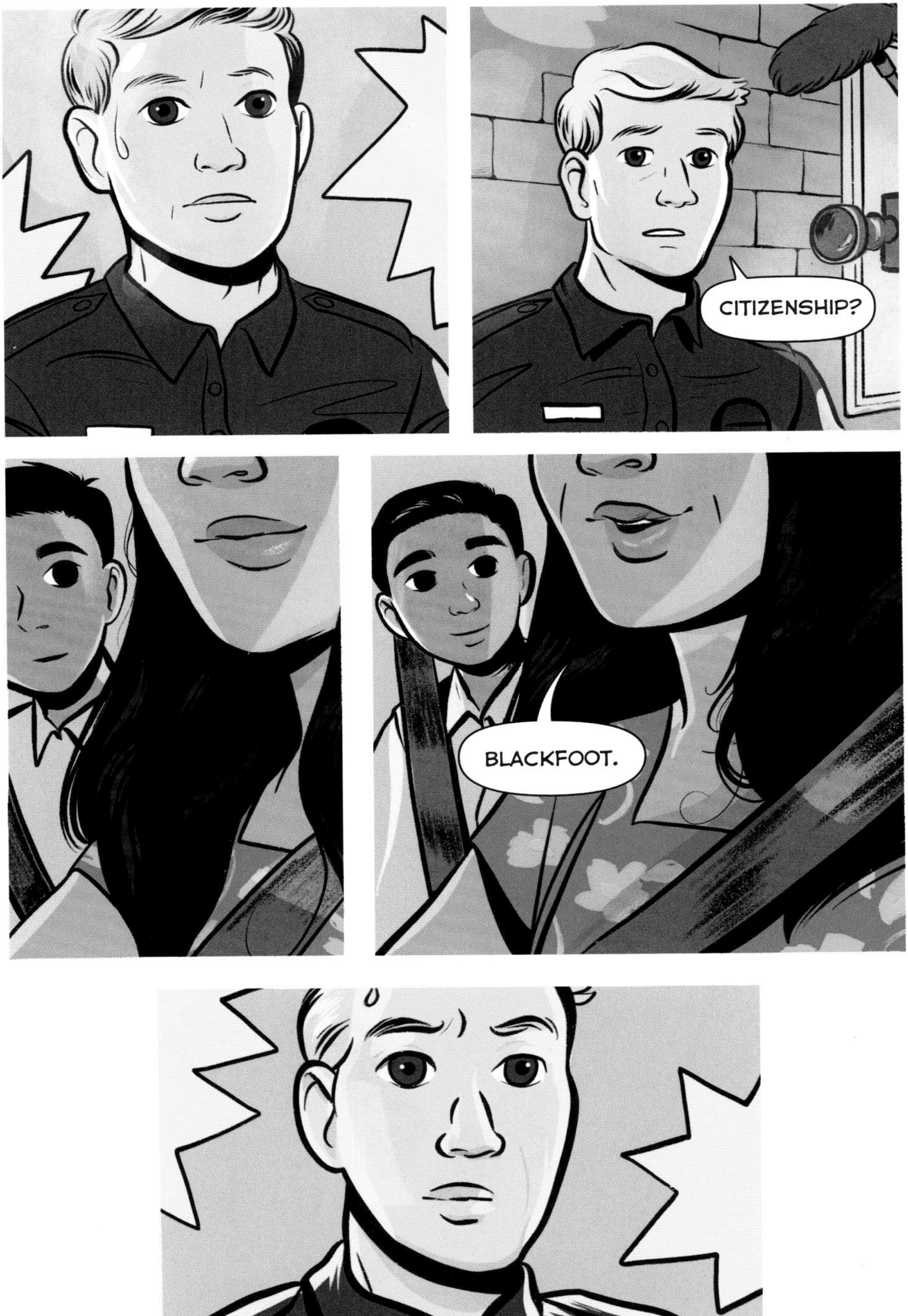
CITIZENSHIP?
BLACKFOOT.

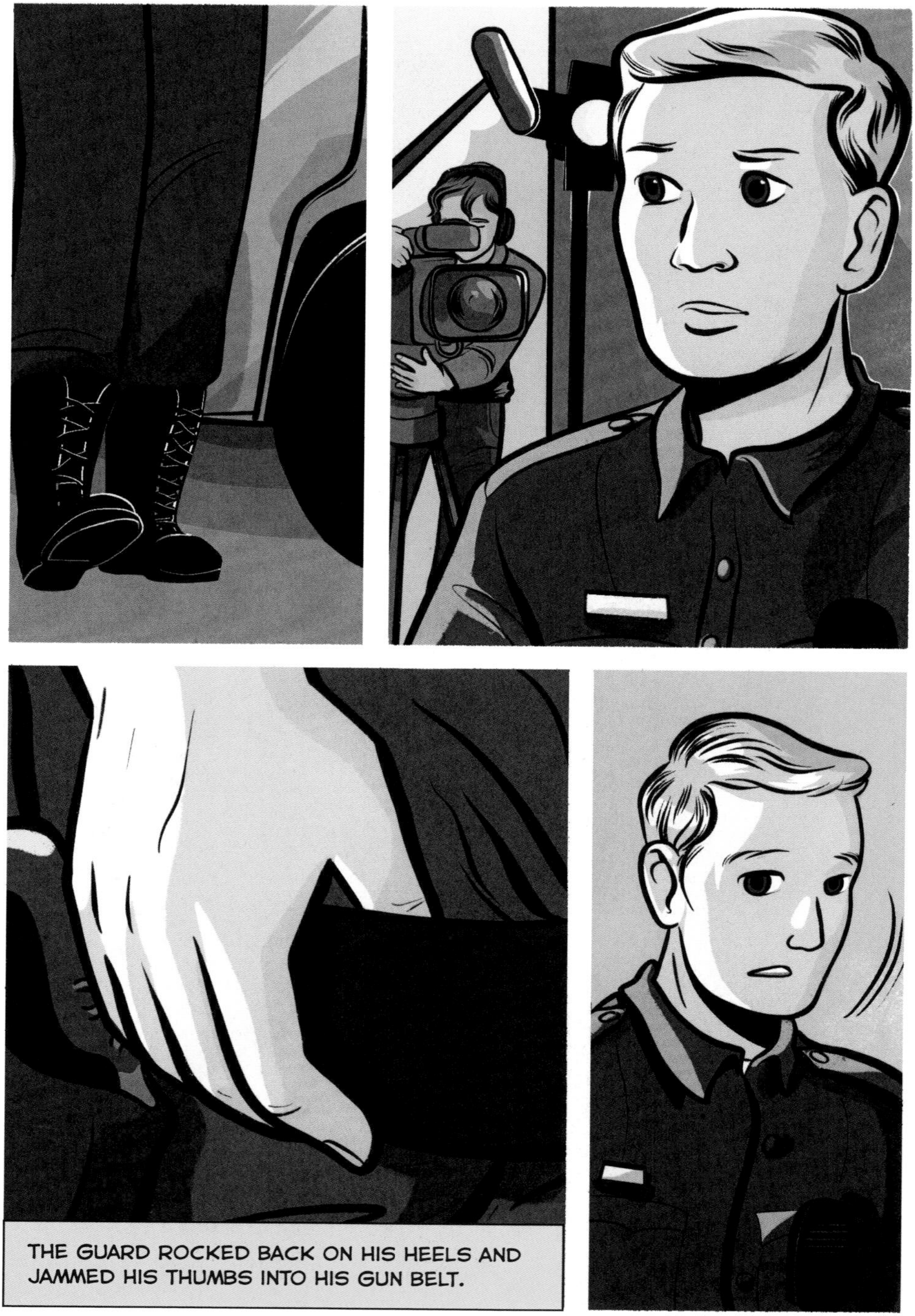
THE GUARD ROCKED BACK ON HIS HEELS AND JAMMED HIS THUMBS INTO HIS GUN BELT.

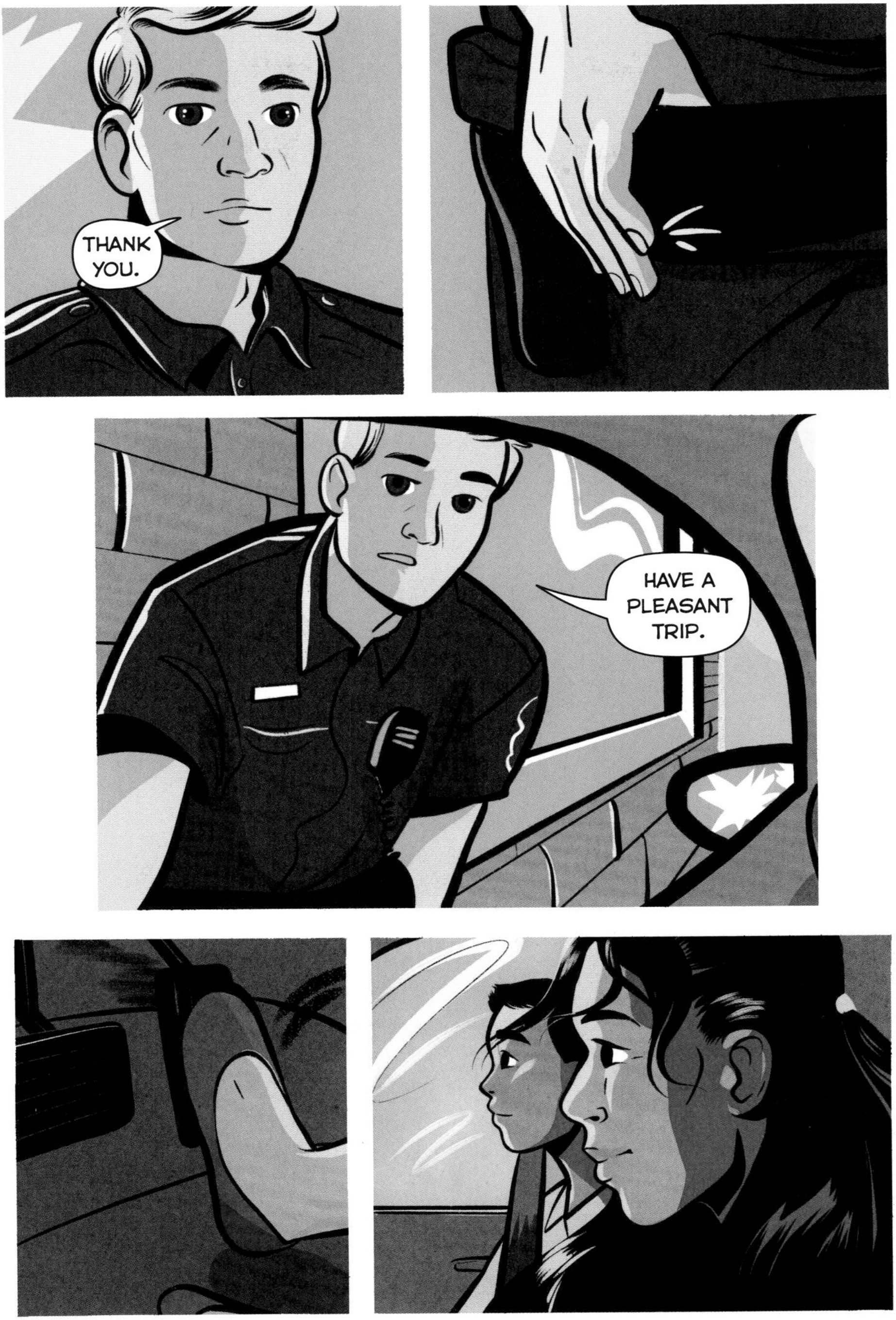
THANK YOU.
HAVE A PLEASANT TRIP.

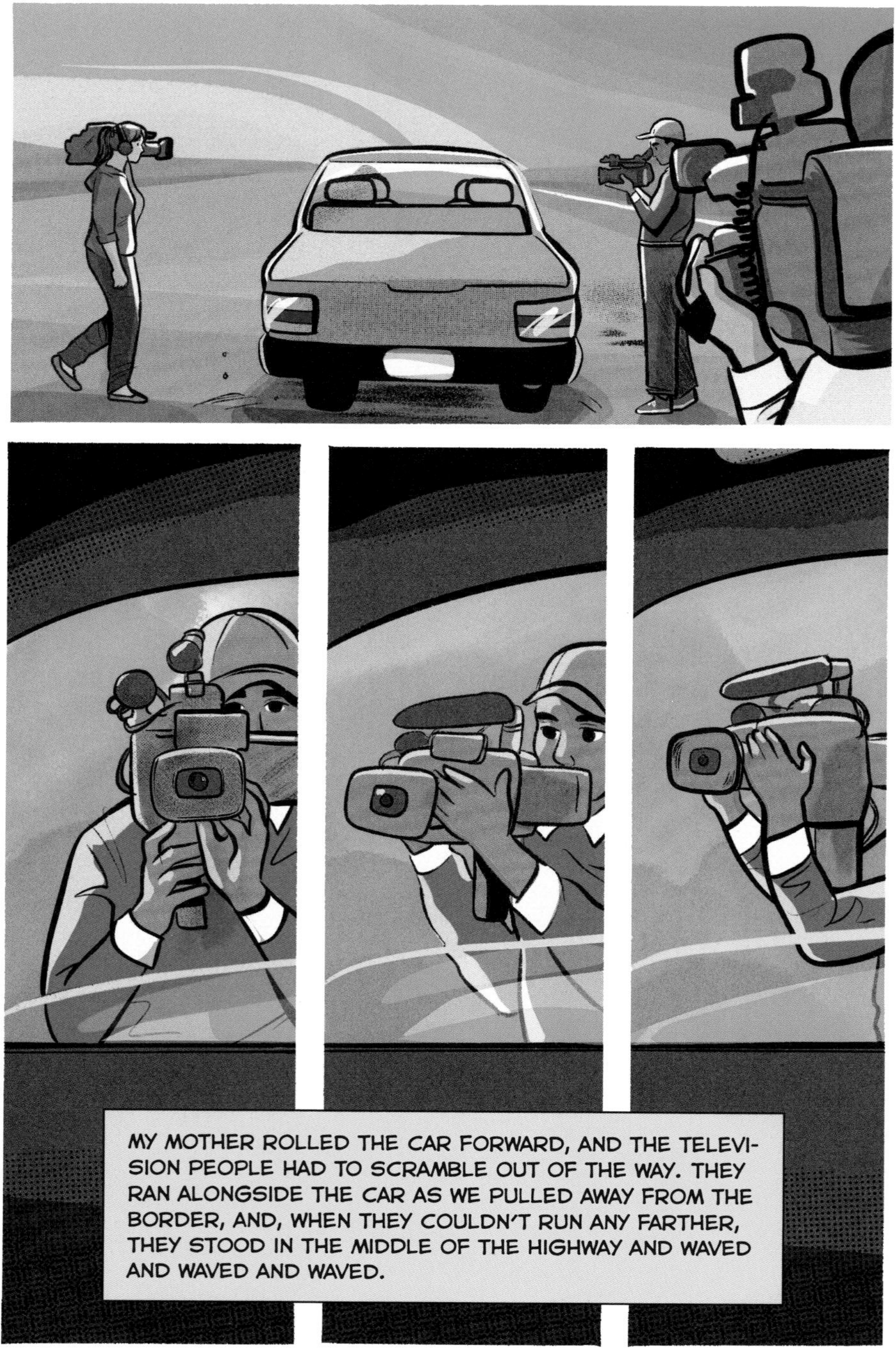
MY MOTHER ROLLED THE CAR FORWARD, AND THE TELEVISION PEOPLE HAD TO SCRAMBLE OUT OF THE WAY. THEY RAN ALONGSIDE THE CAR AS WE PULLED AWAY FROM THE BORDER, AND, WHEN THEY COULDN'T RUN ANY FARTHER, THEY STOOD IN THE MIDDLE OF THE HIGHWAY AND WAVED AND WAVED AND WAVED.

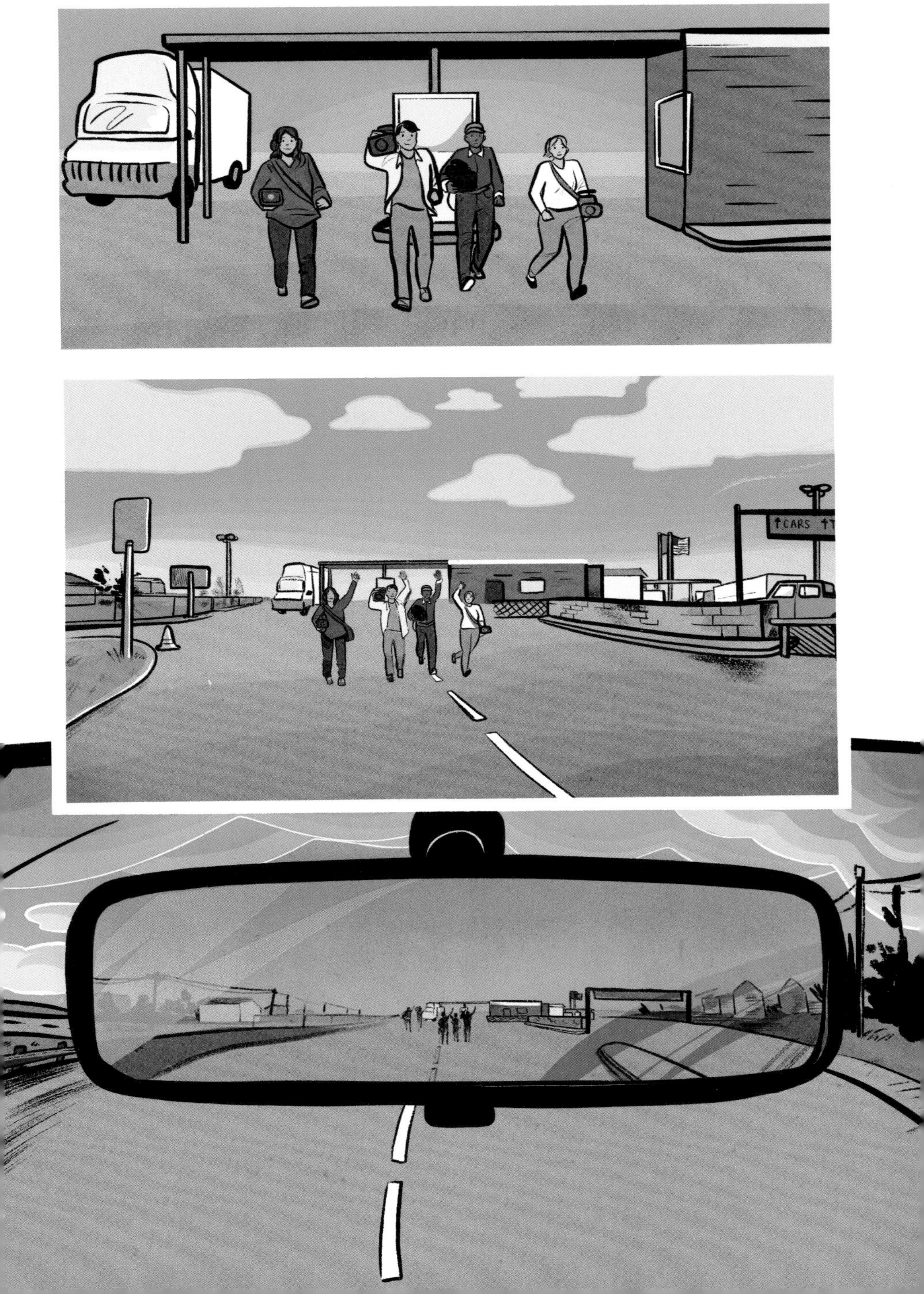
↑CARS

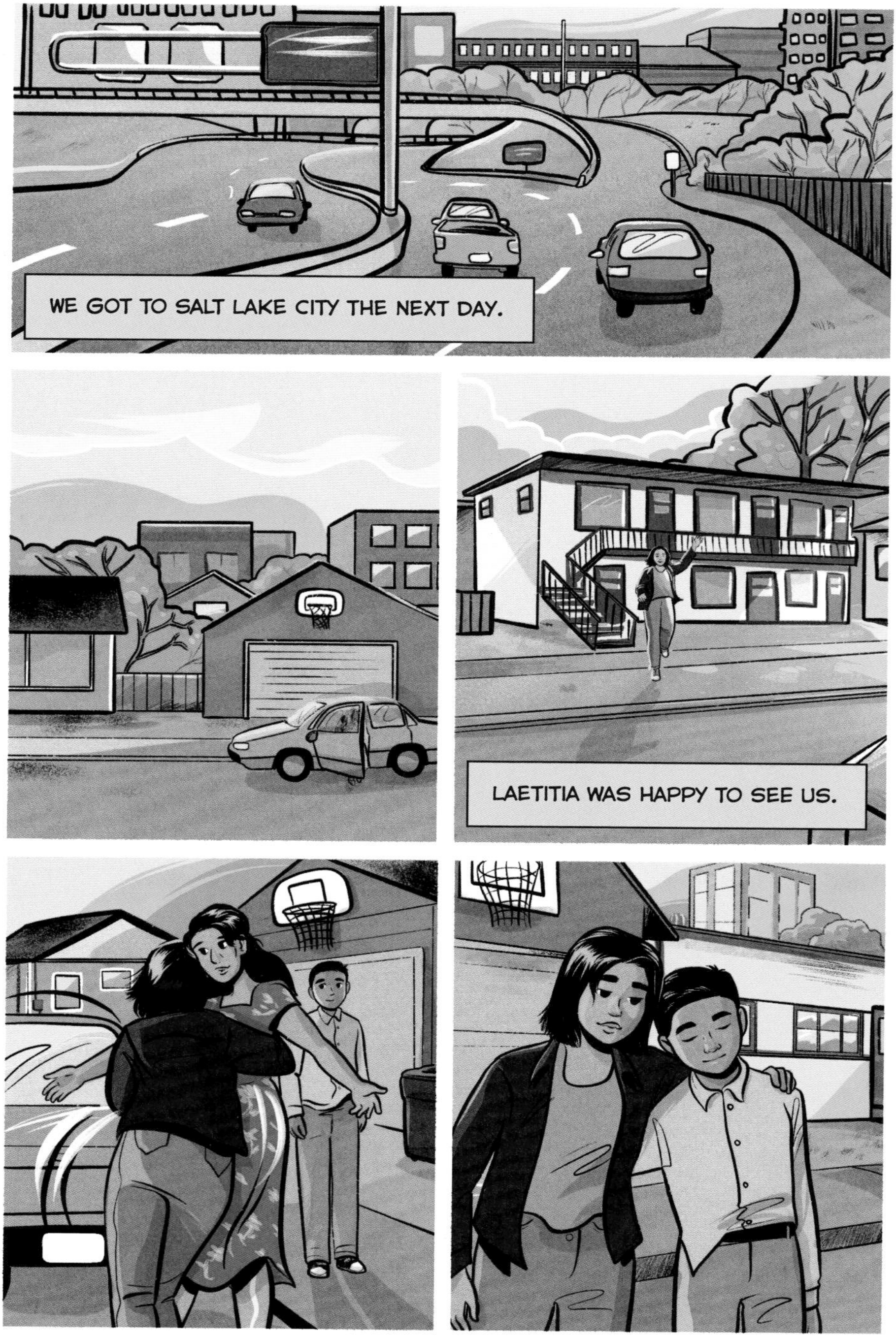
WE GOT TO SALT LAKE CITY THE NEXT DAY.
LAETITIA WAS HAPPY TO SEE US.

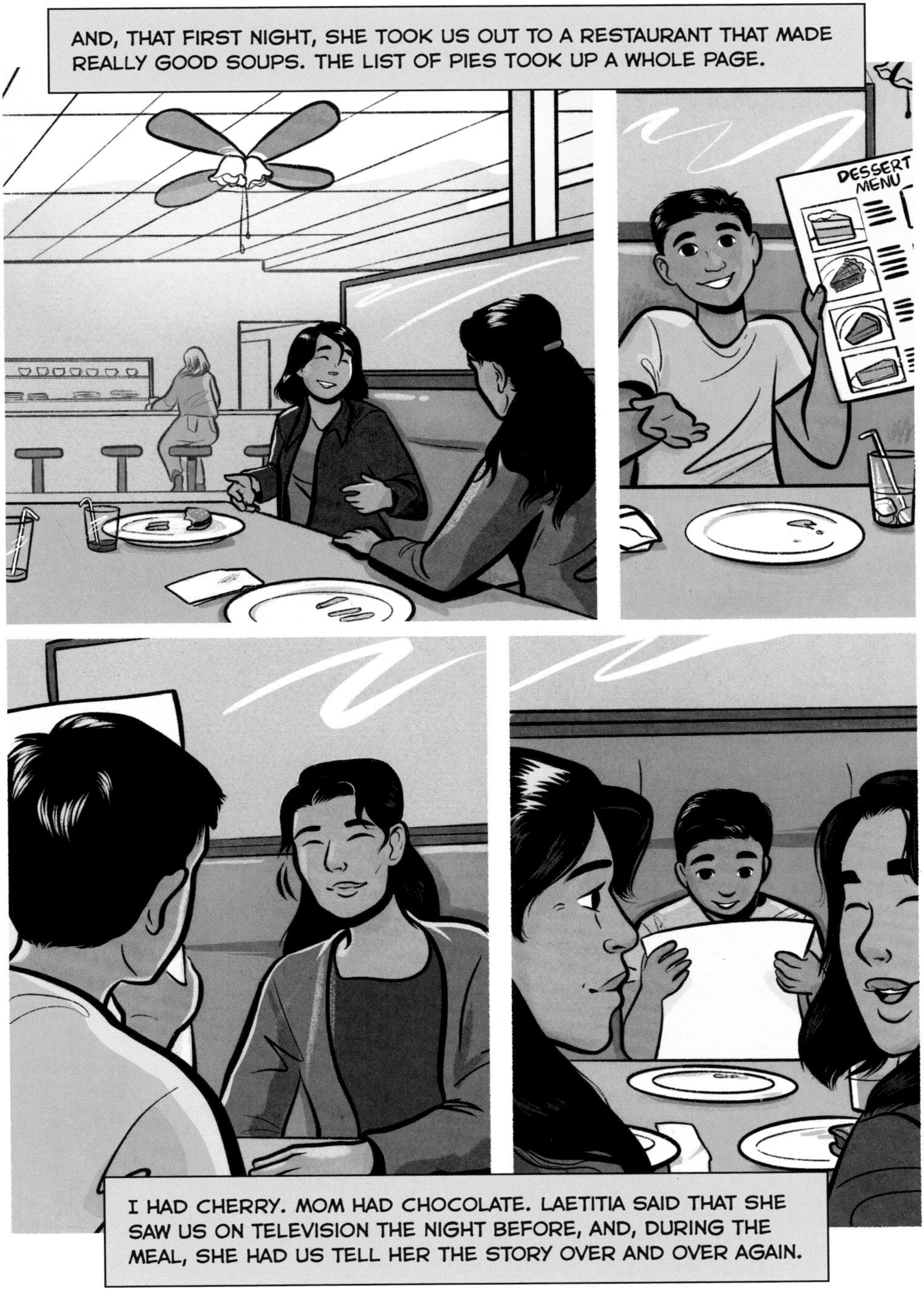
AND, THAT FIRST NIGHT, SHE TOOK US OUT TO A RESTAURANT THAT MADE REALLY GOOD SOUPS. THE LIST OF PIES TOOK UP A WHOLE PAGE.
DESSERT MENU
I HAD CHERRY. MOM HAD CHOCOLATE. LAETITIA SAID THAT SHE SAW US ON TELEVISION THE NIGHT BEFORE, AND, DURING THE MEAL, SHE HAD US TELL HER THE STORY OVER AND OVER AGAIN.

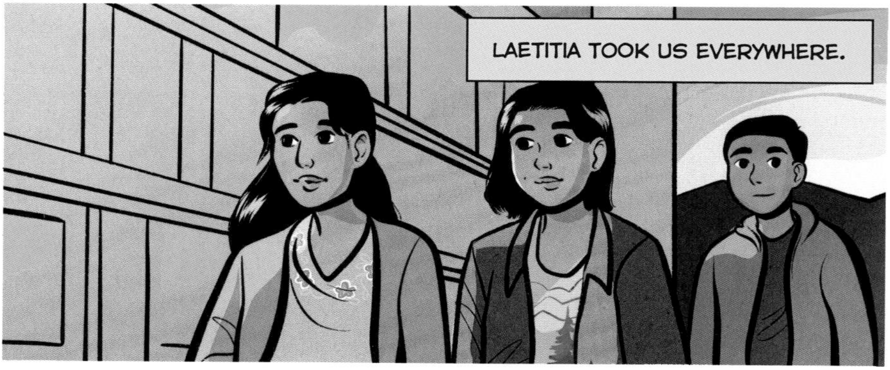
LAETITIA TOOK US EVERYWHERE.

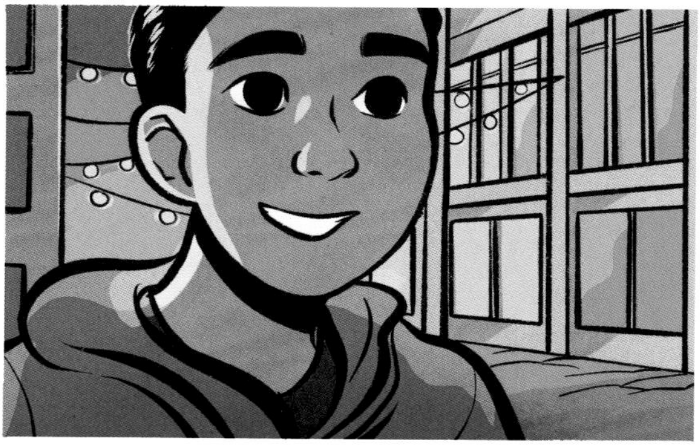

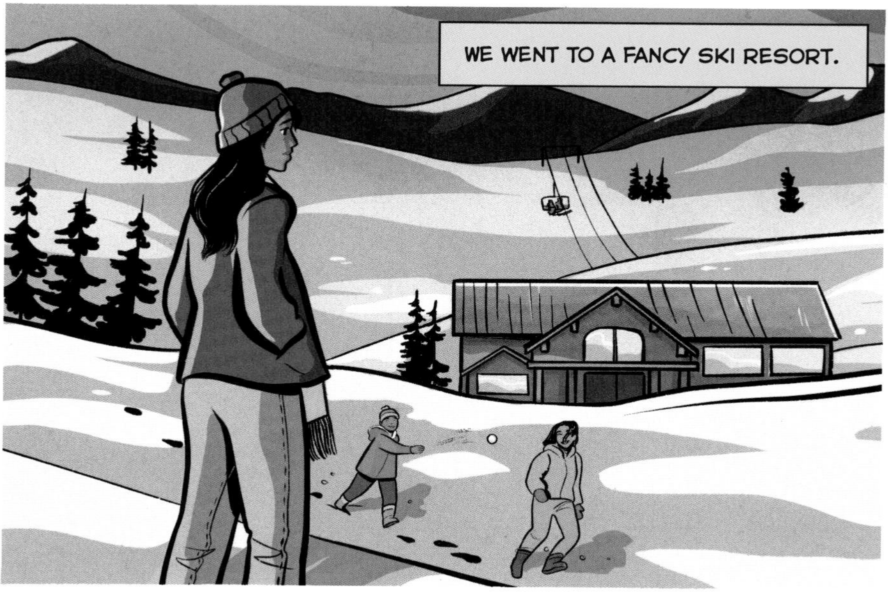
WE WENT TO A FANCY SKI RESORT.

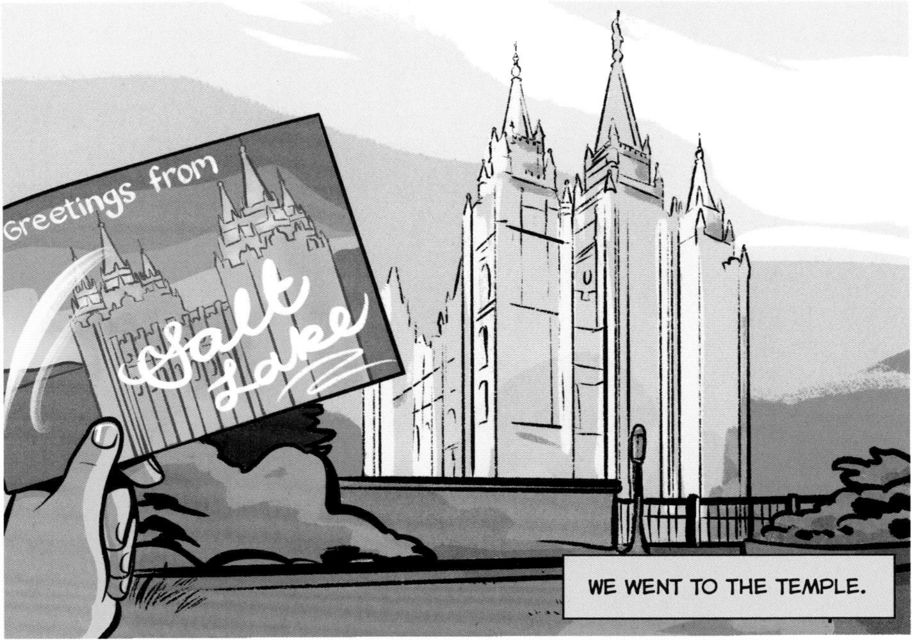
Greetings from
Salt Lake
WE WENT TO THE TEMPLE.
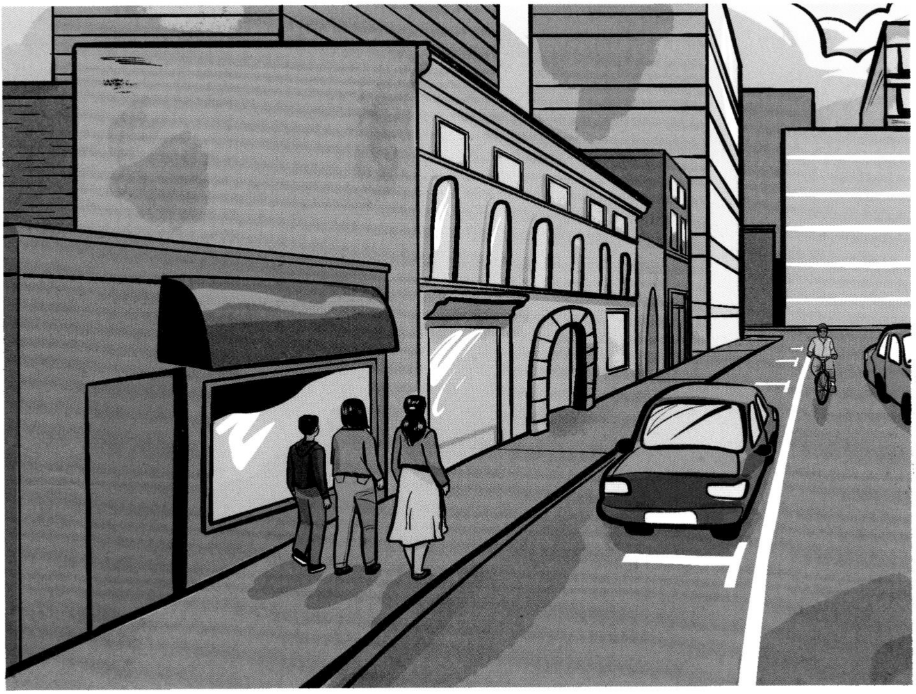

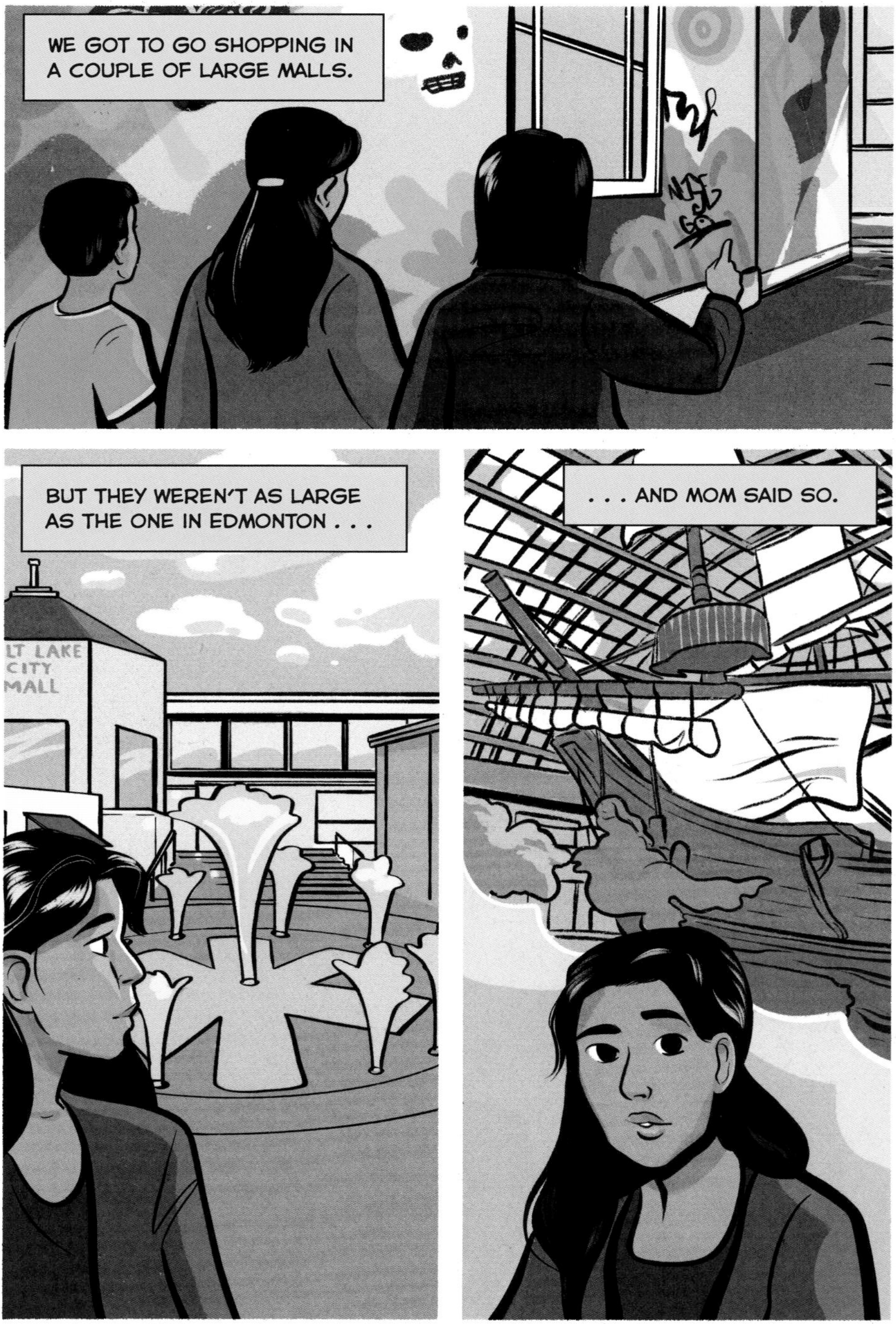
WE GOT TO GO SHOPPING IN A COUPLE OF LARGE MALLS.
BUT THEY WEREN'T AS LARGE AS THE ONE IN EDMONTON . . .
LT LAKE CITY MALL
. . . AND MOM SAID SO.

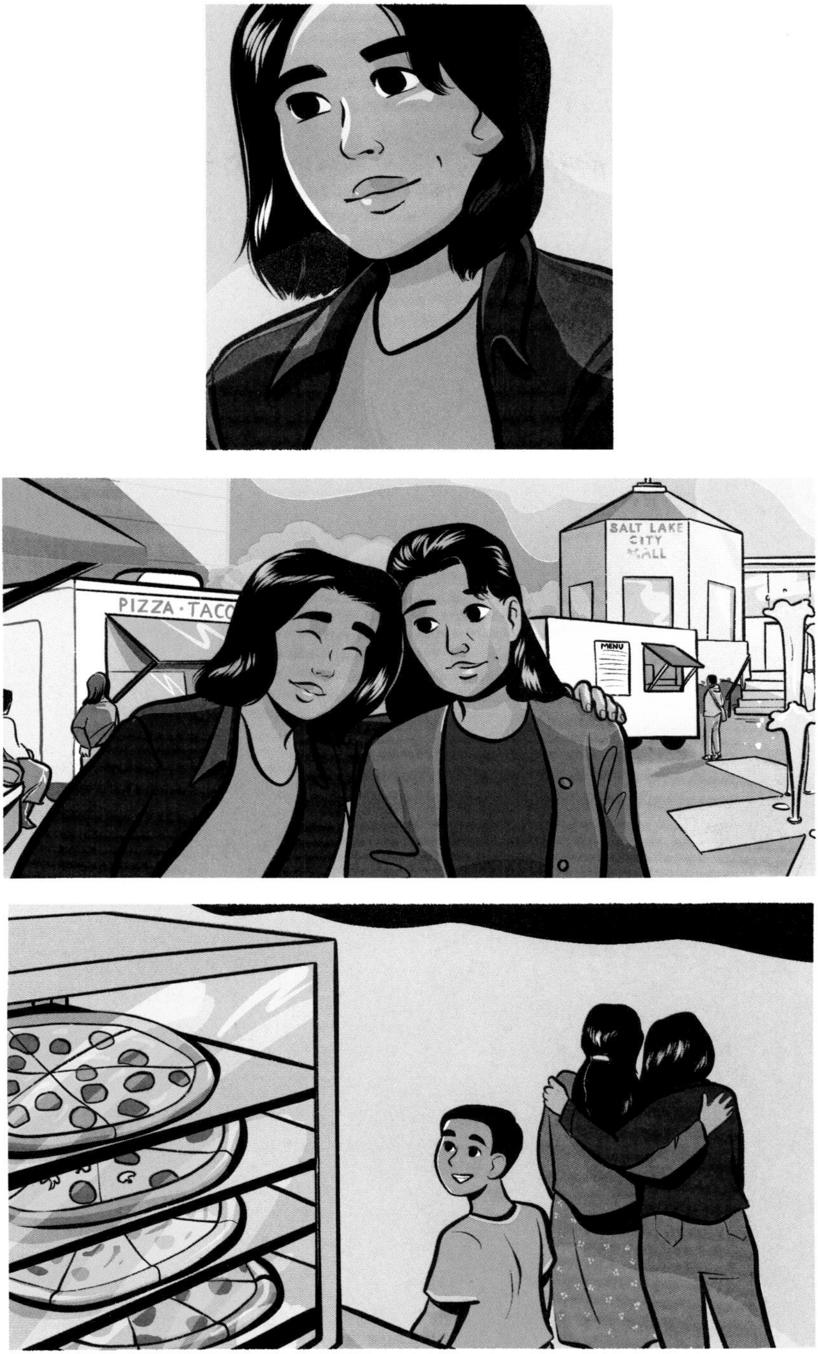
PIZZA · TAC
SALT LAKE CITY MALL
MENU

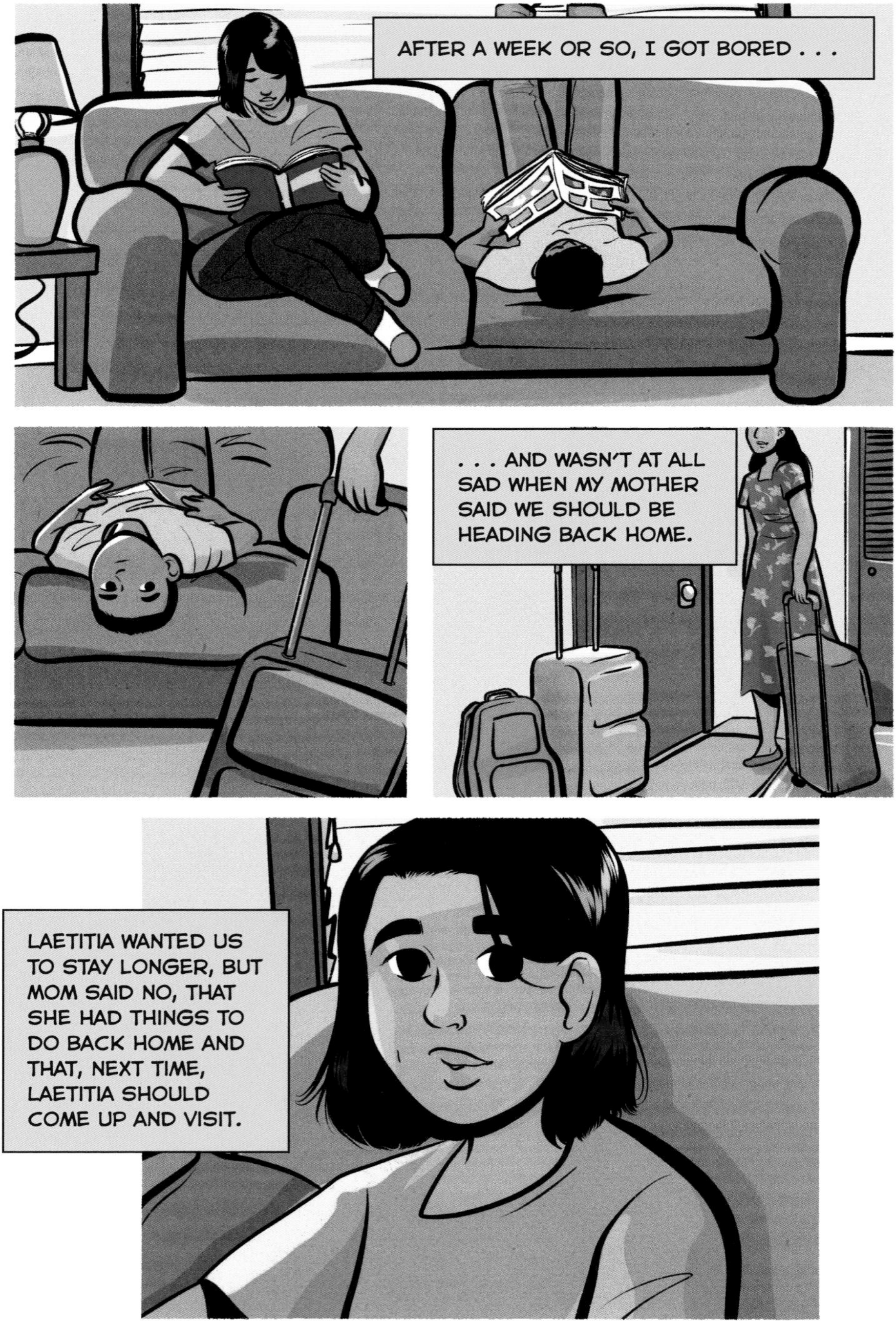
AFTER A WEEK OR SO, I GOT BORED . . .
. . . AND WASN'T AT ALL SAD WHEN MY MOTHER SAID WE SHOULD BE HEADING BACK HOME.
LAETITIA WANTED US TO STAY LONGER, BUT MOM SAID NO, THAT SHE HAD THINGS TO DO BACK HOME AND THAT, NEXT TIME, LAETITIA SHOULD COME UP AND VISIT.

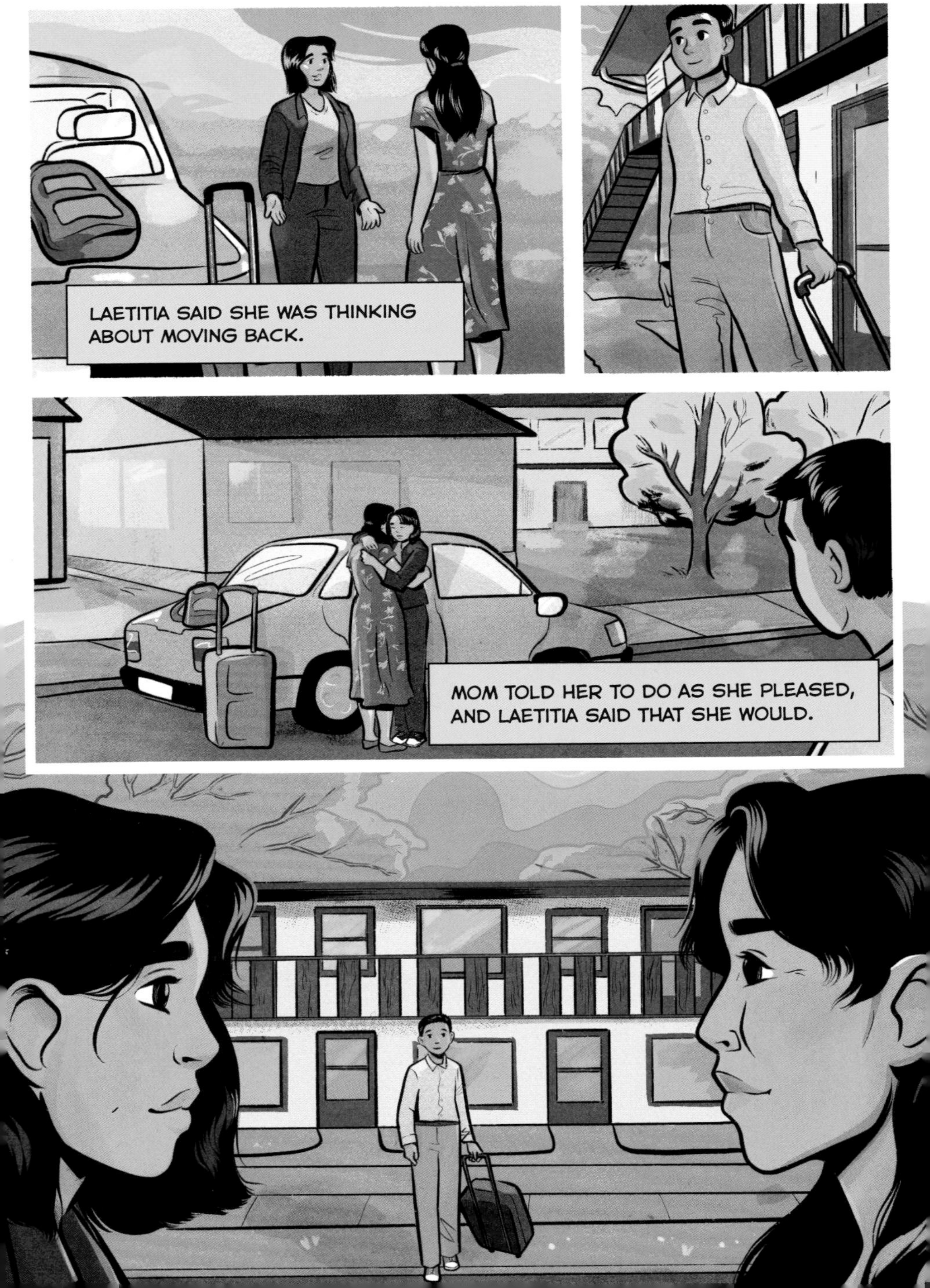
LAETITIA SAID SHE WAS THINKING ABOUT MOVING BACK.
MOM TOLD HER TO DO AS SHE PLEASED, AND LAETITIA SAID THAT SHE WOULD.

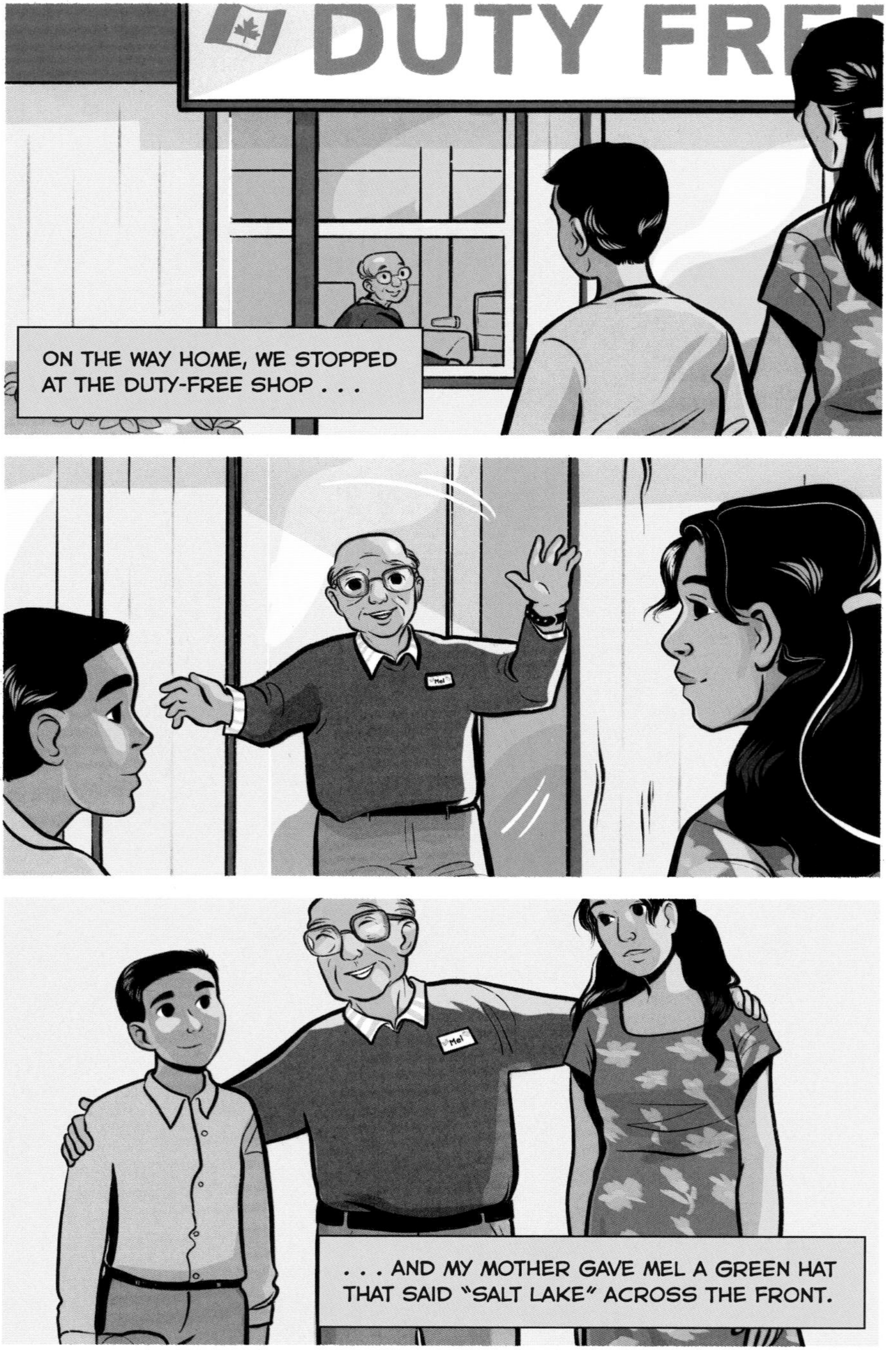
DUTY FRE
ON THE WAY HOME, WE STOPPED AT THE DUTY-FREE SHOP . . .
Mel
Mel
. . . AND MY MOTHER GAVE MEL A GREEN HAT THAT SAID "SALT LAKE" ACROSS THE FRONT.

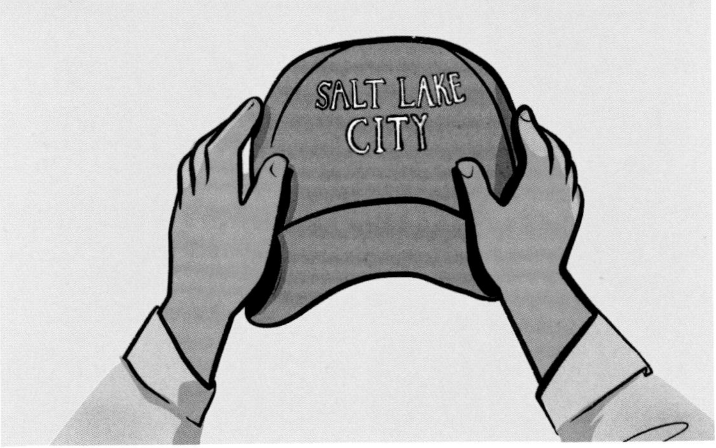
SALT LAKE CITY

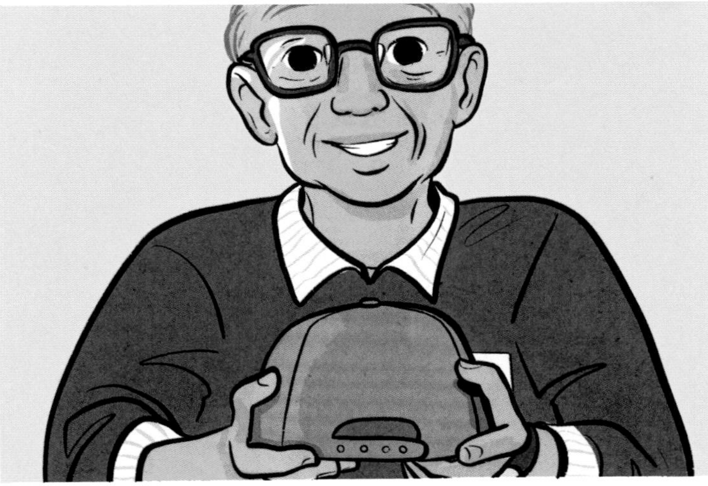

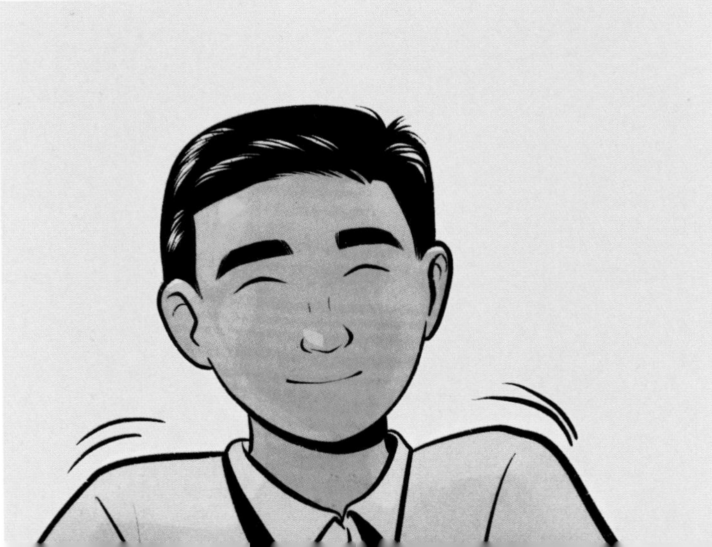

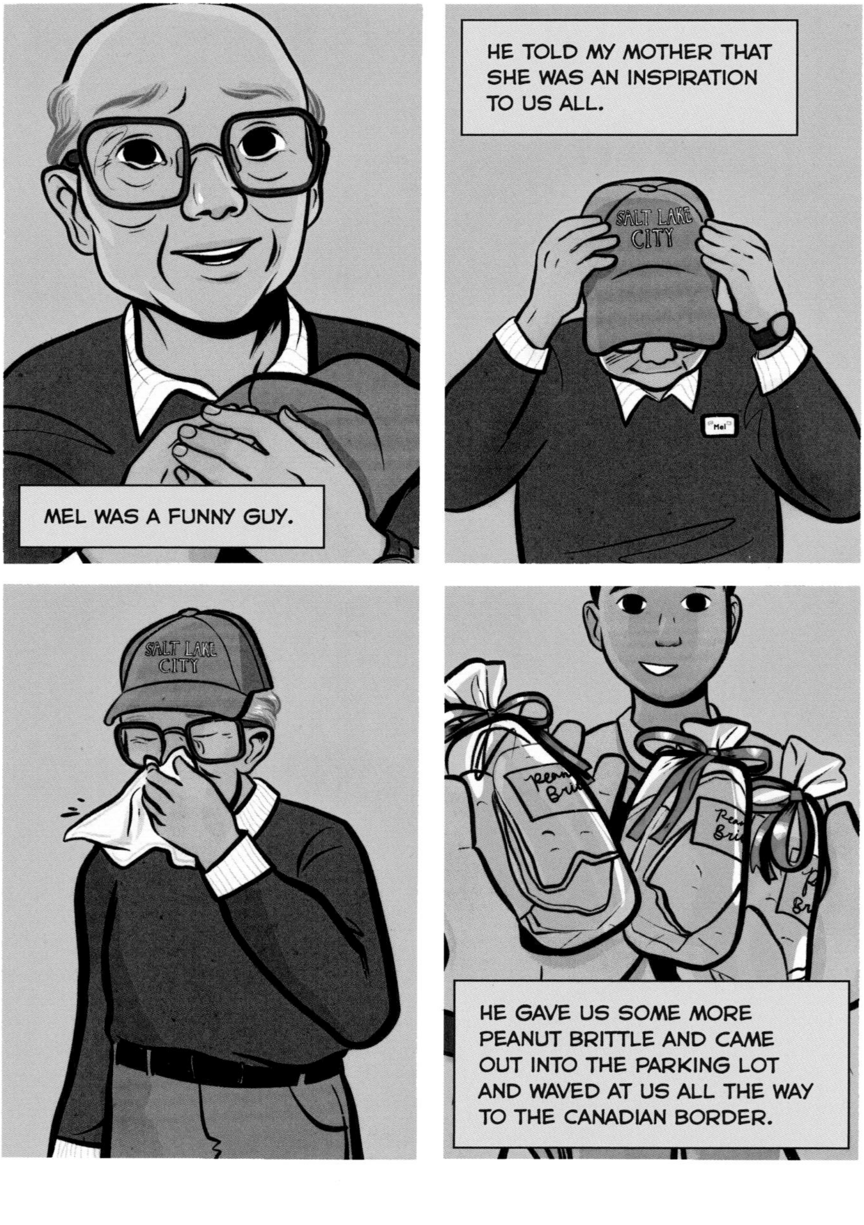
MEL WAS A FUNNY GUY.
HE TOLD MY MOTHER THAT SHE WAS AN INSPIRATION TO US ALL.
SALT LAKE CITY
Mel
SALT LAKE CITY
HE GAVE US SOME MORE PEANUT BRITTLE AND CAME OUT INTO THE PARKING LOT AND WAVED AT US ALL THE WAY TO THE CANADIAN BORDER.

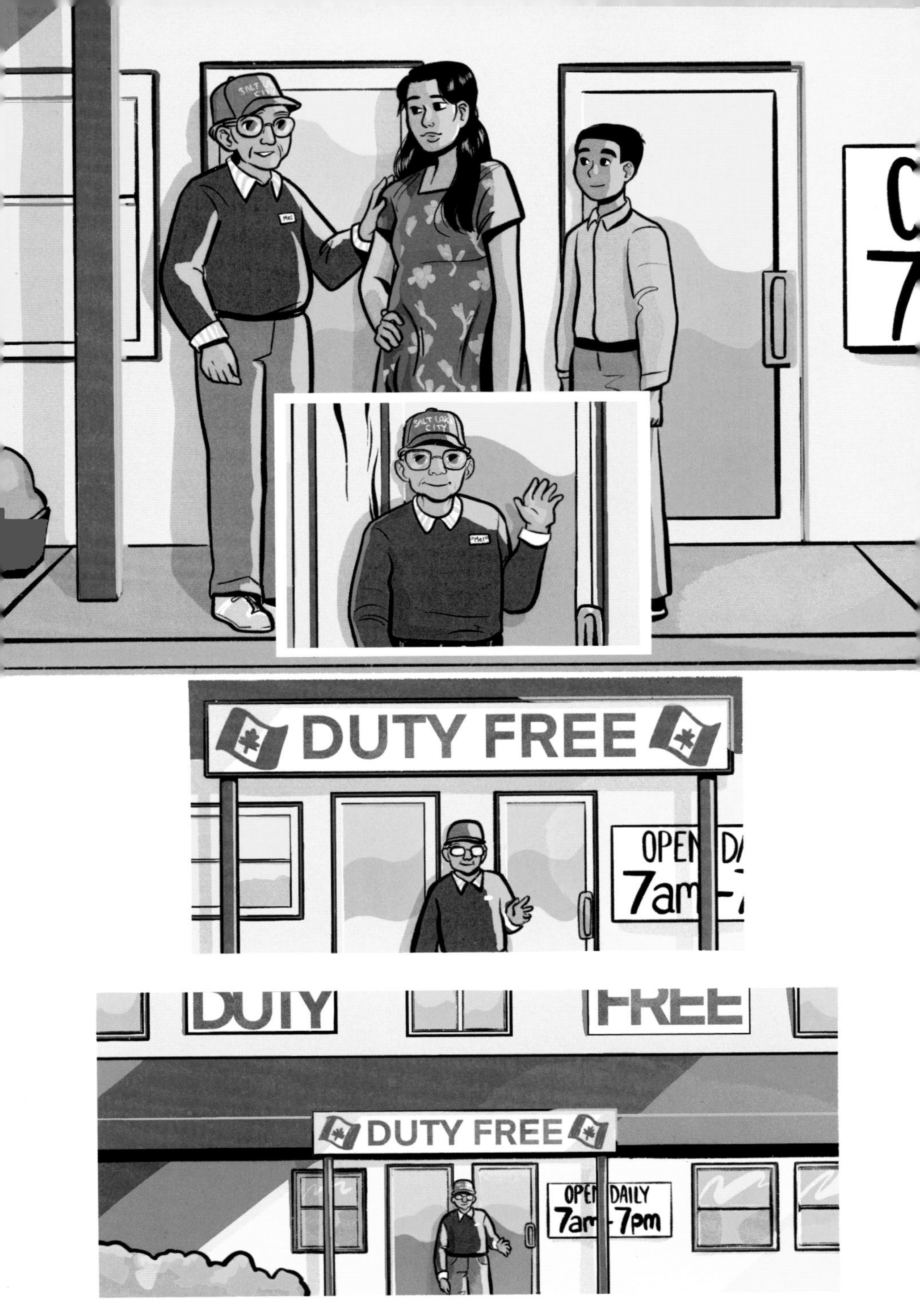
Mel
DUTY FREE
DUTY FREE
OPEN DAILY
7am-7pm

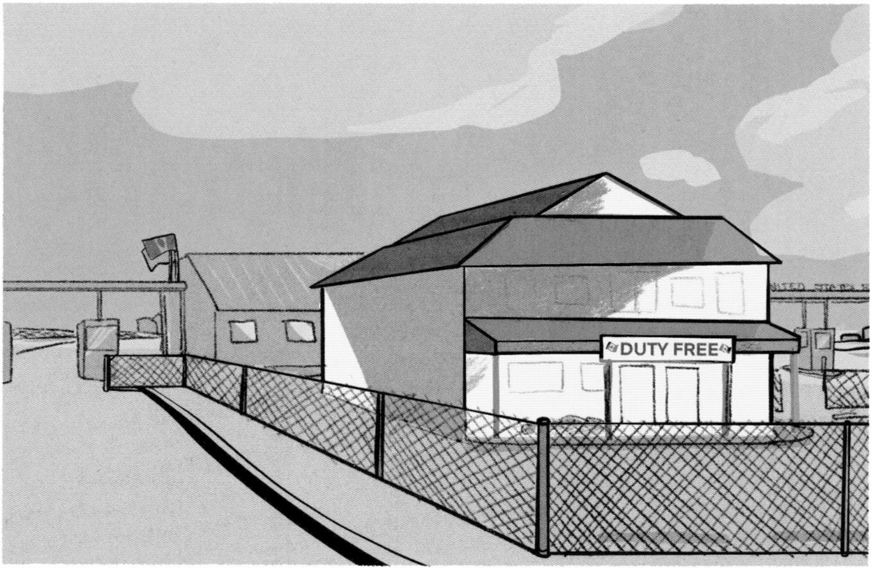
DUTY FREE

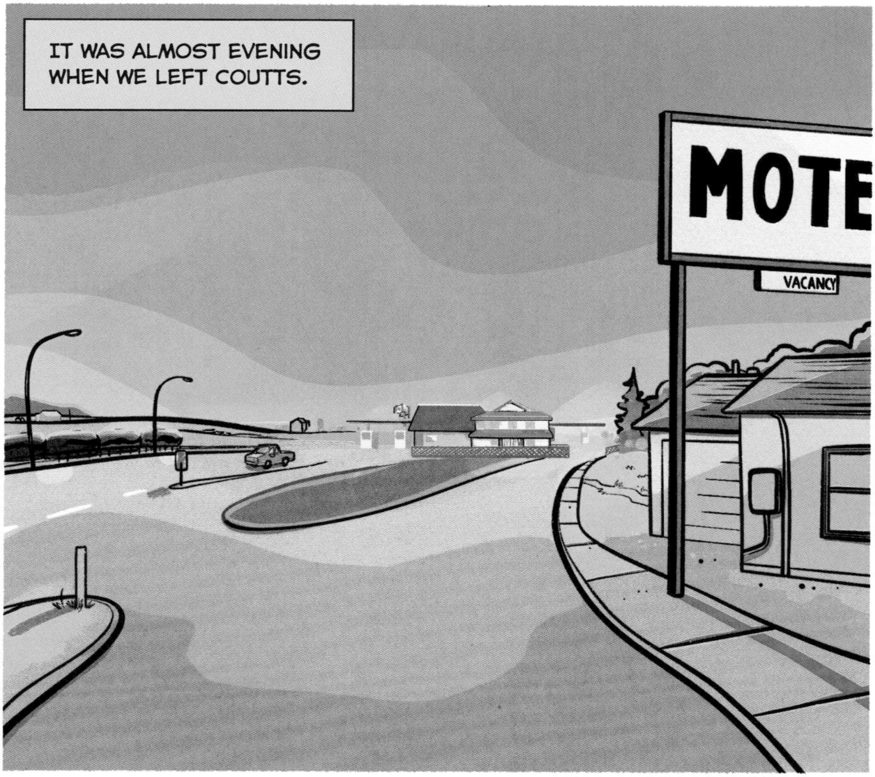
IT WAS ALMOST EVENING WHEN WE LEFT COUTTS.
MOTE
VACANCY

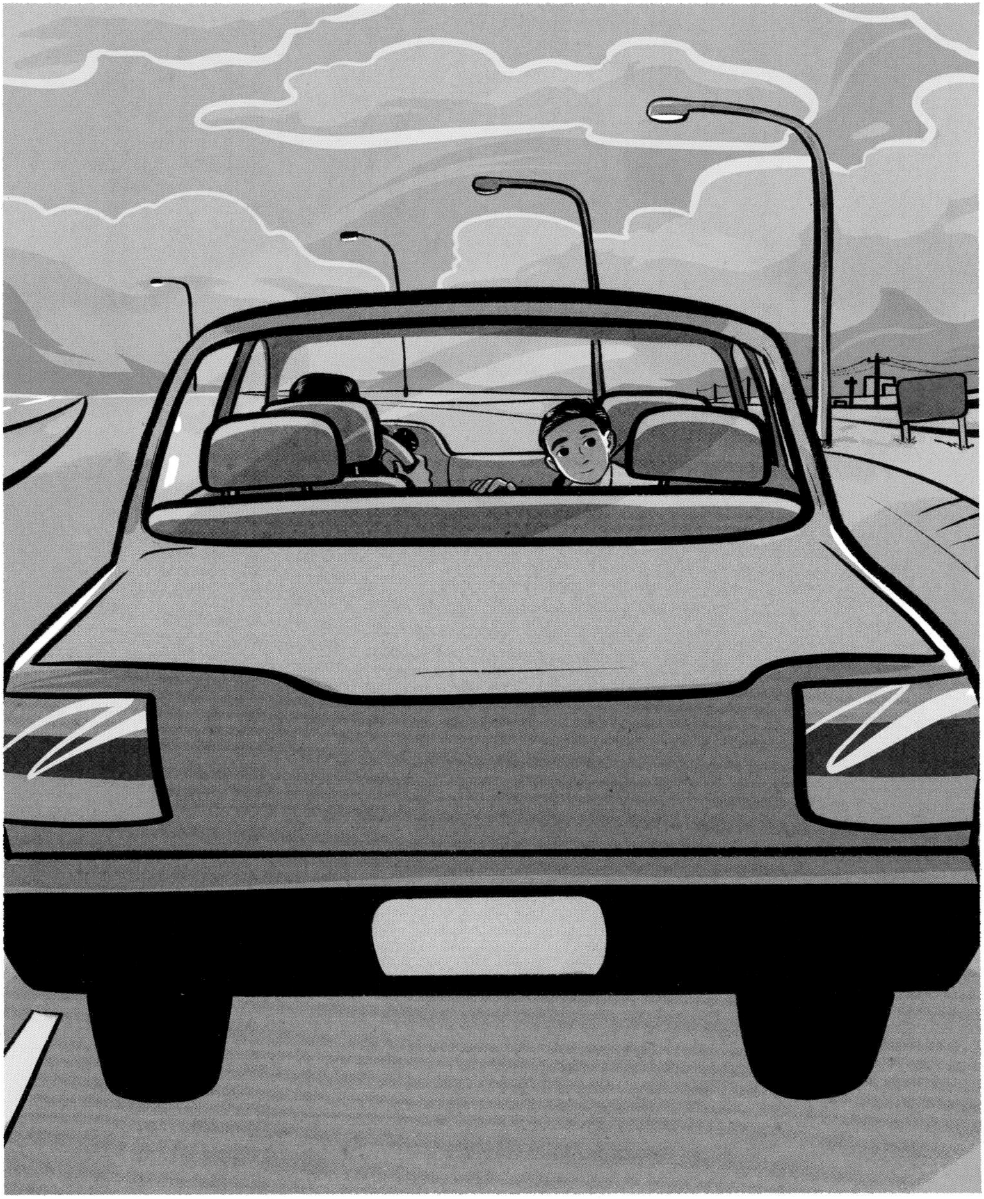

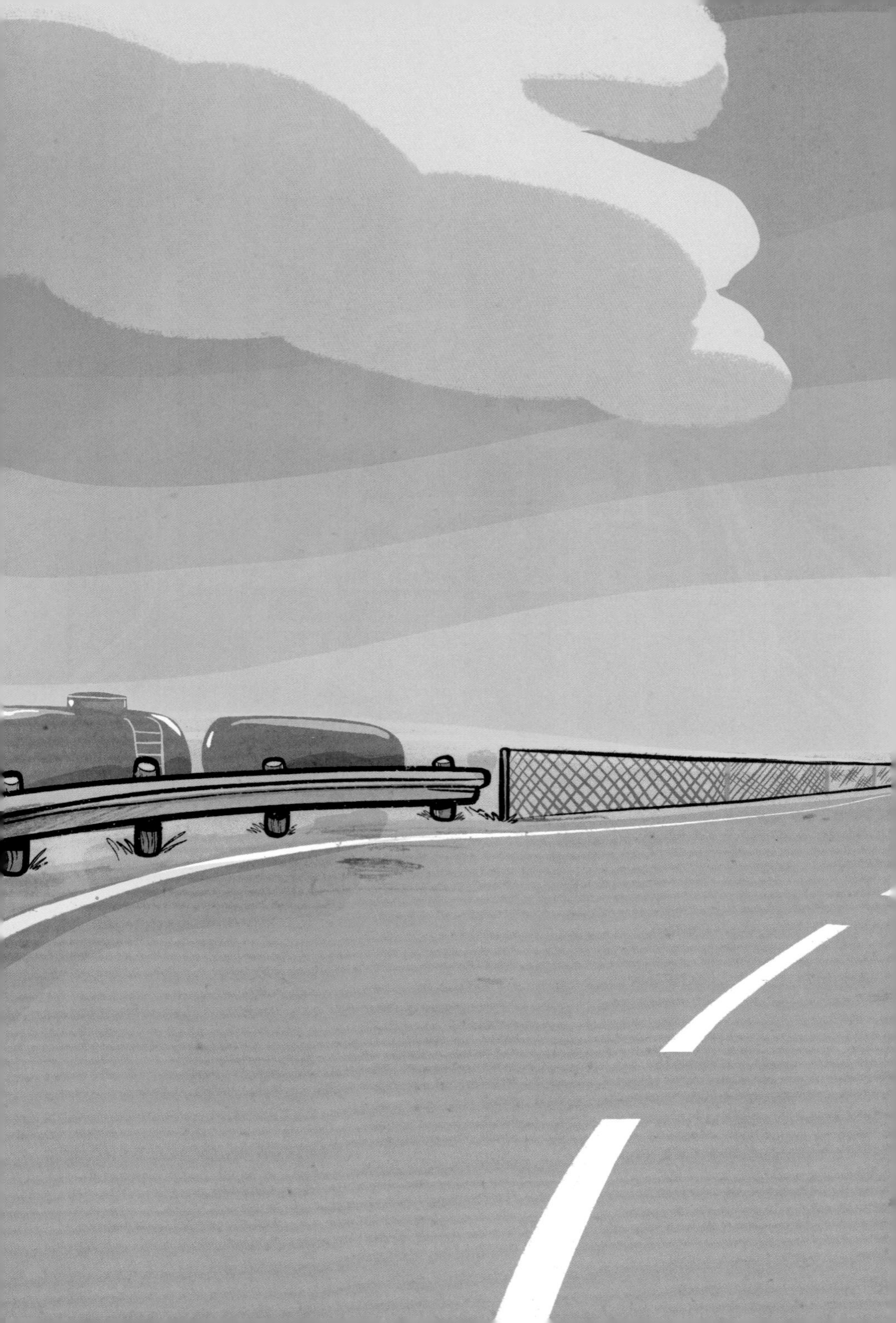

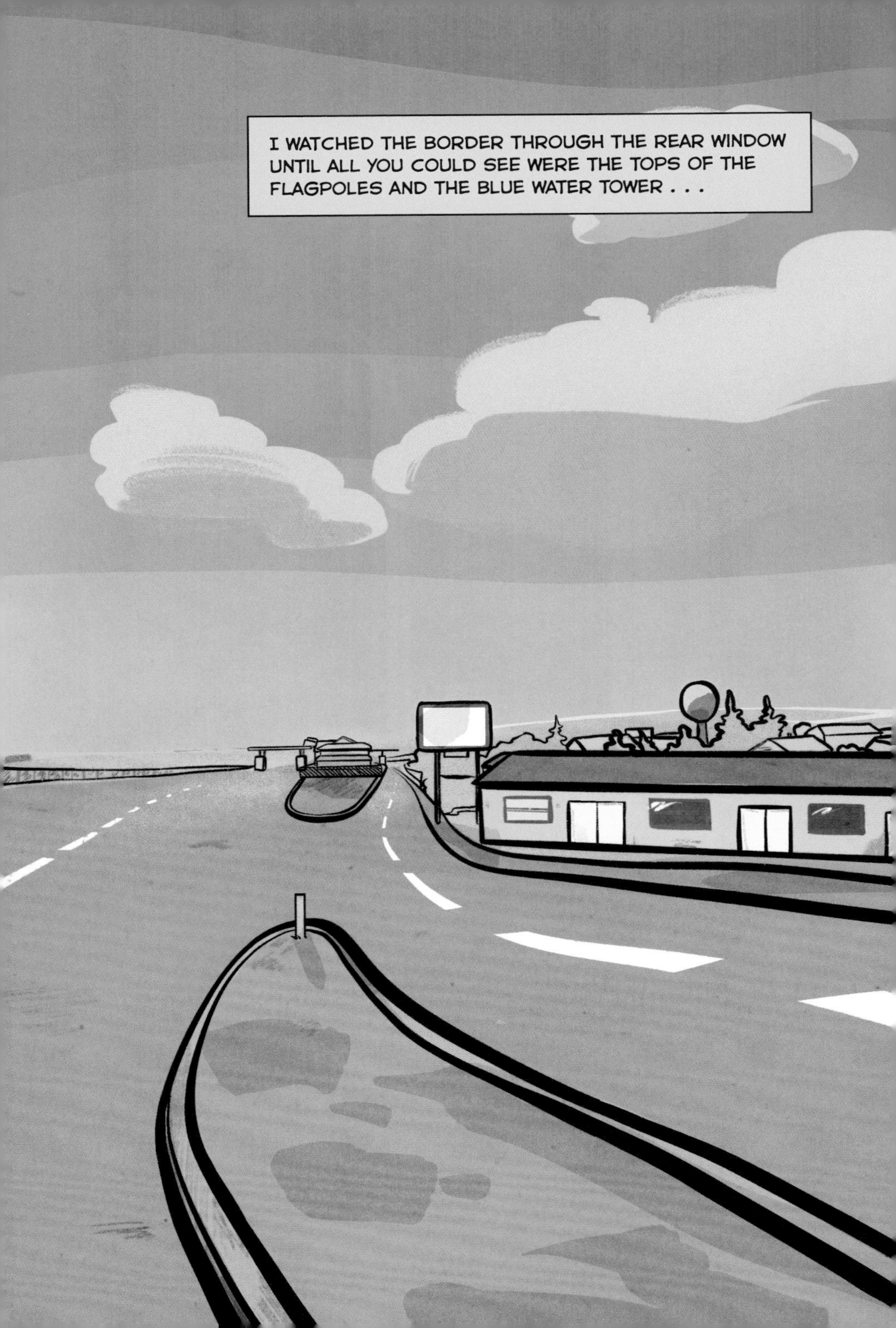
I WATCHED THE BORDER THROUGH THE REAR WINDOW UNTIL ALL YOU COULD SEE WERE THE TOPS OF THE FLAGPOLES AND THE BLUE WATER TOWER . . .

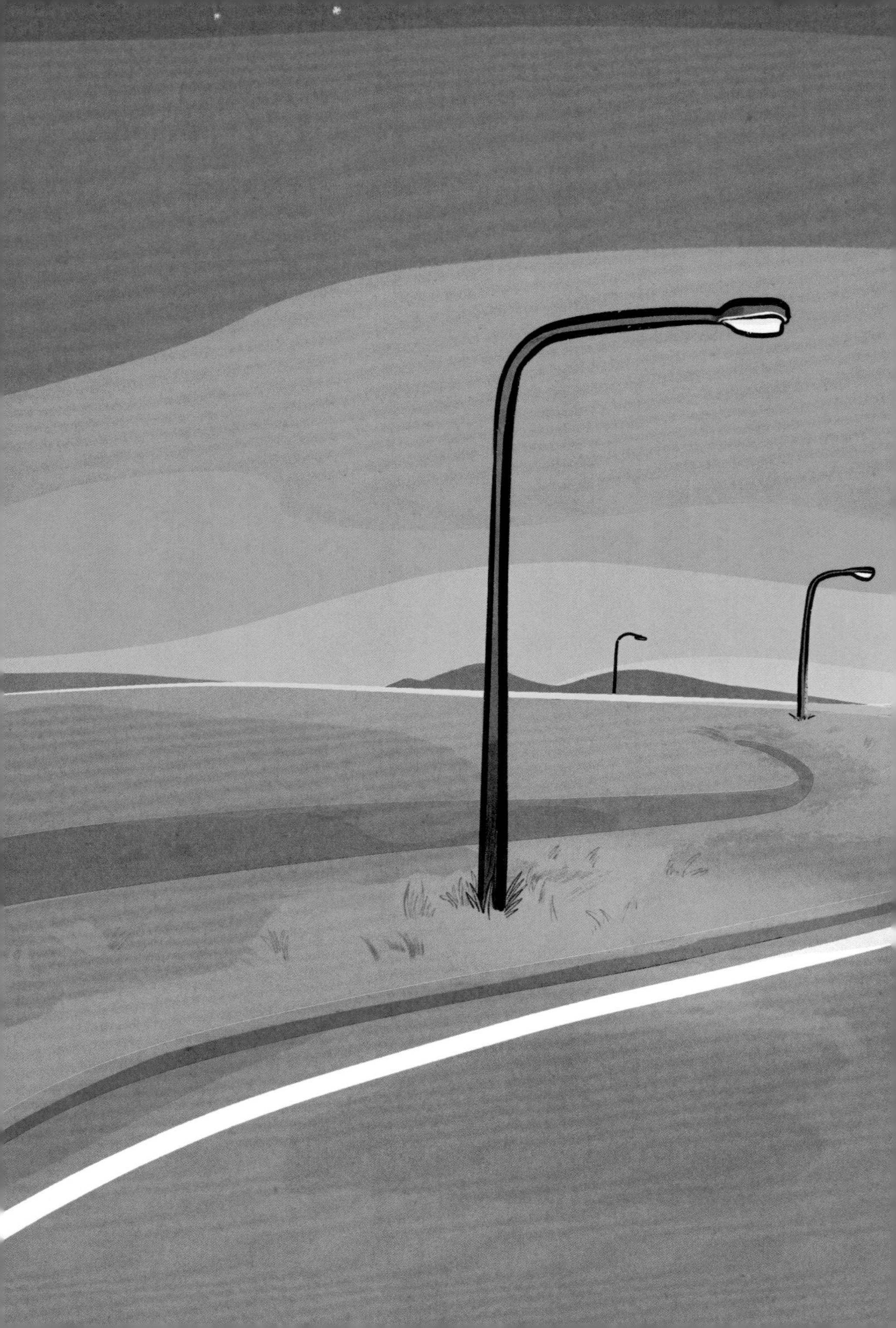

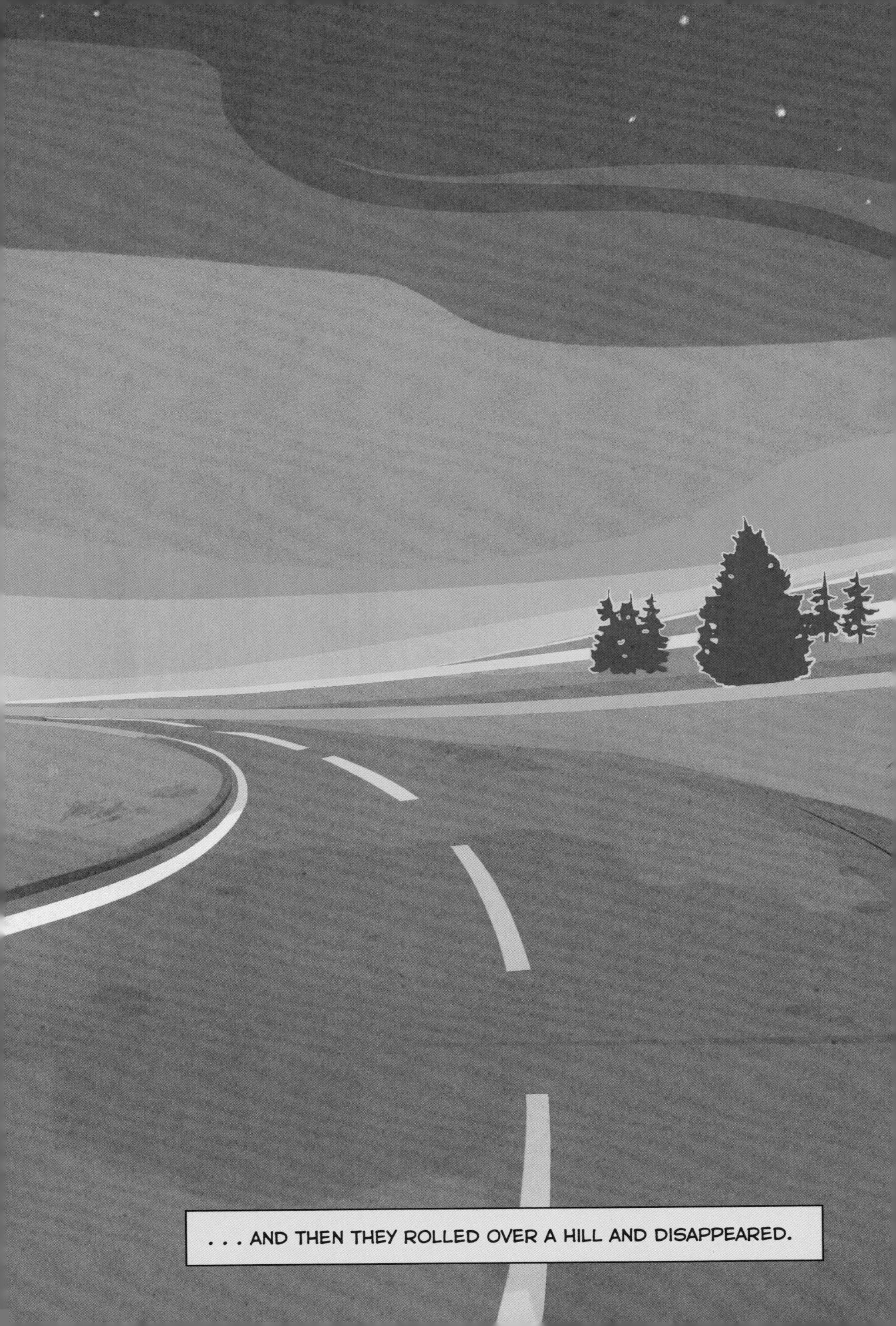
. . . AND THEN THEY ROLLED OVER A HILL AND DISAPPEARED.

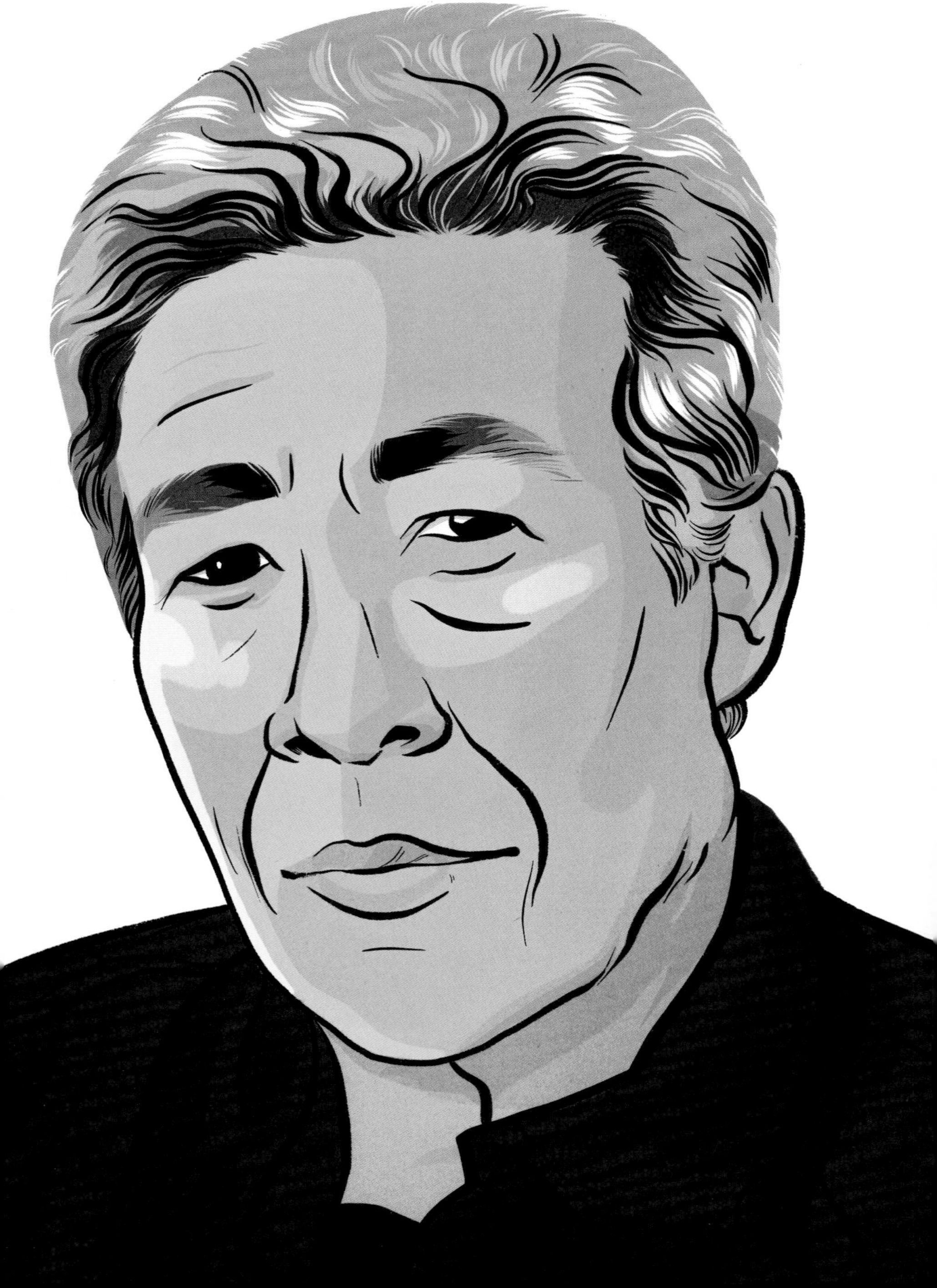

THOMAS KING IS AN AWARD-WINNING NOVELIST, SHORT STORY WRITER, SCRIPTWRITER AND PHOTOGRAPHER OF CHEROKEE AND GREEK DESCENT. HIS CRITICALLY ACCLAIMED, BESTSELLING FICTION INCLUDES *MEDICINE RIVER*; *GREEN GRASS, RUNNING WATER*; *TRUTH AND BRIGHT WATER*; *A SHORT HISTORY OF INDIANS IN CANADA*; *THE BACK OF THE TURTLE* (WINNER OF THE GOVERNOR GENERAL'S LITERARY AWARD FOR FICTION); AND *INDIANS ON VACATION*. HE IS ALSO THE AUTHOR OF THE BESTSELLING NONFICTION WORK *THE INCONVENIENT INDIAN* (WINNER OF THE RBC TAYLOR PRIZE). HIS FICTION FOR YOUNG READERS INCLUDES *A COYOTE COLUMBUS STORY*, ILLUSTRATED BY WILLIAM KENT MONKMAN; *A COYOTE SOLSTICE TALE*, ILLUSTRATED BY GARY CLEMENT; AND *COYOTE TALES*, ILLUSTRATED BY BYRON EGGENSCHWILER. A COMPANION OF THE ORDER OF CANADA AND THE RECIPIENT OF AN AWARD FROM THE NATIONAL ABORIGINAL ACHIEVEMENT FOUNDATION, THOMAS KING LIVES IN GUELPH, ONTARIO.

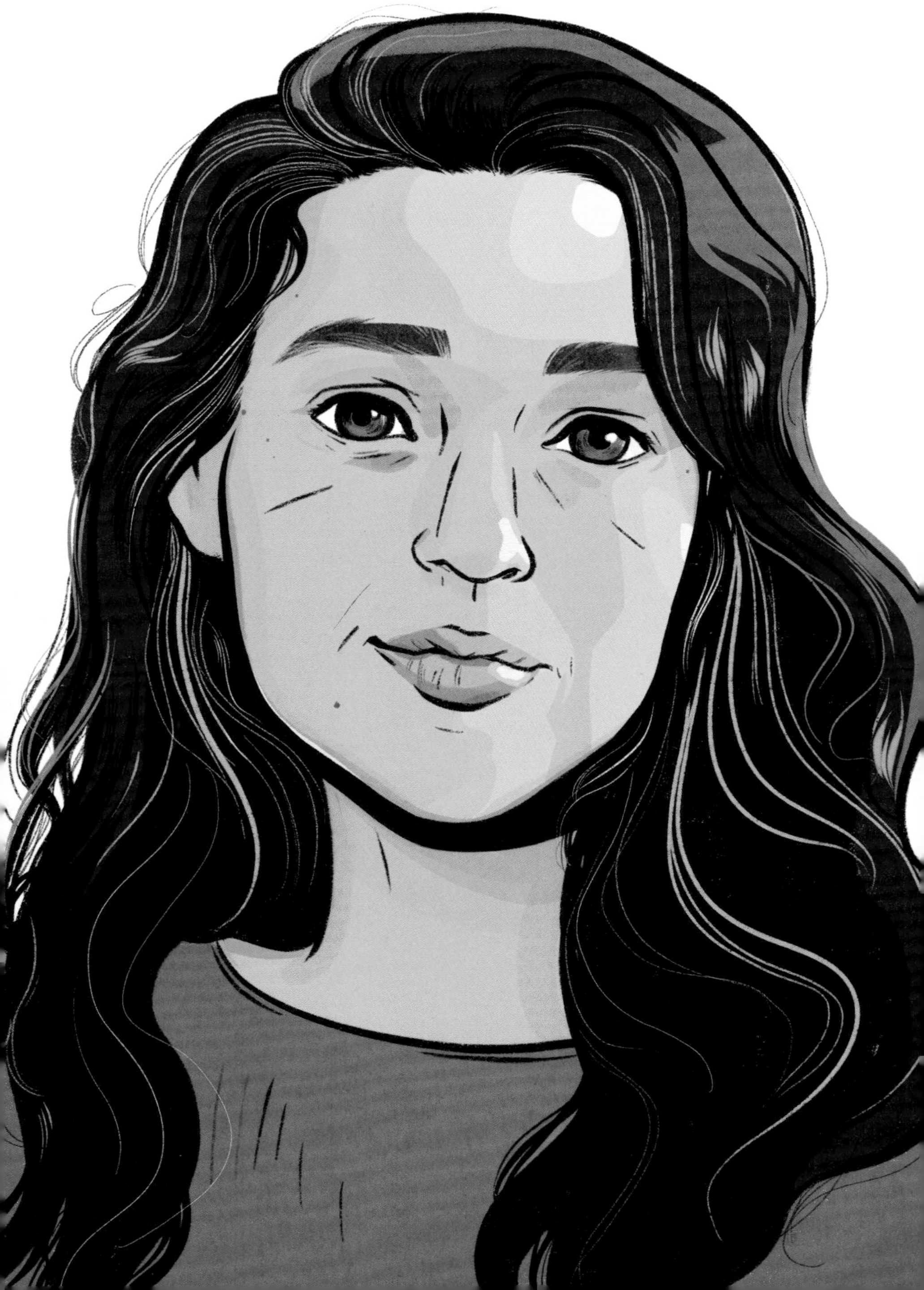

NATASHA DONOVAN IS A MÉTIS ILLUSTRATOR ORIGINALLY FROM VANCOUVER, BRITISH CO- LUMBIA. HER SEQUENTIAL WORK HAS BEEN PUBLISHED IN *THIS PLACE: 150 YEARS RETOLD,* AND THE *WONDERFUL WOMEN OF HISTORY* ANTHOLOGY. SHE IS THE ILLUSTRATOR OF THE AWARD-WINNING GRAPHIC NOVEL *SURVIVING THE CITY,* AS WELL AS THE AWARD-WINNING MOTHERS OF XSAN CHILDREN'S BOOK SERIES, AND THE FORTHCOMING PIC- TURE BOOK BIOGRAPHY *CLASSIFIED: THE SECRET CAREER OF MARY GOLDA ROSS, CHEROKEE AEROSPACE ENGINEER.* SHE LIVES BY THE NOOKSACK RIVER IN WASHINGTON STATE.

OTHER WORKS BY THOMAS KING

Fiction

Medicine River
Green Grass, Running Water
One Good Story, That One
Truth and Bright Water
A Short History of Indians in Canada
The Back of the Turtle
Indians on Vacation

DreadfulWater Mysteries

DreadfulWater
The Red Power Murders
Cold Skies
A Matter of Malice
Obsidian

Nonfiction

The Truth About Stories: A Native Narrative
The Inconvenient Indian: A Curious Account of Native People in North America

Children's Illustrated Books

A Coyote Columbus Story, illustrated by William Kent Monkman
Coyote Sings to the Moon, illustrated by Johnny Wales
Coyote's New Suit, illustrated by Johnny Wales
A Coyote Solstice Tale, illustrated by Gary Clement
Coyote Tales, illustrated by Byron Eggenschwiler

Poetry

77 Fragments of a Familiar Ruin

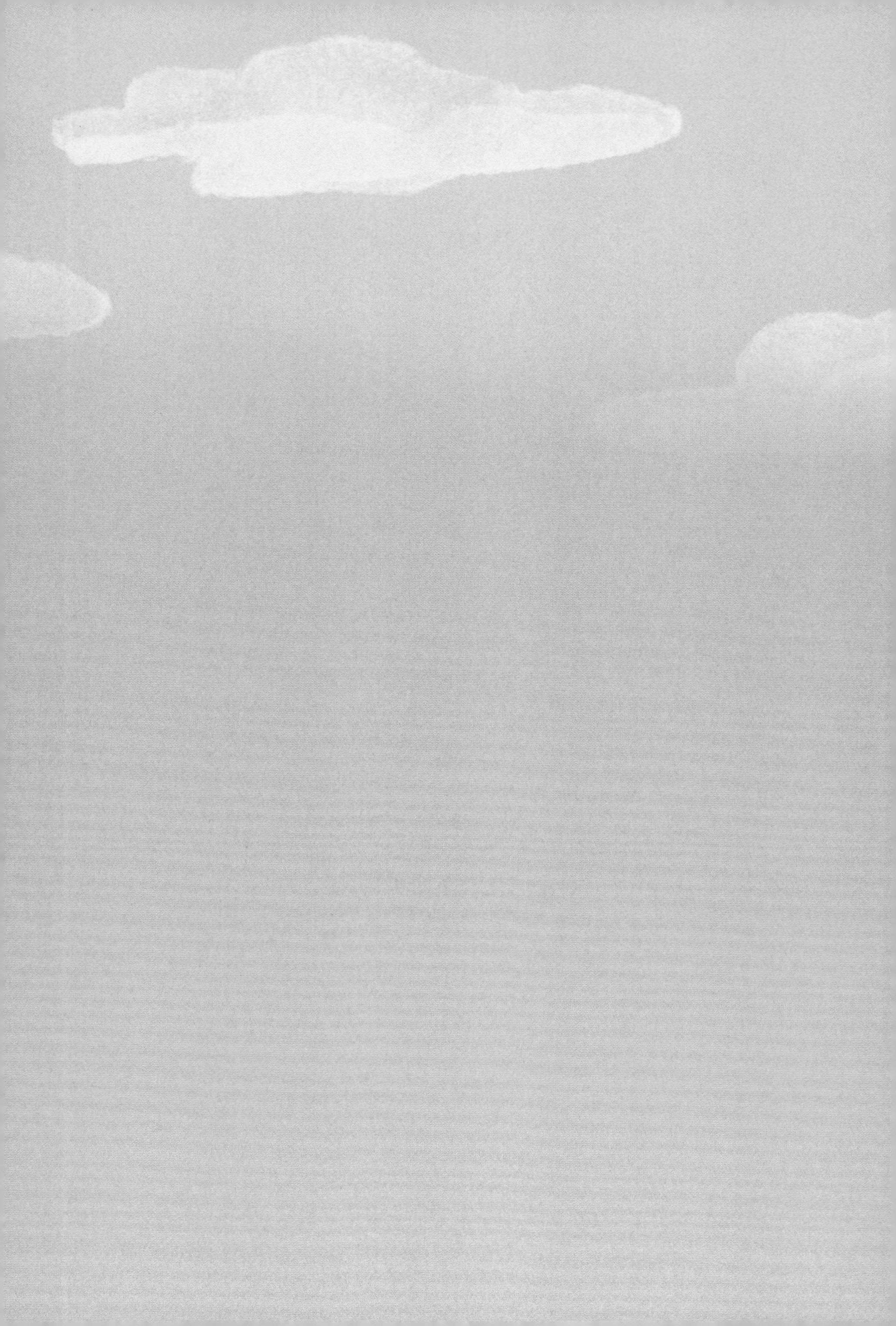

OTHER WORKS BY NATASHA DONOVAN

Anthologies
The Other Side: An Anthology of Queer Paranormal Romance
This Place: 150 Years Retold

Mothers of Xsan Series (written by Brett D. Huson)
The Sockeye Mother
The Grizzly Mother
The Eagle Mother
The Frog Mother
The Wolf Mother

Graphic Novels
Surviving the City (written by Tasha Spillett)

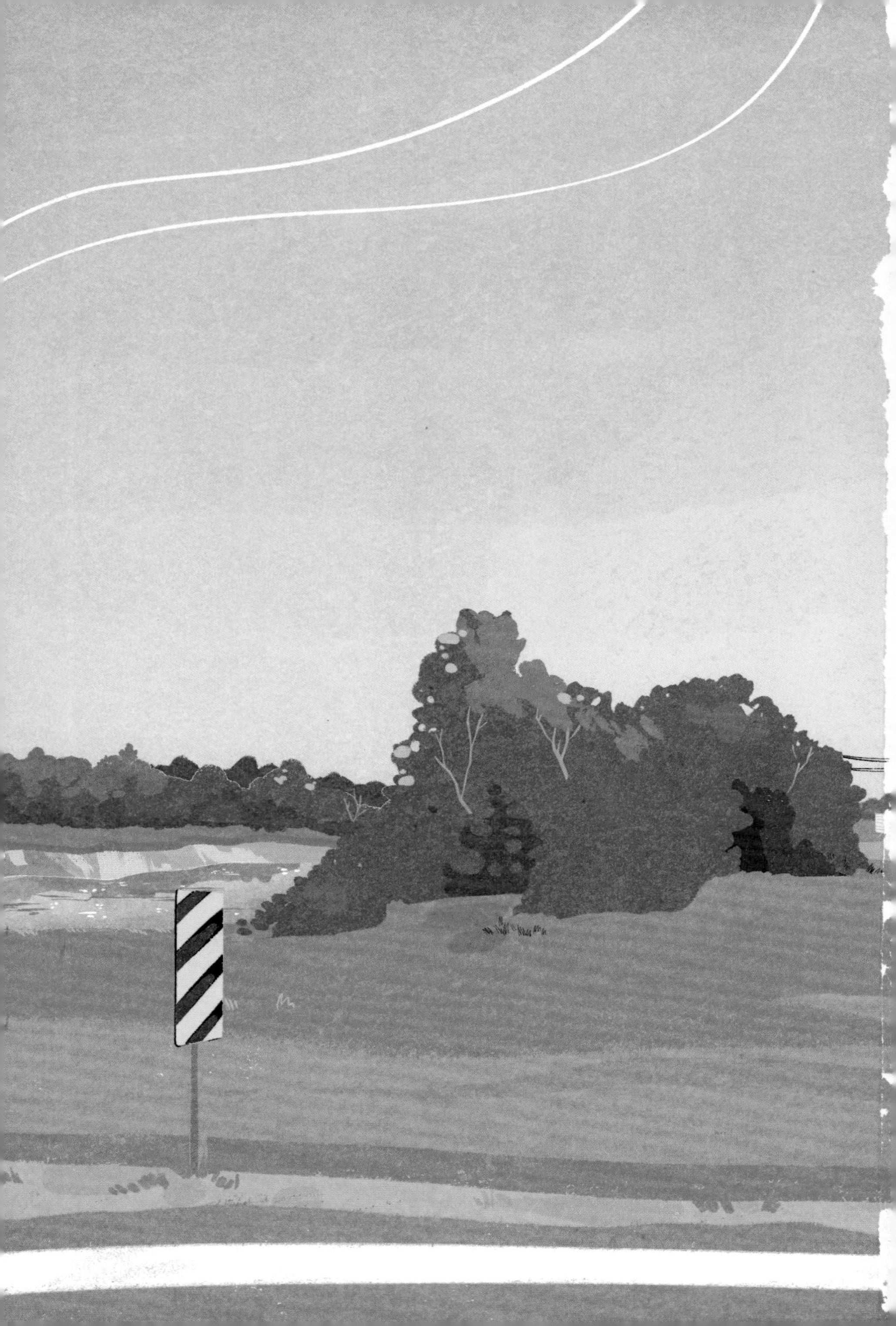